BRAINSTORMED

BRAINSTORMED

A NOVEL

VLADIMIR LANGE

RED SQUARE

This is a work of fiction. The events, characters and institutions
portrayed are imaginary. Their resemblance, if any, to real-life
counterparts is entirely coincidental.

Published in the United States by
RED SQUARE Press / May 2018

Library of Congress Cataloging-in-Publication Data
Lange, Vladimir.
Brainstormed : a novel / Vladimir Lange.—1st ed.
p. cm.

ISBN 978-0-9760398-3-9   (hardcover)

_____

Red Square Books are published by Red Square Press.
Its trademark, consisting of the words "Red Square"
and the portrayal of the square, is registered with the
U.S. Patent and Trademark Office and in other countries.
Marca Registrada. Red Square Press
11331 Skyline Drive, Santa Ana, CA 92705

_____

Printed in the United States of America
10 9 8 7 6 5 4 3 2 1

First Edition

In loving memory of my father Anatol

BRAINSTORMED

PROLOGUE

Lizzy was startled out of a sound sleep. The iPad by her bedside signaled a message. "Amy's Café across from the hospital. He's crossing the street now."

Jeezzz... Twice now, by the time she got there, the man was gone. Another miss and there goes the gig, she thought. Lizzy wiggled into her jeans, slipped on her hoodie, grabbed the iPad and dashed downstairs, hoping that this time the aging Four Runner would start on the first try. If things went well today, she'd treat herself to a more reliable conveyance.

The aroma of freshly baked cinnamon buns spread into the parking area. No wonder the poor patient slipped out of the hospital three times a week. Who could resist? Lizzy heard her empty stomach grumbling.

The wireless bud in her ear was hissing before she even reached the café door. It was a high-pitched voice, the audio too distorted to tell if it was a man or a woman. "Inside. Second guy in line."

Lizzy breathed a sigh of relief. *Made it*. She turned her head and scanned the lot. Was her contact here too? Watching her? Whatever. Less chance of getting stiffed.

The café was crowded. The man in line was in his fifties. His ragged overcoat hung off his thin stooped frame almost far enough to conceal his hospital-issue blue scrub pants. Below the baseball cap, grey stubble was growing over a two-inch fresh surgical scar behind his right ear.

She got in line, her heart pounding. *Here we go.*

It had started with a simple message on her FaceBook page. "I hear you're a cyber whiz. I hope you can help me." A few e-mails later, and she was looking at a two K offer—just to access some new medical gizmo in some guy's head. "It's a Bluetooth link to his computer. I want to see how it would look on his screen. Can you do it?"

Duh. She was better at hacking than her boyfriend Spike, and he was considered a real techie. And it wasn't like she had to do something illegal—like Spike, who she suspected might have sold credit card numbers before they met. Then there was her roommate Angie, who made astronomical figures modeling for rich Newport Beach men, in "photo shoots" that lasted all night. Screw that. At least this was semi-legit. Probably industrial espionage by a competitor. The part time job in the dog lab was helping with books and lunches, but two whole grand would go a long way toward making up what her pre-med scholarship at UCI was not covering.

The man was moving toward a booth, a tray with three buns, dripping with frosting, and a tall steaming something shaking slightly in his hands. The face was gaunt, the eyes hollow. "Psych ward escapee" was written all over him.

Lizzy grabbed a black coffee, slipped into a booth where she could still see him, and flipped the iPad open. After a few keystrokes, the URL of the man's implant appeared on her screen. Her fingers worked the screen, but nothing happened. Damn. The gizmo had its own medical encryption. Sweat beading on her forehead, she typed,

Dotwrite (ast)/Search // impl.nbmc

Nodename= getNodename (LX)

The man wolfed down the first bun, wiped the drips off his lips, took a sip, and started on the second one. At this rate he would be done before she got in. Lizzy typed faster.

gopher://nbmc:port/path?query_string#fragment_lx

A window popped open. "Name: Jeremy Rogers" appeared in small block letters in the upper corner. Lizzy smiled. Hello, Jeremy.

The voice rasped in her ear bud again. "Show me what you have so far."

The contact definitely sounded like a hands-on customer. Just let me do my job.

"Just name," she typed in.

"Show me."

She activated screen sharing, sending an image of what was on her screen to the caller. She was glad she didn't have a way to reply verbally, or this session could turn into a gabfest. That's not how she liked to work. Why had this gig been outsourced, anyway? Because the device required close physical proximity? Or because the client didn't want his or her electronic fingerprints all over this job? Oh, boy . . . Lizzy was the lucky outsourcee. She would worry about it later, she decided.

The image on her screen was a parade of multicolored lines, like the brain tracings of the dogs in the physiology lab. At least it was familiar territory. Under the lines was a set of sliding controls, like the ones on her iPad. Not two grand worth of info, but that was not her problem.

"Try moving the controls," the voice said.

She felt a shiver sweep through her. "NFW," Lizzy mumbled. The deal was, log on and watch. No way was she going to mess with the man's brain implant. Did they think she was nuts?

"An extra five hundred if you move the controls," the voice said. "Just slide your finger across."

Lizzy started hyperventilating.

"It's nothing but a monitor. You won't hurt anything."

The man took another sip, and started wrapping the remaining bun in a napkin.

"A grand. Just move the sliders, Lizzy."

He was standing up, fishing in his pocket.

A thousand bucks. It was just a monitor, like Dr. Strand used for vital signs when the dogs were anesthetized, she thought. She had worked one of those before. She typed in "Two thousand."

"Done," the voice said.

The man deposited some change on the table. Then he leaned over, picked up the cup.

"Now," the voice urged.

Trying to control the fine tremor in her hand, Lizzy slid her fingertip across the screen. One of the sliders moved. A yellow line gave a quick wiggle and moved up on the scale.

The man drained what was left in the cup, placed it back on the table, and started buttoning his jacket.

"Try another control."

Lizzy felt like she was on a winning streak on Jeopardy. "Another control for a thousand," she typed. Tuition was taken care of for another year.

The man continued buttoning up. Whatever the device was supposed to do, it wasn't very dramatic, she thought. She pushed the new control slider to the far end of the scale. Another year of college, four years in med school, and she would be doing this kind of work for real. She wondered how much the implant cost the man, and whether he could afford it, and how exciting it would be to help a patient. She noticed that the green line was running flat along the upper edge of the scale. Ooops. She slid the control back in place, but the line didn't budge. She tried again. The line squirmed like a snake and went back up again.

When she looked up, the man was hurrying toward the door, his gait unsteady. An elderly woman was walking in. The man shoved past her and blasted through the door without stopping.

Lizzy stood up so she could see him. The man was outside, heading toward the busy Pacific Coast Highway, staggering as if he were drunk. Before she had time to panic, the man stepped off the curb into the path of a speeding Ferrari.

Lizzy's hand flew to her mouth as she saw the man being scooped up by the car's low hood like a hamburger on a grill. The body flew into the air, flipped, and plunged head first onto the asphalt, the cinnamon bun splattering next him, the napkin carried off by the breeze.

Gasps spread across the cafe. "Oh, my God!" "Call 911." "Did you see that?"

She was on her feet, out the door, and in her car before panic overcame her. Oh shit, oh no, oh shit. Mercifully the Four Runner cranked over on the first try.

"Good job," a man's voice said from behind her. "Now let me have the iPad."

Lizzy felt warm liquid escaping between her thighs. "That wasn't the deal," she managed, trying to sound as confident as she could.

"It is, now," the man said. "There's ten thou in here." An envelope appeared over her shoulder. "Includes the iPad. Just drive around the corner."

NFW, Lizzy thought as she grabbed the door handle. Words from self-defense class flashed in her mind. "Under no circumstances let them take you to a secondary crime scene. They're more likely to kill you . . ."

"If you don't want to drive, I will." A hand clamped the back of her neck like a vise.

"I want . . ."

A smelly rag choked out her cry.

 **01**

ONE YEAR LATER

A pair of aviator sunglasses floated across the cockpit. Mauricio reached out, his arm unsteady in the decreased gravity, and slid them back over the bump in the bridge of his nose. Then he twisted the yoke, flipped the plane upright and rammed in the throttle. The roar of the single supercharged engine filled the cabin. The plane responded, pinning him against the seat as it rocketed into the dawn sky. He smelled the scent of oil and fuel and felt the metal straining, relishing a rare moment of peace.

Far below, the freeways lay like casually abandoned double-stranded necklaces—shimmering red rubies on one side, rich orange topazes on the other. Thousands of commuters inching to their day jobs like determined ants. To the west, toward the Pacific Ocean, thick fog lay in a layer of whipped cream, concealing the concrete jungles of tall buildings and wide boulevards of Newport Beach. For a moment he let himself imagine how the real jungle of his boyhood home would look like from the air.

In the distance the jagged black outlines of the San Gorgonio Mountains carved the deep orange horizon. A small cloud flared like a bonfire, telling him the rising sun was moments away. He kept the plane climbing until a blinding orange crescent emerged from behind the hills, gilding the filigree of wispy clouds above it. Sunrise.

"Manhã, tão bonita manhã," he hummed, knowing the Brazilian lyrics paled by comparison to the majesty of this morning. It was an awesome sight, the flight to honor the anniversary of his sister Dora's death.

At the top of the climb, he pulled the throttle back. The cabin grew eerily silent. The plane decelerated, stopped and hung suspended, as still as a raptor floating on an updraft.

He sat motionless, weightless, waiting. The plane groaned, hesitated, then began a backward slide, flipping on its back, tumbling like a wounded bird, plummeting out of control toward the barren hills, the rocky protrusions growing larger, exploding in the windshield.

Just like Icarus, he thought, recalling the mythical hero who aspired to soar with birds. Using feathers and bee's wax, his father built Icarus a pair of wings. "Be humble, my son, and do not fly too high," he cautioned. But the young man disobeyed. He leaped off a cliff, spread his wings and flew up, and up, reaching toward the sun. Angered by the man's hubris, Helios the Sun God heated the wax until it melted. The wings disintegrated, plunging Icarus cartwheeling to his death.

He had built this plane himself, bolt by bolt, selecting components to his own liking. It had been a welcome relief from the long hours of surgery at the hospital, before the all-consuming work on the LX neuronal implant came into his life. He named the plane Icarus. Was it a reminder to respect the limits, or a challenge to exceed them? He didn't know himself.

He watched the altimeter whirring past the thousand-foot mark. Nine, eight, seven . . . The air screamed across the airframe. At two thousand feet, the sun sunk back behind the hills. Sunrise undone. The clock turned back. What he wouldn't give for a chance to turn the clock thirty years back.

The spinning terrain was a kaleidoscope that dominated his vision.

He felt his pulse accelerating, the lungs gulping air, the adrenaline flooding. In a few seconds, he and Icarus could turn into a tombstone of aluminum and flesh.

Another hundred feet.

At least he would have a tombstone. Nothing marked the site where Dora died. Nothing but floating lily pads. And it was his fault.

The rocks were closer.

A radio call intruded into his moment. "Seven Seven Mike Bravo, So-Cal Approach. Are you on frequency?"

He wrenched Icarus out of the dive, the blood sluicing from his brain, the G-forces tearing at his every organ. For a few labored heartbeats, light turned to darkness.

"Seven Seven Mike Bravo, So-Cal Approach."

He knew he had to press the mike button, but pinned by gravity, his thumb wasn't moving. Instinctively, he pumped his legs, chasing the blood back to his brain. Daylight returned. Hilltops receded. Icarus leveled off and the G-forces released their grip. "This is Seven Seven Mike Bravo," he managed. "Go ahead, So-Cal."

"Confirm this is Dr. Mauricio de Barcelos."

"That's affirmative." Alarms went off in his brain. Traffic controllers never used names. How did they even know?

"Switch to one-two-two-point-eight, sir, for a landline patch," the professional monotone recited. "It's your hospital with an emergency call."

"Mau . . . Bruce . . . need you . . . accident . . ."

The static made the words unintelligible. He took a deep breath. "Say again, Bruce. Slowly."

Bruce was Chief of Psychiatry at Newport Bay Medical Center, and Mauricio's counterpart in the LX neuronal implant study for the past five years. High-strung by nature, Bruce was prone to calling about complications that were often imaginary.

"Head . . . not sure what . . ."

"What happened?"

Static. Something garbled, then, "Weasel called Talon . . . You need . . ."

Now Bruce had his attention. If Administrator Isaacson, The Weasel, and the incompetent surgeon Charles Talon were involved, the potential for both a PR and a clinical disaster was enormous. "Who. Is. The patient?"

More garbled words, but there was no mistaking the panic in Bruce's voice. "Not over radio . . . Get here . . ."

His brain raced through the possibilities. A software crash? A subdural bleed? A suicide? Whatever it was, the golden hour—the magic sixty minutes after the event, when corrective measures were the most promising—was ticking away. With Talon in charge, probably uselessly. He had to get down fast. He glanced out, calculating. Fullerton, the little airstrip where he kept Icarus, was just ahead, but it would be an hour drive to Newport. The Orange County John Wayne Airport was by far the closest to the hospital, lay buried in fog.

Approach Control was back on the air, annoyed. "Mike Bravo, So-Cal Approach. State your intentions."

He realized that he hadn't been listening. "Mike Bravo requesting clearance direct to John Wayne."

"John Wayne is reporting visibility one-fifty, ceiling indefinite. Airport is below minimums," the controller rattled off. "Long Beach is six-fifty and one mile. Fullerton is clear. I suggest Fullerton."

He glanced at the deck of clouds cloaking the coastline. With a hundred and fifty feet of visibility, it would be like diving into a bucket of milk.

His mind reconstructed Bruce's fragmented message: "I cannot tell you who she is on the radio, but get here and save her, or it'll be a catastrophe." He pressed the mike button. "So-Cal, Mike Bravo ready to copy clearance to John Wayne."

Minutes later, everything outside the windshield turned white.

02

M AURICIO FELT THE FAMILIAR SHUDDER of the airframe as Icarus punched into the cloud layer. The bright skyline turned to amorphous gray. Now all he had to guide him to the ground was a cluster of multicolored gauges. The Instrument Landing System could guide him down to 250 feet above ground—right at the height of several of the 25-story buildings in the vicinity of the airport. After that, the instruments were useless. Descending lower without seeing the runway would be playing Russian roulette.

"Here we go," he whispered. Just a routine instrument approach, he reassured himself. This one was going to require bending a few rules and risking his life, but for a good reason.

But then he was used to breaking rules. His innovative neuronal implant had far surpassed any currently available antidepressant drug. Even dysfunctional suicidal depressed zombies had been rehabilitated to near-normal function. Only foot-dragging by the FDA kept it from being available to many more of the sixteen million men and women incapacitated by depression.

"Mike Bravo, contact tower now on one two six point eight," the controller was saying. "After your missed approach, climb to three thousand and turn right two seven zero."

Your missed approach . . . The man was already assuming he would not be able to land in this weather. "Have a good day," he snapped back. You're talking to the wrong guy. If one of his patients' lives was at stake, he was going to make it, no matter what.

He listened to the engine humming evenly. Icarus descended through 800 feet, the fog so thick he couldn't see his wingtips.

Five hundred feet, ILS needles still locked on the centerline. There was nothing to do but follow the glide slope down and hope the clouds were not all the way to the ground.

Bruce had been unwilling to reveal specifics as what awaited him. With the FDA's paranoia, any complication, even an unrelated accident, would be used to send the project into revision hell.

Concentrate. Fly.

At 400 feet he ventured a glance outside. Gray.

"Mike Bravo, we have the approach lights on full," the tower controller said, his voice attempting a soothing tone. "Report runway in sight."

No runway.

Whatever it was, he would have to prove to the FDA that it was not an implant malfunction. That could take months. Maybe years.

Think about the approach. Or you'll have your own malfunction.

He was 300 feet above rooftops, freeways and power lines. All he could see was gray. Flat, featureless gray. Fifty feet left until safe and legal flying would turn into mortal danger.

A shrill beep pierced the cockpit. The DH light flashed on the panel. Two hundred and fifty feet. Mandatory decision height: see the runway or climb and head for the alternate. The erratic needles were now nothing but a best-guess of his exact position. He pressed the mike button. "Uh, runway in sight." Not really, but it was close enough to the truth.

"Mike Bravo, clear to land runway two-zero right," the tower controller said. "Understand you do have runway in sight."

Almost. Any second now. He was sure of it.

One hundred and thirty feet above ground. Give or take fifty. No sign of runway. No lights, no beacon, no flashers. He was hurtling along at over one hundred miles an hour, blindly skimming very hard objects.

"Calma, Mauricio," he whispered. Stay calm. It was not different from delving into a patient's gray matter with long probes. One neuron at a time. Don't let them see you sweat. That was the operating room mandate.

One foot at a time, his ship continued its relentless descent. He realized he had a death-grip on the yoke and made an effort to wiggle his fingers. Sticky sweat oozed out.

Eighty feet. Give or take fifty.

A flash of yellow light burst through the side window. It vanished, then reappeared, now as a string of yellow blurs. The unmistakable glare of runway lights.

He yanked the power and shoved the nose down. Almost immediately, the wheels struck asphalt. He let out the breath he didn't realize he had been holding. He released the grip on the yoke, wiped the sweat off his hands on his pants, and rolled onto a taxiway.

Red flashing lights emerged from the fog and raced toward him. He made out the outlines of two police motorcycles followed by a massive black SUV. He slammed on the brakes. Busted?

"That's your ride," the controller explained.

As the Suburban raced north on Pacific Coast Highway, Mauricio took in the large radios, the gun rack, and the man and woman sitting up front, their shoulders blocking his forward view. "You're not hospital security?" he asked, wondering about the ground transportation that Bruce must have arranged.

The woman turned to face him. She was an attractive short-haired redhead, with high cheekbones that set off her large brown eyes. "I'm

Gayle Morris," she said, skirting his question.

He noticed her eyes dart up and down him with obvious disapproval and distrust. He was dressed in his casual flying-on-my-day-off outfit: old gray sweat pants, a sweat shirt dotted with airplane oil, and his old running shoes. He shifted uncomfortably and ran his fingers through his hair in an attempt to organize the curly mess. Mercifully, Gayle turned forward again.

Minutes later the motorcade whipped around a corner, and the eight-story shape of Newport Bay Medical Center floated out of the fog—a massive structure poised on a rocky promontory overlooking the Pacific.

The car screeched to a halt at the Emergency Department entrance, Gayle leaped out and his door swung open. Only now he noticed the gun holster on her hip. He found himself looking at her for an extra moment.

"Good luck, Doctor." Her voice cracked. "Do your best." Her eyes were wide with fear.

03

THE AUTOMATIC DOORS of the Emergency Department whooshed open. Warm air laced with the scent of floor cleaner blasted his nostrils.

Mauricio turned to the woman with the gun, who had accompanied him on the ride up. "Thanks, Gayle, I'll take it from here."

He hurried inside.

Someone tugged at his sleeve. "Wait up, Mau!"

He glanced over without breaking stride. Chief of Psychiatry Bruce Levine, a roly-poly man in his early fifties, was normally upbeat and jovial. Now, disheveled and breathless, his cherubic round face flushed, his limbs jerking, Bruce looked like one of his own patients in the throes of an anxiety attack.

"Mau, I . . . I fucked up," Bruce panted, trying to keep up. "I knew she would try again, sooner or later . . ."

"Who, Bruce?"

Bruce glanced around and lowered his voice. "You never met her. She didn't get the wire. She was in the control group."

Mauricio felt his shoulders relaxing as a wave of relief swept over him. The emergency had nothing to do with the LX implant.

"I shouldn't have . . ." Bruce stammered, trotting alongside. "Oh, man . . . That's why I called you. Mau, you have to save her!"

He paused with his hand on the door to the trauma area. "Hang in there, Bruce. Let me see what's going on and . . ."

A nurse flung the door open from inside. "Dr. B, you better get in there . . . Dr. Talon just called it."

"Called what?" Bruce paled. "Is she dead? Oh, my God. Mau! Do something."

Mauricio followed the nurse inside.

As the inner door was closing, Bruce yelled, "Save her, Mau. Please!"

The moment Mauricio stepped into Trauma One, he knew things had gone terribly wrong. Nurses, techs, scanners, fluid pumps were everywhere. The smell of recent trauma treatment frenzy—body odors, cleaning fluids, body fluids, blood, and the acrylic aroma of newly ripped sterile packages—permeated the air. But hardly anyone was moving. It was like a movie set of a battle scene after the director had yelled, "Cut."

"Dr. B's here," one of the nurses called out.

"Good morning, everyone," he nodded. He could see the pain of failure etched on the half-dozen faces that turned toward him. They looked like weary soldiers who had just lost a battle.

Charles Talon's billiard ball-bald head looked up from an iPad. "Dr. Barcelos," Talon said, his voice frosty. "To what do we owe the pleasure?"

Talon was twenty years older than him, and at six-foot-four he was almost a head taller. As former Chief-of-Staff at NBMC, the man behaved like a semi-divine authority.

"Bruce called me," he explained as he worked his way toward the patient's gurney.

He and Talon had butted heads on many occasions. Former cardiothoracic surgeon, Talon had lost most of his skills, but none of his friends, who included the wealthiest people in Newport Beach. Name-the-building-after-me wealthiest. So Talon remained on the staff and occasionally wound up in situations that were clearly above his skill grade.

"Oh, yes. The shrink," Talon smirked. "He was pretty freaked out. But there's not much to do here." Talon gestured dismissively over his shoulder. "We're just breathing her . . . Waiting for her Ob to get here, so he can take the baby out. At least we'll save the kid."

Mauricio eased his way through the crowd and approached the gurney. "What's her story?" he asked no one in particular.

"Thirty-four-year-old married female . . ." one of the nurses began reciting.

Maggie, the head nurse on the shift, a perky brunette with almond eyes who had always been the friendliest, took over. "Dr. B, the paramedics brought her here on Dr. Levine's insistence. The patient fell or was pushed from a third story balcony . . ."

He frowned. Newport Bay Medical Center was not a Level One facility. Trauma cases went to Mission, just minutes down the road. Why was this trauma patient here?

Talon interrupted. "She didn't fall, she jumped. Bruce should've institutionalized her a long time ago. Now we have a mess on our hands."

Without acknowledging the remark, Mauricio moved to the head of the gurney. The patient, a young female, attached to tubes, lines and monitors lay with brain-dead stillness. Her head was resting on bloody bandages that had been hastily cut off but not removed.

The face looked vaguely familiar, but it was hard to be sure, with the swelling and distortion of her features. On the left side of her head, a four-inch gash—the raw edges still oozing dark red blood—highlighted the area where her skull was slightly indented. The sheets had been pulled back and her engorged breasts rolled in rhythm with the hissing respirator.

His eyes took in her bulging belly. Like a bolt of lightning, a disorienting image ground his thoughts to a halt and hurled them to a different time.

Dora, fifteen-years-old, pregnant. A pregnancy that had been allowed to proceed, because that's how things were thirty years ago in the small Brazilian village where they lived. And now Dora was dead, and it was his fault, and damn it all . . .

Não deixo você morrer, flashed through his head, as he stared at the comatose woman lying in front of him. I'm not going to let you die.

He became aware of someone tugging on his arm.

"Dr. Barcelos?" Maggie's normally smiling eyes telegraphed concerned.

"What?" His mind inched back to the present.

"Dr. Levine wants to know if he can come in."

He waved the irrelevant question away and spun toward the computer console. "I need to see her CT," he snapped, typing his access password.

"Don't have a CT," Talon said.

"Really?" Did the idiot not order one?

"CT's down, Dr. B," Maggie explained. "The tech is working on it right now."

He reached for the ophthalmoscope on the wall. A nurse snatched the instrument out of its cradle and slapped it briskly into his hand.

Talon gave a loud smirk. "You go right ahead. Doctor. But I already checked. It's squash in there. The boys said her pupils have been dilated and fixed most of the ride here... I pronounced her . . ." He glanced at the clock. "Hmm, about five minutes ago." Talon crossed his arms. "A real shame."

Mauricio felt his pulse quicken. For Talon, doing nothing was always the safest choice. He clenched his jaw to avoid blurting the thought out loud.

He pressed the ophthalmoscope to his eye and leaned to an inch from the woman's face. The smell of fresh blood and vomit filled his nostrils. Her pupils were indeed fixed in a wide-open position and unresponsive to the bright beam. Brain death was imminent, or already there. Inside the eyes, he could see micro-hemorrhages from the oph-thalmic vessels—tell-tale signs of sudden deceleration that occurred as she hit the ground. The small round spot where the optic nerve connected with the retina bulged like a mushroom trying to break through. Intracranial pressure is up. Not good.

He straightened and took in the rest of her. Young, healthy, pregnant. I'm not going to let you die, damn it.

He picked up a limp arm and ran his fingers over the cold, clammy skin. He zeroed in on her wrist, where parallel white lines were criss-crossed by angry red ones.

He felt the gears engaging, his mind sorting the facts.

According to Bruce, she was in their clinical trial, the direct comparison of his LX neural implant to the leading antidepressant, Anadep. She qualified, so she must have had a confirmed diagnosis of severe TRD—treatment-resistant depression. But she must have been randomly assigned, as dictated by the clinical trial protocol, to the Anadep arm of the study.

Obviously, with little success. The wrist scars spoke of at least two attempts to end her life, years apart. The current trauma was not a mere call for attention. This woman had been determined to end her life. And now she had apparently succeeded, and was brain dead. At least according to Talon.

Everything around him began to move in slow motion, as his brain raced ahead to what needed to be done. Yes, the woman had head trauma. But a concomitant effect of antidepressants could not be ruled out. Certain drugs would dilate the pupils, even without the head trauma. Absent of a CT scan, he had to go with instincts.

He flashed a light at her immobile eyes and checked for pupillary reflexes again. He thought he spotted a faint reaction in the left eye. The shrinking of the pupil was faint, but not imaginary. The woman was not a goner yet. Not in his book.

"Burr hole set, please," he ordered.

Three people rushed toward the shelves.

"Burr hole?" Talon exclaimed. "Are you out of your mind, de Barcelos? The woman is dead. I pronounced her!"

"Then we'll call it a post-mortem examination, Charles."

Talon puffed his chest and towered over him. "You're grandstanding, Doctor."

Mauricio ignored him and turned to the nurse at the monitors. "Fetal heart?"

She gave a thumbs-up sign.

"Drill's ready," a technician announced, thrusting the instrument tray forward.

"O-two sat at 97, BP 110 over 70," another nurse called out.

While he pushed his hands into the gloves, Maggie slipped a plastic face guard over his head. "There."

Feeling the new surge of energy in the room, he took the scalpel that Maggie held ready, and let her douse the area with Betadine. He wiped off the excess with a sponge.

"Here we go."

He made a small incision in the scalp just behind the depressed area, revealing the hard cream-colored surface of the cranium. The tech handed him the drill. He motioned for Maggie to pull back the edges of the scalp and pressed the drill bit against the exposed bone. There was a brief buzz and a faint odor of burned flesh. Then a tiny pop as the bit penetrated the outer layer of the temporal bone. Then softness, then another pop. The bit was in the subdural space.

He pulled out and held his breath. His heart did an extra beat when a thin fountain of blood, dark-red and thick, sprung out of the drilled orifice across the gurney and onto the floor.

"Bingo," Maggie exclaimed.

"Lucky guess," scoffed Talon.

The stream continued for several long moments, then tapered off.

"Big one," he said, estimating the hematoma that had been crushing her brain to be a minimum of two hundred cc's. A cupful that was about to crush the life out of the brain in the confined space.

The bleeding stopped. He waited. For an eternity, there was nothing but the uneven chime of patient's and baby's monitors. He checked the pupils. They were as minimally reactive as before.

Come on. Work with me. Another moment passed. No one was moving. He ground his knuckles into her sternum. Nothing. "What's her name?"

"It's Lori." Maggie's tone implied that he should know her. Why would he? She hadn't been his patient, until now.

He sunk his thumb next to the girl's shoulder joint, in the Spockgrip designed to elicit pain without injury, and shouted into her ear. "Lori, can you hear me?" There was no response. He squeezed harder. "Lori!"

An electric jolt raced through his body as Lori's right arm fluttered off the gurney.

Not a goner.

"Open your eyes, Lori." For an endless second, nothing happened. Then one eyelid drifted open. The eye wandered, and then focused on him.

There was a collective gasp, and then a cheer filled the room.

Mauricio felt his shoulders relaxing. "That's better," he said, as casually as he could manage. He stepped back, released a quiet breath. Lori was not out of trouble, but not dead. He would take her to the operating room and clean up the fragments.

He was stripping his gloves when a thought flashed. Did Maggie say Lori? Suddenly the features coalesced into a familiar face. The short-cropped blond hair, the angle of the jaw.

He took two fast breaths, then calmed himself.

Lori Caldwell Thorp. The daughter of the President of the United States.

04

Mauricio caught sight of Bruce, staring at him across the room wide-eyed and expectant. At that instant he understood why Bruce had summoned him. So far what he had done was textbook intervention. Any competent brain surgeon would have done the same. Bruce was expecting more. But there was no way he was going to do it.

"It's not going to happen, Bruce," Mauricio snapped when they were huddled in a small consultation room adjacent to Trauma One. Beyond the glass partition Emergency Room and Operating Room, teams moved silently, preparing Lori to be taken up to surgery. "Not going to happen," he repeated.

"I understand, Mau," the psychiatrist nodded with the passive-aggressive look Mauricio hated so much.

"You called me in to make sure she didn't die of the head injury on Talon's watch…"

"I called you to save her."

"Mission accomplished. She's saved. I'm going to take her to the OR, debrid the fragments . . ."

"Hey, it's okay. You don't even have to do that. I'm sure Talon would be happy to do it."

The thought of letting the incompetent surgeon work on Lori was revolting. "I started, I'll finish. But then she's all yours."

Bruce gave a quick nod of agreement. "Right. Till she tries again."

"Double her Anadep. She's in our clinical trial, and you love the drug. Seventy-six percent success rate, as you are so fond of reminding me."

"I had her on the max dose already. She's the twenty-four percent where it doesn't work." Bruce paused. "Mau, the wire is all that we have to offer her."

You're probably right, he thought.

They both looked through the window as the nurses prepared to move Lori.

"Do you know what her odds are?" Bruce was asking.

"Of surviving the brain injury? From what I see they're…"

"Of surviving her next attempt," Bruce interrupted. "You know there will be a next attempt. What are the numbers?"

He searched his memory. "This being her third go-around…?"

"Fourth, counting the two wrist slashing and the overdose."

"Something like ninety percent?"

"Actually, ninety-seven percent mortality on a fifth attempt." Bruce paused, as if to let the information sink in. "Lung cancer has better odds!"

"You'll just have to watch her more closely."

"Yeah, that really worked," Bruce smirked. "Secret Service twenty-four/seven, and she still managed to fly off the balcony."

Mauricio glanced over his shoulder into the adjacent room, where the young woman's pregnant belly glistened under the overhead lights.

Dora was four months pregnant when she died, he reminded himself.

"It's a matter of time till she's back on that gurney, Mau, and next time she'll go for something more effective." Bruce held two fingers to his temple, and then mumbled something that sounded like "drowning."

The word felt like a gut punch. Drowning. Like Dora.

"What did you say?"

"Nothing. You know what she needs, Mau." Bruce's voice was seductively low. "Sooner or later, she needs the implant."

If it were Dora, would he risk it? he asked himself. His reputation, his career, the future approval of his LX implant were all at stake. His pulse was hammering in his head. Yet he knew the answer even before the issues gelled.

"Okay, Bruce. I'll break protocol and do it."

Bruce's face relaxed and he breathed a sigh of relief. "It's the best choice, Mau. I'll schedule her. Six weeks?"

Mauricio looked at the psychiatrist. "Six weeks?" The man was clueless, but he wasn't a surgeon. He glanced through the glass wall. In Trauma One, two orderlies were steering Lori's gurney toward the door. He pushed the intercom. "Hold it."

He felt like Icarus about to leap off the cliff.

"Maggie, send someone to my OR and bring down the head scanner. And a couple of wire kits. And see if you can get Mel to come in."

On the other side of the glass, Maggie's jaw dropped.

"Just do it." When he turned to Bruce, the man's satisfied smile had morphed into panic.

"You're going to do it now?" Bruce gasped. "Right here in the ER?" "Are you crazy?"

Crazy? For a moment he was tempted to point out the obvious: You should know; you used to be my shrink. But this wasn't the time or place.

Talon barged into the room. "I forbid you," Talon yelled, his deep voice filling the confined space.

"I don't need your permission."

"I'm in charge," Talon persisted.

"Not since her personal physician here asked me to take over."

"But Mau," Bruce pleaded, "I didn't mean now. I meant eventually, once she's stabilized . . ."

I wish it were that easy. "We can't wait," he snapped. "If I'm going to do it, it's now! Before her brain swells even more. Before it's pea soup in there, and I can't find the landmarks." He forced a calming breath before going on. "Bruce, her window of opportunity is about to slam shut, for months. When she recovers, she'll try again. We both know it."

Bruce was panting. "Let's just wait . . ."

"Think of the liability to the center," Talon hissed through clenched teeth.

"I'm thinking of the patient," he shot back.

Talon pressed on. "You're not going to stick your experimental wire into the President's daughter." Talon made experimental sound like leprosy. "Not without her informed consent."

"She's in the study. She signed for both Anadep and LX before she was randomized to the drug."

That seemed to stop Talon's next rant. He turned to leave, but stopped at the door, his finger pointing. "If something goes wrong . . ."

"How much more 'wrong' can it get, Doctor Talon? You pronounced her dead already."

05

Mauricio rolled his stool closer to Lori's gurney, positioned her head in the scanner frame, and one by one he tightened the screws that would hold her head immobile throughout the procedure.

Here in the Emergency Room setting, the neural implant paraphernalia felt out of place, and working without his regular team was awkward, but he was racing against time.

He punched a button on the monitor console. The minute the three-dimensional multicolored image of Lori's brain appeared on the overhead monitor, his heart sunk. The distribution of colors told him that her brain, in response to the severe deceleration trauma, was already swelling. The anatomical landmarks were turning into fuzzy clouds.

It's not too late to call it quits . . .

He bent down to confirm the alignment of the insertion device, and then straightened up, unrolling his shoulders. He was about to reach for the drill, but hesitated. All eyes were on him, and there was nowhere to hide, so he leaned forward. Holding his left hand concealed, he made a fist, with the thumb pinched between his index and middle finger. "Faz figa," he whispered under his breath. The good luck sign of his childhood years in the Amazon.

He held his right hand out, and a tech slapped the electric drill into his hand.

No bailing out now, he thought as he began to drill an access port through Lori's mastoid process, just behind her right ear.

The odor of burning flesh and bone filled his nostrils. With it came the calm relief of being on familiar ground. But slipping a neural implant into brain mush was not familiar at all. Acute head trauma, semi-comatose, pregnant. The number of possible complications, some life-ending for her, all career-ending for him, was endless. He was walking on the razor's edge.

Mauricio remembered one of his patient's sayings, "Come out to the edge; it's less crowded out here." The man had severe mania, but there was truth to the statement.

He exhaled slowly and finished drilling the hole. Establishing an entry was the easy part. Navigating his way through the fog of a deformed brain was a different story. He handed the drill back.

"I'll take the wire now, Maggie."

Maggie snapped open the sterile LX package. He eased out the six-inch-long strand and inspected it. The hair-thin wire encased in a clear flexible poly sleeve slid smoothly between his fingers. He threaded it into the insertion device, and made sure the filament release mechanism was cocked. He focused on the large overhead monitor. The outlines of the cerebellum and corpus callosum were even fainter now. Swelling was setting in, fast.

He glanced at Maggie, wondering if she realized the difficulty ahead. "Dim room lights, please."

The room went dark and quiet. Only the beeping and the whooshing sounds betrayed the signs of life. He advanced the plunger of the insertion platform. On the screen, the tip of the LX slowly slid into Lori's brain cavity.

"EEG on, please," he ordered.

"I'm looking for the control . . ." a nurse mumbled. "I'm sorry Dr.

B. We don't normally . . ."

He suppressed a frustrated breath. "Press the second button from the left," he said, his eyes on the screen, where the tip of the LX was quivering gently, in sync with Lori's pulse. "Now slide . . ."

"EEG captured," said a raspy voice with a vestige of Scottish brogue.

He didn't need to look up. Mel's voice was unmistakable. Immediately, he felt more relaxed. With his competent, level-headed software designer and programming expert by his side, the way ahead was suddenly less daunting. "What happened to never missing your morning spin in the wild blue yonder," he ribbed Mel.

"Hey, Big Red and I were up way before you," Mel mumbled. "I came in to work on code, and heard you were doing a solo."

"Will never happen again, I promise," he said in mock contrition. "Be a sport, ping her with 20 millivolts."

"Reaction nominal at 20," Mel responded. "Not sure why you're doing the download outside my lab, but hey, you're the expert."

Mel had been adamant about LX procedures being done only in the confines of his lab, specially shielded from any radio or wi-fi interference. But right now it wasn't an option. "We'll reset it later, if you want," he offered.

The wire continued snaking slowly into the brain, millimeter by millimeter.

"Thirty."

"You're still good."

"Deploying filaments, watch for gamma and theta spikes."

"None."

He continued, his whole body frozen in concentration. It was like threading the eye of a needle, while holding the thread with a long bamboo pole.

"We're good on the vitals, Dr. B," Maggie added.

The tip responded obediently to the gentle guidance of his fingers, as it worked its way among the labyrinth of brain structures, its normal anatomy distorted by the rapidly increasing swelling. For Lori it was not a moment too soon.

"Three degrees left," came Mel's quiet suggestion.

"I see it."

The tip of the wire reached the target zone. "Yes," he congratulated himself silently. Step one. "Deploying."

Mauricio discarded the sleeve and moved the flange forward, deploying the electrodes. On the screen, five hair-thin wires fanned out from the LX tip, snaking toward their respective areas.

"Lines are good," Mel reported on the tracings of brain activity in the familiar shorthand they had honed over years of working side by side.

This was the most complex part of the procedure. The five filaments that emerged from the tubular structure of the LX wire would now settle in the various intended brain regions. From there, electrical microcurrents would cast out a net of interacting fields, stimulating various cells to release neurotropic agents, adjusting the brain chemistry far more precisely than any antidepressant drug could. It was that easy. If only Lori's brain were a little less distorted.

"Now the module." He took a flat, quarter-sized shiny device from the tray and clamped it on to the protruding end of the wire. With a swift sweeping motion with a Kelly clamp, he carved out a small pocket under Lori's scalp and slipped the module inside.

"And a stitch. How's the contact, Mel?"

"Five out of five," Mel reported after checking the Bluetooth connection between his console and the implanted module.

Mauricio stood up and rolled his shoulders, wondering if he had just dodged a bullet or hung himself. Time would tell.

"Good job, everybody. Thank you."

He slipped off his gloves, shoved the gown into the bio-bin, and headed toward the door.

The shriek of a monitor froze him in mid-step.

"BP's climbing!" Maggie called out. "180/100."

Mauricio felt his gut cramping. In an instant, he was back at Lori's side, pulling on a pair of gloves that miraculously materialized in his hands, checking her pupils, examining the LX protruding from her scalp, and scanning the monitors. He searched his memory for another instance when hypertension had occurred after an LX implant.

When he met Mel's eyes, he was squinting slightly. The only other time he had seen Mel squint was nanoseconds before two planes crashed at an air show.

Maggie glanced at him. "Would the LX do that?"

He shook his head. He had never seen malignant hypertension after an implant. His shirt was sticking to his skin, as cold sweat ran down his back.

"Manitol IV, push up her FIO2, hold the fluids," he fired off, trying to keep his voice even. "CT up yet?"

"Not yet," Maggie said.

"BP is 200/120," a tech yelled.

Alarms were shrieking, both at bedside and in his brain.

Perhaps one of the filaments had gone astray and was sending impulses to the blood pressure regulating centers. Or some anomalous cross-wave interference was tricking her brain into a false-stress response. But he had eliminated those side effects long ago, in his early experiments on dogs. Just so that it wouldn't happen in a patient. And it hadn't happened. Until now. In the woman he had risked his invention and his career to save.

From imminent success to terminal disaster, in one easy deviation from protocol, flashed through his mind.

"Fetal heart 175," the tech announced. "Up from 140 a minute ago."

His mind spinning, he scanned the EEG streaming across the monitor. He noted gamma wave distortions that spoke of stress, but the LX output was normal.

"Mel?"

"Tailspin."

"No shit."

"210/120! Fetal heart is accelerating . . ."

Oh, shit.

He felt like he was flying, but the controls had snapped and the plane was tumbling toward the rocks.

"Stop her fluids," he ordered, knowing it would make little difference.

A drop rolled down his forehead and dripped on his sleeve.

He ran down the differential diagnosis. Brain swelling . . . A reaction to one of the drugs . . . Kidney trauma . . . Ruptured spleen . . .

He pulled back the sheets and felt Lori's belly. His mind dredged through every obscure cause of increased blood pressure he had ever encountered in his training. Suddenly he sighed in relief.

Preeclampsia!

It hadn't been the LX that caused the problem. It was the paradoxical rise in blood pressure that some women experienced during labor.

"Mag citrate," he said. "Push fifty IV now, then every three minutes. Tell the OB team to join us in the OR."

All around, heads were nodding as they remembered the sudden blood pressure spike that sometimes struck women in labor.

"Near miss," Mel said calmly.

Mauricio rolled his shoulders. A very near miss indeed. "Now the easy part. Brain surgery." As he stabilized Lori's wire for transport to the operating room, he noticed that his hand was shaking.

06

Picking out bone fragments from Lori's brain was like pulling spaghetti out of the sauce, without disturbing the sauce. His muscles ached from sitting hunched over the microscope, virtually motionless. Maggie's brief shoulder rubs offered only temporary relief.

As far as he could tell, nothing important had been destroyed. At one point Lori was even able to mumble, "My baby?" When he told her that the OB had performed a Cesarean section and delivered a healthy seven-pound girl, she managed a contented groan. Whether Lori's mental state would improve enough for her to be a good mother was now pretty much up to the implanted LX.

By the time he finished the debridement, it was nearly evening. The surgeons' lounge was deserted. He settled in front of one of the computers and began dictating. "A Leksell stereotactic frame was applied using local anesthesia. Images of two-millimeter thickness without overlap were reconstructed in three dimensions using the Medtronic neuronavigation software . . ."

Ten minutes later, he was done. Slipping a white lab coat over his surgical scrubs, he stepped out into a quieter and darker nighttime corridor.

As Mauricio approached the recovery room, two Secret Service agents blocked the door.

"Hold it, sir," said the man.

"It's okay, he's the doctor," the woman replied.

He recognized the pretty redhead from the morning ride and smiled a greeting. "Gayle, right?"

She smiled back. "Yes, the agent in charge of watching over Mrs. Caldwell-Thorp." She pressed her back into the door to open it for him. "Thank you," she mouthed, as Mauricio stepped into the room.

The recovery room had been cleared of patients. Two more agents stood by the wall, their eyes watching him intently. He recognized the First Lady even from the back. She stood by her daughter's gurney, smaller and frailer in person than she appeared on TV.

"Mrs. Caldwell? I'm Dr. de Barcelos."

She turned. He was struck by her poised demeanor, despite puffy eyes. Without a word, she reached out, took his hand and held it.

"Will she be . . . okay?" she managed to say after a long silence.

"It's hard to say this early after head trauma, but . . ."

She squeezed his hand. "I mean later."

"Mrs. Caldwell, the success we've had with the LX has been very encouraging."

He saw her nod without enthusiasm. Years of disappointing results must have taught her there were no miracle cures.

"As soon as we do the programming of the implant, we'll know how she responds," he reassured her.

She narrowed her eyes. "What programming?"

"The programming that tells the LX how much stimulation goes to each area of the brain. I need Lori to be awake to participate."

He noted the First Lady's blank stare. "Didn't Dr. Levine explain this, when he admitted Lori into the study?"

Patty Caldwell shrugged. "He might have. It's been six months. It feels like six years, you know. All I remember is that they were running a comparison between some brand new drug that he said was amazing and would make Lori's life so much better . . ."

"Anadep. Yes, the drug had just been approved as the anti-depressant of choice. The LX had to compare favorably in this study, before it could get its own FDA approval."

"And did it prove to be as good as Anadep?"

"The LX has surpassed the drug in many ways," he said, searching for how to break the news. "It works as well or better in most cases because it can be instantly adjusted to the patient's needs. And it has almost no side-effects."

Patty Caldwell's eyebrows rose as she waited for more. "You don't need to dummy it down for me, Dr. Barcelos. I used to be a nurse."

"Okay, then." He flipped open his iPad. In well-practiced medical language, he explained how the micro-currents generated by each filament created a net over the key psychotropic areas of the brain. How changing the timing and the intensity of the output from each of the five filaments enabled the device to achieve an almost infinite combination of results. How the feat was comparable to adjusting a myriad of medications simultaneously, instantaneously and reversibly, until the perfect combination was found.

"Instead of drugs, you're using electrical impulses to force the production or suppression of certain neuro chemicals," she paraphrased him.

He smiled at the sudden understanding reflected in her eyes. "And best of all," he went on, bringing up a new screen with a row of sliding controls, "Lori will be able to fine-tune the output herself, using a bluetooth connection between her computer and the control module implanted under her scalp. Everything's adjustable—including sleep cycles, adrenaline levels, serotonin output . . ."

"Astounding," Patty Caldwell whispered. "I thought I knew it all after dealing with Lori's . . . condition. For four years. But this . . ."

He nodded. Astounding was a term many of his colleagues had used. At least the ones who listened to his explanation without rolling their eyes and walking away. In reality, the idea was no more astounding than the Parkinson's pacemakers and the anti-seizure brain implants that had been commonplace for over a decade.

"And that's all the therapy Lori will need?" she asked skeptically.

"I'm sure Dr. Levine is going to want to meet with her regularly. But in principle . . ." He held up his palms. "The LX should hold her. If she needs more . . ." He made an air-quote sign, "'medication,' she can adjust the inputs herself."

Patty Caldwell absorbed the information. "I wish Dr. Levine had been more forthright about the advantages. I would have chosen the LX."

"It wouldn't have made any difference," he said. "That's why we had her sign the consent for either. Then the computer chose. Blind randomization. It's the only way to ensure that human bias doesn't affect the results of the clinical trial. Dr. Levine could not have reassigned her to LX instead of Anadep. That would be tampering."

Her eyes flashed with anger. "Where I come from, Dr. Barcelos, there's always a way. And if the implant is better, that's what . . ." She stopped herself. "So how long has your implant been around?"

Oh, boy, he thought. "Uh, technically . . . We're still awaiting the FDA's decision."

She fixed him with her deep-set hazel eyes. "You're saying you put in an unapproved device into my daughter's head?"

Mauricio cleared his throat. "Well, technically, it was approved, at one point, but . . ."

At that moment Lori groaned in her post-operative stupor, and they both instantly snapped to attention, reaching for her hand and looking her in the eyes. Their hands touched.

"Lori?" They said at the same instant.

He scanned the bedside monitors. When he looked up, Patty Caldwell's expression had softened.

"You went out on a limb for my daughter." She squeezed his arm. "I won't forget that."

He gave a barely perceptible nod. She had no idea how far out on the limb he went. Someday, he might confess to her that he had never done this procedure on a patient with severe head trauma, as an emergency procedure, outside his operating room. Someday. Maybe when Lori's newborn had graduated from college.

"If it's as good as you say, what was the hold up?" Caldwell asked.

He shrugged. "A year ago the FDA agent died in a motorcycle accident the night he was supposed to sign the papers."

She glanced at him. "In New York, right? I remember. A hit-and-run. Tom had dealt with him at the FDA. "Sanjay . . . ?"

"Sanjay Shrinivasan." Mauricio had never met the man, but their frequent e-mails and Sanjay's empathy for Mauricio's challenges had forged a friendship. "His successor demanded another hundred cases. That's what I've been doing."

"So, how many left?"

"Out of the hundred? Seventeen."

She rolled her eyes. "Sounds like a technicality."

More like cover-your-ass paranoia by the newcomer, but the FDA was omnipotent. There was no appeal process, and no end to how vindictive they could be if he crossed them. "Rules . . ."

"You strike me as someone who doesn't need to be reminded that rules are meant to be broken, Dr. Barcelos." She paused, and then added in a low voice. "Would you like me to ask my husband to look into it? See if the process can be . . . expedited?"

He glanced up without raising his head. FDA approval meant future patients could be treated without the draconian qualification requirements, without the agonizing uncertainties of randomization. Thousands of patients now suffering from Treatment Resistant Depression would benefit, practically overnight. Cash would start flowing back into his depleted operational funds. His struggles would be over. He chewed on his lower lip.

"What're you afraid of?" the First Lady was asking. "I can't imagine you're enjoying running this . . . this stupid bureaucratic gauntlet."

The prospect of a life without obstacles was novel and frightening.

He busied himself with Lori's monitors, and then started toward the door. "Let me think about it, Mrs. Caldwell."

"Dr. Barcelos?"

"Yes, Mrs. Caldwell?"

"The re-election campaign is in full swing, and the last thing the President needs is to be accused of preferential treatment. If the LX is good enough for our daughter, it should be available to all." She paused, contemplating something. "I'm not supposed to give this out," she said reaching into her pocket. "But here." She handed him a card with nothing but a long number written on the bottom. "You can reach me on this twenty-four-seven, anywhere in the world."

Their eyes held for a moment. "I hope you say yes, Dr. Barcelos," she said, turning back to her daughter.

07

MAURICIO STEPPED OUT OF THE RECOVERY room to the sound of, "Uh, Dr. Barcelos?"

He blew out a frustrated breath. Shelly Isaacson's falsetto voice was unmistakable. The hospital administrator, a diminutive man with a scraggly goatee, was hurrying down the hall toward him, his short legs moving double time.

"I'm deeply concerned, Dr. Barcelos," Isaacson blurted out when he caught up with Mauricio, tension lines etched across his wedge-shaped face. He swung open the monogrammed leather case of his iPad and pointed to a headline. "'NBMC surgeon experiments on First Daughter'," he read. "'Unauthorized use of untested device.' 'California hospital practicing voodoo medicine.'" He slammed the iPad closed. "Do you realize the embarrassment these claims bring to this hospital?"

"Not as big an embarrassment as her dying on our operating table, Shelly."

"But that wouldn't be our fault, would it?" Isaacson snapped. "I'm not in the market for another fiasco, like last year."

"That was your nursing staff that let my patient slip out of the hospital and wander into traffic. Not my fault."

"Well . . . Anyway I just called Human Resources. Got Beatrice out of bed. First thing Monday morning, we're hiring a PR person. I need to undo . . . try to undo the damage you've caused."

The man's erratic movements reminded him of a weasel he had once seen, that was accidentally self-trapped in the chicken coop back home.

"And stop smirking," Isaacson snapped, his voice even more shrill. "Show some appreciation! If it weren't for this hospital . . ."

"Yes, Shelly, I remember. Without you, I'd be practicing my 'voodoo medicine' in Haiti."

Isaacson missed the irony. "Exactly. I gave you a lab when no center would give you a broom closet for your cockamamie idea."

"You gave me a lab because you knew the LX would put you on the world map."

Isaacson barked a laugh. "You think you were my first choice? I wanted Dumas. You wouldn't be here if your friend Professor Beck hadn't put in a good word for you."

"And funded the Anadep-LX study, which is now employing two dozen people, and keeping your beds full. Why is this suddenly a problem?"

Isaacson rolled his head and ran a finger around his already loose collar.

"Because the minute Cendoz finds out that NBMC proceeded with . . . What did The Register call it? The 'Unauthorized use of untested device,' they're going to yank their grant so fast it'll make my head spin. And then what? How do you think we keep our doors open then?"

Mauricio picked up the pace, doing his best to keep the harangue from derailing his good mood. "Well, with Sun Val Assemblies' help, we have close to six hundred LX kits, sitting in storage, just waiting for the Fed's nod to ship out.

Isaacson's consternation was palpable. "You had them made already?"

He chuckled. "What do you think Mel and I have been doing while we're waiting for the FDA? We're all set to go."

Isaacson shook his head. "That's a big if."

Mauricio stopped and stared him down. "Not with a grateful First Lady asking me if I want her husband to 'See if the process can be . . . expedited'."

The administrator blinked. "She did?"

"She did. And I'm wondering if my being at NBMC might not be the right fit anymore."

Isaacson winced.

Mauricio pressed the point. "Maybe when I exhibit at Neuro-Sciences Convention next week, I'll put the word out that I'm looking to relocate."

"Dr. Barcelos, that is not necessary. This is about the need for a good PR person to control the media spin, nothing more."

Mauricio was going to rebut about not needing a muzzle, but he let it pass. "Fine, Shelly, spin away. I'll go take care of my patients."

08

THE VIDEO OF THE ENCRYPTED CONNECTION remained blank, concealing the caller's appearance, but the woman's voice was crisp. "Perhaps we could meet." Al detected the hint of a German accent. "You may find the opportunity worthwhile."

This was the third encrypted communication of the morning with a woman who had identified herself simply as "K" and indicated that she worked for a small special-needs PR firm based on the East Coast. Al was intrigued.

Two hours earlier, he had been peacefully enjoying a cyber-chess game. "Bishop on h5 takes pawn on f3. Check." His voice was picked up by one of the computers on his desk. The notation, Bh5xf3+ appeared on the screen. Then the three-dimensional graphically animated objects—faithful replicas of the exquisitely carved ivory and mahogany pieces on the board in front of him—shifted positions to reflect the move.

His black bishop slid two squares diagonally and touched a white pawn. With the sound of shattered glass, the pawn disintegrated into a shrinking pile of shiny shards, and vanished. A ping confirmed that the move had been transmitted to the cyber-chess player halfway around the world.

He looked out the window of his third-floor studio apartment to watch the gray waves of the Pacific Ocean, while patiently anticipating the opponent's response.

His friends could never understand his patience, or his passion for the game. "Get a life, Chessman," they would say, making the word chessman sound derogatory, like he was loser. He could not share with them the excitement he felt in dominating opponents, in decimating their strength, in inflicting humiliating defeats.

The message that flashed on the screen made him sit bolt upright. "Bh5xg4+, O-O." O-O was a castle move, but the king could not castle in this position. He realized he was looking at a coded message from a business contact. More notations came streaming in. It added up to: "Your services wanted on a personal sensitive medical project."

"Chess game, sleep," he ordered the computer.

The screen went black and the reflection of his face stared back at him. The nose and jaw came from his Afghan father's gene pool, or at least what he could tell from pictures. The mane of black hair that he kept in a ponytail, and the green eyes, were from his mother's side. In pictures she was a spitting image of the Afghan girl on a National Geographic cover years ago. The furrows crossing his high forehead were his own and made him look older than his thirty-two years.

Medical project. Medical was all he handled nowadays. Helping one pharmaceutical manufacturer hack into another's research facilities, or stealing blueprints for a new surgical robot—it paid the bills and supported his mission.

Personal sensitive medical project? Those invariably turned out to be the most lucrative. A CEO's concealed illness needed to be investigated for its impact on the company's stock. A VIP had to be compromised with disclosure of an illicit affair. The variety had been endless.

He dictated the reply. "We only deal by referral." The computer displayed the message. "Send," he said.

The names of three recent clients appeared almost immediately. He was not dealing with an amateur. The new contact seemed legitimate. "I might be interested," he dictated. "Details."

"Here is the background." She gave a website address. "I'll contact you."

"Computer, open site," he ordered.

A simple home page flickered on. He scanned it. LX, Inc. was some sort of Ma-Pa outfit listed at a P.O. Box in Santa Ana, California. No funding, no PR savvy was written all over it. There were a few photos of the device. A catheter and a bouquet of tiny colored wires, with some sort of flat little control box attached. A screen with multicolored lines and confusing psychobabble labels. In the corner, a mug shot of a man in his early forties. The boyish smile made the age uncertain. Probably the president, CEO, inventor, and chief bottle washer, Al decided.

The computer droned out the name. "Maw-REE-cee-oh de Bar-CE-loss, em dee."

"Enlarge photo."

There was something likeable about this Maw-REE-cee-oh. The intense eyes and tall forehead spoke of a driven intellectual. A kindred soul. His skin was almost as dark as Al's. The nose, slightly deviated to the left—perhaps a poorly healed fracture—belonged to someone confident enough not to care about appearance. The curly black hair was low-maintenance. The kind of man women went to, like moths to a candle.

He felt a momentary pang of envy. Men like Barcelos garnered attention and recognition even when their accomplishments were insignificant on the world scale. His own cause had worldwide implications, but had to be kept secret. He would never be honored with a headline like "Generous Donor Rehabilitates Hundreds of Invalid Middle-Eastern Children." He would never be able to post on

Facebook about what he had done for the Injured Children's Fund. That hurt.

A screen saver image floated up. It was a map of Badakhshan Province, a chunk of mountainous terrain between Kabul and the Pakistani border. The map was dotted with red triangles. Nine one-room schools that doubled as orphanages. Shelters where children could find treatment for their injuries, and learn to read and write. Nine safe-havens he had funded with his own money.

More images. Young children, playing in the dirt. A girl wearing a t-shirt, dragging her toy—a plain rock on a string. A couple of teens, chasing a soccer ball made of bunched-up paper, each wearing a shiny above-knee prosthesis. Another girl, perhaps eight, carrying a legless youngster almost her own size in her one good arm.

He gritted his teeth. She was his favorite. One of these days he would figure out how to bring her here to be fitted with the new prosthetic arm developed by the US military. At least a scintilla of good would come from the American war effort.

He pushed off and stood up, wincing at the sharp pain that shot up from where the prosthesis met the flesh of the stump, six inches above where his left ankle used to be. After fourteen years, he was almost used to the phantom pain from poorly healed nerve endings. But on cold mornings, like today, the injury still ached. If people knew of his shelters, they might assume that his injury, like the Afghan children he helped, was from the war. It was a war, but of another kind.

Walking as evenly as he could, he crossed the simple studio apartment to the corner that was the kitchen. He liked simple. The beige granite countertop was immaculately clean. Seven mixing spoons made of olivewood were arranged in a brass vase. Three copper pans, polished to perfection, hanging from hooks above. Only the dented aluminum tea kettle, which allegedly belonged to his dead Afghan father, still smudged with campfire smoke, stood out as a vestige from another era of his life.

Across the counter, the window overlooked Ocean Avenue with its meandering path, lined with palm trees. Beyond, down a steep cliff, was the wide band of sand of Santa Monica Beach.

He selected three deep red heirloom tomatoes from a basket on the windowsill, then opened the refrigerator, extracted three Persian cucumbers, and lay all on a wooden cutting board.

He sliced the tomatoes and the cucumbers into half-inch pieces of equal volume and doled out the cuttings into a wooden bowl, discarding the few odd-sized pieces. He added three splashes of olive oil and sprinkled in a pinch of Dead Sea salt, massaging the coarse grains between his fingers. Holding the bowl in one hand, he tossed the contents into the air. Six times, without dropping a single morsel.

He was about to walk out on the tiny terrace and enjoy the breakfast when the computer pinged again.

"You may find the opportunity worthwhile," the woman was saying, her disembodied voice floating from the blank screen. He tried to paint a pictured. Probably in her fifties. Slim. Energetic.

He pulled up a map to his favorite meeting place and hit Send on his laptop. Then he picked up the salad bowl and limped out into the sunshine.

09

MAURICIO PARKED HIS AGING VOLVO XC-90 SUV in the narrow alley that separated his condo from the neighbor's, and entered his garage through the side door. Letting the sun bake the car's blue paint to a cracked grey finish was a small price to pay for the chance to convert part of the garage into exercise space.

Practicing his martial arts in a public gym—or anything resembling fighting, anywhere near others—made him feel instantly and uncontrollably sick to his stomach. He felt that way since he left Brazil, even though it was all behind him now. As much "behind" as he could put it.

The mountaineering pack filled with climbing gear, suspended from a rafter, made a cost-effective punching bag. He could have created more space by getting rid of some of his ex-wife Diane's old belongings, like her beloved stair-stepper, or the road bike, but somehow there was never time. So the stuff remained, mixed in with several sets of scuba tanks, two ice axes, a pair of expedition boots, and his mountain bike. And the dog food bowl that he kept, for those rare days when Diane asked him to babysit Lexie.

The rest of the garage was his laboratory. Shelves with tools, benches with electronic test equipment, wires and circuit boards, old prototypes and boxes full of parts occupied every square inch. It was not unlike how the LX neural implant occupied every one of his neurons for the past ten years.

He would never forget the ah-ha moment when the idea for the neural implant came to him. He was attending a lecture by Anne Powell, the neuropsychologist who developed the magneto-encephalograph. The MEG was a brilliantly simple device that could alter behavior by using a pair of rotating magnets to induce electrical currents deep within the brain. "Internal mini-electro-shock therapy," as she jokingly described it. The prohibitively expensive equipment, and the reported side effects that bordered on the supernatural, made the widespread use of the device impractical.

As he sat listening to her and doodling diagrams on his laptop, the solution came to him: why not use implanted electrodes instead of an external beam? If he attached the wires to a pacemaker . . . and sent the therapeutic current where and when it was needed . . . Deep Brain Stimulation, DBS, had been used since the late 1990s for Parkinson's disease and for seizure control. Why not for depression?

The initial response from his colleagues was dismissive. "Mau, nobody is going to let you shove a wire into their brain. We have drugs."

Drugs? Really?, he thought. What about the eight million people in the US alone who had Drug Resistant Depression? People who simply shuffled through life, bringing no joy to themselves or others? Or the 20,000 who still submit to the ravages of electro-shock therapy every year, because nothing else, absolutely nothing, could relieve their symptoms? Tell them about the wonderful drugs.

He stopped trying to persuade disbelievers, and set out to prove his case. Within a year he had built a working prototype, from existing components already in use in FDA-approved devices. Right in the garage of the home where he and his now ex-wife Diane lived, doing most of the work during the nights when he was not on call.

The principle was simple. The results astoundingly successful.

However, bringing the LX to market had almost killed him with frustration. After this morning? Who knew; maybe the journey was over.

He let himself into the house, went upstairs to the bedroom and flipped on the TV. Diane was standing in front of Newport Beach Medical Center, microphone in hand. ". . . The hospital declined to confirm the reports, citing HIPAA rules of patient confidentiality."

Keeping his eyes on the image, he began stripping off his surgical scrubs.

"KNTO was able to ascertain that First Daughter Lori Caldwell Thorp underwent surgery for head trauma, and received an experimental implant designed to control certain psychiatric conditions . . ."

Three years ago, he was standing exactly on that spot when he noticed the handwritten note on the bed. "There is no room for me—for us—in your career. I'm sorry, M. I can't do this anymore." She had underlined us. There was a PS: "Happy twelfth." That was yesterday, their twelfth anniversary. He had been in the lab, working on the LX, for three straight days and nights. And he hadn't even noticed the day.

Diane was continuing the coverage. "According to Sheldon Isaacson, the NBMC's spokesperson, Lori Caldwell Thorp is expected to make a full recovery. Her husband, an Air Force Colonel now stationed in Germany at Ramstein Air Base, has been notified and will probably return . . ."

He stepped into the bathroom and turned on the shower.

"That took serious cajones," Mel had said as he was driving Mauricio to John Wayne International, where he had abandoned Icarus that morning.

"Yes, it was dicey there for a second, with the swelling."

"I meant telling the First Lady that her daughter's implant was not FDA approved."

"She was okay with that."

"Okay enough to send some cash our way?"

He looked over at Mel, who turned away and grumbled something under his breath. His guard went up.

"What?"

Mel worked his jaw back and forth. "Sun Valley Assemblies got bought out."

He sat up. "What do you mean . . . bought out?" Sun Valley Assemblies, the small but impeccably reliable fabricator located in nearby Santa Clarita, had been assembling LX wires for him since he first started. They were more than vendors. They were friends.

"I mean they're doing someone else's production, as of yesterday. So the 540 in the warehouse, plus five in the OR, is all the wires we have left."

"When were you going to tell me this, Mel?"

Mel shrugged. "It's not your job to worry about production."

During early animal research days, he cobbled LX prototypes together in his own garage, from various outdated medical components. Later on, for the Phase One human clinical trials, he and Mel spent long nights assembling LXes in a vacant sterile operating room. The final Phase Three regulations demanded a formal manufacturing process. No Sun Valley Assemblies, no wires, no patients, no FDA approval, no loans, no wires . . .

"I'm on it," Mel was saying. "I have a fix on another place."

"As long as we can assure quality."

"So China is out?"

"Not funny."

Mel grinned. "The new place is in the Midwest. Fast, reliable."

"Go with it."

"Would've, except they wanted two hundred grand just to get started."

He winced. "You're serious?" He had designed the LX to be affordable. The wire itself was the same wire that was used in the latest Parkinson's implants. Off the shelf, by the yard, practically. The control module was a more complex version of the one in cardiac pacemakers.

The only component that made the LX unique was the software. And Mel and he installed that for free. Still, they needed a certified manufacturer.

"Where am I going to come up with $200K?"

"There's always VC money," Mel offered.

"Venture capital over my dead body. Talking about losing control and selling your soul."

"So what then?"

"Let them bill against future sales. I have nothing else left to mortgage."

Mel shrugged. "I offered. They aren't willing to risk the cost of tooling up on a non-approved device."

"We'll get it approved, Mel."

The car pulled into the parking lot, and Mauricio stepped out.

"Have fun at the party tonight," Mel said. "And say hi to the Becks for me. Both of them," he added with a mischievous grin.

Mauricio paused on the curb at the airport entrance. "So who bought Sun Val, Mel?"

"Allegedly some foreign investor."

"Why can't we buy the wires from him?"

Mel looked away. "Grapevine control says the new owner has an exclusive." Then he added, "With K&K. They'll be retooling to service the Nuvius line."

"Those greedy K&K bastards," Mauricio thought as he scrubbed in the shower. They owned a hundred other companies, including Jean-Jacques Dumas' Nuvius, his only neural implant competition. And now they were clearly angling to preemptively put him out of business.

10

MAYNARD BECK LEANED ON THE BALCONY balustrade and inhaled a Cuban cigar. From here he could see the long line of limos, Ferraris and Bentleys that snaked up Beverly Lane toward his hilltop estate. The myriad of tiny lights that his wife Anabela had the staff place throughout the gardens, twinkled like constellations against the dark foliage. Garden bling. Nice touch, he thought.

Fragments of animated conversations and the din of champagne glasses competed with the orchestra playing inside. He surveyed the colonnaded patio below, where tuxedo-clad men and bejeweled women meandered among silent auction tables. Three hundred of his closest friends gathered under the pretext of raising funds to rehabilitate a swatch of Amazonian rainforest raped by Cendoz during the harvest of a key ingredient for their drug Anadep.

He worked his knees, trying to loosen the joints worn to bone-on-bone by marathons that he had ran well into his sixties. The tuxedo fit him perfectly, but the Italian-made alligator-skin shoes that Anabela ordered for him, pinched the instep. They make you taller, Maynardee, she cooed in her lilting Brazilian accent. So what if he was no longer six-foot-two. Compared to most of his peers, he was in better health. And, thanks to Anadep, in far better wealth.

Ten years ago he was at the apex of his academic career. Professor of clinical pharmacology at Harvard Medical School, author of close to two thousand articles, a world-renowned speaker. He was the awe and envy of colleagues.

He pulled on the cigar again. Yes, he was a force to contend with.

He was mere weeks away from attaching the last two molecules to AD5639, synthesizing a revolutionary antidepressant that would have been the hottest innovation to come out of Harvard since ether anesthesia.

Then came the scandal that brought his meteoric rise to a humiliating halt: a love affair with his chief researcher. It would have been a non-event—he was 55 and widowed, she 45 and unhappily married. Consenting adults, except that the dean of the medical school had designs on the same woman, and she had turned him down flat. The fat twerp prevailed on the righteous bastards at Harvard, and the board forced Beck to resign.

Their big mistake.

He left disgraced and disempowered. His lover followed, with the formula for AD5639 on a flash drive concealed in her bra. Two years later he founded Cendoz, a wholly-owned company, whose only product was Anadep, a drug that differed from AD5639 just enough to frustrate any attempts by Harvard's legal posse to recapture the patent, but that wasn't the end of it.

The FDA approval came with a thick string attached. Back then President-to-be Thomas Caldwell was the Boston District Attorney, and he made sure Harvard got their share of the revenues—a sizeable percentage every year. He never forgave Caldwell, and had backed his opponents in every election during the man's rise to the White House.

Overnight Anadep became a fabulously successful drug. The gold standard against which other methods would be measured, for years to come. Now it was gobbling up a lion's share of the thirteen billion dollar a year antidepressant market. Paying tribute to Harvard every year still irked him. It was another score to settle. But it could wait. The next election was coming.

Beck blew out a cloud of smoke and straightened. No sign of Mauricio.

He turned to the woman standing next to him. "What do you think, Jo? The First Doctor is too good for his old friend?"

She shrugged, her always imperturbable face bland. "A sudden connection to the First Family can do strange things to a person."

That was Johanna. His faithful colleague of fifteen years, she could always be counted on a blunt assessment. His colleagues didn't call her Ice Queen for nothing.

He saw Mauricio, bounding up the steep cobblestone driveway. He recognized him by the gait—light, energetic, assured.

I used to walk like that, flashed through his mind.

Mauricio looked just like he did the day Beck summoned him to his office to inform him that he had failed biochemistry, and that Harvard Medical School was not for him.

"You should look at other options," Beck had suggested.

"I only want to do research in neurology at NIH," Mauricio announced.

"Mr. de Barcelos," Beck had said, emphasizing Mister to remind the young upstart how far he was from being a doctor. "You obviously don't have what it takes to master things you cannot see—like molecules. But you are very talented with things that you can see. I don't want your talent wasted."

"It's brain or nothing."

The dogged determination reminded Beck of himself in his younger years. It would be a waste of a brilliant mind and an indomitable drive to let this one go. "Have you considered neurosurgery?"

That suggestion turned out to be a pivotal point in Mauricio's career. And it made Beck feel responsible for ensuring the young man's future success.

He remembered Mauricio asking him to perform his hooding at the graduation. The ceremonial placement of the cap and hood on the newly minted graduate could only be done by a close relative with a doctorate degree. Even now, twenty years later, the memory brought tears to his eyes. *The son I never had.*

He now watched Mauricio work his way through the crowd toward the main entrance. A petite blond in a floor length emerald green gown, the back scooped out to her waistline, intercepted him.

He could recognize Diane from a mile away. The relentless reporter was probably asking her ex-husband for an exclusive on the First Daughter's event. It'd be a huge coup in her quest to become anchor. *That's all this case needs,* he winced. *More notoriety for his damn wire.*

Below, another woman glided up to Mauricio. He didn't need to hear the words. The woman smiled at Diane, while her left arm wrapped around Mauricio's waist, then slowly slid lower. He watched as Mauricio discretely inched away. Moments later, the woman pulled him away and they disappeared into the crowd. *Bitch.*

"Your princess," Johanna smirked. "Remind me why you put up with it?"

Beck rammed the cigar into a sand bucket. His wife's flirting was irritating, but he knew she'd never risk her life of luxury by cheating on him.

"Want to say hi to Mauricio?" he asked instead.

"Later. I'm sure I'll run into him." She pecked him on the cheek and strolled out of the room, her gait confident as if she owned the place.

He watched her lithe, athletic figure till she disappeared, then headed for the stairs, trying to stand straight despite the pain in his lower back.

Anabela da Silva de Beck was easy to spot. Tall, curvy and radiant, she practically melted her way through the crowd. In one of her manicured hands, she clutched a pair of high-heeled Louboutins, the red soles matching her fingernails and her lips. In the other she held the hem of her Givenchy gown, hiked high up on the well-tanned and well-toned thigh, and a tumbler of what Beck suspected was probably not plain Perrier. She was practically dragging Mauricio toward the dance floor.

"Darling, look who I found!" Anabela chirped as soon as she saw him. "Mauricinho is taking me dancing."

"Later, Cara," he said, trying to keep the edge out of his voice. "Mau and I need to talk."

Anabela pouted but released her prey. She blew him a kiss, turned and, hips swaying, melted back into the crowd.

He shook Mauricio's hand. It struck him that twenty years ago he was tall enough to look down on the young man's curly black hair. The hair was still curly, but now they stood eye to eye. He felt himself straightening by reflex. "Walk with me."

The security guard nodded politely as they stepped down from the colonnaded patio onto the gravel path. The noise of the crowd receded.

The luscious gardens stretched into the darkness. Crickets drowned out the distant beat of dance music. The scent of eucalyptus filled the air. Beck inhaled. *All mine. The mansion, the gardens. The crowd. Even Anabela.*

"Did I ever tell you how proud I am of how you ran your project? It took real balls to pass on all the VC money."

"Venture money is heroin. Don't try it, you'll get hooked," Mauricio recited what Beck had once told him. "I'm a good student, Professor."

Yes, a good student. And there is so much more I could have taught you. We could have been a team. Your device, my drug. An empire.

"Did you know that even my company tried to buy you out?" he said.

"Why would Cendoz want to buy my LX?"

"Because a couple of my overpaid idiots saw that K&K bought that Dubious or Nuvius, or whatever that French jerk invented. So they decided we should own a med device too. I guess they thought yours fit the bill," he chuckled. "Monkey see, monkey do. Monkeys now looking for another job. I'm glad you said No."

Suddenly his foot gave way, and he had to steady himself on Mauricio's forearm. Damn the raisers on the damned alligator shoes. "Let's sit."

He gathered his thoughts. What had happened this morning was a game changer for both of them. He put his hand on Mauricio's arm. "From now on, you'll never be able to say that you owe me." He smiled at Mauricio's bewilderment. "You've always claimed that by pushing you into neurosurgery, I saved your ass."

"You did, Professor. And I do owe you. I don't know where I'd be if ..."

"Fine, I'll take the credit for that. But what you did by sticking your wire into the President's daughter ..."

Mauricio stiffened.

"Relax. I know HIPAA makes you tongue-tied, but you can listen. In my time, we took the Hippocratic Oath—do no harm, help your patients, respect your colleagues. Now, it's HIPAA this, HIPAA that. Fuck them and their rules. Anyway with Electronic Health Records anything worth knowing is even more accessible." He paused, then continued, "Anadep is a good drug, but there are patients out there that no drug in the world can help. That's where devices like yours pick up the slack. The more lives that we, collectively as professionals, can save, the better the entire healthcare industry looks to the public. And with damned Caldwell snipping at our heels, calling pharmas greedy monsters, we need all the good PR we can get."

Beck felt his blood pressure rising. The government had thrown Big Pharma under the bus. Drug development was one of the few industries that this country could still claim was superior to the rest of the world. It was one of the mainstays of the economy. Its very survival was now threatened by unfair patent limitations and manufacturing quotas that Caldwell was trying to enact. All for the sake of garnering a few more votes from the unemployed. Shit, if Caldwell would just leave them alone, the new factories would bring enough jobs . . .

Beck cut the mental diatribe short. It was one point he and his protégé did not agree on. He changed the subject. "Damn Bruce Levine. He should never have put the President's daughter on Anadep. Not with her history."

"She was randomized," Mauricio pointed out. "The choice was the computer's, not his."

"Randomized my ass. The shrink wanted the attention! Let me be the doctor to the First Daughter. Let me prescribe her drugs. Let me cure her."

He slowed, to control his wheezing. Any two-bit researcher had ways around 'randomized' protocols. They tried to suggest that to Levine, but no, he couldn't lay low and keep her out of the study. What if the President's daughter had died while being treated with a Cendoz drug? 'PR disaster' wouldn't begin to describe it.

He leaned toward Mauricio and lowered his voice. "This morning, young man, your wire was my lightning rod. You saved my ass."

11

MAURICIO DID NOT ENJOY THE LONG DRIVE from Beck's Beverly Hills mansion down to Orange County. As soon as he walked into the house, he made a beeline to the kitchen. A dirty coffee mug and a couple of plates were in the sink, but he was too worn out by the day's events to care. He opened a cabinet and pulled out a bottle. He had kept himself from drinking at the party, knowing he would be scrutinized, particularly after this morning's heroics, as some of the guests referred to it. But now it was his time.

He poured a generous dose of cachaça into a tumbler. The pungent aroma of the sugar cane liquor, so much more flavorful than other rums, always reminded him of hot summers helping his father work the small sugar cane patch that the family had carved out of the rain forest.

He filled the glass with ice cubes and added sugar. He reached for the fruit basket. "Shit." The limes, the key ingredient for the caipirinha he had been craving all night, were gone.

For a moment he considered going next door. The slightly overweight and often underdressed neighbor seemed to have an endless supply of fresh limes and free time. Over the past few months, she had become a neighbor-with-benefits, and a safe alternative to the persistent overtures from his female co-workers.

But tonight, he was in no mood for such benefits. All he wanted was lime juice. He bent over the trash can and rummaged through the discarded cartons, the used paper towels and the wilted lettuce leaves. Near the bottom, he found three lime halves. He squeezed what juice was left into his glass, picked up the cachaça bottle and walked outside.

The backyard was little more than a cement patch around a small elongated pool, with an attached Jacuzzi, the rising steam glowing in the cool air. The breeze felt refreshing on his sweaty body. In the distance, the lights of Orange County spread like a glimmering carpet.

An airliner whooshed low overhead, engines throttled back on its descent into John Wayne Airport. It was one of the last commercial landings before noise abatement regulations closed the airport for the night. His eyes followed the flashers to the runway, barely visible in the distance. Soon the fog would roll in again and cover the coastline for most of the night. The coastline, the airport, and NBMC.

He took another gulp and closed his eyes, enjoying the burn. His stomach empty except for a dose of morning coffee and spare nibbles of party finger-food, and the buzz was building, fast and furious.

He leaned on the railing, feeling the liquor pleasantly permeating his entire body. His mind replayed the morning as a kaleidoscope of disconnected images. The call, literally out of the blue. The drill sinking through the skull, irreversibly committing him to a course of action, crossing of the medical Rubicon. The LX filaments spreading along their assigned tracks, throwing Lori the electronic lifelines to a better life. The tentative relief on Lori's mother's face.

He topped off the glass with more cachaça and swallowed half of it in one long pull.

As his mind relaxed, the morning slowly came into focus. It could have been a career- ending, self-esteem-shattering, dream-destroying disaster, but it had been the right thing to do. And he had pulled it off.

Rocking unsteadily on his feet, he picked up the bottle and raised it in the general direction of NBMC. "Parabéns!" he toasted. "Congratulations. You did well, Barcelos."

This triggered a recall from this evening's party.

"Congratulations," Beck had said when he told his mentor of the First Lady's offer to help fast-track the FDA approval. For some reason, tonight the cold stare of Beck's steel-blue eyes—the legendary gaze that petrified his med school classmates—sent a chill down his spine.

"Congratulations," Beck repeated, raising his empty glass. "Lady C does it again." Then Beck paused and looked away. "Lady C indeed." It sounded dirty on Beck's lips.

"No doubt who wears the pants on Pennsylvania Avenue," Beck ranted on. "From nurse to White House. Now she has you in her back pocket. That should come in handy, when Tom Caldwell starts pushing his healthcare bill."

"It was not about that, Professor," he had tried to protest, surprised by Beck's anger. "She just wanted to . . ."

"Bullshit," Beck spat. "Our Prez would love nothing more than to drive all manufacturers out of medicine. What's the idea? Make the taxpayers pay the millions we lose on products that never see the light of day? The business risks we take, the expensive failures . . ." Beck had been on a roll tonight.

He took a gulp, then a second one, trying to forget his mentor's ranting.

"You made the LX so simple, any chimpanzee can slip one in," Beck had said. "The minute the Feds say go, every Jo Blo with a doctor's shingle is going to want your wire. 'Come to Podunk, and we'll give you the presidential treatment.' I sure hope your warehouses are full."

Warehouses? How about two shelves' worth in his OR?

He had told Beck about the anonymous buyer who bought Sun Val Assemblies, and about his suspicion that it was a thinly disguised effort by K&K to strangle his supply line. Beck looked away and seemed to plunge into deep thought.

He remembered the Professor's alligator-skin shoes circling slowly as if he were trying to loosen his ankle joints.

"Listen," Beck said finally. "Money speaks. If K&K is behind this, you'll need funding, or the rich bastards will bury you. Let me see if I can arrange a grant for you through Cendoz. No strings attached. We'll call it educational or unrestricted or something, so there is no stink of control. My legal eagles will figure it out." His mentor's eyes looked at him with deep concern. "You're so close, Mauricio. I don't want to see you fail."

Another airliner passed overhead and he imagined how it would feel to levitate off the ground and chase the plane into the black sky. He put the bottle down as carefully as he could. Holding on to the railing, he walked to the Jacuzzi, stripped off his clothes, and eased himself into the warm water. Moments later, the mind-numbing cachaça buzz enveloped him like a cloud.

Money speaks. They will bury you.

He was staring at the marble floor of Beck's mansion, considering the offer, when Beck's shoe filled his vision and derailed his thinking. Now his mind flashed to another pair of alligator boots—the ones belonging to the rich cattle rancher back in Brazil. The boots were shining, despite the red dust of the dirt floor.

"Arrest this boy," the man was yelling. "I'm going to bury the little bastard."

The terrified boy stared at the man and his four teenage sons lined behind him, murder in their eyes.

Money certainly spoke that day. And four months later, Dora died.

I owe you, Sis, he thought just before his mind went blank.

Dora kissed him lightly on the cheek, and tiptoed into the forest, her bare feet silent on the carpet of fallen leaves. She made her way to the shore, untied the canoe, and paddled out to the center of the lake. The moon was shining. Red reflections of alligator eyes surrounded her. Dora stripped her clothes, folded them carefully, and placed them on the bottom of the boat. Her last gift to her family. She ran her hand over her bulging belly and crossed herself. Then she looked up at the stars, and let herself slip into the river.

Her screams were muffled by the splashes of caiman tails, and the crunching of bones in powerful jaws.

Mauricio awoke, coughing up chlorinated water.

"Culpa minha," he whispered. It had all been his fault, and he had carried the burden for three decades, determined to fulfill the promise he had made when he learned of Dora's meaningless death.

When did his work turn into an obsession? He couldn't remember when the realization that no self-flagellation would wash Dora's death off his hands had morphed into a drive to achieve something monumental enough to honor her memory. Dora's memorial, his LX project, seemed so close to completion, but without help, it threatened to crumbled like a house of cards. Had he been too hasty in implanting the LX in Lori? Did the question, Would you do it for Dora, cloud his judgment and led him to attract visibility that neither he nor his invention were ready for?

He felt a moment of panic. Did I make a mistake?

He shook off the dream and the anxiety, and refocused on what happened that morning.

"That's all?" the First Lady had asked when he told her he needed only seventeen more cases to meet the Fed's demand. It had been an unreasonable demand, dictated by bureaucratic paranoia. If it were not for Sanjay's death, the LX would have been approved by now.

He studied the few dim stars above.

It could be approved. All he had to do was accept her offer. Or he could hold out, until Dumas' device got its own approval, and the K&K marketing monster plowed him into the dirt.

One hundred seventy-six successes. Seventeen lousy cases to go.

It was close enough.

As soon as the sun broke the horizon, he could wait no longer. He dialed the phone number the First Lady had given him.

"Is something wrong with my daughter?" came the instantaneous reply. There was a dull whine in the background. "I'm on a quick trip to DC, but we can turn around . . ."

He began explaining his predicament, and his hope that her offer to help speed the FDA approval was still good. She interrupted before he got far.

"I already spoke to Tom. Consider it done."

12

Pedaling slowly, Al picked his way among runners, bikers and skaters jostling for position on the concrete boardwalk that ran along Santa Monica Beach. Seagulls circled low, competing with the homeless for fast food discards. A salty breeze blew off the white-capped waves.

With every down stroke, the pain around the prosthesis rekindled the memory of the car bumper crushing his leg against the garage door, and then the endless string of unsuccessful surgeries, culminating in an above-ankle amputation. He tried to keep the pain from unbalancing him. Control, Al. It's all about self-control.

He wore a dirty jacket on top of a gray tattered T-shirt, torn janitor pants, and jogging shoes that he had once rescued from a trash bin. Just another thirty-something homeless person. Even the bike was rusty, and the front wheel scraped rhythmically against the fork. The outfit would add an interesting twist to his upcoming meeting. You could tell a lot about people from the way they treated a man down on his luck.

He rode south, passing under the Santa Monica Pier, the ancient Ferris wheel turning slowly overhead. In the distance, multimillion dollar yachts and small sailboats paralleled the shore. An occasional small plane from nearby Santa Monica Airport droned overhead. The haves almost mingling with the have-nots.

Ten minutes later he reached the chess park and slowed down. On the paved platform on his right was a chessboard as large as a basketball court. A dozen children giggled and jostled as they pushed man-sized pieces from square to square.

Further down there were rows of concrete tables, with chessboards inlaid into their tops. Most of the players and their audiences looked just like he did: dirty, disheveled and destitute. But unlike him, they were true homeless. He knew many of them personally from his frequent trips here. To play, to watch a good game, or to enjoy the company of men whose IQ scores were far higher than their credit scores.

He stopped at one of the tables where two men were perched over a board, their arms dashing from chess piece to timing clock and back in a speed-chess match. A mental battle in full swing. So elegant, so intense.

He walked his bike to one of the far tables, sat down, pulled a cloth bag out of his pocket, set up the chess pieces, and began a speed game against himself. The solo endeavor never failed to produce the adrenaline rush that had a paradoxically calming effect on whatever challenge he was facing. And the upcoming meeting promised plenty of challenges.

The on-shore breeze had picked up and the temperature dropped. He was on his third one-man game when he spotted his contact.

Interesting. An athletic, elegant, woman in her late fifties was heading toward him. The face was a chiseled mask with high cheekbones and a firmly set jaw. Boardroom, not bedroom, he decided. She wore a simple jogging outfit, with loose sweat pants and an unbuttoned jacket. Under her left arm she held a rolled up yoga mat. The brisk pace and the focused stare in the intense brown eyes made it look like she was heading at him.

He tensed and began to stand up.

The woman's face softened into an amiable smile as she extended her hand. "I'm Kay."

The handshake was all business, without a hint of revulsion at his homeless outfit. Score a point for the woman.

"My associates call me Al," he said.

She sat across from him. "Thank you for meeting on such short notice."

Was the slight German accent real? The self-assured manner certainly was. Most of his clients were ill at ease on the first meeting. This one was as calm as if she were sipping tea at Shutters on the Beach with a girlfriend. Give her another point. He preferred doing business with seasoned pros.

"Jordan spoke highly of you."

He gave a quick nod. She had done her homework. He relaxed and let part of his brain escape back to the serenity of the chess game. Ng1-f3, Bc8-f5, Nb8xc6, e5xd4 … There was an instant soothing effect as the moves came in rapid succession, helping dissipate the pent-up energy.

Kay began to summarize the project. "The neural implant we want you to look at just got a big publicity boost."

"A given, when you're dealing with a member of the First Family." Al said, without taking his eyes off the board, letting her know he too had done his homework.

"Potentially, the new visibility may pose a business threat to my client. We need to make this implant … Shall we say, less attractive to the public."

His hands worked the pieces faster. Ng1-f3, Bc8-f5, Nb8xc6. He liked this woman. She was the first client who didn't ask him to stop playing and listen. Add another point for her.

"My client is small, but he is prepared to offer a hundred thousand dollars to derail this competitor."

First person to mention money is the needy one. "Five hundred," he said without looking up and without pausing on the next move. "I take cash only."

Technically, that wasn't true. Once he had been hired by the wife of the CEO of a surgical supply company, to hack into the man's computer and find enough dirt to throw the prenup out the window. He got paid in prosthetic limbs, delivered directly to his Injured Children's Fund. Apparently it was something about a tax-deductible donation. To this day he took pride in knowing that forty-two dirt-poor Afghani children were running around with the latest prostheses, each worth close to fifty grand.

"Half a million?" Kay gave a chuckle. "We want you to discredit him, not buy him. My client doesn't have that kind of big bucks."

Wb8xc6. The white bishop blew off the black pawn. Blacks were losing. He took a deep breath. Give her one more chance. "Who is your client?"

"I'm sorry, Al, but client identity is on a need-to-know basis."

He felt the blood rush to his head. "I work on trust." What he did was unique. Cyber espionage was much more about people skills than programming skills. It was far more productive to infiltrate the CEO's assistant's mind, than the CEO's computer. When it came to this social engineering skills, he was among the best, thanks to his adoptive Russian father, a former GRU operative. And he expected to be respected and compensated accordingly. "I need to know who I'm dealing with."

"The client's name is not negotiable." Her voice projected control, making it that much more infuriating.

A slow vibration spread up from where his right foot used to be.

Bc8-f5, Rb8xc6x. Black rook moved up field. Check.

Don't take it personally. She didn't mean to underestimate you.

"Your small client is backed by a mega-conglomerate. One of their corporate jets, a late model G600 Gulfstream, tail number N8KK, just landed forty-five minutes ago." He nodded in the direction of the Santa Monica Airport.

Any high-schooler could pull up any flight plan using Flight-Tracker.com. And he didn't need to be a brain surgeon to learn, with a

few keystrokes before the meeting, what Lady Kay conveniently neglected to mention.

LX and its competitor, Nuvius, were the two leading neural implants in clinical trials, FDA approvals pending. Nuvius was part of
K&K, a Fortune 500 giant who owned hundreds of products, anchored
around three highly profitable pharmaceutical manufacturers serving
the Alzheimer's, Parkinson's, and tranquilizer markets. Judging by the
clinical trial results he had found on the public-access FDA site, the
device's approval was imminent. The only puzzling fact was that even
at full production, the brain device was projected to account for only
one-point-seven percent of K&K's business. It was not a big-ticket
item. For some reason it was important enough for this woman to be
here.

"The jet brought your client's entire marketing team to the National
Neuro-Sciences Convention that starts next week at the LA Convention Center."

She looked positively placid at what he thought was revelatory in-
sight on his part. Give her a point for cool under pressure.

"You won't draw me into a guessing game about the client's I.D.,
Al."

"I am not guessing. I know." He obtained that information by
phone from the girl at the FBO, who had arranged the limo service for
the arriving jet. A little social engineering went a long way. That's why
I get paid the big bucks.

"And it seems that your small client has the largest booth at the
convention. So the price just went up to six hundred." He wasn't sure
whether it was amusement or amazement that he saw as she studied
his face.

"Five it is," she said smiling.

Fuck you. He began gathering the chess pieces. Suddenly her hand
was on his.

"Cool your jets, Al."

The voice was soothing, but the grasp far stronger than he expected in a woman of her size. "I'm not finished." She unrolled the yoga mat and produced a flexible smart-pad. "There is more in it for you than you think."

As he listened, his interest in the project, and respect for the woman grew.

"Why don't you go back to the person you used last year?" he asked when she was finished.

"Several reasons." She paused and glanced away. "One of them is that cyber-security is much tighter now that the program is on the Cloud. We know where the implant's Achilles heel is, we just can't get to it," she admitted. "Besides, the idea isn't to start crashing patients randomly."

"Because you don't want to spook the doctor into cranking up security," he offered.

"Exactly. So I want you to start with four or five targets. All different, none linkable to an LX malfunction. You'll create a few situations; they'll get written off to various unrelated causes. Then, and only then, we leak a secret internal memo about the vulnerability of the device . . ."

He looked up from the board and finished her sentence. "The media eats it up, and the implant becomes a four-letter word in the public's mind." He liked her strategy.

A faint smile flashed on her lips. She tapped the screen. "Start with these."

He eyed the short list of names on the smart pad. Several were familiar to him from political news. "A little too prominent, no?"

She stiffened, barely perceptibly. "Let me worry about the who. Your job is to figure out the how. I'll give you more names, as we find additional suitable candidates."

He was going to bring up his fee again, but she interrupted.

"Most of these cases will feature bribery. Money is a great distraction. As you know," she added. "Big sums. Yours to keep."

"How big?"

"Each big enough to fund at least one orphanage."

His breath caught. How the hell did she know about ICF? Talking about doing the homework.

"The money will be transferred directly to your charity, if it's okay with you. Tax deductible to the client," she explained.

It was okay with him. The half mil he had asked for had just tripled or quadrupled. Something didn't add up. He was good, but not that good. There was more afoot here.

"Why me?" There were other talented and more affordable hackers out there.

"Honestly? Your people skills are even better than your hacking skills." She paused.

"And?"

"And I know a few things about you that the FBI might find interesting."

He heard the faint clicking from the prosthesis as his foot began to shake. He forced the leg against the concrete bench. "Such as?"

"Your extracurricular activities, for one."

"Damn you."

"Don't damn me. Thank me. It will be a win-win." She got up. "And Al, a few moves back, black pawn c5 to c6 would've been better." She smiled. "It's hard to think on both sides of the fence, isn't it?"

It took a dozen more games, played out with increasing frenzy, to calm his nerves after Kay's departure. A precarious balance of power was established, but it was not in his favor. Do the job, collect the money, get out.

He packed up and rode away. As he negotiated a turn, he spotted a familiar silhouette up ahead. She was jogging, long legs barely touching the pavement, her buttocks snapping tight with every stride, the setting sun backlighting her luscious strawberry-blond hair.

He rolled up behind her, the sight of her breasts bringing back fond memories of the two "encounters."

"Hello, Marci!"

The woman jerked away as she recognized him. She jogged off the path onto the sand and picked up her pace.

Al tried to follow, but the bike got stuck in the sand, and he nearly fell off, catching himself on his bad foot.

Slowly he turned around. He was damaged goods. It could be revolting for a young woman as pretty as Marci to wake up to a one-footed cripple. At that moment, rejected by one woman and manipulated by another, he felt particularly crippled.

The pain from the stump was becoming unbearable. The pain in his soul was worse.

13

STANDING IN HIS SPACE at National Neuro-Sciences Convention exhibit hall, Mauricio found it difficult not to be overwhelmed by the endless landscape of exhibit booths, large and small, stretching around him as far as he could see. For anyone even remotely involved in neurology, neurosurgery, psychiatry, psychotropic pharmacology or neural devices, NNSC was the most important scientific trade show, selling opportunity, learning forum and schmooze fest in the world. It was attended by every serious, curious, or underemployed professional, or any surgeon looking to rack up CMEs—the mandatory Continuing Medical Education credits needed to retain a license. For him, it would be the official coming-out party for the LX. It was exhilarating and frightening at the same time.

"The improvement my daughter has made is nothing short of miraculous," the First Lady had told him when he called asking for help. "To keep that from others would be a crime. Tom said he would personally drag the FDA director out of bed, if need be, to get immediate approval."

Three days later he received a phone call. "This is Don Fiaschetti. I'm calling to inform you that the committee voted to approve your neural implant, effective immediately." The man said it with all the enthusiasm of someone being forced to eat a rotten egg. "You'll get the letter soon." Then he added in a lower voice, "And Dr. Barcelos, just so you know, this is over my dead body. So if something goes South, don't look at me to take the fall on your behalf." The director hung up.

Just like that, the dream had turned into reality. A lump formed in his throat as he reedited his exhibit materials, deleting the cursed: "Not for Sale—Investigational Use Only" labels. The goal had been achieved. Years of battles and sacrifices had finally born their fruit. His promise to Dora had been fulfilled. He was so happy, he was ready to do cartwheels.

With time to spare before opening, he surveyed his diminutive exhibit space. A modest backdrop with a few hastily printed posters, a stack of pamphlets, and a monitor hooked up to his laptop, playing the LX video. All of it dwarfed by the K&K edifice looming across the aisle, its giant screens promoting dozens of drugs and medical devices. Like a camping tent pitched next to a three-canopy circus, he thought. It felt like that the day he tested for his black belt as a ten-year-old: determined not to show that he was scared out of his wits.

At 9:00 A.M. the exhibit was announced open. He watched as a mass of attendees, some dressed in impeccable Armani's, others in mismatched jackets, comfortable jeans or in elegant pants suits, rushed through the doors flashing their badges at the guards.

But instead of scattering across the convention floor in search of free handouts, or irresistible incitements usually offered by the megaexhibitors, a phalanx of them headed in his direction. Moments later he was the epicenter of a noisy crowd clamoring for his attention, peppering him with questions, and fighting over the small stack of handouts he had brought along.

He fired back answers as best as could.

"Yes, you can order now."

"No, it is not difficult to learn."

"Yes, it has been approved by the FDA. Recently." Very recently.

"It will be reimbursable as soon as third party payers fall in line with the FDA approval."

"The technique is based on principles any neurosurgeon should have mastered already."

He was not used to being the center of this kind of attention. It was like being in a different world, he thought, glancing around and realizing his little booth was surrounded by potential buyers.

At one point a tall woman caught his eye. She stooped slightly, as if to blend in with the crowd. From what he could see, she wore a conservative white blouse, and no makeup or jewelry. The intense gaze was bit disquieting.

She noticed that he was staring at her, and her eyes darted away. When he looked back in her direction, she was gone.

More questions, more answers.

"It's cloud-based. The entire system is hosted by CloudFort."

One answer drew laughter from many. "No, I have not received death threats from any psychiatrists for putting them out of business. Not yet, anyway."

Those without questions just stood around, reading the brochure or watching the video playing on the screen.

There she was again. The striking part of her face was the jaw, firmly set, thrust slightly forward, telegraphing stubborn determination.

What the hell, he wondered, trying to figure out where she fit in the doctor-nurse-tech-vendor continuum. The outfit was too conservative for a vendor from another booth. The face too expressive to be a physician. Instead of a purse, she had something that looked like an elegant attaché case slung casually from her shoulder. Creative-advertising type? It was not uncommon for competing companies to spy on each other's sales pitches, but she had been there long enough to have heard all he had to say.

He was about to call on her, when he sensed a change in the crowd. Heads turned, conversations stopped, questions abated. A cluster of mostly young, mostly male physicians moved closer. In the center was Jean Jacques Dumas, his 5-foot-4-inch figure almost engulfed by his entourage. The man was dressed in a striped dark grey Armani suit that complemented his pale skin. The perfectly grayed temples distracted effectively from the barely visible face-lift scars. The red Italian silk tie was tied with a perfect knot. A matching kerchief protruded from his breast pocket, above a name tag decorated with a rainbow of ribbons: speaker, board member, president elect . . .

"Docteur de Bar," Dumas drawled with a heavy French accent, eyeing the exhibit. "How's our amazing Amazonian doing? It's been a long time, oui?"

Not long enough, he thought.

Jean Jacques Dumas and he first crossed paths during his residency, when he dared to question one of Dumas's diagnoses, in front of younger residents.

Their paths collided a year later. Right in the middle of a challenging case, Mauricio had jerry-rigged a simple retractor that saved the day and earned him an accolade from the crusty professor of surgery who was struggling with access to a vessel.

"You should patent this," the old surgeon said.

Dumas offered his enthusiastic guidance and persuaded him to accept development funding from a venture capitalist. "He's a friend of mine. He'll make you rich," Dumas assured him.

Three years later, Mauricio walked away owing the venture capitalist $25,000 in fabricated R&D billings, while K&K, where young Dumas was listed on the advisory panel, began marketing a very profitable device that bore an uncanny resemblance to Mauricio's invention.

That was ten years ago. Today Jean Jacques Dumas' Nuvius was part of the K&K conglomerate. Despite huge infusions of cash, the Nuvius Deep Brain Stimulation paddles, designed to treat a variety of psychiatric conditions, including depression, were still languishing in clinical trials.

In principle, the idea was not that different from his LX. Tunable micro-currents were used to reset the depressed brain. The two silver-dollar sized discs had to be implanted on opposite sides of the head, and the soap-bar-sized controller bulged under the chest skin. These were minor drawbacks, and Dumas' articles dating back six years revealed that the device was far superior to any anti-depression treatment available back then.

Mauricio couldn't help wondering why, with a ten-plus year head start, did the Nuvius not beat the LX to market. Was it the excessive zeal of K&K's medical-legal team, or an interior bureaucratic snag that kept the Nuvius from even being submitted for FDA approval? Either way, he suspected that Dumas' abrasive personality did not help grease the path.

"When I heard that our parent company bought Sun Val and cut off your supply," Dumas was saying, "I was . . . was . . . vraiment faché. Really furious," he repeated, glancing at his retinue for confirmation.

"How exactly was it that you heard about it, JJ?"

Dumas smiled. "Jungle drums, my Brazilian friend." He made a quick drumming motion with his hands, and winked.

Mauricio let the reference to his origins slide.

"Yeah, a real bummer about your wire supply," Dumas droned. "And you'll need a bunch, now that the Caldwells are supporting you."

Supporting me? He let that slide too. Behind his back, he could hear Dumas' retinue chatting and laughing as they watched the video.

Dumas moved closer and lowered his voice. "Listen, K&K asked me to let you know that they would be willing to help you out. Maybe even consider an acquisition."

Calma, Mauricio. He forced himself to take a calming breath. "It's not for sale, JJ."

Dumas rested a hand on his shoulder. "It's not too late. In the right hands, that little wire of yours . . ."

He could hear the pounding crescendo of his own pulse. He shrugged Dumas' hand off his shoulder.

"The little wire is not for sale," he said more insistently.

Dumas smirked. "If I were you, I'd consider their offer. K&K can buy enough advertising to make you invisible."

"Hey, Dr. Busselas," somebody yelled, "the video died. We haven't finished watching."

He moved to the computer that served as the video source. The screen was flashing something that resembled an error message. "d2-d4 d7-d5."

He tried several keyboard commands but the screen remained frozen.

We wouldn't be having this problem if you clowns hadn't played with it.

More keystrokes. Nothing. He clicked on the error message itself. For a few moments, nothing happened. Then the screen came alive and a photograph appeared in the left upper corner. By the time he recognized that he was looking at a silhouette of a nude woman leaning on a rock, more images flashed on. Nude torsos, artistically composed and mysteriously lit. Breast, legs, buttocks.

There were scattered exclamations and chuckles behind his back.

"O-la-la," Dumas said.

"What the . . ." He tapped more keys, but the bizarre show continued to unfold. A woman spread-eagle, face-down on a gravel surface, wrists bound with a coarse rope. Faceless nudes, tied to beams. The images floated onto the screen like falling leaves, settling slowly, revealing details.

Dumas's voice behind him. "Mon ami, I had no idea . . ."

More laughter.

He ducked under the display table, searching for the power source, and wishing he could just stay there. It was mortifying. At least twenty people must have seen what was on the screen. By tonight, it may as well be on a billboard. Neurosurgeon to the First Family is a pervert.

He found the power cord.

"Dr. Barcelos?" The voice was rich and throaty.

Go away. "One moment please ..." He yanked the plug out of the socket and crawled out from under the table.

The dark blond mane was inches from his face. Two enormous blue-grey eyes stared at him through the wild curls. The mystery woman was back.

The rest of the crowd had thinned, or he didn't notice them.

14

"THESE ... THESE ARE NOT MY PICTURES," Barcelos mumbled, his face beet-red.

I know, Leoni wanted to say, but couldn't. Her instructions had been to upload a file to this man's computer. Only now was she seeing the contents. Long-suppressed memories of other nude pictures exploded in her mind, fanning her with anger. Not your pictures, not my choice. She cursed the day years ago that led her to become an unwitting participant in this bizarre charade.

She saw Barcelos studying her, his eyes squinting in growing suspicion. Instinctively, she pressed the attaché case with the concealed SmartPad against her flank and forced a friendly smile. "Hi."

His eyes darted to her badge, dangling from a lanyard between her breasts, and then shot back up to her face. Now he looked even more embarrassed. She felt a moment of sympathy for him. The pornographic parade, clearly designed to compromise him in front of colleagues and customers, would knock the confidence out of any man. Then to be caught looking at the part of her body where the eyes of so many other men had been lost before ...

"I'm Mauricio de Barcelos."

She could tell he was making a monumental effort to recover his composure. The voice was tense, and had a definitely Brazilian accent. The defined cheekbones, slightly almond-shaped dark eyes, and that curly hair spilling down his forehead. There was something boyishly endearing about this man.

"Are you familiar with our neural implant?" The opening of the sales spiel sounded far more confident than she would had expected under such embarrassing circumstances.

Job completed. Now is a good time to just walk away, she thought, but the warm glow in his dark brown eyes kept her legs from moving. "Leoni Wakeling," she said, reaching out her hand.

His handshake was firm and sincere. The eyes continued probing. She felt a wave of panic. He's going to ask me what I do. Or what I did, and why . . . To distract him, she blurted out the first thing she could dredge up from watching the video before she crashed it. "I was wondering how you came up with the idea that intermittent stimulation of the hippocampal area can potentiate serotonin release?"

His eyes flashed with surprise and renewed interest. He must have taken her for a colleague, she thought, as he launched into a detailed narrative. Relieved, she assumed her best attentive-listener posture.

Sentence by sentence, his excitement grew. ". . . So the technology enables the patient . . ." His hands were like an orchestra conductor's, punctuating important points, outlining anatomical structures, and directing her attention. At first she responded with suitable Hm-hm's and I see's. A few minutes into his presentation she realized she was actually understanding his innovative approach and enjoying the pitch, and wanting to know more. Like a tractor beam his excitement had captured her and pulled her into its energy field.

I don't need this.

It was not what she had expected or wanted when she was given this assignment, and neither was this man. Maybe it was the charisma he radiated, but Barcelos looked far younger than his stated forty-one years. Certainly younger than her at forty-four, although people told her she passed for thirty-something. And he was nothing like the stereotypical arrogant surgeons she had encountered more than once in her PR career. Even though he was no taller than she was, his wide shoulders and narrow waist were statuesque. The curly hair spilling in disarray down the tall forehead . . . Quit it, Leo. She chased her thoughts back to the task at hand. Look like you had nothing to do with the pictures, and move on.

". . . Think about not taking drugs, not seeing psychiatrists. Think about being able to work, play, enjoy. Now that we have FDA approval . . ." He was a kid talking about a long awaited toy finally found, all wrapped up under the Christmas tree, and ready to use.

She became aware that his eyes were looking at her. Not at what she was, colleague or vendor, but who she was. The back of her neck smoldered under the hair, and she hoped she wasn't blushing. She stepped back. I really don't need this.

"I need this," she was thinking five years ago, when a male colleague suggested going out for a drink. Just to talk. He was a freelance IT consultant for the medical PR company where she was working as a developer of social media. Even though he was probably a whole twenty years younger than she was, he was a good listener. With her pending divorce from the husband of twenty years, she needed to talk about being treated like a possession, berated for being unable to con-ceive, and discarded for a younger woman . . . She was about to be thrown out without financial support, thanks to a prenup she was young and naïve enough to sign. She suspected that his interest in her was more than casual, but being pursued by a younger man was a welcome boost to her battered self-esteem. She needed it.

"You need this," the man was saying when she woke up in the mid-dle of the night, naked, with no recollection of how she got to his apart-ment. The caresses she hadn't had for years must have turned her to Jell-O. "Yes. I need this . . ." she whispered as the lovemaking continued.

It had been a moment of weakness that had led to an abhorrent betrayal, leaving her feeling guilty ever since. An act that she swore she would never repeat, until the text she had received yesterday.

"Did I lose you?" Barcelos was asking.

"Sorry . . ." There was something incredibly nurturing about the way he was touching her arm.

"I get carried away," he said. "Tell me about your work."

Several physicians were gathered around the booth, shifting their bodies impatiently, waiting for their turn with him, but his eyes were focused on her. Oh, boy. The interest seemed to be mutual. No, no, no. A personal involvement with the man whose computer she had just hacked was the last thing she needed. Why weren't her legs following instructions to walk away?

"I'm in public relations," she said. "My company helps start-ups with social media." It was part true. That was what she used to do before she had to leave the job.

"Oh . . ." A look of disappointment swept across his face.

She cringed. She had misled him with her interest. "I know I'm not supposed to be bugging you," she managed.

"That's right; you are not, Ms. Wakeling. This is a professional convention. There is no soliciting here."

His anger from the porno fiasco was being refocused on her.

"Sorry I took up your time. And the pictures? Don't worry about them. I'm sure your PR person will handle it for you . . ."

"I don't have a PR person, and I don't need one. And you should leave, before I call security."

Last thing I need. She raised her arms in resignation and backed away. "I'm really sorry, Dr. Barcelos. You'll never see me again."

Not until she was in the safety of a stall in the ladies' room, did she exhale. She pulled out her SmartPad and texted. "Done. Pix uploaded, doctor discredited. Now honor your promise and leave me alone."

Remembering how scarce her funds were, she restrained the impulse to smash the SmartPad against the tile floor and stomp her heel through it. She felt dirty. As dirty as the day she opened the FedEx envelop from the young consultant and saw the pictures he had taken of her their night together.

She sat on the toilet till her heartbeat returned to normal.

When she emerged from the Ladies' Room, Barcelos was standing there. Her panic returned. He's determined to bust me.

"Ms. Wakeling?"

"Yes?" There was the hand again, reaching out and touching her, the tingling spreading up to her shoulder, her chest . . .

"I'm sorry," he was saying.

She cleared her throat. "For what?"

"For being rude. The way I reacted to your being a . . . a . . ."

She relaxed. He looked so flustered. She had trouble hiding a smile. "For my being a vendor?" she offered.

"How big is your company?"

"Honestly? It's just me. I used to work for a big med-marketing outfit, but they downsized me."

His eyes held hers, and she thought she saw a flash of compassion.

"I'm sorry I was so hard on you," he repeated. "Good luck in your search." He started to move away, but stopped, reached into his jacket and pulled out a card.

"If you want, call my hospital. They may have openings in . . . publicity, or so they tell me."

She took the card. "Why are you doing this?" she couldn't help asking.

He shrugged. "You look like you could use a break."

15

"I STILL CAN'T BELIEVE YOU LET DUMB ASS have a hundred wires," Mel grumbled as they were changing into scrubs in the surgeons' locker room.

Mauricio had wondered how long it would take Mel to bring it up. The demand had skyrocketed in the days since the convention, and Rosie, swamped with orders had to be frugal in doling out the 500 or so left in stock, until the new fabricator could deliver their first batch. Truculently, Dumas had placed his order under his nurse's name. By the time Rosie had figured it out, the wires were on their way. Not that we had a choice, Mauricio thought.

"If we said no, Dumas would be bellyaching about restriction of trade, Mel. Do we have time for that? He's a good surgeon; he won't screw up."

"I'm not talking skill," Mel shot back. "I'll bet the minute he gets them, he'll have five techies in his lab trying to reverse-engineer the damn thing."

"Let them," he shrugged. "It's not the wire; it's the software that makes it unique. And that's locked solid at CloudFort."

"Yeah, well, I don't trust that outfit either."

He hid a smile. Mel had been more and more protective of the project, particularly since a patient had walked into traffic and died a year ago. "Would you rather have the programming running through the old server downstairs?"

"Worked fine before," Mel grumbled.

It had, until Isaacson had made a point that cloud-based technology—what the mega-systems like Amazon and Expedia had been using for years—was more cost-effective. CloudFort, who had been handling all NBMC's Electronic Medical Records, and CT and MRI studies, became the host for the LX as well.

"I'm going to watch the Frenchman's cases like a hawk," Mel was saying.

"Speaking of hawks," he changed the subject. "Our old friend General Brad Oakley rolled by our booth."

"Still around?"

"Strong as ever, and a fancier wheelchair. Wanted every single wire we could spare, overnighted."

"To Uncle Sam? Why?"

"Good solution to their major cause of death."

"Depressed soldiers offing themselves?"

"Yep. Suicide. Even after we brought the troops back."

"Just make sure Uncle Sam pays up front," Mel said. He started to close his locker door but stopped. "Want to see a cute mug?"

Mel pulled out his iPad and cued up a photo. "Adorable little devil, isn't he?" Mel's sun-browned wrinkles spread into a smile.

"Adorable," he echoed, glancing at the picture of a very plain nine-year-old on a bicycle, and trying to conceal his amusement with Mel's new parental instincts. "I take it the trip back East went well?"

Mel ran his hand over his crew cut. "Let's just say my daughter is back in rehab, and Martha and I are going to have our grandson living with us."

That was Mel. Enough energy to take care of everything.

His arms held high, still dripping from the scrub, Mauricio pushed his way into Operating Room Seven. Sandy McBride, a woman in her forties, was strapped into a surgical chair in the center of the room. Seemingly oblivious to the lights, monitors and staff that surrounded her, she stared blankly at the ceiling. Her face had the potential to be attractive, but the pale skin was oily and peppered with blemishes. The hair was matted, revealing patches of scaly scalp. The body was doughy and amorphous. Scratches on her forearms spoke of cats that were probably as unhappy as their owner. He was glad the computer had randomized her to the LX arm of the study. She needed it.

High time to get this lady on track, he thought. "Mrs. McBride," he said as cheerfully as he could muster, "We'll have you out of here in no time."

Sandy gave a small shrug. "Take your time. I have no place to go."

"What about your cats, Mrs. McBride? Don't they miss you?"

"They'll manage."

He eyed her. All the signs were there. Loss of interest in her surroundings, feeling of worthlessness, an inability to experience joy. It led one way and one way only: to a black hole with very slippery slopes. He knew the view from inside that hole. No desire to set a goal. No strength to crawl out. No future. Nothingness.

The cascade was frighteningly familiar. Once he too had been close to the edge himself. With Bruce's help, he had managed to skirt the abyss until the LX came into his life and gave him a renewed purpose. For others, winning the battle was far more difficult.

"We'll get you better, Mrs. McBride," he said confidently.

Two scrub nurses covered Sandy's head with a sterile drape and aligned the opening with the pre-shaved part of the skull. The anesthesiologist squeezed a few drops of sedative into the IV line. Since the brain had no pain fibers, he would keep Sandy awake through most of the LX insertion.

"You're going to feel a little sting," he warned as he prepared to inject the local anesthetic. He glanced at Mel, sitting behind the large observation window in his shielded programming room, and waited for the thumbs up.

A tech wheeled the scanner around and positioned the C-shaped retaining frame over Sandy's head. He tightened the three screws into the outer layer of Sandy's skull and gave the head a gentle tug to make sure it was immobilized.

"Mrs. McBride? You're going to hear a little buzz," he warned as he revved up the drill. "Just like a dentist's drill."

Sandy stirred under the drapes. "I can't stand dentists."

His fingers sped through the familiar procedure. By comparison to Lori's emergency insertion, this was a walk in the park. The monitor screen showed the tip of the LX at the edge of the skull, penetrating deeper. He watched as the wire continued working its way into the brain. The tip passed the hippocampus, the parahippocampal gyrus, the subcallosal singulate gyrus . . . It was like flying past familiar landscape.

Sandy twitched. "I just had a weird sensation. Like my legs were running."

Good. He was on track. "That's normal. Keep telling us what you feel. It'll help us stay clear of certain areas . . ."

"What areas?" Another twitch. "Phew. I felt that!"

He made a small correction and the wire slid into the target zone. It was calibration time. Every brain-wire interface was different, so the placement had to be tailored to each patient. But once set, the contacts had proven to be uncannily reliable.

He signaled to Mel that Sandy was ready for the test pulse that would confirm that the impulses fired by the filaments were reaching their brain targets.

"What did you do?" Sandy exclaimed. "I feel . . ."

"What?"

"I feel . . . lighter somehow."

He looked up and Mel winked. Target hit.

During his first runs, when the impulses were generated by an external computer, it always surprised him how even a test jolt would result in a mood boost that lingered for hours. Now, it seemed commonplace.

All he had to do now was to hook up the control module. The command center of the whole system would generate the electrical impulses that would regulate a variety of chemicals that Sandy's brain produced.

He took the quarter-sized device from the scrub nurse, and turned it upside down. "Alpha eight three seven," he said, reading the serial number.

"Check," Mel's voice confirmed from the control room.

Sandy moved. "What?"

"Nothing, Ms. McBride." He made a rotating gesture with his index. Let's move. Without the software upload, a module was nothing but ten bucks worth of chips, not smart enough to drive a coffeemaker. Behind the glass, Mel was punching buttons.

He connected the module to the end of the wire protruding from Sandy's head, pressed gently with both thumbs, and slipped the entire assembly under the scalp. Four dissolvable stitches and it was done.

It was almost disappointing how little skill was required. But that had been the idea behind his design. He wanted it to be a simple, by-the-numbers procedure, so that any semi-competent surgeon could learn it in a couple of tries. See one, do one, teach one, as the surgical mantra went.

"Device detected, identified, and locked," Mel announced over the intercom. "Uploading Version 4.1."

Moments later the computers beeped in unison. Sandy's module was ready to be programmed.

"Almost done, Ms. McBride," he said. "We need to give you a little identification mark. The medical tattoo we talked about."

The nurse handed him the coder and pulled back the drapes, exposing Sandy's flank. He pressed the device against Sandy's skin. "This will sting, but only for a second."

"I've had tats before," Sandy said. "What does this one look like?"

Who knew? A nice lady from Pasadena sporting tattoos. He exchanged an amused glance with the nurse.

"It's invisible, Ms. McBride." He pulled the trigger and waited while the device tattooed a QR icon on Sandy's flank.

"Lights . . ." he started to say, but the room was already dark. He aimed the UV beam of the bar code reader at Sandy's flank. In the darkened room, the tattoo, a two-inch image of the Quick Recognition square, glowed a deep cobalt blue, the labyrinth of crisscrossing lines encircling the snakes-and-staff of a small caduceus.

The computer beeped twice.

"We have a match," Mel announced over the intercom.

"You did great, Ms. McBride," Mauricio said, peeling back the drapes and watching Sandy squint at the light. He slipped off his mask and gave her arm a reassuring squeeze. "My colleague Mel and I will see you a little later to get the device adjusted."

"That's it?" Sandy beamed. "Well, bless you. It takes me longer to get my prescriptions filled."

16

By the time Mauricio made rounds, dropped in on Lori, and dealt with emails and new orders, two hours had passed and it was time to work on Sandy's final calibration.

He punched in the code to the surgeons' lounge, changed into scrubs in the adjacent locker room, emerged on the operating rooms side, and headed to Mel's lab. It was an inconvenient access, but LX programming equipment required shielding from radio waves, Wi-Fi fields, and mobile phone emissions.

Mel hadn't arrived yet, but Sandy and another woman were waiting. He noted a twinkle in Sandy's eyes that wasn't there before the procedure. Just a test dose, and already she was looking better, he thought.

Sandy perked up. "Oh, here he is. Pam . . ."

Her companion didn't wait for an introduction. "Hello, Dr. de Barcelos. I'm Pamela, Sandra's older sister. I take care of her."

Pamela's handshake was cold and far too firm. He noted that she had used the formal version of his name, *de* Barcelos, as in *from*. She looked younger and slimmer than her sister, but her face lacked Sandy's soft femininity.

"By the looks of her, my services are no longer needed," Pamela said.

"You can go back to Detroit and take care of Dad instead," Sandy chirped.

"Gee, thanks." Pamela turned to him. "What if this miracle cure doesn't work?"

He studied her. It was the caregivers who were the skeptics. Little wonder, since the LX threatened the security of their position as co-dependents. He did his best to warm up his smile.

"I'd say it would be a miracle if it didn't work, Ms . . ."

"Pamela, it's fine."

Okay . . ." We have so many ways of adjusting the LX that it's rare indeed for it not to work. I think your sister is going to be back to her cheerful self before you know it."

Pamela did a barely perceptible roll of her eyes. "Right."

Some relatives should just stay home. He inhaled and flipped open his iPad. He could identify with depressed patients, but obstructionist relatives had little redeeming value. "Since you're both here . . ." He spoke to Sandy. "Would it be okay if your sister listened in?"

Pamela stepped closer. "Yes, please. So I can help her later."

Don't hold your breath, he wanted to say. "As I'm sure both of you know, depression is caused by a chemical imbalance in the brain."

"I know." Sandy got a word in. "Serotonins and all that."

"Combined with a weak spine," the sister mumbled under her breath.

Who let this co-dependent in, anyway?

"We can restore the balance with drugs . . ." He tapped the screen and brought up a diagram. "Or by using electrical impulses to stimulate certain areas of the brain to release the right combination of chemicals."

"Personally, I'd rather shove pills in my mouth than wires in my brain," Pamela said. "But that's just me."

Sandy made a face. "Obviously, drugs weren't doing the trick for me, Sis, were they?"

He continued. "And that's a much more common experience than people realize. Almost fifty percent—half of the patients—do not get better with drugs."

Sandy flashed a triumphant glance at her sibling.

"Even at their best," he continued, "drugs have a slow onset and unpredictable side effects. Often two or more drugs are required. There's a lot of trial and error. It can take years to arrive at the right combination, and when the patient's metabolism changes you have to recalibrate all over again. By contrast, the output of the LX can be tailored . . ." He snapped his fingers. "At a moment's notice."

"If you can get your doctor to see you, at a moment's notice."

"Ah-ha! That's the beauty of it. The patient can do the adjustments themselves. The LX can dialog with any Bluetooth-compatible device. From any place that has Internet access. You can use your home computer. You can even be sitting at Starbucks with your iPad."

Pamela tightened her lips. "So every hacker can snoop in?"

"Pam," Sandy snapped. "Enough already. Let them try. I've nothing to hide. And it sure beats being a pill-popping zombie."

He noticed tears in Sandy's eyes. She lowered her voice. "Can't you be happy for me? Just this once?"

He touched Sandy's arm, but spoke to the sister. "Many patients do worry about safety. But the LX is protected by a medical encryption algorithm that's even more powerful than what you use for your online banking, for example."

"I just don't see how your filament can control all that."

He held the pad so Sandy couldn't see, and called up a clip from the surgical instructional video he had made for future users and cycled through a few particularly graphic pictures of sliced mammalian brains with wires hanging out.

"There are five filaments. One is inserted in the parahippocampal gyrus . . ."

More graphic pictures.

". . . The other goes into the subcallosal cingulate gyrus, also known as Brodmann's area 25." A nice illustration on the three-dimensional diagram, followed by a picturesque photograph of the real thing, post-mortem. "The third goes into the nucleus accumbens, part of the so called reward circuit that controls dopamine . . ." Another picture of a pre-sliced brain.

Pamela stepped back. "I get it, I get it." Her skin was a shade paler than before. "Is there a ladies' room . . ."

"Let's take it step by step," he said after Pamela dashed out. "Find a comfortable quiet spot. Log on, using a password that you will pick."

"How about Kat . . ."

"Don't tell anybody. And make sure it has at least twelve characters, including upper and lower cases. We need to make this as hard to crack as possible."

Sandy rolled back her eyes, seemingly thinking of a suitable combination.

"Once you log on, the opening screen will have questions about your mental state. Trouble concentrating? Click here. Tired in the morning? Click here. Feeling overwhelmed . . ."

"I got it," Sandy said. "It's the short version of that questionnaire on depression that Bruce . . . That Dr. Levine gives me."

He nodded. "It's sort of like a quick chat with your psychiatrist. Next . . ."

Four colored lines appeared horizontally across the screen. Under each there was an electronic slider that resembled the volume or image adjustment controls on home TV screens.

"The green line controls serotonin secretion," he explained. "Think of it as what Prozac used to do. Or what Anadep does now."

Sandy nodded. "SSRI. Done that."

"Selective serotonin re-uptake inhibitors." He nodded, satisfied that she was familiar with the old class of antidepressant compounds. He touched his finger to the screen and slid the control back and forth. "Adjust as needed. If you exceed presets, the computer overrides you."

Sandy nodded. "Pam had something like that after her back surgery. A pump for pain meds that she could control."

"Something like that," he admitted. "Red line is the new Valium."

"Anxiolytic. Tried those," Sandy said.

"Want to relax before a big event? Slide the control knob, like so. Take a chill pill."

"Self-medication. Been there, done that, too," Sandy said.

"Think of it as self-empowerment, not self-medication," he corrected her. "Last is the green line. For sleep. You decide when to go to sleep, when to wake up, when to take a nap."

"Here, let me." Sandy pushed his hand aside. "I can see I'm going to like this."

He smiled as he watched her run through the steps required to set the sleep cycle.

"When you're done adjusting everything, click here." He tapped "submit." "The information goes to a central computer for processing and generating the right input. Kind of like getting your prescription filled."

The computer pinged. Sandy sat up startled.

"What happened?"

He laughed. The computer just downloaded the new settings into your module." He touched her dressing. "Right here under your skin. You can now log off and go do what you want."

Pam's voice startled them. "Looks like anybody smart enough to work a TV is smart enough to adjust this brain pacer." The woman approached them.

Sandy threw her a withering look. "Who knows, maybe even I can manage on my own."

Pam pretended she didn't hear.

"When the patient logs on for reprogramming," he continued, "all the settings are recorded. In addition to answering a depression questionnaire, there's even a 'talk to the doctor' window. Post questions or comments to our staff—kind of like a message on Facebook, but private.

But in-between logons, you're on your own."

"How long is that, Dr. Barcelos?" Sandy asked.

"Every six hours till it's calibrated. Then daily for a few weeks. Eventually. . ." He shrugged. "Weeks, if you're stable and nothing has changed."

"At least now I'll know where you are."

"Actually, no," he said, wishing Pam's bathroom break had been longer. "We specifically left out the GPS function. It would be too intrusive. We believe in empowering patients, not controlling them."

"What if she doesn't logon?"

"Pam," Sandy chided.

"I'm sure you will be diligent. But, what if?"

What if she doesn't take her drugs? What if she jumps under a car? What if . . . He explained as patiently as he could. "The programming center will detect a missed logon, and alert her physician."

A knock interrupted them.

"Am I too late?" Mel asked easing through the door.

"If you mean did I do your work for you and explained how the brain pacer works, then yes, you are too late," he said, relieved by the diversion. He began the introductions, but Sandy cut in.

"Are you the nice gentleman who called last night and offered me a ride from the hospital?" she asked, smiling coyly.

Mauricio suppressed a grin. Patients were known to have the wildest fantasies in the hours immediately after implant insertion.

"I don't think so, Madam," Mel said.

"Oh, well. He sounded so nice on the phone. I wish I had said yes.

17

MAURICIO SNUCK IN THROUGH the back door, trying not to disturb the gathering. He loved these weekly LX support group meetings as much as he loved inventing and operating. The smiling faces were the payoff at the end of an arduous journey—the process-result cycle. Struggle and achievement.

Bruce Levine had been opposed to the idea of group therapy. "It's not a group sport. Let them see me individually." But studies have proven that social interaction was an effective addition to any antidepressant therapy. He prevailed, convincing Bruce that the group discussions offered valuable insights into how the implants were performing. "Publish the results. It'll make you famous," he teased Bruce.

About twenty men and women sat in a circle facing Bruce. The regulars, many with their significant others, plus a couple of newcomers whom he had only seen in surgery.

Kevin Sharp was talking. "Don't look for me here next week." Kevin was a compact man in his forties, with the quick movements and sharp gaze that spoke of an above-average intellect. "I got slapped with jury duty again."

Kevin's wife, a plump, sun-dried woman with a belly that muffin-topped out of her jeans, stroked his hair. "Waste of time, this jury duty thing," she said to no one in particular. "Kevy was so looking forward to catching up at work."

Mauricio pitied the defendant. Kevin had no patience for anything that wasn't honest and by the book.

He had liked the man from the day they met.

Bruce had introduced Kevin as a retired mechanic.

"Unemployed A and P," Kevin snapped. "Unemployed. Not retired. I wasn't ready to retire. And I'm an A and P. Airframe and Power plant licensed mechanic. Not a car grease-monkey."

"Unemployed A and P." Bruce corrected himself.

"It's not right," Kevin fussed again. "I've bust my ass all my life, and then . . . this. The little bit the wife and I saved, all blown on my treatment. Not right," he repeated.

Mauricio spotted a petite woman sitting with her back to him, a luscious mane of red hair spilling over her shoulders. Gina Roslyn. The very first patient he had enrolled in the study. She hadn't missed a meeting in the three years since her implant. She turned. Her eyes lit up. She leaped up, tiptoed to him, wrapped her arm around his shoulders and planted a kissed on his cheek.

He tried not to blush. That was Gina's usual greeting. Hot redhead to the core. She waved her left hand inches from his face. A pea-sized diamond sparkled on her ring finger. He mouthed proper admiration and hugged her waist. Gina beamed back, and floated back to her chair, her butt wiggling.

He barely managed to hide a proud grin. He had met Gina's boyfriend Peter when they came for the preliminary discussion about whether she would qualify for the study. Peter came across as a supportive and loving partner, despite Gina's severe depression. Now they made a good couple, Peter's level-headed attitude balancing Gina's flamboyant personality. And now Gina was happy and getting married. Treatment results didn't get better than this.

Bruce concluded the meeting and Mauricio stood up. "I want to thank all of you . . ."

Everyone turned.

"On behalf of Dr. Levine and myself, I want to thank those of you who trusted us enough to be among the first to enroll in the trial." His breath caught and he cleared his throat. "It's you who made it possible for thousands of others to return to normal activity, to enjoy life, and to . . ."

The door flew open and a teenager with a pierced lower lip, and hair that obscured half his face sauntered in, clutching a SmartPad in one hand and a skateboard in another, charged in.

"Glad you could join us, Spike," Bruce greeted him coldly.

"Whatever," Spike grumbled as he stumbled noisily to one of the chairs. "I'd a been here sooner, 'cept . . ." Spike snorted. "Except some shithead fu . . . screwed with my program."

Mauricio rolled his eyes. "Nobody screwed with your program, you malingerer," he thought.

Spike, a.k.a. Jules Karp, was one of the more recent additions to the trial, and had been a programming problem from the start. He had come to NBMC a year ago, on the heels of his girlfriend's disappearance. "She was abducted," he kept yelling. "She went to meet someone at the A Cafe and never returned."

Spike had a long history of poorly-managed depression, and several attempts to end his life. Since he was so unbalanced by his girlfriend's disappearance, Bruce enrolled him in the study, and he was randomized to the LX group. With careful monitoring and frequent LX program adjustments, Spike pulled through, and now was working for the Geek Squad, making house calls on ailing computers. Nice kid, except that he claimed it was his God-given right to adjust his neural implant settings to suit his whims.

"It's my head, dude," Spike had argued with Mel.

"Be happy we fixed it for you. Dude," Mel growled.

"All I want is to make it to my job by six a.m., is all. I know there's a way to fix my gizmo."

"There is. Don't stay up all night playing your vidiot games," Mel said.

"But I see it right here. The sleep thing. You guys put a limit. I should be able to changed it if I want to."

"Not going to happen," Mel said.

"And how come I can't post my tracings on Facebook?" Spike persisted. "That'd be so rad. Like, I could share how my brain works with all my friends. Maybe we could do a mind melt and . . ."

Mauricio was sure Mel had been tempted to throttle the guy on more than one occasion. After their last session, he told Mauricio, "I think the bastard tried to bypass one of the controls. Took me an hour to reset the mess. I wrote in an extra set of limits, just for him."

"How did he manage to bypass the preset limits?"

"Who the fuck knows. I'm going to review the record later."

While Spike complained, Mauricio pulled up his record on his own iPad. The Alpha channel was pegged at the limits. That would lead to maximal corticosteroid output. No wonder the kid was bouncing off the walls.

His thoughts were interrupted by the sound of skateboard wheels. He looked up. Spike was gone.

18

THE QUIET STREET IN PASADENA was already dark when Pam's Prius rolled to a halt in front of the small Craftsman-style house. Sandy flung the passenger door open, stepped out and headed up the driveway.

"Sandy, wait." Pam hurried around the car.

"Stop babying me; I'm not an invalid," Sandy said, as she fought for control of the small bag of personal stuff she had taken to the hospital that morning.

"You just had surgery!"

"A minor procedure, not surgery. Let go!" She made her way up the short flight of stairs, her sister close behind, and unlocked the door.

The odor of garbage and cat urine overwhelmed her. Several cats—all Tonkinese, tan-furred and blue-eyed—sauntered up to them and rubbed against their legs.

Pam grimaced. "How can you live like this?"

Sandy winced. How indeed? Those wasted years would be all behind her now. Already she could feel the black blanket lifting. If only she had connected with Dr. Barcelos sooner. "Come back tomorrow. You won't recognize the place." She turned to the cats. "Okay, kids.

Mamma is back, and Mamma's gonna scrub this place down. And then you're all getting a bath." Did she really own that many cats? Was she nuts?

She dropped her purse on the couch and used her foot to shove aside a pile of dirty clothes blocking the hallway. Her reflection stared back from the mirror. "Yikes." She tugged on the bags under her lower lids. "I need to have them snipped off." She turned to Pam, who was still standing in the foyer, looking down at the cats as if they were rats. "Do you think I should have them snipped off? Look . . ."

"Why don't you get your life in order first, Sandra?"

"That too. Seriously. I'm having it done. The eyes. Next month. Then I'm getting a new picture, and going back on Match.com. Wanna go too? I'll write your profile."

"What the hell did they give you at that hospital?"

She grinned. "They said it was a starter dose."

"We'll be scraping you off the ceiling if you get any higher."

"And I'll be loving every minute of it."

Coming from where she was just yesterday, the manic euphoria was like a drug-less high. That gorgeous hunk Mel had warned her that things would stabilize in the next few days. The high was the body's way of getting used to the neural implant. At first, she would need to connect herself to a computer every six hours and fine-tune Mel's initial settings. By next week, she could cut it down to just a once-a-day tune-up, he had assured her. Later on, it would be weekly, or as needed.

It felt so good, she shuddered.

"San, listen, you had a long day," Pam was saying. "Get yourself some tea with honey, and go to bed."

"Speaking of honey . . . And speaking of going to bed . . ."

"Alexandra Penelope McBride!"

"What? I'm just going to e-mail Robbie. See if he wants to come play tonight." The thought brought a warm sensation between her legs. "Hmm," she groaned. The wetness was starting. It had been months. A year probably. Holy moly, it felt wonderful.

"The man is a pervert," Pam said.

"And your point is?" For Pam, anything beyond an air kiss was perverted.

"And he broke your heart."

She considered that. Robbie could've stuck around when she was down and out. Depression was like diabetes, Dr. Levine had said. It wasn't her fault. Robbie could have been her rock, but he bolted. If he weren't so damn good in bed . . . "Time to get even," she mumbled. She glanced at her sister.

Pam looked exasperated. "They told you, no exercise, no sex, not even bending down the first day ."

"What if I just lay flat?"

Minutes later, Pam was heading down the driveway. At her car, she turned. "You want breakfast tomorrow?" she yelled.

"Not sure. Depends . . ." Robbie might be talked into an all-nighter. "I'll call you." She waved goodbye, closed the door, and headed for the laptop sitting on the dining room table. She had a lot of lost time to make up. Starting with Robbie.

Two hours later, with the music blaring and stripped to skimpy undies and barefooted, Sandy was pushing a vacuum across the room and dancing a la Tom Cruise in Risky Business.

Robbie won't recognize this place, she thought. She would show him what he walked away from. She would make him regret dumping her when she got sick.

She thought she heard the doorbell. She turned off the vacuum, walked over to the radio, turned down the music and listened. Silence. Then heavy footsteps receding down the wooden porch stairs.

Shit, I almost missed him.

"Robbie!" she yelled, running to the door. It was time to get even with the son of a bitch. "Robbie, come back here," she yelled flinging the door open.

19

As Mauricio neared Lori's room the morning after the support group meeting, he saw the tell-tale thick cables snaking along the hallway. A hand-written sign was taped to the door: "ON THE AIR. QUIET PLEASE." He smiled. The day after Beck's party, he had called Diane. "The patient we discussed . . . She and her mother would be delighted to give you an exclusive on discharge day." Diane had leaped at the chance.

The now familiar Secret Service agents, posted on either side of the door, did a perfunctory metal scan with a hand-held sensor and waved him on. He silenced his phone and tiptoed in.

The room was packed with news crew staff—some leaning on walls, some sitting on the floor. Several light stands and a roll cart with a TV monitor blocked his way. Beyond them, a tall woman with her hair pulled tightly into a bun blocked most of his view of Diane, standing in front of the TV camera. In the background, in a Norman Rockwell tableau, two nurses and the First Lady were hovering around Lori and her baby. A six-day growth of hair concealed Lori's surgical scars. The baby smacked her lips, looking for a breast.

"... An illness that affects twenty-one million adults in the US alone," Diane was saying. "In the general population, depressive disorder is second only to heart disease. And among military personnel, it's the single most prevalent cause of disability."

He glanced at the monitor screen, where Diane was replaced by dated clips of desert battles, fighter jets taking off carriers, then by elaborate graphics. The station must have pulled an all-nighter preparing the visuals for this one, he thought.

The tall woman's back finally turned, offering him a better view. Diane was on a roll. "Today, antidepressants are an eight-billion-dollar-a-year industry. That's billion, with a B. And that's just the three or four pharmaceutical companies that produce Zyprexa, Epraxa, Wellbutrin, and a handful of others. There's no telling how that number will change with the recent introduction of a new product, Anadep—one of the most effective and most expensive—drugs in the medicine closet."

He noted that, and as promised, Diane didn't reveal that Anadep was the drug that Lori was taking when she tried to kill herself. NBMC's attorneys had threatened to scuttle the whole interview if she even hinted at it.

"Brian, according to my sources," Diane went on, addressing an off-screen anchor in the studio, "the total cost for a typical neural implant procedure ..."

Again, no names were mentioned. He was glad the piece wouldn't sound like a promo for the LX.

"... Plus five years of follow-up, will cost less than what patients—or their insurance companies—are now paying for just two months of drug therapy. Staggering savings, over the years. To say nothing of the decrease in psychiatric admissions. It's certainly good news for the HMOs, who will benefit from the much lower payouts ..."

The tech at the monitor ran his index finger across his throat, signaling an imminent commercial break.

The baby started crying. Lori blushed, fumbled with her shirt, brought the baby to her breast, and then leaned back with a contented smile.

Madonna and child. He thought he would explode with pride.

Minutes later, Diane asked Lori, "Take us to the moment when you realized you couldn't take it anymore."

Instantly, Lori's eyes filled with tears. "Standing on that balcony, I'd have never thought it possible. I'm just so sorry I . . . my baby . . . I came so close . . ."

Patty Caldwell stopped her with a gentle touch.

"It's been hard for her, and for us. But I'm confident that with the implant, better times are ahead. The President is already working on legislation that will make it possible for the millions who are suffering with this terrible disease—often using up their lives' savings on ineffective drug therapy—to enjoy the benefits of this wonderful device. This development dovetails with the President's plans to reduce medical cost by curtailing the obscene profits made by some of the pharmaceutical . . ."

Mauricio cringed. Patty Caldwell was known to be as rabid as the President about the Big Pharma issue. Her daughter's discharge day wasn't an appropriate forum for that discussion.

". . . And I personally want to extend my compliments to Don Fiaschetti, Director of the Food and Drug Administration, for pushing through with a timely approval, in record time. As for me, I'm going to spend time with my daughter and my granddaughter."

"A White House stay for the entire First Family?" Diane asked both of them.

The First Lady glanced at her daughter.

Lori shook her head and answered first. "No. No White House for me. I don't want to intrude on Father. He's busy with the upcoming election," she added with ill-concealed harshness.

Patty Caldwell's left eye twitched and she glanced anxiously at Diane.

On the monitor, he saw a predatory flash of interest in Diane's eyes. For an instant, it looked like she was going to delve deeper into the family's strained dynamics.

"We hope to see both of you very soon on our morning show," Diane said sweetly. "Make it all three of you," she added, as the camera zoomed in on the newborn's yawn. "Back to you in the studio, Brian."

The cameraman signaled a cut and everyone in the room started shuffling at the same time. He exchanged glances with Diane and nodded a thank you. It wasn't like Diane to pass on an opportunity to explore a potentially juicy angle, but what a wise, classy move to resist the temptation.

He was about to sneak out, when the tall woman turned.

He recognized Leoni Wakeling from the NNSC convention. For a moment, she froze. Then her lips started moving but there was no sound. "I followed your advice and called . . ." she whispered as she stepped closer.

He was about to welcome her aboard, when he heard Patty Caldwell's voice. "Dr. Barcelos, do you have a second?" He put up a just-a-minute finger.

Mauricio walked over to the First Lady. She drew him toward the window and lowered her voice. "Lori doesn't know, but I have arranged for extra supervision. Round the clock. But still . . ." She looked him in the eyes. "Do you think it's safe to leave her at home?"

"Mrs. Caldwell, I think Lori is back on track. Her mood has been excellent; her depression scale scores are completely within normal limits. The implant is working. Dr. Levine told me he's sure . . ."

Patty Caldwell's eyes flashed with anger. "She almost died on Dr. Levine's watch. I want to know what you think."

He thought for a moment.

"She's ready, Mrs. Caldwell," he said simply.

Patty Caldwell smiled. "When we're not in public, please call me Patty."

"That's what I call access," Diane mumbled, as he stepped over to her side.

He hid a smile. Nothing gets past this woman. They watched the monitor as the camera recorded the exit procession of the patient, baby, First Lady and a Secret Service escort. They were followed by nurses, attendants, and Shelly Isaacson, who had appeared at the last minute and was tagging along trying to look relevant.

Diane touched his arm. "If this piece doesn't get me a couple of brownie points at the station, nothing will," she whispered.

The camera was still rolling on the stragglers, when a young heavy-set woman pushed her way through the door. He recognized Rosie, his administrative assistant. He held his breath. Rosie looked panicked. Rosie was never panicked.

For a moment, she stood still under the lights, her enormous eyes scanning the scene, drops of sweat glistening on her chocolate skin, the bouffant hairdo looking windblown.

"Dr. Barcelos, we have . . ." She noticed the cameraman waving frantically. She froze, and then recovered. "You didn't answer your phone," she hissed.

He raised his finger to his lips.

Rosie lowered her voice to a whisper. "Sandy M's sister just called. They're down in the ER. She found Sandy in bed, unconscious."

20

Sandy McBride lay motionless, breathing evenly as if in a deep sleep. A vital signs monitor beeped quietly. A single IV led into her arm. Mauricio took her hand. The skin was warm, the pulse strong and steady. She did have several bruises on her face, perhaps from a struggle.

Chad Michaels, the ER physician, started to brief him. "The sister came to breakfast, found her on the bed unresponsive, and called the paramedics. Her vitals are within normal limits; she does have some facial contusions. Labs so far show nothing; tox screen is pending. Head CT looked unremarkable to me, but the radon hasn't seen it yet," Chad added.

"Did you do a rape kit?"

Chad nodded. "No evidence of sexual activity."

"Pacer tracings?"

"Couldn't access them. Our UV reader is still on order. I was hoping you could bypass ..."

Mauricio flipped open his iPad, punched in his password, logged on to the LX website, entered his administrative access code, and pulled up Sandy's record.

He studied the multicolored lines of the preceding twenty-four hours as if reading a book.

Chad looked over his shoulder. "Spaghetti factory."

"From what I can see," he explained, "all was well until 9:04 P.M. last night. Then . . ."

At that point, the tracings were scrambled beyond recognition. Now, that's spaghetti, he thought. The mess reminded him of an earlier dog implant, when the dog got into a fight with a bigger animal and was dragged around like a rag doll for several minutes before he could break them up.

Sandy's anomalous tracings continued through most of the night. By the wee hours, the knotted lines return to a normal pattern.

"I've downloaded what's on the module," he said. "We'll run the tracing through our programs." Mel could squeeze information even out of a real spaghetti bowl. "Can I see the CT?"

Chad pulled up a set of images on the bedside monitor.

He studied the screen, and then zoomed in on a small area around the tip of the LX. "I'll bet you a buck that's what did it."

"What?" Chad asked.

"That's fresh bleeding." Trauma just jumped to the top of his list. "Something dislodged the tip after we sent her home. Could be from the facial trauma."

"Or the headboard," Chad suggested. "Sister fessed up that our patient had invited an old boyfriend over."

What part of "no heavy exertion" did Sandy not get? And with a boyfriend who apparently beat her up? You can cure depression, but ensuring common sense . . . He shook his head.

"Okay, we'll go with a diagnosis of trauma-induced LX malfunction. I'd give her ten of decadron, repeat every two, and keep head elevated. You know the drill. In a day or two that local bleed will settle down."

He worked the settings on Sandy's LX page, adjusting them slowly to avoid shocking her system. Moments later, Sandy stirred and her eyelids fluttered open.

"Hi, honey," she mumbled, looking at him through heavy eyelids. She repositioned her legs and closed her eyes again.

"Well, we seem to be in NAD," Chad commented. "I'll go check on the tox screen."

No Acute Distress, indeed, Mauricio thought after Chad left. He shook her shoulder. "Ms. McBride . . . Sandy."

She opened her eyes again.

"What were you thinking, inviting a boyfriend over for sex?"

Sandy rolled her head without raising it from the pillow. "I'm sorry, Dr. Barcelos. I remember cleaning house—but I was very careful not to bend down, like you said."

"But you invited your boyfriend over and apparently that didn't go over well. You have bruises on your face."

"That's what my sister said."

"You could have bled into your brain . . ."

"I screwed up, Dr. Barcelos. Never again, I promise."

She seemed genuinely contrite.

"Thing is, I don't remember what happened," she added. "The whole evening is a blur. Except that I remember being pissed at Robbie. For leaving me. And . . ."

She raised her head a little off the gurney and checked the room, then lowered her voice. "And being . . . You know . . . Okay. I admit. I was horny as hell, waiting for Robbie. It's been months." She paused. "I think there was a knock on the door. Then nothing. I don't even know how I got upstairs. But I remember the paramedic."

"That was this morning, Sandy."

She wiggled her nose, and stared at something on the ceiling. "He had this soothing voice," she mumbled, her voice husky. "Telling me to lay still. That everything was all right. Just kept repeating . . ."

He shrugged. "Probably trying to settle you down while they moved you down the stairs to the ambulance."

She studied his face. "If you say so. I thought it was last night. But the whole thing is foggy." Suddenly, she smiled mischievously.

"Worst part? I don't remember having sex. What's the fun in that?"

He was at the nurses' station dictating his report, when he heard a scream coming from the direction of Sandy's room.

"No, please . . . Help!"

He dashed down the hall, Chad and two nurses on his heels.

Sandy McBride was wrestling with two female deputies who were trying to cuff her wrists.

A skeletally thin middle-aged man watched the scene.

Sandy cried out when she saw him. "Dr. Barcelos, don't let them."

"What's going on here?" Mauricio exploded.

The man blocked his way. "I'm Detective Blanchard." The detective was several inches taller than him, despite the hunched over posture that gave him an avian look.. "Sorry about the disturbance," Blanchard said. "We'll be gone in a minute."

"Gone where?"

"Not your concern, Doctor. Police business."

His jaw muscles tightened. "Here it's all medical business, until I say it isn't. If that's all right with you, Detective."

"I don't know what happened," Sandy pleaded.

Blanchard interrupted her. "Remember, you have the right to remain . . ."

"Help me, Dr. Barcelos."

He held up his hand. "Ms. McBride." He turned to Blanchard. "Detective? May I have a word with my patient? In private?"

"You can see her at the station," Blanchard snapped. "After we get her booked."

One of those, he thought.

"No need for handcuffs, Detective. She's a sick woman. She's not running."

"Not your decision. We checked her house. She had a bag packed.

Wallet, meds, laptop. Don't tell me she's not a flight risk."

This wasn't going to end well for Sandy. He took a deep breath and made the most empathetic face he could manage. "Yes, of course. I understand. Police business. I'm only concerned that the implant might retro process through the singulate gyrus while you're driving her downtown, and cause a paradoxical dysencephaly."

Retroprocess through the singulate gyrus? Paradoxical dysencephaly? Where did I come up with that crap? he wondered.

"Whatever," Blanchard barked. "We'll deal with it when we get downtown."

He gave a resigned nod. "It may be difficult, in the car. Particularly when the projectile vomiting ... Oh, well." He raised his voice enough for the deputies to hear him. "And if she aspirates and dies ..."

He shook his head. "Detective Blanchard, you wouldn't want that on your conscience, would you?"

Blanchard's neck veins bulged. His yellowish eyes telegraphed a clear message. I know what you are doing, and I don't like it.

"Two minutes," Blanchard hissed, and then nodded to the deputies. "Outside. Watch the exits."

Mauricio draped his arm around Sandy's shoulder and helped her back onto the gurney.

"What happened?"

Tears streaming down her face, she whispered, "They're saying ... they said ..." She let out a volley of sobs, gasping and chocking on her tears, and started to sag forward off the gurney.

He held her up.

"I don't know how it happened..."

"Ms. McBride ... Sandy ..."

"I didn't do it, Dr. Barcelos. I... I don't think I did it..."

"Shhh. Just take a deep breath and tell me. "Did what?"

"He ..." She choked on a sob, and then blurted out, "He said I killed Robbie."

21

"A HELL OF A FIRST DAY ON THE JOB," Leoni thought as she watched the deputies leave empty-handed. The doctor's most famous patient was being discharged on national TV, just as the most recent patient was being arrested on a murder charge. Her job was to keep that off TV. Good luck.

She saw Mauricio storm by, agitated, on the phone.

"…Not letting her out, Bruce. Bullshit charge…Get the hospital's attorney on this…"

This was definitely not a good time for her reintroduction as the new LX spokesperson. She could just see his reaction. "Every time I have a problem, you're there." She waited till he was out of sight, then made her way down to the lobby.

She had been determined to make this job work. Fascinating device, worthy cause, a great opportunity to spread her PR wings again. But it had nothing to do with the inventor, she assured herself. Even though every time she thought of Mau—Mauricio was a mouthful, she had decided—the skin on the back of her neck warmed up. That she didn't need, but the job itself promised to be rewarding. And best of all, she was now free of the blackmailer.

How did it happen? "That's what you get for being a softie," she had chastised herself countless times, "and talking to a guy just because he walked with a limp." Then she would add, in the interest of full disclosure, "That's what you get for being needy, and melting just because a twenty-something made a pass at you."

"I need a favor," the computer guy had texted her the day after she slept with him.

"Leave me alone," she texted back.

His reply was a picture. She recognized herself, naked, with a man's back blocking part of the view.

"I need two files from your boss's office," he said when they met at a nearby coffee shop.

"You're the IT, get them yourself."

"I can't. They're paper files. All you do is go in . . ."

She bolted from her chair. "Over my dead body."

"Over your naked body. . ." the man corrected her, scrolling through several more pictures on his iPhone. "You don't want this in your husband's hands before your divorce is final, do you?"

Her pulse was racing with anger and fear. Out on the street, penniless after twenty years. The prospect was daunting.

He gave her shoulder a gentle squeeze. "Look, all you have to do is scan ten pages. He'll never know."

"He has security cameras," she protested.

"I'll take care of them. I am the IT guy after all," he smiled.

Late next night, she made her way to the Penthouse and used the access code to let herself into the boss's office. The room was dark, the sound of her footsteps muffled by the thick carpeting. She glanced up to confirm that the little red lights were off on the three cameras. She made it to the old-fashioned file cabinet, located the files, started feeding them through the scanner . . .

Suddenly a muffled sound came from the direction of the recliner that faced out toward the bay window. A guttural gurgling. She made out the outline of her boss's bald head.

"Dr. Crowley," she gasped. "I was just checking . . ."

The man didn't budge. She inched closer, hoping what she heard was snoring. A crimson streak was running down his scalp, dripping onto the rug.

Oh my God, oh my God. She rushed back to turn off the scanner and tripped on a heavy object. She picked it up. It was the malachite ashtray Crowley had brought from a trip to Argentina. One corner was covered with sticky liquid. Blood. She slammed the ashtray on the desk.

The phone rang. An ear-splitting sound that sent ice water through her veins.

"Get out. Security is coming."

"They'll know I was in the building."

"I'll fix that. We'll say you were with me all night."

As the days went by, Crowley recovered. No suspect for the attempted mugging was ever identified. The blunt heavy object used to inflict the injury was not found. She had been torn about turning herself in, but the man talked her out of it. "You did nothing wrong. Why risk a lifetime in jail?"

She couldn't face Crowley when he returned to work after a month of rehab. She quit, citing personal reasons. On her last day, the man intercepted her in the parking lot. "Don't worry about what happened," he said, leaning over her car window, his face inches from hers. "I pulled the recordings and hid the ashtray. It'll be our secret."

Her heart paused. "What recordings?"

"Security."

"But. . . The cameras were off."

A faint smile swept across his lips, and she knew the bastard had rigged the cameras and collected the ashtray with her bloody fingerprints all over it. He had her.

He leaned in and kissed her on the lips before she could pull back. Then he straightened and limped away.

For two years the IT guy sent her weekly requests to go out with him, to get to know each other. The thought of being with him was revolting. She replied with monosyllabic negatives. The specter of the security tapes hung over her like a storm cloud. Eventually he stopped asking. She was beginning to think it was all behind her, when the phone call came the previous week.

"There is a trade show. I'll get you a badge. All you need to do is embarrass a physician. The security video will be in your mailbox by the time you get home. Then you'll never hear from me again."

"The video and the ashtray."

To the man's credit, he delivered. When she got home from the convention, she found a package on her doorstep. Inside was a DVD and a Ziploc with the malachite ashtray. A simple message was scribbled on the disc. "You're free to fly away, butterfly, but please let me thank you by taking you out to dinner."

She texted him. "If I ever hear from you again, I'm going to the cops." She hoped the bluff would work.

In the lobby, the reporters who had gathered to cover the First Daughter's discharge had returned, like sharks sensing new prey. By noon, the story of the woman's arrest will be in every news feed and every tweet, she thought. Right next to the story that both women have the same neural implant.

She held her breath when she saw Barcelos emerge from the stairwell. As open as he was, he'd just make a mess. He must have noticed the press because he headed in the opposite direction. A couple of reporters followed. She knew the others would too.

Shit.

She swept her hair back, took in a deep breath, and stepped into the center of the lobby. "Ladies and gentlemen." Her voice projected over the din. "I'm Leoni Wakeling, spokesperson for the neural implant project. If you have questions, fire away."

22

THE WHEELS OF THE VAN GROUND to a loud halt on the desert gravel. Al stepped out and let the door slam shut. In the deep silence, the sound reverberated from the mountains in the distance. A flock of turkey vultures spiraled into the early morning sun. A gust of desert wind carried away the odor of burned engine oil, replacing it with the scents of juniper and mesquite.

He found an elevated spot and squatted with his back against a rock. The cold rough surface chilled him right through his cotton shirt and thin sweater. He exhaled slowly, and let his eyes linger on the landscape, in an effort to still his mind.

Mojave Desert, just a hundred miles north of the metropolitan sprawl called the Greater LA Area, might as well have been on Mars. Rocks and Joshua trees, furnace-hot in summer, snow-covered in winter. It was God-forsaken territory, where scorpions and sidewinders and desert rats far outnumbered humans.

"Just like Badakhshan Valley," he thought every time he came here, recalling the pictures of the sun-scorched province in Afghanistan where his mother Soraya had spent her childhood.

Even before the Soviets invaded in 1979, Soraya's parents had moved to Kabul and managed to enroll her into the University. Years later they gave their blessing to her marriage to a young professor who would become Al's father. A father who joined the Mujahedeen to fight the Soviets, and vanished into the hills in 1986, leaving his pregnant wife to fend for herself. He was reported killed in the last spasm of rebellion against the occupying Soviet forces.

When Al turned two, his mother took a job at the Russian embassy. He couldn't blame her. As a widow, she had no one to turn to, and a child to support. They were the enemy, but they paid her salary.

Eventually she married a Russian coworker, Maxim, a communications expert, who had a daughter, Svetlana. She was a few years older than Al. Even as a toddler, he remembered being fascinated by her beautiful blond curls. Besides reminding him of his homeland, or photos of it, what had attracted him to this desolate spot were the abandoned borax mines. There were miles and miles of shafts that burrowed into the rocky soil, branching and spreading in all directions, like man-sized gopher holes. After his first visit, he had returned often, and spent long days exploring the passages, imagining the stories these tunnels could tell.

One day, while concealing his car from view between two mounds of debris, he stumbled on an entrance to yet another mine. He explored the convoluted passage and found the far end sealed by a rusted gate. Beyond, he could see a spacious cave. A flat floor, almost smooth walls, and a ventilation shaft told him it had been a miner's shelter, long ago deserted.

He fell in love with it and spent months enhancing the space with gas heating, a water tank, and a small gas generator, so he could have lighting, a TV and a computer. Then he had rigged up an antenna and hacked into a communications' satellite for cable and Internet access.

It nurtured his soul to think that by living in a desert cave, even if only for a few hours a month, he was following in the steps of his ancestors. Even without the luxuries, it was far better living than what most children enjoyed in Badakhshan, he often reminded himself, thinking of his Injured Children's Fund.

The vibration of his cell phone jolted him to the present, the caller ID instantly reminding him of last night's terrible outcome. He sent the call to voice mail. He would report in when he was ready. On his schedule.

The Kay woman had agreed to a half mil on behalf of her client. Plus commissions, as he decided to call the money that would supposedly come with many of the successful cases. He flashed to the map of orphanages he had funded. Nine so far, in ten years. With luck, this project would double that number in a few months. He would deliver as promised—he always delivered as promised—but he wasn't going to be at her beck and call 24/7. Bitch.

He picked up a pebble and tossed it absentmindedly at a nearby cactus, but missed.

This de Barcelos guy was going to be a challenge. In the past week he had read everything the doctor had written on the LX.

"Since depression is associated with increased activity in the subcallosal cingulate gyrus (SCG), a brain area involved in mood regulation," stated one of Barcelos' articles, written several years back, "the possibility of directly modulating the output of the SGC and, consequently. . .

Al's dictionary app had been working overtime.

"Deep brain stimulation with implantable electrodes," one piece concluded, "is a versatile and easily reversible method of modulating the activity of dysfunctional brain circuits."

And so on and so forth.

He was impressed by the remote control aspects of the device. It was a superbly designed system. Not bad for a ma-pa outfit. You couldn't just waltz into NBMC's basement, bribe the IT nerd and help yourself to the data. The cyber-security was better than in most banks. It was going to take all his skills, he realized, to gain the needed access.

And that was just the beginning. Lady Kay's instructions were to explore specifically the sleep cycle alterations, and its potential for hypnotic suggestion. The woman must've been a medical researcher, or more than some fixer type. He'd look into it.

He tossed another pebble, and this time hit the cactus.

He had been right about Barcelos being reluctant to ask the NBMC IT people to remove the virus bearing the pornographic pictures from his computer. The doctor had decide he could avoid further embarrassment by doing it himself. Big mistake. The malware that Al persuaded Leoni to upload, seemingly deleted, was now firmly ensconced on the good doctor's laptop computer.

Even with access to the doctor's computer assured, he still needed a functioning LX, in a real patient, to penetrate the Cloud where the records resided. It would be next to impossible to cover his steps if he used Barcelos' computer as an entry point.

It took him all of thirty minutes to learn everything he needed to know about the several recently implanted patients. Thank you, Facebook. Thank you, LinkedIn.

Cat Lady, aka Sandy McBride, was the perfect candidate. She lived alone, was naïve, easy-going. It seemed that all he needed to do was show up and talk her into letting him fiddle with her computer to gain access to her programming. From there, he was sure he could worm his way into the Cloud, and the rest of the patient data. And then he could explore how the LX could best be used to execute his assignments.

Sticking a flashing red light on the roof of his van, and donning a white coat made the job even easier. "We picked up an emergency call from your implant, Ms. McBride. Dr. Barcelos sent me to adjust your settings . . ."

It should have been the easiest social engineering job imaginable. He had done his due-diligence. He was ready for anything. But he hadn't been ready for finding Cat Lady practically naked.

He had to make an effort to act professional, telling her to get dressed before he could come in and help her adjust the neural implant settings on her laptop. That cost a few precious minutes.

Once he persuaded Sandy to log in, he had felt like a pro manipulating her tracings. A couple of tweaks on the sleep channel and the woman was out. He relocated her to the couch.

To his dismay he found that the firewalls at CloudFort would not crumble as easily as he expected. It was clear that he would have to spend some time experimenting with Sandy's programming to worm his way into the main system.

Just as he settled in for an extended hacking session, he heard the pounding on the front door and a man calling out to her. "Damn it, Sandy! If you wanna get fucked, open the damned door."

By the time Al made it to the kitchen to persuade the intruder to leave, it was too late. The clearly inebriated Robbie was already inside, charging at him with clenched fists.

He panicked, grabbed a knife from the counter, and raised it in defense just as the man lunged at him. Al felt the sickening sounds of escaping air and bone rubbing on metal as Robbie impaled himself on the long blade.

Al had no choice but to log off and get out of there. At least he thought to punch Sandy in the face a couple of times to make it look like there had been a physical confrontation that led to her killing this visitor. The bitch even scratched his face, calling him Robbie.

Damn Robbie. Dead for no reason.

Al winced and tried to chase the thought away by reminding himself of all his dead friends and countrymen. And his own father. Dead, for no reason, except national greed. At least his mission was a noble goal, not a meaningless pursuit of territory.

Still, it was humiliating. He should've researched the subject better, even tapped into her cell phone to catch this invitation. "Dumb shit," his adoptive Russian father would have said.

He exhaled and forced himself to refocus. Now he would have to search for another suitable candidate. This time he would be sure to choose one that he could spend time with. A subject that would serve not just as a portal into the Cloud, but as a live specimen on whom to explore the limits of what he could or could not make the LX do. In situ, so to speak. Lady Kay had hinted that the assignments were going to grow increasingly complex. He was determined to go forward fully prepared to exploit this opportunity.

He looked at the Joshua trees silhouetted against the clear morning sky, at the birds circling in the distance. After his initial failure, he needed an ego boost, but he didn't dare call Leoni. She wouldn't answer his call, just reject him again, adding fuel to the fire. His leg began to twitch. Don't make me do it, Leoni . . .

When and if he really needed her, he had a way to enforce his will. She would answer his call then. She would have no choice.

23

Mauricio stopped in the middle of the isle of the Boeing 777's luxurious first class and double-checked his seat assignment. Sure enough, 3A. For some reason he had been upgraded from the sardine section. The prospect of the red-eye to D.C. suddenly became much less unappealing.

The plush window seat did nothing to allay his concern about Brad Oakley's cryptic message that had arrived that morning. "Come see your tax dollars at work. Signed, Brad. PS: I could tell you, but you wouldn't believe me."

He stared out the window, watching the ground crew load the last of the luggage. Was Brad's show-and-tell going to be unbelievably good or unbelievably disastrous, he wondered?

On top of Brad's summons, the memory of the previous week's confrontation with Detective Blanchard over Sandy McBride's arrest was adding to the stress. His mind had assumed the worst. The LX had malfunctioned. She had committed a crime during a psychotic episode caused by an implant misfire. It would be a first in his experience. The CT scan from her ER visit had confirmed bleeding around the filaments. Did the erratic output cause a psychotic episode? Could it have pushed her to kill Robbie?

He remembered breaking out in a sweat when Blanchard came up to them and announced that his two minutes alone with her were up, and they were taking Sandy downtown. The detective left him no choice. He had to put his foot down, raise his voice, make up a bunch of medicalese mumbo jumbo and force Blanchard to seek approval from his superiors. While the detective stepped away, he summoned Bruce and got the psychiatrist to place Sandy on a 72-hour hold in the psych unit at NBMC.

Blanchard had been livid. He barked orders to the deputies and then stormed out, his final glance leaving no doubt about his feelings. Made an enemy, Mauricio remembered thinking. Vai te fuder. Go fuck yourself, he decided, trying to dismiss the event. But old tapes of his childhood encounter with authority started replaying in his head, spawning an irrational fear that had been haunting him for days.

Now the 72-hour hold was over. The last he heard, the hospital attorney managed to keep her out on bail. Mel was still analyzing the LX tracings and figuring out what really happened.

"Please raise your seatbacks to an upright position . . ."

He leaned his head against the window and closed his eyes, determined to fall sleep as soon as he could.

"Eu so perto do Rio Azul . . ." he thought, visualizing himself near his old home on the Rio Azul. "It is evening, I am walking down the path. . ." The ritual, honed by years of interrupted sleep during residency, began to work its magic.

An image of his home appeared. It was a one-room dwelling built of eucalyptus logs, topped with a straw roof, and perched on six-foot-high stills to survive the high water of the river during the rainy season.

Now he was walking toward the birdcalls beckoning him into the forest. The birdcalls grew louder. He recognized the croaking call of a toucan. Bats streaked through the darkness.

His muscles were relaxing.

All around, giant Kapok trees reached to the skies and obscured the stars. He stepped gingerly, his bare feet feeling the familiar ground. He glanced back and saw the flickering fire.

The vision was interrupted by a bump as a body landed in the seat next to him.

No body. No seat. No plane. He must have bumped into a tree trunk . . .

He woke up with a sweet citrus scent teasing his nostrils, and something tickling his face. The cabin was dark and the plane was in level cruise, the engines humming evenly. He brushed off the offending tickle and sensed a body next to him.

He forced his eyes open and studied the shape. A woman, her back toward him, her thick hair spilling toward his face. She rolled over slowly.

His eyes popped wide open.

Leoni.

Her eyes opened, inches from his. She jerked back, sat up and smoothed her blouse. "Sorry. I hope I wasn't snoring."

He eyed her, waiting for an explanation.

"I was late boarding; you were asleep, so I didn't wake you."

This didn't answer his tacit question.

"I see Rosie didn't tell you," Leoni added. "I wanted the upgrade to be a surprise."

"Did I miss a memo?" He stared at her, trying to make sense of this situation.

"It's my fault," she said. "I should've let you know I was coming along."

You think? he wanted to say.

"I really didn't get a chance to explain myself back at the hospital, with all the confusion."

He gave a quick nod. He had intended to seek her out after Lori's discharge and welcome her, but Sandy's attempted arrest prevented that.

She continued, "After the convention, I took your advice and called. They had an opening in PR."

"Nice of them to check with me first," he said.

"The job wasn't with you. A Dr. Talon needed help with fund-raising. But when it came up in the conversation that I had met you at NNSC, I got reassigned to you. The job description included being able to tolerate stressful work conditions and excelling in damage control. Or something to that effect." She raised her palms in resignation. "My specialty. I said I'd take it."

Her hand flew to her mouth. "I . . . I didn't mean it that way. I'm really looking forward to working with you."

In the dark, he couldn't be sure whether she was telling the truth. He snorted. "It still doesn't explain why you're here."

She glanced away. "Hmm, Mr. Isaacson said something about you being . . . headstrong."

"You met The Weasel? That must have been an interesting interview," he said, his eyes darting involuntarily down Leoni's long legs, curled up in the seat. The sight would have made Weasel's day, no doubt.

"At least he didn't yell at me," she pointed out.

He winced at the thinly disguised reference to his own meeting with her. "So you're here for damage control?"

She nodded.

"I'm not a rabid dog, you know. I don't need a muzzler."

Leoni's lips quivered with suppressed laughter.

"What's so funny?"

"Those are exactly the words Isaacson used."

24

"CLOUDFORT. TIMOTHY DAVENS speaking. How may I help you?"

Timothy was one of four attendants working CloudFort's switchboard. After a month of stellar performance as a new hire at the world-renowned cloud-computing giant, he had been promoted to graveyard shift supervisor in an obscure low-activity medical section. The entire plant was entirely automated, and he knew he was little more than a law-mandated ornament. It wasn't exactly the physician's assistant job he was hoping to get after working so hard at online vocational courses, but it paid the bills. With healthcare in flux, he had high hopes of soon finding the job of his dreams, where he could play doctor. At least CloudFort was a large, reputable company that provided health benefits and training in Information Technology that would serve him in the future.

The caller sounded like a nervous intern at a minor hospital.

"Timothy, I'm Sam Nightingale. I'm a nurse here at St. Joe's in Tucson, Arizona . . ."

Yes, Sam, that's where Tucson is, Tim sighed. Arizona.

"We have a patient that has a brain pacemaker of some sort . . ."

Tim drummed his fingers on the keyboard, waiting for useful information he could input. Get to the point, man.

Suddenly, a blood-curdling scream came from Sam's end of the line. Tim bolted upright in his chair.

"Oh, oh, standby . . ." Sam's voice said.

Tim heard the phone slamming on a counter. More screams. It was a woman's voice, in pain, but the words were unintelligible. Then Sam, yelling an order to someone.

"Talk to me, Sam."

"We're getting Dr. Barcelos now," Sam stammered. "She's a Newport Bay Medical Center patient."

More screams.

"How can I help you, Sam?" Tim asked, and this time he meant it. A real medical emergency with a live patient. Much more fun than an incompetent IT with an inane question.

"Well, it's kind of a confusing story. We've been trying to piece it together. We called the husband, and he said . . . well, even before that . . ."

More screaming in the background.

"Yes, so?" Tim prodded, wishing he could trade places with Sam the Slow Witted and show him how a real healthcare provider worked.

"He's driving in. Six hours away. . . But he gave us her password."

Ah, finally, a CloudFort connection, Tim thought.

"From what our doctor thinks, she's in a stem overdose. Pacemaker malfunction."

More screaming, moaning, and pleas for help. A psychotic episode, Tim diagnosed proudly. I should've been a doctor. Treat with Thorazine and . . .

"It's a pacemaker-induced psychotic episode."

Ah-ha, what did I say, Tim thought.

"So we have to log on to the hospital server at NBMC. . . so we can reset the inputs . . ."

"Did you?"

"Their server is down … We called her doctor, Dr. Barcelos, but he is unreachable, flying somewhere." Sam's voice was getting more frantic. A large object crashed in the background.

"The physician covering the implant program for him, Dr. Bruce Levine, said that CloudFort is the main server …"

Tim was already logged on to the NBMC account. "Nothing I can do to help you," Tim said flatly. "HIPAA rules, you know." You could invoke HIPAA to cover anything. Fifth Amendment on steroids.

"Look, all I need is for you to clear access to this one patient. I have all her data, her passwords …"

"Only if the hospital client or her physician authorizes. I recommend you get …"

"Stand by," Sam yelled. "Martha, get anesthesia in here. STAT!"

Pause. Tim felt his adrenaline racing.

Sam was yelling at his nurse. "I don't give a shit. Oh, boy …"

Pause. Moaning.

Sam's voice came back, more forceful. "Work with me, Tim." He seemed to have a plan of action. "I have the patient's pacemaker logged on to St. Joe's computer. I'm sending you a link, so you'll know this is legit."

Tim's fingers raced over the keyboard. An email with the return address of www.SaintJosephofMercy.org appeared on the screen. The body of the email contained a link that looked like a device IP address. Tim clicked on it. Lines of code raced across his screen.

</div>DepR</pharm></p><meta
http-equiv="Content-Type" "text/html;
charset=UTF-8" /><meta name="neural" =
"LXmod tr><td>Row 4, and <dfn title="LX">access …

"See it yet?" Sam asked.

"I see it."

"See the patient data?"

"Yes …"

"I'd put her on the line but as you see, I can't ... So I'm inputting her private password ..."

Tim's screen flashed LX ACCESS ESTABLISHED.

"Tim, all I'm asking you to do is pull up her record ..."

"That'd be a confidentiality breach. I could get fired."

"Tim Davis, get me your supervisor."

"I am the supervisor."

"Obviously, you're not medically trained, Davens," Sam said. "So let me explain ..."

"Actually, I happen to be a Certified Physician's Assistant," Tim interrupted.

"Oh, assistant. What, you couldn't make decisions on your own, so they didn't let you into med school?"

Tim's temper flared. "Listen, Nurse Sam," he started, making nurse sound as insulting as he could. "I make the decisions here and ..."

Another muffled scream then nothing.

"Oh, shit ..." Sam's voice sounded frantic.

Then Tim heard the words that always excited him.

"Code Blue, Emergency room. Code Blue, Emergency room."

The next thought that flashed through Tim's mind was not so exciting. The woman is going to crump, and that Sam guy is going to pin it on me. "Sam? Hello, Sam," Tim yelled into the receiver. He heard only sounds of commotion. "Hello?"

Not good, Tim thought. What was it that Sam wanted? Link to the patient's record? The man had the patient and the patient's password. What harm could it be to give him access to the record?

Sam was back on the phone, barking. "We're doing CPR ... You get me your boss. Now. Or our attorneys will make sure that the only assistant job you get will be at Starbucks. For the rest of your life."

What harm could there be, Tim thought. That's what CloudFort was supposed to provide. Instant access to records, from any system, anywhere in the world. That's why clients paid the big bucks. Perhaps the bosses would praise him for independent thinking. It would look good on his resume . . .

"In the interest of patient welfare and safety, I'm making the decision to allow the access," Tim announced, salvaging what he could from his insulted dignity. "Send the link and I'll punch it in from this end."

In the back of his van, parked on a side street, Al was typing as fast as his fingers would move.

StJoe</LX.RossG></p><meta http-nor= content="CloudFort> <td>Row 4, and <dfn title="LX"

He checked the screen, and hit 'send.'

"On its way."

Moments later, the "LX//KR467 tr>CF*6^^ message confirmed that his computer was engaged in a lively exchange with the CloudFort server.

He pumped his fist and mouthed, "Yes."

He was already savoring Lady Kay's probable reaction. "We've been trying for a year. And you got in on the first try?"

Admittedly, it had taken two tries, if you included the Cat Lady. But there was no need to reveal details of failures past.

It was social engineering at its best. Human insecurities and jealousies and greed were far easier to manipulate than software. He thanked Tim, told him he had just helped save the woman's life and that he would send in a commendation as soon as he was done restoring the patient's heartbeat. Then he hung up.

So far, it had been a successful first step.

The subject's shopping history that was there for all to see on Facebook and Amazon eventually provided a link to her computer and the Post-it note on which she kept her passwords. Including the one for her LX settings. Then dimwit Tim came through as expected. All he had to do now was tweak the patient's sleep channel, and wait for her in the tenants' parking lot. If step two went as planned, she should lapse into a light sleep and let him guide her into his van.

Step three would be to take his time and use her implant as the Trojan Horse he needed to move freely about CloudFort. He was on track, but time was running short. The first assigned case, was due to happen any day. And Lady Kay did not strike him as someone who would accept a failure.

Al played another segment of a woman's voice screaming from one of the files he had downloaded to his laptop and gave himself an Oscar for sound mixing. Then he slipped behind the wheel and drove on, feeling redeemed after the Sandy failure.

25

MAURICIO AND LEONI WERE MET at Dulles International by a female military aide. An hour later, they were trotting behind General Brad Oakley's wheelchair as he zoomed down the hallways of Bethesda Naval Hospital at breakneck speed.

"New ride, I see." Mauricio pointed to the computer screen mounted in front of Brad.

"Always improving," replied a computer-generated voice.

Yes, he thought, Brad Oakley was always improving things. If he couldn't serve his country on the battlefield, he would continue charging forward with equal vigor in the research field.

The man had dedicated the early part of his career to returning aviators to active duty as soon as humanly possible. His success rate was legendary. If you were a wounded pilot, your chances of returning to flying increased ten-fold if you had Oakley for a surgeon. One night he was making a dash to a field hospital to attend to an injured pilot, when an IED took out the bottom of his Humvee and turned Oakley into the wheelchair-bound mute he was today.

But instead of opting for a comfortable retirement, Brad became the poster-child for the newly developed cortical implant. The device, first used in 2008, but vastly improved over the years, consisted of a small set of electrodes implanted into the brain of quadriplegics. Neurons, glions, and other brain cells grew around the implant like ivy on a building, forming enough connections to enable the patient to interface wirelessly with a computer and control a wheelchair and other devices. A speech generator did the rest.

The neuron-to-electrode bond was the same principle that Mauricio had relied on to enable the LX to bond to the brain: eventually the implant would become a natural extension of the organ. He often talked to Brad about future possibilities—both for the LX and for Brad's own cortical implant technology. The man's intellect was astounding, but he found that it was the relentless, obsessive drive that most attracted him to the general.

"Your own publicist," Brad's computer-synthesized voice was saying. "Moving up in the world."

"Not my idea," he answered. "But I'm not complaining." He glanced at Leoni. "At least not yet."

Brad led them on a quick tour of the main ward, where his recent implant recipients were lounging, playing computer games, or watching the news.

"You've been busy," Mauricio noted, amazed how many patients his friend had managed to treat since he received the shipment of LX wires barely ten days earlier.

"We had a backlog," Brad said. "My boys had no trouble learning the technique. It's not like it is brain surgery." Brads monitor flashed a cartoon designed to replicate a laughing face.

After posing for a photo op for Leoni's public relations benefit and a brief interview, Brad wheeled up to face her. "I am delighted to have met you, sunshine," the computer voice said. "But now I want to show my friend how we are going to win the next war with those fucking towel-heads." The monotonic computerized speech gave the statement a sinister note. "May I steal your doctor for a few moments?"

"Not mine to steal," Leoni shrugged, seemingly undisturbed by the summary dismissal.

The guard at the control post held out a small tray and Mauricio relinquished his phone.

"Only prescreened, pre-approved devices are allowed in," he explained. "Sir."

"This is beyond classified, Mau," Brad said, as they cleared two more control posts and entered a warehouse. "Only showing you because you need to see this with your own eyes."

The room had a large flat console and several display monitors. One of the walls had a one-way glass. Beyond the glass, he saw a set of four stations that resembled fighter aircraft cockpits, complete with pilot seats, panel displays and controls. The spaces where the windshields would have been, had semicircular screens instead. In two of the mock cockpits men wearing flying helmets worked the controls.

"Let me show you what they're seeing," Bradley said. There was a quick flickering of Bradley's communication screen, and then the consoles inside the control room came to life.

Mauricio saw simulated targets crisscrossing in all directions. Crosshairs moved as the pilots took aim. Tiny flares marked the kill-shots.

"Interesting," he said to humor his friend. It was less interesting than PlayStation's Combat Ace. For this he had traveled cross-country?

"'Interesting?' That is all you have to say?" Brad's synthetic voice couldn't quite convey his frustration, but his eyes did. "Look closer."

He scanned the display. His jaw dropped. "Brad, are you out of your friggin mind?"

26

Mauricio and Leoni made the 8:00 p.m. flight back to Los Angeles with time to spare, and settled in adjacent seats.

"You don't need to fly me around in first class, you know," he said, picking at the warm nuts that had been served immediately after takeoff.

"First class makes you more of a player. My job is to buff up your image," Leoni said.

"I didn't know my image needed buffing," he snapped, with more vitriol than he had intended.

Leoni bit her lip. "I see your meeting went really well," she said finally.

It didn't take a brain surgeon to detect the sarcasm. "It went fine." There was absolutely nothing about the meeting that he could share. He turned to examine the black nothingness outside the window.

The conversation with Oakley was gnawing at his gut. There was one thing the general had been right about: Mauricio wouldn't have believed him unless he had seen it.

The visit replayed in his head: The small digital clock on the pilots' panel, showing 36:24:11, and ticking up. The graph, hovering around the top of the scale at the 95% mark, reflecting strike accuracy. Plus, the relaxed faces of the test pilots at the simulator consoles.

"Thirty-six hours," Brad's synthesized voice had said. "These guys have been going for thirty-six hours. Nonstop. Only food and bathroom breaks. They could've flown to the Middle East and back. Twice. And still be awake long enough to get laid."

Mauricio's mouth had dried up as a foreboding engulfed him. "LX implantees?" he asked, not sure he wanted to hear the answer.

Brad's screen displayed an edge-to-edge grin. "I call them my AAA boys. Awake, alert, accurate. We adjusted sleep cycles, optimized for REM sleep, tweaked a few things."

He was so stunned he found himself reciting the obvious. "We have built-in overrides. No one can program more than eighteen hours of waking time."

"Did. Done. Works like a charm." The electronic eyebrows wiggled in a Groucho Marx parody. "It's the military. We have hackers too, you know."

"You're insane!"

The eye winked. "Been called that."

His pulse hammered in his ears as his anger grew. "The LX isn't approved for this."

Oakley wheeled closer. Their faces almost touched. He could smell the man's acid breath—result of his liquids-only diet.

"Keeping pilots awake on long missions has been top priority since Gulf One. We used drugs in Iraq. Uppers. So they could fly out, do a bomb run, fly back, repeat. Guys flew twenty hours at a stretch. Thirty sometimes. With no sleep. Whatever it took."

He was speaking as fast as his processor let him.

"So mistakes happened. You think friendly fires were computer malfunctions? Weapons systems errors? Not. It was some poor sleep-deprived slob trying to get his last functioning brain cells to talk to each other. Remember when we bombed a dozen Canadians to smithereens, back in Iraq? Or the hospital in Syria? Amphetamine-induced pilot error. Hush-hush."

"Get more pilots, then."

"You're joking. It takes years to train them. Over three mil apiece. Scarce commodity, Mau. That guy on the right?" Brads' chair pivoted toward the room beyond the glass. "Lieutenant Michael Fox. One of only three men qualified to fly the new F-28. Ten thousand hours. What, you think I can pick up a replacement on Craig's List?"

There was an awkward pause.

"I designed the LX so depressed patients could function normally," he said finally. "Normally, Brad. Not to play Top Gun."

"That is where we differ. You're happy to rehab any unemployed housewife. I want to help the cream of the crop."

He realized that arguing the relative value of the lives of others, with a man who would gladly give his many times over for a cause he believed in, was useless. "If you are waiting for applause, Brad, it's not coming."

The chair spun back toward him. "Mau, I need your help with a function my techies haven't been able to crack."

"Help you?" he snapped. "Help you destroy my project?"

"Help me make it safer."

"It was plenty safe before you started screwing with it."

"Mau, if you help me figure out how to adjust the sleep channel and insert more REM sleep, the pilots will tolerate it better."

He wished he had never sold the wires to this man.

"No one needs to know," Oakley's voice was droning. "Just for my fly-boys. Let's push the envelope, enhance your product. Call it LX/M. A civilian-military version. Very in nowadays."

He spoke again, with less conviction. "We don't know the dangers of long-term sleep deprivation ..."

"Thirty-six hours is long-term? You don't remember working thirty-six hour shifts in our residencies? And the dangers to those guys?

You mean like above and beyond being shot at? Those dangers? These are fighter pilots, Mau. They volunteered. It's their life. Those two begged me to get them back into action. At any cost. If they're giving all they have, I'm going to do the same, till my last breath."

A tear had formed in one of Oakley's eyes, and he tried blinking it away. "I'm on borrowed time anyway. I'm going to help protect this country now and in the future, if it's the last fucking thing I do!"

On the general's motionless face, the eyes were burning with determination.

"And in case you're wondering," Oakley's computer said, as if the man could read his thoughts, "it's all cleared, all the way to the top. And I mean top. There isn't a damned thing you can do to stop me. So you might as well help me."

He had wondered if Caldwell had been so impressed with the effect of the LX on his daughter that he authorized the military to take the device one step further. Or was there another "top" that Oakley was alluding to, that had nothing to do with civilian authority?

Mauricio continued to stare out the window. In the distance, lightning flashed occasionally under the clouds, giving them a surreal appearance.

Just recalling Oakley's ultimatum made his blood drum in his ears. The fact was that there was little he could do. The General was determined—and evidently authorized—to extend the limits of the LX with or without Mauricio's blessing.

Exposing Oakley's rogue experiment would jeopardize the entire project, frighten hundreds of current users, and dissuade thousands of others from ever considering the implant. "Mrs. Smith, that little wire in your head? Uncle Sam can use it to keep you up all night." Talk about mass panic.

On balance, getting involved was the lesser of two evils. At least he could ensure that certain safeguards would be built in to protect the pilot's health.

And there were upsides to Brad's idea. After all, that's how technology progressed. Someone took an existing device and adapted it to a new need. What Oakley was proposing was not radically different from what he himself had done: used Parkinson-style implants to control brain chemistry. Sleep regulation was one of the intended capabilities of the LX. Why not sleep reduction?

It was a heady proposition, and he had to rein in his imagination. If the LX was to be pushed to new frontiers, the brilliant and well-intentioned Brad Oakley was the man to do it.

"Only a limited trial, and only military volunteers," Brad had assured him.

"I'm not going to have your men out on their own for thirty-six hours, without close monitoring," he had insisted. "I'm going to have Mel build in safeguards. Your pilots will need to log in frequently." He hoped these conditions would sour Oakley's interest, but no luck.

"Mau, we have so many remote links to the cockpit, it'll be like having the pilot sitting in our programming lab."

He faced his old friend. "If I have your word that it will be for your pilots' use only, I'll have Mel work on the code and send you a restricted version."

The lightning outside the airliner's window struck so close, it blasted through his closed eyelids like the noon sun.

Icarus was soaring, its feather wings flapping in the sunlight.

27

LEONI KEPT STEALING GLANCES in Mauricio's direction. From this angle, the small deviation of his nose looked more pronounced. She wondered how he had broken it, and why it hadn't been repaired. And why he had been giving her the cold shoulder ever since he returned from his tête-à-tête with the General.

Meeting went fine? Really?

His foot-tapping and the deepening furrows on his forehead told her of his tortured thoughts. She could practically feel his pain.

She wished for a moment that they were cramped closer together in coach. She reclined her seat, managing to brush his elbow with hers. No response. As if she weren't there.

The whole day with Oakley felt like she wasn't even there. The instructions Isaacson had given her specified that she should stay by the doctor's side and take over in case the press showed up. Her own agenda was to gather material for a soft-and-fuzzy piece about the civilian-military interaction for the LX web page she was starting to build. Oakley's plans for her turned out to be different. Run along, little girl. She had hoped she could at least get some private time with Mau, but the man seemed oblivious to her.

She bumped him with her elbow again. "Earth to doctor."

His eyes swung around toward her.

"Did you get into a bind again, Dr. Barcelos?" she asked innocently.

He inhaled as if to respond, and then his lips spread into a plastic smile. "Sorry, I must have dozed off."

Right, she thought. Dozed off. "And dreamt about your meeting?"

This time the response seemed more sincere. "About feathered wings."

At least that was believable. "Icarus," she suggested.

He gave a double take. "Something like that," he admitted.

She had learned the plane's name from Rosie, along with a slew of other tidbits. His legendary memory for patients' faces, his failed marriage, his currently nonexistent love life. "Not that every gal on the staff, married or not, hasn't tried," Rosie confided, then lowered her voice and added, "some say he may be gay."

That he's not, Leoni wanted to say.

Feeling like a teenage stalker, she had spent quite a few evenings with a glass of wine and her laptop, learning all she could about him. She had even looked up the town of Barcelos on GoogleEarth. It was deep in the Amazon, had a population that was smaller than her condo community, and was surrounded by rain forest and an endless network of rivers. The posted photos made it look like a jungle paradise.

He was silent again, staring out the window. Perhaps her comment last night about him being headstrong had hurt his feelings. But giving her the cold shoulder wasn't opening any paths for reconciliation. Maybe he just didn't like her personally? Let's have that out, right now.

She sat up in her seat. "Dr. Barcelos, do you ever wonder what it feels like not being trusted to do your job?"

He shot her a what-are-you-talking-about look.

"I took this on," she continued, "because I wanted a job that feeds my soul. God knows, I've had my own bouts with depression. But I need to feel like I'm part of your team, not the enemy. I want to be a good public relations person for you. I want your implant to be in headlines around the world. If that's not your vision, why don't I just quit?"

She heard his quiet exhale.

"I thought you were Isaacson's watch dog."

That was a slap on the face. "Not a watch dog. Damage control is a different animal. I want to do this job because I believe in your product. And in you. Not that you seem to care."

Might as well let it all out. "Who do you think has been fielding all the calls from the media, your ex included, in the past week? Who kept Sandy McBride's arrest from being headline news? Who spent three hours on the phone today wrangling rumors about the runaway bride?"

He sat up. "What runaway bride?"

"Gina, the red-head. Your favorite. Fiancé Peter called your office, all freaked out. Rosie passed it on to me, being that you were oh, so busy with your general friend."

"And?"

"I talked to him. Turned out it was some prenup jitters."

It had been more complicated than that. Peter had described the fiery argument they had about wedding invitations, and Gina's threat to run away to her sister's. Work called because Gina hadn't shown up. He called the sister to learn Gina wasn't there either. He was on his way to report her as a missing person to the police.

Leoni wound up having to call Mel and persuade him to check Gina's record. Gina's exact location was not determinable, but Mel pointed out that her log-in session was on time, and she had attached a short message assuring everyone that she needed a little time to herself, and asking Mauricio to persuade Peter to be patient.

Another headline had been averted.

She tried to add a little levity to the news. "What is it about redheads that makes them crazy, anyway?"

His eyes seemed to be studying every detail of her face. She imagined her under-eye bags and the messy hair, and wished the cabin were even darker. She had gotten virtually no sleep on the overnight flight, and instead of resting, spent the down-time in DC on the phone, and working on a new splash page for the LX website. Leoni had planned to surprise him with the new visuals on the flight back. But here he was, sulking like a teenager.

"Why are you staring at me like that?" she snapped.

He gave a little shrug and smiled.

"I was wondering . . ." he said. "What do you think about creating a Facebook page for the implant?"

Her jaw dropped. How was that for synergy? She didn't think he even knew about Facebook, recluse that he was. She had intended to get cracking on the social media front the minute they got back. And here he was, already thinking ahead.

"You said social media was a special interest of yours," he was saying. "Maybe you would like to set up something for us?"

Leoni eyed him. Oh, now it's us? You've no idea how I'd love to do that, she thought. "I'll consider it," she said and turned away. I'm not going to melt for you, she thought. She let a few moments pass, then found the call button and pushed it.

"I'll have a Bailey, extra cream on the side," she said when the attendant came. "And, Hemlock for him," she added with mock seriousness. Then she leaned toward the attendant and whispered the other order into her ear.

"By the way," she said when the attendant left, "while you were visiting, I called Diane. The Cat Lady Murder Mystery has been solved. I thought you may want to know. To help clear the clutter in that head of yours."

"What happened?"

"They decided that the kitchen knife found stuck in the boyfriend was indeed hers, but the fingerprints were not hers. So looks like Sandy McBride is off the hook."

He looked at her and she thought she detected a hint of gratitude. There is so much more I can do for you, if you could just trust me, she thought.

The drinks arrived. His was a glass tumbler with ice cubes, served with a fistful of sugar packets, and a plate with four limes, sliced in halves.

"Dr. Barcelos," she said turning her whole body so she was facing him, "if you could stop being such a tight ass, and trust me, you may find that I'm a very . . . more useful than you think."

She pulled two small bottles out of the bag by her legs and poured the contents into his glass. "Took me two hours to find cachaça in TSA-approved three-ounce bottles." She made a face. "You can squeeze your own limes."

28

O<small>N THE WALL-SIZED SCREEN</small> of the dimly lit cavernous basement of the hospital annex, the heads popped up one by one. The second weekly video-conference for LX providers was starting. Mauricio and Bruce Levine listened, each with their own iPads. Nurses scribbled notes, and two IT guys worked the logistics of the multicenter video linkup.

"Eighteen implants. One failure, placed back on Anadep." The label under the man's image read Russ Greenberg, Pensacola, FL. Mauricio recognized one of the first surgeons who had stopped at the booth at the recent conference. An early adopter.

"Only one complaint," said John Goodson, a neurosurgeon from Boston Medical Center.

"Only one?" Mauricio teased. BMC, often referred to, only half in jest, as the Mecca of Medicine, was home to some of the most demanding prima donnas in the medical world.

"One complaint," Goodson repeated. "It was not NIH."

The faces on the screen laughed. At the Mecca of Medicine, "NIH" was a common complaint about new products. "We don't like it because it was Not Invented Here."

Alvaro Cabral from Duluth was next. "Forty-seven cases. Four equivocal, if you go by HRSD-17 measurements. One failed to respond but requested a second implant. I'll update you next week."

Mauricio watched the graphs on the big screen as they updated to reflect each report. The Hamilton Rating Scale for Depression was a commonly accepted measurement of response. By that standard, LX's therapeutic success rate was hovering in the 85-87% range. A miracle cure by any standard. Finally, the world was going to believe him.

Gillian Landis popped up. "One hundred and forty two so far."

Mauricio and Bruce exchanged glances. The woman doctor was a machine.

Gillian changed her screen to show off a few of the tracings.

Suddenly Mauricio sat up. "Can you play that back? That last tracing?"

Gillian did. "What?"

He turned to the IT guys. "Blow it up, please."

"The little drop out? I saw something like that in one of our patients," Goodson said. "Looked like an artifact to me."

Mauricio reviewed a very fuzzy enlargement of the patient's Delta channel tracing. "Nothing, I guess." He punched a few keys on his iPad to capture the segment. While Gillian ran through the rest of her cases, taking more than her allotted time, he replayed the tracing. On the small screen, the defect was little more than an easy-to-miss hairline blip.

He chewed on his lip. The shape, though fuzzy in the blow up, was hauntingly familiar. He wasn't endowed with a photographic memory like many of his Harvard Medical School classmates—Goodson among them—but he seldom forgot an image. "Your memory is great," Mel always teased him, "but your recall sucks." Familiar meant it was stored somewhere in his brain. All he had to do was find it.

He forwarded the captured segment to Mel's lab, with a simple "Your thoughts?"

Mel's reply came moments later. "I saw them too. Was able to reproduce on a bench test. Most likely an insulation artifact. One of ours, Kevin S, has the same. Will dig further. I'm on it."

The sound of Gillian's voice brought him back.

"The screens, Mau," she was saying, "we love those new screens of yours."

He looked up. "What screens?"

"The new home page. All my patients commented on it."

An elegantly designed image now filled the big screen, where the old simplistic LX home page had been. Leoni's work. The woman didn't waste time.

"Didn't know you had it in you, Barcelos," Gill was saying.

"Not me, my PR person."

"Well kudos to him then."

"It's a her."

"Oh," Gill said, her eyes smiling mischievously. "Of course, it's a her."

He hoped the room was dark enough so no one would suspect him of blushing.

"Hey, Bill," Gill changed topics, "When is Mass General going to open a satellite clinic in DC? To treat the VIPs?"

Goodson looked confused.

"I heard Vice-Pres Spencer checked in recently."

"Then you probably also heard that the White House spokesperson said it was a routine physical," Goodson snapped.

"Long trip, just for a physical."

"He's from Boston originally. And we're here to discuss implant patients only."

"Still . . ."

Mauricio shook his head. Those two had never liked each other, and Gill was not one to pass an opportunity to rib somebody from the Mecca of Medicine.

Bruce cleared his throat. "Uh, if I could have a turn here. Our results . . ." He briefly outlined the NBMC cases. "I'm not sure whether to classify this one as success or failure."

Mauricio stopped thinking about the mysterious artifacts and perked up.

"One patient is AWOL, for marital, or rather pre-marital issues," Bruce was saying.

Gina's record appeared full-screen. Her sessions were longer than usual—almost double in duration—but on schedule. The HRSD-17 depression scores reflected Gina's usual perky disposition of the post-implant years. Happy. The notes she had been typing into the comments section at the end of every session were cryptic, but positive.

Where the hell are you, Gina, he wondered.

Bruce was going on. "... I feel comfortable classifying her results as a continued therapeutic success. So out of twenty eight patients this week ..."

Under the table, Mauricio made a good luck figa with his fingers and hoped the missing Gina would remain in the success column.

29

THE SHRINK'S VOICE HAD A HOLLOW digital sound. "One patient is AWOL, for marital, or rather pre-marital issues."

Al leaned closer to the computer and turned up the volume. Barcelos' cell phone was probably in his pocket, across the room from Levine, so the background noise made it difficult to understand what was being said. But it was better than nothing.

Converting the smart phone to a listening device had proven simpler than expected, thanks to the doctor's lack of paranoia. The malware that had been uploaded to the laptop at the convention, leaped to his Smartphone the minute he used it to check email. How did they manage to spy on people before the internet, he wondered.

"I'll put her in the success column," the shrink was saying.

Al smiled. "And in mine as well."

"A nationwide total of four hundred and twenty eight new patients this week . . ."

Lucky dog, Al thought. The speed with which the LX had been adopted by the medical community was as astounding as the results it delivered. Simple, cheap, effective. The more he learned about what

Barcelos had created, the more respect he had for the doctor. Surprisingly, the man did not turn out to be an arrogant jerk like Dumas, who was conspicuously absent from the videoconference. He knew the doctor's team had done at least half a dozen LX implants, and would be expected to report in.

The scraping of chairs signified the end of the conference. Suddenly a new but familiar voice came through Barcelos' phone.

"Bonjour! Sorry I'm late. I had an important meeting with investors."

Barcelos' voice. "We're pretty much done. Do you have something that can't wait till next week, Jean-Jacques?"

"Actually, yes." Dumas' voice sounded more abrasive than usual. "It's not good, de Bar, not good."

He noted that Dumas was the only one who called Barcelos "de Bar." Maybe the man couldn't think of another way to pervert the official "de Barcelos," as in "from Barcelos," the small town where he was born. He was willing to bet that Dumas—or Dumb Ass, as Mel called him—would never set foot in a place so uncivilized.

"One patient fell asleep at the wheel," Dumas said. "Crashed his Ferrari going a hundred-twenty on the interstate."

Silence. Then Barcelos. "I'm so sorry to hear it. Is he okay?"

"Survived."

Al could have sworn Dumas sounded disappointed that the crash hadn't been fatal.

"Here's the tracing."

There was beeping, and Al wished he could have a visual.

"Damn it, J.J.," a woman said angrily. "I know this guy. Owns a bail bond business. An alki-bum with a dozen DUIs. I tried to have our DMV yank his license. He must have gone from state to state till he found you. What were you thinking? He's not LX material!"

"He passed out, so I have to file . . ."

Barcelos again. "Fell asleep or passed out?"

Dumas. "It's not clear."

"Tox screen?"

"Uh . . . Allegedly blood alcohol of .23."

Woman's voice. "Need I say more? Don't you do backgrounds before you implant?"

"Yeah, well . . . It's still a complication with an implant recipient, and I have to report it."

The man had an ax to grind, and Al could understand why. Barely two weeks after its release the LX was wiping out any future potential for the Nuvius, Dumas' own implant. Strange, because from the articles he had read about the Nuvius, it sounded like it should have claimed its leading role a long time ago. And yet there it was, stagnating in R&D. So was fucking Dumas trying to subvert the competition by implanting the LX into people who did not qualify?

"Go ahead and report it." Barcelos. He must have taken the phone out of his pocket, because the voice was loud and clear now. "And next time consider being more careful in your patient screening."

Al heard footsteps, then the door closing.

Minutes later the GPS tracker on Barcelos' phone showed him heading across the hospital. Probably to the operating room, Al decided. There were patients on the schedule.

He got up from his chair and stretched.

Between the cell phone and the intermittent access to the doctor's desktop, when the hospital ITs let their guard down and failed to sweep the system, the volume of information coming at him was sizable. Whatever conversations he didn't catch real-time, were captured by a recorder, transcribed by the speech recognition program, scanned for select key words and flagged for his later review. Just like what the NSA was doing.

The doctor's accomplishments made him wonder just how far he could have gone, what he could have created, if he had stayed in school. His Russian stepfather had said he was smart enough to do anything.

Al flashed back to the chess lessons with Maxim. "Chess builds character. Builds strength. Helps you in all aspects of your life." Within a year of starting, he was his school's champion, playing five games simultaneously. Blindfolded. Like the legendary Russian chess master Alekhin. He enjoyed the victories, but found even more satisfaction in his stepfather's rare praise.

Despite the overly strict discipline, he had respect for the man. At the end of the Soviet occupation of Afghanistan in 1989, Maxim, now married to Soraya for two years, realized how much damage the occupation had done to his wife's country. He defected to the Americans with whatever military secrets he had, in exchange for an entry visa to the US for the entire family.

Al vaguely remembered a late night drive across the desert and a meeting with some Americans. Then came the long trip, a year somewhere in Maryland, and finally their relocation to Thousand Oaks, California.

Feeling displaced after the move, Al and his adoptive sister Svetlana grew closer. Even though she was four years older, the age difference seemed offset by Al's precocious maturity. By the time Al turned 15, a romance developed, obvious to all and a source of anger to Maxim. One confrontation was particularly painful to remember. Maxim had pinned him against the wall, and hissed. "Leave Svetlana alone. She is not for you."

"I don't know what . . ." Al had protested feebly.

"Don't be a dumb fuck," Maxim grunted. "Stop, or you'll see what happens."

Al shuddered and forced himself to forget what did happen.

After the disastrous final encounter with Svetlana, Al found himself out on the streets, destitute and deformed.

The imam at the mosque that Soraya and he had attended had taken him under his wing, relocated him from the Valley to Los Angeles, and helped arrange the countless foot surgeries. None was successful. Eventually, the foot had to be amputated.

The imam helped him find jobs—first menial cleaning work, then tutoring rich Russian and Iranian kids in Beverly Hills in math, chess, and computer skills. Even though his proceeds were meager, Al donated half to the mosque.

One Friday the imam called him. "Brother, do you want to help with a truly generous gift?" All he had to do was access a CEO's home computer and copy a few files."

Al completed the assignment when he went to give the fat little son a chess lesson. He hacked the host's wi-fi network while demonstrating moves on a computerized chess game, downloaded the files, and delivered them to the imam.

The next day the CEO made an unexplained one-million-dollar donation to the mosque. Al's share was a mind-blowing one hundred thousand dollars.

"There is a reason your real name is Khalim al Zafir, Al," the imam had praised him. "Khalim the Victorious. I see great deeds in your future."

Al had told the imam his mother's story, about how his father had named him, before he went off to fight the infidels.

Al bought clothes, a new car, and got an apartment. He drove by a UCLA student hotspot, where Svetlana attended school. He waited until she left; he didn't dare limp into the bar. She saw him, and just walked away. He followed her down the street in his car, until she alerted friends: "That cripple won't leave me alone."

Al drove off to escape a beating. He still wasn't good enough. He needed to accomplish something more amazing to regain his self-esteem.

He called the imam. "More assignments," he demanded. "And from now on, your share for providing the contacts will be only ten percent."

"Why so greedy, brother?"

"Because I am the best. And because ..." He told the imam about his plan. Most of the proceeds would go to a new cause: helping rehabilitate Afghan children who had been injured as a result of the fighting. The Injured Children's Fund was born. Finally, he had a goal worthy of Khalim the Victorious.

Since then, his successes had continued. His revenues and his clout skyrocketed. There were now nine orphanages he had funded and close to a hundred and fifty kids who had been rehabilitated with his earnings. But he had remained unknown. Irrelevant.

And here was Barcelos, making headlines helping depressed people who couldn't deal with their own problems.

The thought of being unknown and irrelevant infuriated Al. It was time to appear on the radar screen. At least as an anonymous enigma.

He cued up a chess game, worked a few keys, and pushed send. Chew on that one, Barcelos. The cryptic message, much more subtle than the gross images often posted by hackers, would not garner recognition and praise, but at least it would feed his soul.

Suddenly he heard Barcelos' phone ringing.

Mel's voice. "Come on up to the lab. I want to show you what I found on Kevin's tracings."

Barcelos. "Now what?"

"Two more artifact gaps last night, like the ones you sent me."

"Shit. On my way." Click.

Shit indeed. Al had tried to be slow and methodical, avoiding leaving any trace of his visits to the patient records, but Lady Kay had insisted he rush along. As a result, a few tell-tale changes had made their way into the patient's record. And Mel spotted them, almost immediately.

The Kevin assignment had been simple, from a programming and a social engineering perspective. But Lady Kay had rushed him. "Closing arguments start today. Jury deliberations can go anytime in the next day or two. I want him ready."

She hadn't given him enough time to figure out how to better conceal the Delta gaps. But he took comfort in knowing that the odds of

Mel and the good doctor figuring out the real purpose for the gaps were a-million-to-one.

Al heard a pounding sound coming from the phone. Probably Barcelos hurrying up the stairs. On the display, the GPS traced him through the surgeons' lounge, then the OR hallways. OR Seven. Damn it. He was headed into the lab.

"Mel. Speak to me," Barcelos said.

Al held his breath, wondering what Mel would say about the anomalies in the Delta channel that he must have spotted.

"Here is . . ."

The sound went dead and the GPS blip vanished. Al kicked the desk with his good foot and swore under his breath. Barcelos must have entered Mel's electronically-shielded lab.

There was little left to do here. He shut down his computer and headed for his car. His Mojave lair, now converted to a testing lab, complete with a real live test subject, awaited him. There was much work to be done.

30

It WAS CLOSE TO MIDNIGHT and Mauricio, sitting in his office, was just getting around to the mystery of the bizarre tracing anomalies.

The meeting in Mel's lab had not been revelatory. "I still think it's a filament insulation problem," Mel said.

It was only a momentary dropout in the Delta channel. Like a pause in a heartbeat, or an engine miss. The shape of the artifact looked familiar—his brain told him he had seen it before—but he couldn't place it.

"Perhaps there is a glitch in the code at the central control end?" he said. "What if something got corrupted on the program stored at CloudFort?"

"Unlikely. But I'll humor you and ask CloudFort," Mel said. "I have the weekly pow-wow in the morning. Want to join us?"

He wouldn't miss it for the world.

Mauricio now powered up his office computer and cued up Medscape. Thirty minutes and hundreds of keystrokes later, he found the image he was looking for. The squiggle looked exactly like what he and Mel had noted.

"Son of a bitch."

The image was in a Clinical Neuro-Physiology article written by one J.J. Dumas, MD eight years earlier. During tests of prototype of his deep-brain stimulation paddles, Dumas had observed what he called "Sleep wave anomalies." In close-up, the anomaly looked like a carved-out gap, with distinctively rolling edges and a concave bottom.

Interesting, he thought, rubbing his forehead.

The article noted that when the paddles were tuned to a certain frequency, and placed at certain angles, depth of sleep decreased. Like a patient momentarily waking from anesthesia, enough to become aware of his surroundings, or hearing what was being said, then dosing off again. The article went on to say that during this state some of the patients were able to follow simple commands that they subsequently did not remember. There was no long-term effect on depression, as measured by the depression scale. "These episodes are therefore of no clinical significance for the intended use of the device," Dumas' article concluded.

Of no clinical significance, my ass. No unexplained anomaly was ever of "no clinical significance." To him, the disturbing question was: Were the Delta anomalies caused by a filament contact defect, or a software malfunction?

He clicked on the author's name to see what other pearls of wisdom the man might have to share with the world. The long list filled the screen. He scanned a few of the more recent ones, but all had to do with obscure details specific to the Nuvius, and all ended with some version of "Additional research needed to determine clinical significance." No wonder the device was still awaiting FDA approval.

There were no other mentions of the anomaly.

His brain wandered back to the car crash of Dumas' patient. Did Dumas make a judgment error in patient selection? Or was the bastard trying to sabotage the LX?

He blew out a heavy breath, anger beginning to bubble inside. That went way past malpractice, straight to felony.

He leaned back in his chair, and suddenly saw a figure standing in the doorway. Leoni.

He waved her in and started to clear a chair next to his desk. He hadn't met with her since the DC flight almost a week earlier.

"I didn't mean to intrude," she apologized.

"Not an intrusion." Actually a very welcome break. "I meant to stop by . . . You got lots of kudos today, with the new splash page."

Her cheeks pinked up. "It's a start." She perched on the edge of the chair. Her knee touched his, then bounced back.

He tried to move, but the space was cramped.

There was an awkward silence.

"Is this how you spend your evenings?" she asked.

"Usually I work at home," he said.

More silence.

"Why so gloomy?"

His shoulders sagged like a collapsing circus tent. This woman didn't mince words. "It's all moving so fast," he heard himself verbalize for the first time since the LX was approved.

"I thought you like fast."

"I like under control." He paused. "Three weeks ago I was the only one doing the implants. Now . . ." He flung his arms out. "It's a free-for-all."

"Most inventors wouldn't complain."

"I'm not complaining. Just . . ."

She cocked her head and waited for him to continue.

"A little scared," he confessed. What was it about this woman that made him dig deeper?

She nodded. "I noticed. After your DC meeting. And now too."

He glanced away. Was she a mind reader? If he were superstitious, he would be worried. "Thank you," he said.

"Thank you?"

"For noticing." He turned away, now completely embarrassed by his admission.

"I notice . . ."

Leoni stopped herself in mid-sentence. "I notice because I care." She was here to bounce an idea off him. Not to get personal.

She shifted in her seat, felt their knees bumping and jerked back.

Flustered, she went with the first thing that came to mind. "Any suggestions of what I can do better? With the LX home page? I want to make sure it all fits with the theme. Colors are really important mood setters and I want the visitors to appreciate . . ."

She realized she was babbling, and that he seemed amused by her discomfort. That made it even worse. "Sorry, you have work to do. I should be going anyway."

"Did you have a chance to think about expanding the website?" he asked.

Chance to think about it? That's all she had been doing, ever since they broached the subject on the plane.

"Maybe on the Facebook page," Barcelos was saying, "you could add something personal. Like an electronic version of our support groups."

It was exactly what she had been thinking. She sat up. "If you cue up the hospital's site, I'll show you a few things I've been working on."

"Let me just save this." He touched the keyboard.

Suddenly the screen changed to a three-dimensional chess game, with a message in script: Want to play?

He stared at the screen, looking flustered.

"I didn't know you play chess," she said. That was an interesting tidbit Rosie hadn't shared.

He shook his head. "Did as a kid. Not lately."

Then what's that, she wanted to ask. Maybe he considered chess too nerdy a pastime for a hands-on guy who opened brains and flew planes. She smiled. "Welcome to spam for brainiacs."

She was about to show him how to get on the website prototype, but the deep furrows in his forehead told her it was not the time. She stood up. "I'll show you tomorrow. You should get some sleep, Dr. B," she added.

When she reached the door, she glanced back, but he was already deep into his work again.

Mauricio turned back to the screen before the door closed. The chess game was gone, replaced by the last Dumas article he had read.

The image of the chessboard was still etched in his mind. He had played enough chess in grade school to see that the game was in its early stages, and that whites were down several pawns plus a bishop. It was entirely out of character for the bombastic Frenchman to add any levity to his bibliography. He had no intention of humoring Dumas by analyzing the position further, or responding with a move.

His mind flashed to the scene in The Thomas Crown Affair. A very hot Renee Russo and a catty Pierce Brosnan locked in a game of chess more erotic than any naked romp could have been.

Did Leoni play chess? He should have asked her to stay. How inconsiderate. She was eager to show him the site she must have worked on so hard, and he just blew her off.

Tomorrow, first thing, he would go see her and apologize.

31

Mauricio and Mel sat with the impeccably clad, square-shouldered CloudFort representative at one of the outdoor tables at Amy's Café, across the street from the hospital. The sun was shining, seagulls crisscrossed the crisp blue sky, expensive yachts rocked gently in the marina. The tantalizing aromas of coffee and freshly baked cinnamon buns wafted from inside the small building.

Mel was going over the issue of storage capacity at the cloud computing facility. "You guys erase it all after twenty-four hours," Mel complained, "so I have nothing to go by, unless I can get to the patient's module itself, and that isn't always easy."

"At CloudFort," the rep said in a polished newscaster's voice, "we offer a variety of service levels to meet every client's needs. What I recommend . . ."

Terabytes, metatags, scuzzy drives, blah blah . . . Mauricio's eyes glazed over a while ago. Now they were in Mel's world. The rep sounded as incomprehensible as Professor Beck did when he spoke of carbon rings, amyl hydrates, and transcarboxylation back in biochemistry classes. He inhaled the crisp air, and let his mind relax.

Earlier, when he had brought up the unexpected appearance of the chess game on his screen, the rep had practically laughed out loud. "Ancient technology. Think online shopping. I order a dress shirt, and a dozen ads for shoes and belts pop up on my screen. They know who's looking. They know what you want. They can reach you anytime they want."

"But why a chess game?"

The rep shrugged. "Because there is a record that you once played chess? Or bought the movie about Bobby Fischer the chess champion?" He grew more enthusiastic. "Hell, they can sort people by the brand of toothpaste they use, and the car they drive to the drugstore."

That still didn't answer his question. "Why was the chess game linked to a medical article?" Mauricio persisted.

"You tell me, Dr. Barcelos," the rep laughed. "Crazy folks are your specialty."

Dumas certainly qualified. Crazy as a fox. "I just want to be sure these crazy folks, as you call them, don't find their way into patient records."

"At CloudFort?" The rep straightened up with an air of superiority. "Now you're crossing into the realm of the impossible." He proceeded to describe the cyber defenses CloudFort had in place in terms that Mauricio found to be irritatingly complex. It was a rehash of the sales pitch they had heard when CloudFort came down to solicit their business a year earlier.

"Nobody is getting into our system, Dr. Barcelos," the rep concluded. "Even with the LX's unusually high—I'd say, unprecedented—incidence APTs and DDOSes."

Why can't he speak in normal English, Mauricio thought. "AP whats?"

"Advanced Persistent Threats? Attempts to get into the system?" The rep exhaled and looked like he was going to roll his eyes. "Think of somebody turning a door handle to see if it's locked," he said as if speaking to a child. "You had a sudden increase, about two days ago."

"Surprise, surprise." Mel threw Mauricio an I-told-you-so look. "I knew Blondie would futz it all up."

"Later, Mel," he snapped.

Ever since the video conference, Mel and Leoni had locked horns over her LX home page.

"Ms. Leoni, here, has put a target on our backs," Mel fumed.

"The LX needs visibility," Leoni shot back.

"Oh, yeah, visibility!" Mel sneered. "How did you word it in your intro? 'Impregnable to unauthorized access?'"

"Getting their brain implant hacked is every patient's number one concern," Leoni countered. "I wanted to dispel that fear upfront."

"'Virtually impregnable' is catnip to a hacker. Every pimple-faced geek on the planet is going 'Oh, yeah? Impregnable? Let me try.' Or don't they teach you that in PR school?"

"At least I went to PR school. And cloud access is . . ."

"The cloud?" Mel snapped. "The cloud, where if you hack in, you can access all your patient records at once, instead of having to work at it, one by one? That cloud?"

Mauricio looked from one to the other more amused than annoyed. Cloud computing had been in use in medicine for years. The principle was simple: the information was stored in server farms—giant ware-houses with enough backups and physical and electronic protection to make Fort Knox look like a 7-Eleven.

Cloud computing enabled instantaneous access from any terminal, anywhere. There was only one obstacle to wider acceptance—human paranoia about loss of control. In that battle, Mel led the charge. "Don't need it, don't trust it, don't want it," was his mantra.

"Please don't confuse CloudFort with something like Facebook, Linkedin, Groupon . . ." the rep was saying. "Now, those are wide-open portholes to serious incursions. Friend the wrong person, and it's like letting a fox into a hen house."

"So what do you make of these attempts on our system?" Mauricio interrupted.

The rep threw his chin up dismissively. "Expected and irrelevant. Medical devices have always been targets. You might've heard of the case, back a couple of years? Two doctors hacked into a patient's pacemaker and stole her bank account?"

"Are you referring to the JAMA article," Mauricio corrected him, "by two physicians who gained access to a bedside insulin pump, using a frequency scanner they bought at Radio Shack, to illustrate the vulnerability of medical devices?"

"Yes, that one," the rep admitted. "Let them knock all they want. I can assure you, when it comes to protecting you, CloudFort is on the forefront . . ."

Mauricio cut into the diatribe "But for argument's sake . . . Say, you're a very persistent hacker . . . How would you get in?"

"Into CloudFort? I'd pick an easier target. Say, the Pentagon," the rep laughed.

"I'm listening," Mauricio said, not laughing.

The rep studied the seagulls circling above, and shrugged. "I'd use one of the devices that are already recognized by the system, like one of your patient's implants. A couple years ago, the Chinese stole Boeing's blueprints by way of a printer in one of the engineers' offices. It was one of those programmable CN-48s that practically think for you. A guy came in, pretended to be a repairman, and slipped the malware into the system. Full access, in no time."

Mauricio glanced at Mel for reassurance.

"Cyber security is what we're all about," the rep droned on. "We're constantly monitoring what comes in. To upload malware takes time. So if something is hidden in the transmission, the session will be longer than it should be. Say, ten seconds, instead of five. At CloudFort, we have scanners designed to filter out anything that even remotely looks like hidden code." He paused and leaned closer. "To get inside Cloud-Fort, Doctor, you have be invited, or you have to be already approved. You can rest assured that your records are safe, Doctor. We haven't had a security breach in three hundred and forty days. That's more than the Pentagon can say."

He wanted to ask how Mr. CloudFort would feel if he told him he hadn't lost a patient in a whole year, but decided not to press the issue.

"I'll be honest, Dr. Barcelos." The rep leaned forward. "In the cyber environment we live in, nothing is impossible. Remember Stuxnet, a few years ago?"

Mauricio knew the story. Allegedly Israeli cyber-experts wrote a piece of software so sophisticated, it knew how to search out and affect one specific target: the little black box that controlled the speed of the centrifuges that Iranian nuclear engineers were using to concentrate uranium. It didn't get more specific than that. Worst of all, he heard that the source code for Stuxnet was in the public domain, for anyone to adapt to their own use. Son of Stuxnet controlling medical radiation therapy devices, anyone?

"When we plan our defense strategies," the rep continued, "we always have to ask ourselves, who has anything to profit from the access? Hackers who have what it takes to invest the computing time—I'm talking thousands of hours—most of them go after high-value targets—like bank accounts. Records of mentally ill patients?" He wrinkled his nose. "Not so much."

32

GINA FELT THE VIBRATIONS in the cave walls before she heard the rocks crunching outside. She opened her eyes. Not that it made a difference. The space was as black as the inside of her eyelids, even though she had managed to wiggle her head out of the black sack that the attacker had placed over her head.

The crunching outside stopped. A thud reverberated down the long tunnel at the far end of the cave. A car door.

She rolled over on the futon and shivered as her toes touched a cold packed-dirt floor. She cinched the tie on her sweat pants and bundled tighter in the sweat shirt. What time was it, anyway? What day?

More details of the past two days came into focus.

She had dressed to go out for her yoga class. At exactly 8:35 she was about to unlock her car. Then, all went blank.

When she regained consciousness she was on the floor of a van. The ride was long. First freeway-smooth, then on rocky ground, the vehicle rolling from side to side, making her sick. Then the deep bump of a ditch, a door sliding open, the crisp morning breeze, the dead silence, the scent of rocks and Joshua trees. She realized she was in the desert, which is where she and Peter first made love.

When the man pulled her out of the van she braced for the worst. He was going to rape her, kill her, and bury her under a Joshua tree. Peter, help me, she wanted to scream.

But the man was strangely polite. "Just working on a project," was all he would offer as explanation. "Please be patient and don't try to interfere. I'll take you back as soon as we're done." The voice was soft, but the firm grasp spoke to his determination.

"Done with what?" she wanted to know.

"With the project. It may take a day or two."

Then came the stagnant air of what was probably a cave. And a long day that stretched into a sleepless, blindfolded night.

At some point she must have been given water and food, because she didn't feel hungry. By the time she woke up again, on what must have been her second day, the bag was back on her face, and her hands were tied behind her back.

At least since she had managed to rip the damned bag off she could breathe easier.

She heard the screech of a metal gate, swinging open, then closing. Then a bolt sliding back in place.

Footsteps. Uneven. Step-clunk, step-clunk . . .

He was back.

The beam of a flashlight played off uneven whitewashed walls. A muffled motor chugged to life. She heard a switch flip. She had to close her eyes when the lights came on suddenly.

When she opened them, she saw a swarthy man in his thirties standing next to a generator. His face registered annoyance. "You had to remove the bag, didn't you?"

He eyed her up and down. A look that sent shivers up her spine. "You must be cold."

The man placed a grocery bag on the wooden table, walked over to the far corner—step-clunk—opened the valve on the propane tank, lit a match, and fired a burner.

He served the food. A crisp tomato and cucumber salad, a bowl of humus, pita bread, still warm. He opened a thermal container. A spicy aroma filled the confined space.

"I hope you like lamb," he said, dispensing a generous helping of steaming stew.

The man was a mystery. Her foggy brain flashed to a scene from Beauty and the Beast. Any moment now, he would turn into a prince, she thought. And take her back to Peter.

"Eat. Then I'll help you log on to your LX site. You and I have work to do. Tonight is the big night for me."

33

KEVIN SAT IN THE STUFFY ROOM where the twelve jurors had been debating Joel Sneiderman's fate for six hours. It was Friday, and tempers were running hot.

"Kevin, how much more evidence do we need, to send this guy to the slammer?" the frustrated foreman asked, for the fifth time that morning.

Sneiderman was a 64-year-old Democratic senator from New York who often visited his mistress in Los Angeles. Six months earlier, drunk and high, he plowed his rented convertible into a school bus, sending it rolling down the hill from Mulholland Drive, killing six of the twelve kids on board, plus his own mistress. It was his fourth drunk driving incident. As was often the case, Sneiderman escaped serious injury. But not the LAPD.

"Kevin, what happened? Yesterday you wanted to convict . . ."

Kevin continued to eat the egg salad sandwich that his wife had prepared. Eggs from their own chickens. Homegrown bib lettuce. Even the mayo was lovingly hand-whipped.

"None of that cafeteria crap, Pumpkin," she said.

For emphasis, she ran her hand into his pants and squeezed his butt. "Go put the guy in jail and hurry back for dessert."

He owed her. He owed the LX. He wanted to kiss her, right now.

"Kevin!"

His mind returned, but the tactile memory of her fingers lingered.

"Why did you change your mind, Kevin?"

He wasn't sure what happened. He did remember that three days earlier, when the sleazebag attorney defending this sleazebag congressman had finally stopped talking, that there was no shred of doubt in his mind that Sneiderman had to be taken off the streets, one way or another. But when he woke up today, he was equally sure that the only fit punishment was the death penalty. No matter how he had tried in the past few hours to agree with his fellow jurors, a voice in the back of his mind kept screaming, "An eye for an eye. Death penalty or nothing."

"Kevin?"

"Yeah. Sorry. I thought about it and decided the man does not belong in the slammer. He belongs in front of a firing squad."

"Kevin," the Foreman said patiently, "we don't have firing squads in this country. We have gas chambers. You heard the judge, the most he could do was life."

"Should've been first degree, aggravated, or whatever they call it, and . . . poof." Kevin made his hand into a gun and shot in the general direction of the courtroom.

"We have eleven for conviction, only you against. Life behind bars is better than a hung jury, Kevin. We don't want to let the man out again."

Kevin heard the words, and they made sense. A hung jury would not serve justice. He considered going with the majority. He even tried to force the words out of his mouth, but all he could think of was the voice in his head repeating "An eye for an eye." It was maddening.

"I'm not against convicting him. As long as he goes on death row," Kevin heard himself saying. Admittedly, he was a bit foggy on the jury instructions. Foggy, period.

Last night had been sleepless, what with the chocolate cake, and the anticipation of winding this jury thing up and getting back to work. The idiot who called at 2 a.m. with a wrong number hadn't helped in the restful sleep department. So, yes he was groggy. But one thing he was sure of. Death or nothing.

Somewhere in the distance, far across the room, the foreman was saying he was going to call the clerk.

When the jury emerged from the courtroom several hours later, Kevin ran head on into a barrage of TV cameras.

"What was supposed to be an open-and-shut case," one of the reporters was yelling into the camera, "against Senator Sneiderman, who ended the lives of seven innocent people, ended in a hung jury, thanks to one man who apparently changed his mind just hours before the final vote."

The phalanx of photographers advanced and he was peppered with questions.

"Why did you vote to acquit?"

"Do you realize the cost of trying him again?"

"Do you have a daughter, Mr. Sharp?"

"And how would you feel if she was killed?"

Kevin blinked at the cameras, the mikes, the unfamiliar faces.

Death penalty or nothing. It had been crystal clear, at some point. Now . . . Kevin shielded his face from the bright lights, and pushed his way through the crowd.

Suddenly, an attractive blond with short-cropped hair grabbed his arm.

"Mr. Sharp, I'm Diane Lasser, Channel 17. Can you share how you came to your conclusion? Tomorrow on our morning show?"

Kevin tried to answer, but his brain seemed to have turned to mush.

"I'm sorry, Ms.," he mumbled. "What conclusion?"

34

ICARUS BANKED STEEPLY, three G's, ramming Mauricio's back into the folded parachute that doubled as the back cushion. The chute was an annoying requirement for an aircraft performing aerobatic maneuvers. He fully subscribed to the school of no jumping out of a perfectly good plane. So unless he screwed up a loop and the wings came off... With his irrational fear of heights that he had revealed to no one, not even Mel, he wondered if he would have the balls to jump, anyway.

A few hundred feet below, the Pacific shimmered with reflections of the rising sun. He watched in frustration as Mel's Big Red, a World War I vintage biplane, streaked below him, rolled over, and vanished from view. He spun his head from side to side, but Big Red was nowhere to be seen. That meant it could only be in one place. Directly behind him. Perfectly positioned for a kill shot.

Mel's voice came over his headset, confirming the suspicion.

"Poof! Wwwzzzzzz ... Splash!!" The sound effects of a crashing plane were Mel's favorite part of their weekly dogfights. "Okay, Ace, that was the last of your nine lives. Big Red returning to base."

He glanced at Lexie, sitting at attention in the seat next to him, strapped into the harness he made for her, her ears cheerfully pointing in different directions, her tongue hanging out.

"Bite him when he lands," he said, giving her a scratch behind her ears.

The dog let out a little whine in response, as if sharing his frustration.

"Next time we'll get him, old lady."

He made it back to Fullerton before Mel did, parked Icarus in its usual tie-down spot on the ramp, and unstrapped the dog.

"Sorry, Lex," he said, rubbing her fur. "No trophies today."

The mutt licked his hand and reluctantly walked out on the wing.

With Lexie waddling at his heel, he wandered over to Mel's hangar, unlocked the padlock on the pass-through door, and activated the motor to raise the hangar doors.

Moments later, Mel taxied up and spun the plane around, blasting him with hot air and the smell of burning oil. Big Red still had most of its original military equipment, but the detailing spoke of an owner who spared no time or expense on his pride and joy. The nine cylinders of the giant radial engine glistened with chrome. The paint shined. The tires looked like they had never touched anything but pristine asphalt.

The eight-foot wooden prop ground to a halt, and the power plant let out an exhausted hiss. With a practiced pull-up, Mel extricated himself out of the cockpit, stepped on the lower wing, and hopped down onto the tarmac.

"What do you know," Mel exclaimed in mock amazement. "You're alive after all! I could swear I saw feathers floating in the ocean."

"One of these days, Mel. I'm not going to let you win."

"On that day, hell will turn into a glacier."

"Yeah, well . . . If I could get a flight in every single morning, like you, I'd be an ace too," he teased, knowing it had taken Mel years of military training to reach his level of competence. It wasn't as easy as, "See one, do one, teach one."

"You should try it. Nothing like the smell of burning oil to clear your head."

Pushing against the prop and the lower wings, they rolled the five-thousand-pound behemoth into the hangar. Mauricio whistled. Mel's hangar, always immaculate, now had a small neat desk with a computer and several peripherals set up in the far corner.

"What's with the new office?"

"Ever tried working with an eight-year-old in the house? I love Mickey to pieces, but when he's around . . ." Mel clutched his head. "Arrrgh!"

Lexie sniffed the air and trotted inside, eyeing the unfamiliar set up.

"So when I'm not at Newport, I'm all set up to work here. If I want to say hi, I just Skype."

"You cabled the hangar for internet?"

"Hmm, not exactly." Mel gave a sheepish grin. "The lady with the sweet-looking twin-engine in the next hangar has Wi-Fi. I change her oil; she lets me log on."

Leave it to Mel, he thought. Frugal and practical. But working on patient information, from a computer that wasn't blessed by the IT guys . . . questionable.

"In case you're wondering," Mel added, as if reading his thoughts, "there is no patient data here. And all my work goes home with me." Mel patted the palm-sized hard drive attached to the computer.

"Still . . ."

"Hey, if they want something, they'll steal it from anywhere. Deal with it. And if you think your CloudFuck friends are safer than my hangar, think again. Besides, I didn't want to be working on this where the hospital IT nerds could find it."

Mel stepped to the shelves and slid open one of the drawers. The handle was neatly labeled "EXIT BOLT WRENCHES."

Mauricio smiled. There was no such thing as "exit bolt wrenches" in aviation. When the LX system was originally turned over to Cloud-Fort, Mel had insisted on keeping a secret access, protected by a twelve-character code. "Every programmer worth his salt has a back door," Mel had explained. He kept the passwords to his secret access door hidden in plain sight.

From where Mauricio was standing, it looked like the drawer contained a random assortment of tools and discarded electronic components. After some rummaging, Mel produced a flash drive.

"Done. Tell the General to be careful."

Mauricio took the flash drive as if it were made of explosive material. Taking another shortcut, he thought.

When he told Mel what Oakley had done, Mel had worked his jaw for a long time, staring into the distance. Finally he said, "You'd have thought of it yourself eventually." The inventor in him was sorry that he hadn't been the first. It would have been an interesting addition to LX's capabilities. Interesting, but not life-saving like treating depression.

Mel's tacit approval went a long way to clearing his conscience about cooperating with Oakley's experiment. With proper supervision and patient selection, the case could be made that it was ethically acceptable. Besides, he reminded himself, that train had pulled out of the station, whether he wanted to or not. It was better to be aboard, in some control, than running behind waving your arms like a clown.

"I've been thinking," Mel said after returning from one of his practice flights.

"Of course you have," Mauricio had replied. Mel was at his most creative when part of his brain was occupied with the task of flying the plane, leaving the rest to invent freely. Maybe there was something to those morning spins around the patch as he called the airport. "And what have you come up with this time?"

"I wrote the program so that the pilot-subject has to be reprogrammed every three hours. With his AAA—Awake, Alert, Accurate—pilots up for the better part of two days, somebody had better be keeping an eye on them. Lots of toys they can mess up in those cockpits, if you're fooling with their sleep cycle."

Mel had used "subject" instead of patient. These were volunteers, not innocent victims of disease, he reminded himself. "How's that going to enable them to fly a long mission?"

Mel scoffed. "Simple. Ground uplink. They've onboard computers that can fly a whole mission under ground control. You think they can't figure a way to interface with the pilot's implant?"

It was a rehash of the conversation he had had with Oakley. These military types, he thought. Nicely done, Mel. Oakley had what he needed to improve his new app. Mauricio could have reasonable expectation that the pilot's well-being would be monitored. It was a tenable compromise.

At that moment Lexie, who was rummaging in one of the corners, let out a yelp.

"Mel, I think you have mice."

Mel shrugged. "Probably. By the way, did I show you the picture of Mickey on the bike?" Mel asked reaching for his wallet.

"Only three times."

"Oh." Mel looked disappointed. "Want to see it again?"

He shook his head and smiled. "You're turning into a marshmallow, man."

"You're just jealous. You and Di could've . . ." Mel stopped short. "Then let me show you this." Mel went to a workbench and lifted a tarp, revealing a partially assembled two-foot-long model of an F-18 fighter jet.

"Grandpa-and-Grandson project. Remote controlled. Will pull twelve Gs without coming unglued."

"Gorgeous." Mauricio stroked the fine finish on the wings, wondering whether Grandson would ever get his hands on the toy. "Speaking of coming unglued," he said, "weren't you a bit too close to the waves on that last pullout?"

Mel grinned. "Where I flew, it wasn't too close unless you got your wings wet."

"In the Gulf you had to, here you don't. Can't afford to lose you, pal." He slapped Mel's shoulder and headed out. "Ate amanha. See you tomorrow."

On the other side of the ten-foot high chain link fence, the Sunday morning crowd of parents and kids were watching the "little airplanes" practicing landings, and listening to the pilot-to-tower conversations broadcast over the loudspeaker.

As Mauricio opened the security gate to let himself out, he noted a man standing just outside, a hefty toolbox in one hand, a cell phone in the other. Medium height, black hair, small mustache, not an ounce of extra fat. He wore jeans and an old blue parka with an embroidered logo: CZ-A. The line under it, in smaller letters, read "Charley Zulu Avionics". The same logo was painted on the toolbox.

He was going to hold the gate open, but the man turned away, continuing a conversation. He pushed the gate locked, leaving Charley to finish the phone call.

Mauricio crossed the parking lot and approached his Volvo. There was a dark blue windowless van parked next to his car. A magnetic sign affixed to the side of the van had the CZ Avionics logo.

Good resource, he thought. An avionics repairman who was willing to work weekends was more precious than a doctor who made house calls.

On his way out, he cruised slowly past the security gate, hoping to spot the man and ask about his rates, but Charley Zulu was nowhere to be seen.

35

"**I** WANT IT OUT, DOC," Kevin yelled, his right hand clawing behind his ear. "Out."

Mauricio tried to sound calm. "Kevin . . ."

He had been summoned to Bruce's office with a, "Someone here would like to say hello to you." Their code for: "Help, the situation is circling the drain."

He found Bruce perched uncomfortably in his armchair, as if ready to bolt. Kevin was pacing, his anxiety saturating the confined office space. His face was drenched with sweat.

"Ah." Bruce perked up. "Dr. Barcelos . . ."

Kevin spun toward him. "No more wire." He scratched behind his ear again. "Nothing personal. I've the highest respect for you. But it did something weird . . . I don't know what, but I want it out."

Mauricio eased himself down on the couch and motioned for Kevin to join him. Kevin kept pacing. "That jury duty thing. The scum walked, and it's my fault . . ."

"And it's bothering you," Bruce said. "Kevin, I'm sure you made the right decision for that time."

"It's not the decision, it's the dream . . ."

"The dream?" Mauricio prompted.

"This morning I remembered that I had a dream the day before the jury verdict. It was about you." Kevin pointed at Bruce. "You were telling me I had to do the right thing. 'An eye for an eye,' you said."

Bruce's eyebrows arched. "Kevin . . ."

Kevin inched away. "You kept saying, 'Kevin, you know it in your heart. Death penalty or nothing.'"

Mauricio glanced at Bruce. Audio-visual hallucinations meant the Alpha or Delta filaments were missing the key foci in the singulate gyrus. It was not an unusual development. In some patients, small areas of scaring formed around the filament tips and compromised the contacts. It was a problem easily correctable in the programming lab, by simply adjusting the outputs. "Mr. Sharp," he said, "let me just check something." He flipped open his iPad and began pulling up Kevin's record.

"What are you doing?" Kevin backed against the wall, his body shaking. "No more programming."

"No programming. Just checking."

"You think I'm crazy, don't you? Well, I'm not. Your wire did something. I'm not a cry baby. I can handle red-hot exhaust pipes with my bare hands." He held out callused fingers. "I had root canals done without numbing. But one thing I know like I know my wrenches: something weird happened. Maybe it's nothing to do with the wire. In that case, my apologies. But I want it out."

Mauricio glanced at the iPad. Tracings were streaming across the screen.

"I said no programming," Kevin shouted.

"No programming, Mr. Sharp." He set the iPad aside. "Again, just checking."

"When can you take it out?"

"Taking the LX out is an extremely risky procedure."

"Took you five minutes to slip it in. How hard can it be to yank it out?"

"Nerve cells are now attached to the filaments. Pulling the wire may cause bleeding."

"So? Bleeding stops. Big deal."

"Intracranial bleeding might kill you."

Kevin stared. "You mean I'm stuck with it?"

"Not stuck. We can turn the module off. Completely. It will stop being a microcomputer and become a . . . a nothing."

"A nothing, sitting in my head?"

"As innocuous as a tooth implant."

Kevin seemed to consider the option. Then his anger flared again. "I don't trust it. Either you take it out, or I will." He stormed for the door.

Mauricio leaped up. "Kevin, wait."

The door slammed in his face.

"That went well," Bruce said. "You treat them; they get better; they stop the treatment; they tank. This one will be back to square one before you know it."

Mauricio winced. "I think his hallucinations were due to a mal-union."

"Doesn't matter what we think, does it? It's in his head, no pun intended. And if somebody as . . . as . . ." Bruce seemed to search for the right word.

"Tough?" he suggested.

"Stoic. As stoic as Kevin just freaked out in front of our eyes . . . It's scary to think how a full-fledged nut would react if he or she got spooked. I'll bet half of them sleep with one eye open, just waiting for the bomb in their head to go off."

He glanced at the psychiatrist. After years of failed drug therapy, LX patients had reason to be emotionally fragile. Still. He shook his head in frustration. "But in Kevin's case, it's such an easy fix."

Bruce shrugged. "Let him cool off. I'll call him. A little talk therapy might do the trick."

Mauricio retrieved his iPad and headed out.

"Hey, Mau?" A complacent smile played across Bruce's lips. "What do you think? Maybe they still need us old-fashioned healers?"

36

Leoni felt a bit awkward asking, "What does he like for lunch, Rosie?"

"You mean, if he takes lunch? Pretty much anything."

"His favorite takeout?"

Rosie puckered her lower lip. "Couple of times he sent me for Brazilian grill."

She got the address and ordered so much that she could have fed the entire staff. Fried plantains, feijoada, and linguiça sausages, and medium-rare picanha, and three other meats in case these weren't to his liking. It was worth the effort just to see the expression on his face when he caught a whiff of what she had brought.

"I figured I better take the initiative, and just show up with lunch," she said, quickly setting out the Styrofoam trays and plastic cutlery. She had checked his schedule with Rosie, and decided to take a chance.

"I didn't even know I was hungry," Mauricio said, making his way across his office to the couch.

Leoni continued, "I was bracing to deal with the press about the holdout juror on the drunken Senator's case. In case they got wind that he had the implant." She popped open a carton. "Feijoada?"

She watched the muscles rippling in his forearm as he dished out a generous portion of black bean stew on her plate and sprinkled it with farofa, a toasted cassava flour mixture. Then he helped himself.

"He was supposed to be on KNTO this morning," she continued, "but he got rescheduled. Did I get the right sausages?"

With the plates full, she perched her iPad between them and touched the screen. "You asked about Facebook? Forget it! Meet BrainPacers.com. A social networking site exclusively for LX patients. An exclusive Facebook on steroids."

Her leg was so close to his that she could feel the heat radiating between their two thighs, like a high-voltage arc. She caught a subtle scent of eucalyptus emanating from his shirt. She forced herself to focus.

"It's a place where implant patients can keep in touch, share information, post comments, update friends about events in their lives, and keep in touch through email or video chats."

He watched intently as she scrolled through the screens.

"Beautiful layout, appealing colors. And simple controls" he said at one point. "Even I get it."

She had no doubt he would. He and Gillian Landis had coauthored a paper showing that social networking ranked in the top three ways to re-engage people who were emerging from depression.

It was Mel who was the skeptic about BrainPacers when she circulated the prototype for approval two days earlier. "We don't need to encourage herd mentality. Why the F would anyone want to wallow in communal misery?" A real albatross.

Barcelos's doubts centered entirely on the privacy issues. But she had cited numerous other medical sites. BeaSurvivor.com for cancer patients; KidsHealth.org for new parents; Diabetes.org for diabetics— the list was endless, and helped her make a good case for why LX should not be an exception.

"And, yes, it's totally separate from the medical data," she said, anticipating his concern. "In addition, it's open to a relatively small, very select community, and it's protected by the same encryption algorithms as the LX system. Twelve character passwords, the works. There's essentially no chance for Facebook-style fiascos, like patient contacts being bought and sold, or shared unintentionally for all the world to see."

To say nothing of the fact that I spent a hundred hours making sure that there could be nothing of use to an outsider, she thought.

"When will it be done?" Barcelos was asking.

"It's ready. Say the word, I push the button, and it goes live."

She wasn't sure what he was thinking, until he said, "Shouldn't we do it together?"

He took her hand.

"How do we turn it on?"

She eased out a silent breath and guided his finger to the launch button.

"I'll keep you posted on the results," she said, her voice thick.

He took his hand off hers. There was an awkward silence as she busied herself with the food.

Seemingly hours went by, and then she noticed that he was staring at her. "Something wrong with my hair?"

"Hmm?"

"You're staring at my hair like it's on fire."

"Just imagining . . ." He looked away.

"Imagining . . ." she prompted.

"What your hair would look like upside-down." He must have noticed her deranged look, because he quickly added, "In the plane, upside-down. In zero G, I mean. I thought maybe one of these days . . . I know we work together, but I take passengers up. It's fun taking people who haven't flown before."

He seemed as flustered by the turn of the conversation as she was.

She wasn't sure about his ability to tolerate that kind of proximity, but she knew her own willpower would be severely challenged.

Just as she was about to ask where they would fly, the intercom buzzed. "Dr. B, Mrs. Barcelos is calling," Rosie said.

She saw him squirm.

"Ask her to hold. I'll be a second."

Mrs. Barcelos. Diane still used her married name outside of her news people circle. "I have to go." She started bagging the leftovers.

"Stay. I'll make it short."

"Yes stay. It will be very short," a voice added.

They both spun around at the sound. Diane's face was in a close-up on the computer screen.

"Hi," Diane said, eyeing him up and down from the screen. "Mau. Ms. Wakeling. So nice to see both of you."

Nice to see both of you? Really? Leoni stiffened on the couch. Even a brain surgeon should be able to see the torch wasn't out on this relationship, at least as far as Diane was concerned. Rosie had assured her their marriage was over. He was divorced, but she wondered how "over it" he really was. She didn't need to have her heart broken by someone still pining . . .

She picked up the remains of the meal, waved in the direction of the screen, and marched toward the door.

What idiot installed the automatic-on for the video conferencing camera, Mauricio wondered as he walked to the desk and sat in front of the computer.

"I see that you and your PR person are working very closely."

He glanced away, wishing he had a good retort, and feeling inexplicably guilty. It was time to let it all go, particularly since it was not just his long absences in the lab that drove the marriage into the ground.

Diane started on the offensive. "Did you take Lexie flying again?" Her eyes turned to slivers, and her lips were tight.

"Di, she loves it."

"I'm sure you think she does. But right after you dropped her off, she barfed all over my living room rug."

"I'll pay for the cleaning. Is that why you called?"

"No," she said, her expression softening. "I want to thank you for hooking me up with the First Lady and her daughter."

"You did a great job," he said. "I had a feeling you and Patty Caldwell bonded."

"Apparently she thought so too, because . . ." She paused with an up-note, her face now softer.

"Yes?"

"Off the record, now!"

"Fine."

"Mau. The First Family is having a little come-to-Jesus next week. Apparently, there're skeletons they want to air out, before the Republicans do it for them, as a pre-election blindside." Diane paused again.

A preemptive strike, he thought. Tom Caldwell had one of the most effective first terms of any president. Job creation, debt reduction, troop draw-downs—the man had no equal in recent memory. To say nothing of cutting healthcare costs by bringing greedy insurance companies and bloated pharmas to their knees. It would be a shame if his reelection were jeopardized by personal issues.

"I got invited to the White House to cover the event! I got an exclusive, Mau. So thank you, thank you, thank you."

"You so deserve it!"

"Don't know about 'deserve it'. I guess they thought I was safer than one of those blood-sucking hacks from Fox News or CNN, who would sensationalize the most minor family issue. Anyway . . ." She trailed off.

He waited.

"I hate to ask. You helped me so much already. But do you have any ins at Boston Medical?"

"What's at BMC?"

"Seems that somebody there leaked the VP's medical record. His cancer's back. He may be off the ticket for November."

Damn. As a very proactive and likable Vice President, Spencer was one of the key assets of Caldwell's administration. A recurrence of his prostate cancer, until now presumed cured, made him a risk his party probably wouldn't take.

"Slick move by somebody if you wanted to put a major dent in the Prez's chances," Diane was saying. "I was hoping you know somebody there who would talk to me."

"I'm afraid you're on your own here, Di." He would never help her fan rumors. She knew better than to ask.

"Too bad. Poor Caldwell is getting it from all fronts. That juror who let the drunken senator walk . . . He was supposed to be on our show this morning. I had an interview all set up."

"How nice." This morning, he was supposed to have been in my office getting his implant adjusted.

"I was looking forward to hearing his side of the story, seeing that the rumors are rampant."

"What rumors?"

"This is off the record, okay? It appears that two-hundred-thousand bucks was donated to an obscure little charity, right after the verdict. Looks like it goes back to one of Caldwell's PACs."

"What does a Political Action Committee have to do with my patient?"

Diane shrugged. "The DA's all over it. Possible jury tampering."

He bristled. "Are you saying Kevin took a bribe?"

"They are. They found e-mails. To your patient from the charity, and to the PAC."

He rubbed his forehead so hard, hairs fell on the keyboard. It was unfathomable. Kevin, taking a bribe? "Where's he now?"

She squinted at him. "You really don't know what happened?"

Oh, shit. "No idea."

"Kevin didn't show, didn't answer his phone."

The hair on the back of his neck stiffened.

"We sent a couple of our guys after him." She looked uncomfortable. "He was in his hangar. It seems that he . . ."

37

Mᴉɴᴜᴛᴇs ʟᴀᴛᴇʀ, Mᴀᴜʀɪᴄɪᴏ ᴡᴀs in Mel's lab, Bruce Levine in tow. "He used a mirror and an x-acto knife to slice his scalp," he explained.

Color drained from Bruce's face.

"Then he grasped the module with a pair of vise-grips, and . . ." He brought his arm behind his right ear and yanked out an imaginary object.

Bruce groaned and made a face.

Mel whistled. "That's brass balls. Did he make it?"

"He's in the OR at Riverside Community. The area around the wire track is mush. But they think the rest is fine."

"Not going to be working on planes, if he lives." Mel's jaw set. "I liked the guy."

Mauricio handed Mel the iPad. "I tried to download him. See if you can find anything." He turned to Bruce. "We should've taken him more seriously."

"The part about the voices, or about taking out his own wire?"

Mauricio gave him a look that could have vaporized a puddle. "You know, sometimes you can be a heartless bastard."

Bruce raised his arms. "I didn't mean it that way. It's just that hindsight can give you an ulcer. There was no way to predict Kevin would be so stupid."

"Obviously, he didn't think it was stupid. He figured since his doctors weren't helping . . ."

Bruce leaned forward. "I know you're blaming yourself. It's a tough business we're in. These people are fragile at the core. Don't kid yourself that you can slip in an electrode, and suddenly their lives turn to roses . . ."

"Save it, Bruce," Mauricio snapped and turned to Mel. "Anything?"

Mel shrugged one shoulder. "We didn't capture enough. The gaps in Delta are there. But I need the whole EEG, directly from the module, to be sure."

Mauricio knew the Electro Encephalogram was the only way to be certain whether the gaps were due to bad contacts at the filament tips, or a result of a programming glitch.

He gnawed on his lip. That would be a totally different kettle of fish. "Riverside promised to send us what's left of the module," he said. "Do what you can." Suddenly a thought flashed through his mind. "And Mel? Check what's happening on the other channels." He turned to Bruce again. "How come we didn't see this coming?"

The psychiatrist thrust his chin out. "Hey, I see the man once a week, tops. Last time he seemed balanced. He didn't say anything about hearing voices."

"One voice. You, calling him."

"I've no idea what that was about," Bruce said. "Patients do transfer their conscience to their therapists, but Kevin . . ."

A bang from Mel hitting the desk with his fist made them turn.

"You were right."

"What?"

"See? During the gap in Delta, I'm also seeing traffic in the Alpha and Gamma channels."

Bruce knotted his eyebrows. "Meaning?"

"Alpha and Gamma areas handle part of acoustic memory," Mauricio clarified. "Goes with the voices Kevin reported."

Bruce looked skeptical. "Kevin only dreamed it was a phone call."

"With what I have," Mel said, "I can't tell if it was a dream, a hallucination, or a real conversation. Sure wish I had that module."

Mauricio didn't know what to make of it. Kevin had described the phone call clearly. Bruce's voice, 'an eye for an eye.' But with one patient tracing, incomplete at that . . . He turned to Mel. "I want you to check all our patients. Find every single D-gap . . ."

"For a change, I'm ahead of you," Mel interrupted. "Running scans as we speak." Mel motioned toward a station where wiggly lines snaked across the enormous screen.

Mauricio winced. "Slow boat." Looking for an event lasting a minute or two out of 72 hours of recording? With the 1800-plus patients scattered all over the country? It was like looking for that needle in the field of hay. "At that rate, you won't live long enough, Mel."

Mel grinned, cuing up a page of code. "I wrote a little app. It scans Delta channel tracings only, looking for the little dropouts. Same as what I would do manually, but at Mach-3 speed."

I don't pay you enough, my friend, Mauricio thought.

"Only thing," Mel added, "Mach speed or not, it still runs about six hours behind."

"Do your best."

"So far I found six tracings with gaps in Delta. Five don't have anything weird in the other channels."

"So all we have is Kevin," Mauricio mused.

"One in a row," Mel confirmed.

Mauricio winced. That left Kevin and his hallucinations or dreams or whatever they were as the only objectively documented finding.

Did one make a pattern?

38

"GOOD EVENING, GINA."

Ah, so it was evening already. Her sleep cycle must be totally out of whack. The long days were wearing, the solitude oppressive. The few books on the shelf were on chess and computers and philosophy. None managed to engage her brain, particularly under the single dim battery-powered headlamp he allowed her. There was the TV, but it only worked when the man was here and the generator was running. He never left it on when he was gone, and as hard as she looked, she couldn't find the key. Other than ruminating over her plans to escape, her days were empty.

It seemed that so were his. On her third evening there, he had asked her to play chess with him. "I'll teach you."

Her brain stalled on the first move.

"That's okay," he said, sounding disappointed. He settled behind his computer and began moving chess pieces on the screen. "Not right," he blurted out suddenly.

She wondered what was not right. That she didn't play or . . .

He continued. "You don't know, but I have helped many. Many. But no one knows that . . . No one realizes that my cause is as worthy as . . ." He trailed off. "Worthier even. I offer new life to innocent victims. To those who suffered . . ." He was pacing, the feet making an uneven scraping sound on the dirt floor. "Not fair," he yelled, flinging a glass at the wall, sending glass fragments flying across the cave.

She eyed a large piece and wondered if it could cut across the man's neck. She bent down to pick it up, but he snatched it out of her hands.

"I'm sorry. I'm sorry," he moaned.

Now he was waving her toward the desk.

"Gina, if you don't mind . . ."

She studied him as he ran a comb through her hair, combing out the matted areas. Almost a prince, she thought, as her hopes were uplifted.

Al eyed her. She was so hopeful, so cooperative. Day four, and she seemed unwavering in the belief that he would soon let her go. Why did she have to remove the damned blindfold? He might have been able to avoid the inevitable. But now . . .

"There." He sat Gina down in front of the computer and adjusted the video camera so her face filled the screen. "No need to worry your future hubby. Smile and look perky."

Knowing that his brief texts on Gina's behalf would soon become suspect and launch a missing person's campaign, he had switched to video recordings. Even skeptical Barcelos seemed to accept them as the real thing when Peter showed him the first message.

"Good one," he said when Gina recorded the message, ending it with "I love you Peter. I'm coming back. Soon." He archived the video.

The rest was more interesting.

He called up Gina's LX page and tapped in her password. Twelve characters, upper and lower case—it was set up by the book, but if you had the real person, what use was the password? Social engineering . . .

He watched as the display flickered, indicating that the computer was dialoguing with CloudFort. Moments later, the connection was established. An attractive display filled his screen. "Welcome, Gina." That must be a Leoni addition, he mused. What a bonus her employment at the hospital turned out to be.

He filled out the prerequisite mood assessment questionnaire on Gina's behalf, and, to give the session an authentic look, made minor adjustments to the channel controls. Putting the LX contact on pause, he opened a file labeled "Queen's Gambit."

A hundred separate documents popped up on the screen. Most have already been uploaded, one by one, to the CloudFort computers. He had converted the instructions to small, seemingly meaningless bits of code, and attached them to Gina's daily programming sessions. They went in undetected, like warriors hidden in the Trojan Horse. He smiled as he imagined how the segments had linked-up inside the CloudFort hard-drives, to replicate the program that enabled him to roam around undetected, accessing the control module programming function of whatever patient he chose. All that for the price of downloading a generic version of the MEDJACK.4 bug, and modifying it to his needs.

The work had paid off. He was no longer perceived as an outside threat to the CloudFort firewalls. He was a legitimate, authenticated device, with an open tunnel to the heart of the LX program.

He was savoring Lady Kay's praise. "Good work. We've been trying for a year. And you got in on the first try."

That's why I get paid the big bucks. Because I deliver. Admittedly, it had taken two tries, if you included the Cat Lady, but he had left that detail out.

He pushed send to upload the last few bits of code. As a final touch, he attached Gina's newly recorded message.

Admittedly, the first two cases that Lady Kay had assigned had not gone off without glitches. Somehow Kevin managed to recall the phone call Al had placed to him during a previously programmed gap in the man's Delta channel. Posing as Bruce, Al convinced Kevin to follow his conscience about what was fair and just punishment for the drunken Senator: the death penalty. Kevin wasn't supposed to remember the conversation, but apparently he did.

The lab tech at the hospital was the same issue. During the Delta gap that he induced in her sleep cycle, Al instructed her to call the *Boston Globe* anonymously and reveal the Vice President's biopsy results, then forget the episode. She had complied. But her emails later in the day made it obvious that she did not forget what she did. And her conscience reared its ugly head, and she wanted to confess. Not good.

Last he checked, she was in deep sleep on her little sailboat, floating out of the Boston Harbor. He hoped the Coast Guard wouldn't spot her. It would be another life on his conscience. One life to complete the assignment that would help many. *It is what it is*, he decided.

He had to get better at this. First Kevin, now the tech. He was going to have to really amp up those Delta gaps. Make the duration longer, fine-tune the sleep level. He hated trial and error approaches, but there was no choice. The LX was a complex device. He hoped that after a few more sessions with Gina, and he would have the technique mastered to perfection.

The payoffs from the cases had been decent and virtually untraceable. Two hundred thou transferred anonymously from a PAC for Kevin. Another 300 for the biopsy results from some outfit in Boston. Those were the bonuses on top of the retainer. Surely, he should be seeing more. He hoped the goose would be laying bigger golden eggs before too long.

"More to come," she had assured him. "In good time."

In good time? What was the problem? The formula was simple. Find somebody in a position of influence, like a Kevin on jury duty. Match them with somebody with a need to control an outcome, like getting a guilty party acquitted. Rig the sleep channel. Make the call. Watch the results. Collect reward.

Hundreds of candidates were at his fingertips, ripe for the plucking. He had the tools that would let him sort the prospects in an infinite number of ways. Down to the brand of after-shave they used, or their pets' nicknames. Or their financial connections, legal or illegal.

Did he really need to wait for Lady Kay's blessing? he thought suddenly. What was the harm in going solo?

His mind turned to a news item that crossed his screen earlier.

"Dems and GOP battling over aerospace contract award: French EADS or American Northrop? With two days remaining before the final selection, the consensus is that the decision, which rests in the hands of a single person, General Schwartz, known as the Top Watchdog, will favor the California-based manufacturer . . ."

Millions at stake. The opportunity was too good to pass. He had two days. Plenty of time to do the homework. And it was a chance to impress Lady Kay. See? I'm not just hired help. I can deliver more than you asked for.

The computer chirped. Gina's last session was over. She was sitting with her head resting on her crossed arms, breathing evenly. Asleep.

What the hell, he thought. He imagined walking her to the bed, undressing her slowly, watching those beautiful breasts slip out . . .

He felt a warm stirring between his legs.

He chased the thought away. There would be time for that. Right now, he was on a mission.

Using Gina's account as entry point, he started working the keyboard.

39

BRIGADIER GENERAL TURNER SCHWARTZ sat at his desk in his second floor study in a suburb of DC, and stared at his computer screen. A bizarre headline stared back at him: "Watchdog General Turns Tail." He tried to remember the events of the preceding 24 hours, but his memory banks were like Swiss cheese—full of holes.

He pulled open a drawer, extracted a pencil and a note pad and began jotting down what little he could remember.

He was certain that the previous day he had been gazing out of the window of the luxuriously appointed cabin of a modified Boeing 727 as it overflew the Mojave Desert on its approach to Edwards Air Force Base. The Southern California sunset was magnificent, coloring the barren rocky hills below a golden brown. Not that different from Iraq, Schwartz remembered thinking.

He had served his country with honor in several hot spots in the Middle East, but his clinical depression had sidelined him to a desk job. Now he was charged with the inglorious task of evaluating military contracts.

Demoted but not defeated, Schwartz proved to be one of the most effective and insightful negotiators. In a tour de force, he was able to single-handedly persuade the commission to reverse the allocation of a mega-contract for a refueling tanker to the European Airbus builder. That move saved 40,000 domestic jobs, to say nothing of national pride. After that master stroke, the Pentagon proclaimed him Top Watchdog of American Interests and Taxpayer Dollars, and younger members of voting committees followed his lead unflinchingly, much as junior officers once followed his orders on the battlefield.

For the thousandth time in the past two years, he mentally thanked Brad Oakley. What years of intensive antidepressant pharmatherapy failed to accomplish, his Academy classmate fixed by pulling some strings and sneaking him into the LX study. More energized and optimistic than he had ever been in his life, Schwartz even started to fantasize about returning to active duty. Brad Oakley seemed to think that a promotion and redeployment was not out of the question. As soon as Turner did his magic on the upcoming contract award.

The decision was simple: should the Pentagon award the manufacture of the engines, landing gear, and a few of the control systems, to EADS—the French aero-defense group that owned Airbus, or should the US keep the much-needed jobs at home, and subcontract the components to California-based Northrop?

"Gee, let me think . . ." Turner once said, staring dreamily at the ceiling, and making the reporters at his news conference break into laughter.

Turner sighed. The charade had to be played, even though most players knew what the outcome would be: no French champagne corks would be popping after his vote was cast.

He remembered walking from the landing strip to his sleeping quarters. He had unpacked, hung his dress uniform, set up his laptop and verified that the Wi-Fi was operative. He went into the bathroom, shaved, found the bottle of little blue pills, and made sure it was within easy reach for the after-dinner entertainment.

That was one of the perks of this position. Since times immemorial, the host—in this case Boeing—attended to every need of the judges. Every need. Not that any of the parties thought that an expensive bottle of wine, or an attractive companion for the night would swing a multibillion-dollar vote, but it was a matter of pride for the hosting company to make the guests feel . . . well, comfortable in every way.

Last year he had been so incapacitated by his depression that he wasn't able to enjoy the company of the attractive young lady visitor that was provided. Even the little blue pill didn't help. Tonight, he was eagerly anticipating a second chance to put that asset to good use.

He went back to the desk, logged on, hit the bookmark labeled "Me" and typed in his password. The program responded with the authentication of his implant. He sped through the familiar questions about how he was feeling, and then verified the channel settings, leaving them as they had been for months. It was working. There was nothing to fix.

As an afterthought, he adjusted his sleep to the new time zone. The visitor was due after dinner. The way he was feeling, he would keep her up well past midnight. He set the go-to-sleep time at 1:00 a.m., the wake-up time for six in the morning, and added an extra cycle of REM sleep to make up for the shortened night. He was, above all, a consummate professional, and he intended to be awake, alert and energized for the morning presentation and vote.

He clicked "submit" and watched as input lines streaming across the screen confirmed that a new set of LX stimuli was being downloaded from the center. His marching orders for the next twenty-four hours. His electronic meds.

He squinted at a hairline blip in the Delta wave line. He reentered the settings and resubmitted, but the dropout remained in the same place. He was about to call the Medical Officer on duty at Bethesda Medical, but the little alarm on the desktop reminded him that it was dinner time.

"To hell with it," Turner thought. So he would wake up for a bit. Big deal. Ever since his college days, a middle-of-the-night interlude had been a most delightful extra. If the same woman was coming to visit him as last time—as the folks had promised—the wee-hours encore would be a memorable experience.

He clicked "accept," and was rewarded with a message:

"Congratulations! We're delighted that you are doing well. Enjoy your trip!"

That he intended to do.

Schwartz made more notes. So far, things seemed to hang together. He vividly remembered the dinner, the walk back to the room, the knock on the door, the tall woman wearing nothing but a raincoat, the passionate lovemaking, the glass of champagne. He also had a clear memory of waking up in the middle of the night, and going another quick round with her.

Then nothing.

Until the flight back, when no one was speaking to him.

Now he was home, it was close to midnight, and the bizarre headlines stared at him from the screen.

"Watchdog General Turns Tail."

He forced himself to re-read the text of the news release, hoping to make sense of what he was seeing.

"In a stunning reversal of his 'keep-jobs-at-home' trend, General Turner Schwartz voted to awarded a four-billion-dollar defense contract to Boeing's bitter enemy, European Airbus owner, EADS. 'Merci,' said the French President during this morning's press conference. 'Merci,' begged the 3000 aircraft workers about to be laid off from Northrop's Southern California plant. As unpalatable as the decision was to President Caldwell, reversing it would create an international incident with the French, and he was forced . . ."

Turner stopped reading, and stared blindly at the screen. No matter how hard he tried, he remembered nothing of what had happened. He sighed. In the end, nobody would give a flying fuck why it happened. Definitely not him. He had failed his country.

There was only one way to deal with that.

40

EARTHQUAKE, WAS THE FIRST THING that flashed through Al's mind. The entire cave was shaking.

Cold droplets formed on his upper lip. The thought of being trapped underground was terrifying. *Run.*

The low rumble built and built, radiating from the ceiling, into the walls, the floor. The propane tank rattled against the wall. Dust started flying in through the vent shafts, filling the cave. He began to cough.

The roar outside grew louder. He moved toward the exit. Turned, glanced at Gina, wondering if he should carry her out. On his stump? He'd never make it.

He hurried down the tunnel, fumbling for the key as he ran. The roar was deafening, the dust overwhelming. He found the lock, opened the gate, and ran the last fifty feet to the cave's entrance.

The blast of hot air saturated with the odor of burning kerosene, a barrage of flying dust and gravel, and a blindingly bright light, hit him at the same time, stopping him in his tracks. He shielded his face with a raised arm.

A giant Sikorsky SH-240 helicopter settled to the ground fifty feet away. The rotors, almost directly over his head began to wind down. The gravel storm subsided, but the air was thick with dust.

What the fuck was that? Military exercises? In this part of the desert?

A figure was emerging from the cloud of dust, silhouetted by the landing lights, throwing a grotesquely magnified shadow that stretched all the way toward him.

Blood drained from his face when he recognized her.

"Out for a moonlight stroll, Al?" Kay yelled over the noise of the idling engines. "Or should I say, moonlighting?"

"How . . ." He felt sand in his mouth. How did she find him? The cave was remote, safe.

"Never mind how I found it, Al. I believe you have something to share with me."

The landing light went out. In the sudden darkness, she was just a voice, but there was no mistaking the anger.

He forced himself to think before opening his mouth. The aircraft's red beacon kept flashing in his eyes, distracting him.

"I was looking for scorpions," he blurted out. "A hobby of mine. They come out at night . . ."

"Not on moonlit nights. They like the dark."

You would know, bitch. . . He was feeling outwitted, and his shock was changing to anger.

"And you need a UV light to find them, Al. To make them glow in the dark. I'm sure you know that. Where is your UV light, Al?" She motioned toward a rock pile. "Sit down," she ordered.

"All I wanted the General to do was swing his vote," Al started explaining. "Then it would be blamed on his being bribed. Like the other two cases. I had no idea he would blow his brains out."

"Human nature, Al."

"But that's not the instructions I gave him . . ."

"Drop it. Messing with the military was an idiot move. Undoubtedly motivated by the two million dollars you got paid by the French."

It was scary. Was there anything this woman didn't know? He was about to point out to her that it took a lot of skill and creativity to match the bidder with the opportunity, and that he had hoped the case would serve Lady Kay's purpose . . .

"You fucked up, Al."

He had a sudden urge to leap up and strangle the woman. I'm not a fuck up. But even if he could overpower her, he would have to deal with the three goons who were leaning on the landing gear of the chopper, just out of earshot, but not out of sight. "I thought . . ."

"I didn't hire you to think. That's my job. You're in charge of execution." She lowered her voice. "Remember our agreement? On the beach? The goal is to create a series of cases of people acting badly for unknown reasons. Only when I say so, do we link it all to the LX . . ."

She was leaving something out. He took a breath. "I assumed the profile of the case matched the others on the list you gave me. And since the window of opportunity was small, and I had no way to contact you . . ."

"What profile?" she snapped.

He could see Lady Kay was bristling. He hid a smile. I see more than you think, bitch. "The juror, the lab tech—they were designed not just to discredit the LX, but to impact the President as well . . ."

She was quiet for a nanosecond, then recovered. "You don't know what you're talking about."

Bull's eye. "I'm sorry. You're right, I don't. I was mistaken in thinking that since the aerospace vote would reflect on the Administration, you'd be pleased." If Caldwell lost the election, he wanted to add, your precious pharma client would be free to continue the criminal price gouging. I could kill two birds with one stone for you, no extra charge.

"You were mistaken. And two cases do not make a pattern, Al."

He gave her credit for fast thinking.

"The goal is to protect our client's business interest from the LX. Period. By involving the military, you could've opened a Pandora's Box of investigation. It was not a wise thing to do."

She reached into an attaché case, and for a second he thought she was going to pull out a gun. Rumors about what happened to the young woman hacker, a pre-med student, no less, a year ago, had filtered down the pipeline to him. Allegedly she was on an assignment having to do with a neural implant.

Al tensed. Lady Kay managed to find his top-secret cave in the middle of the night. There was no telling what else she was capable of.

"Let's move forward," she said. "The Mojave Motel surveillance video of the girl who visited the General ..."

"They don't have a surveil ..." Shit. It just slipped out. Tantamount to confessing it was he who killed her. No one had ever flustered him to this extent before.

Kay smiled. "My guys do. But it's safe, don't you worry." She paused.

Till I screw up again.

She handed him a flash drive. "More cases for you to handle."

He eased out a long breath, trying not to blow up again. The bitch would pay. Somehow, someday. She would pay.

"We have to pick up the pace, Al. I'm going to give you forty-eight hours to get them all in. The first on that list is iffy ..." she added.

"Meaning?"

"It involves a flight up north. Might not go if the storm moves in. You'll see; it's all there on the drive. The other cases are shoo-ins. Particularly for you. "

Flattery will get you nowhere now. He pocketed the thumb drive.

Moments later, the goons were back in the chopper, the blades starting to turn. Before boarding, Kay stopped and turned toward him. Dust was starting to blow again, but she seemed immune to it. Her hair remained perfectly in place. "One more thing, Al," she yelled over the noise. Then she walked back and leaned to his ear. Her voice was clear despite the crescendo roar of the engine.

"That woman you're keeping? She has to go. Now."

"But I need her to access . . ."

"Now."

He stood still despite the gravel hurricane, watching the chopper lift off, cursing the day he met this woman, until the moon and the flashing lights vanished in the cloud of dust.

Al shuffled down the tunnel, blood boiling in his veins. Outmaneuvered. Outsmarted. Outed. Bitch.

He rammed the gate open and made his way into the cave. Suddenly the place seemed dirty, defiled. It was no longer his secret. Lady Kay's spirit permeated the space.

He stood over Gina, still asleep, her chest moving evenly. The sleep of innocents.

He cringed recalling the night when he opened up to her, revealing his feelings of envy and lack of recognition. He had let a bond of sorts form between them. Should never had let it happen.

The Kay woman didn't give him a chance to explain that his success hinged on Gina's LX. Without it, the future of the project would be in jeopardy.

"Get rid of her. Now," the woman had ordered.

You hired me to do a job, don't tell me how. Could he take a chance and disobey? That too could kill the project.

He started pacing. Maybe he could find a way . . .

 **41**

W HEN MAURICIO WALKED INTO HIS OFFICE, Leoni was waiting.

"I need your guidance handling this," she said without preambles. "BrainPacers is buzzing with rumors about the General."

"What General?"

She took two long steps to his desktop computer and clicked the news icon. "That General."

He scanned the headlines. His morning coffee started to burn a hole in his empty stomach.

Leoni kept talking. "General Schwartz did not have a page on BrainPacers, but friends outed to the media that he had an implant. I'm racking my brains about how to keep the LX out of the aerospace contract fiasco. People can make the weirdest connections, and we don't need adverse PR, with the pro ..."

"Where is he? The General?"

"His office said he was on medical leave."

Moments later, Leoni was out of the room, and he had Oakley on the videoconference line.

"When were you going to tell me about Turner?" he snapped.

General Brad Oakley's immobile face filled the top half of the screen, while his computer-synthesized speech came from the speakers. "What happened is need-to-know. You don't need to know."

"The hell I don't. You promised to keep me in the loop."

"I promised that about the AAA pilots. He's not one of the AAA pilots."

"Fuck that. He's an implant patient. Weren't you the least bit curious, why he did what he did?"

"My top dog bit my ass." The image on the screen changed from one of Brad's face, to a headline: Watchdog General Turns Tail. "What else do I want to know?"

The sentences started streaming faster. "That he gave away two billion dollars to the fucking frogs? That three thousand people at Northrop are going to lose their jobs? That all of us lost face? That the President is pissed because it made him look like an idiot?"

Even with Brad's computerized monotone, he could hear the frustration. "How do I explain that?"

He tried to modulate his response. "So what do you think happened? Drugs? Booze? Political pressure? Dementia?"

"I've never seen him do drugs or get drunk. But I've never seen him with a visitor, either."

"What visitor?"

"Don't go there," Oakley responded.

Interesting. "You think the visitor had something to do with the decision?"

There was a pause, then Oakley's voice. "We did track down the broad. In a motel room in Cal City."

He knew the little town, just south of Edwards Air Force Base. A seedy truck stop. Plenty of work for a motivated girl. A man of Turner's reputation blackmailed by a prostitute? He was about to ask if that possibility had occurred to Brad, but Brad was talking again.

"She had a plastic bag wrapped around her head."

His breath caught as an image of Sandy stabbing Robbie flashed through his mind. Cold sweat formed on his neck. He had to remind himself that Sandy hadn't killed Robbie.

His voice was unsteady for the next question. "You think Turner killed the prostitute?"

"He did not."

He let his breath out. "Did you review his tracing?"

"With a fine toothed comb. I'll confess, I was hoping we could pin his actions on the wire. But the readings are nominal. Except for a weird wiggle the night before the meeting."

Mauricio sat up. "Can you describe the wiggle?"

The screen flashed, went blank, and then showed a tracing. A Delta gap identical to the one Mel had found in Kevin's record. "My techs might've missed it," Oakley was saying, "but Turner made a note of it in his write up. Anal Schwartz."

Mauricio's brain was spinning. "Brad, can you get the General to come in? I'll send Mel over there. We need to record directly from his module." If his tracings showed auditory hallucinations, that would make it two in a row. Something to get his investigative teeth into.

Instead of a reply, the image changed. It was a photo of a desk, with a figure slumped over it, face down. A gun lay on the desk. The head had a large defect on the side opposite the gun.

He leaned closer. A wire with a small flat disc was dangling from the hole.

"I didn't even get to chew him out," Brad's voice said. His electronic face was back on the screen, the lips and eyes turned down in sorrow.

42

"How fast can you get the data to us, Brad?" Mauricio had asked after he managed to come to terms with Schwartz's death. It could take ten-to-twelve hours to upload and download the full content of an intact module. "On second thought, can you FedEx it?"

Silence. Then Brad's voice asked, "How fast can you get a man to Los Al?"

Los Alamitos was the little-used military airport fifteen miles from Newport Beach, and about three thousand miles from where Brad was. "What's at Los Alamitos?"

"Your tax dollars at work. Have your courier there in two hours," he added.

Apparently the authorities at Los Alamitos had been notified about his arrival, because Mauricio was escorted out to the ramp just as the F-22 squeaked onto the runway and filled the air with the deafening roar of its reverse thrusters.

Moments later a helmeted figure, holding a small box in a gloved hand, scrambled down the air-stair and headed toward him.

"Dr. Barcelos?" The helmet came off. "I'm Lieutenant Fox."

He recognized the name of one the pilots Oakley had shown him during his visit. AAA. Awake, alert, accurate.

The pilot handed him the package. "From General Oakley, sir."

Mauricio started to thank him, but the man interrupted.

"Thank you, sir for all you've done . . . for the program. Without the impl . . . Thank you," he repeated, giving a smart salute.

Mauricio would have liked to sit down with the pilot and find out how the long periods of wakefulness were being tolerated. He was about to invite the man to the hospital to meet Mel, but the lieutenant spoke first. "I better go hustle the ground crew with the refueling, sir. I promised to take the wife out for dinner and a movie. It's our third anniversary. And I think she's going to tell me she's expecting," he added with a sheepish grin.

Back at the hospital, Turner Schwartz's LX module, still with fragments of dried blood and brain tissue, was pinned in the test stand clamp in Mel's laboratory. The screen displayed a few wiggly lines.

Mel shook his head. "Not much left here."

"Can't you at least pinpoint the time the gap happened?"

"Be happy I'm getting anything, Mau," Mel grumbled. "Shock wave from the gunshot did a job on it."

"Try."

Mel reset the test. More wavy lines, now in slow motion.

"There," Mauricio pointed. "A gap in the Delta wave. Check what's happening on the others."

Moments later, they were looking at the tell-tale signs of audio activity during the Delta gap. The image was time-stamped 06:05 hours.

"Just like Kevin's," Mel said.

"Two in a row," Mauricio confirmed. "But 6:05 a.m. is not the time the visitor was there."

"What visitor?"

"Never mind." According to Oakley, the woman had come in

around midnight and left around 3:30 a.m., so at 06:05 hours the General was alone again.

The recording was moving again.

"Wait a minute," Mauricio said. "Roll it back."

If the General's record was set for East Coast Time, 06:05 was only 3:05 a.m. in California. That meant that the woman had been there at the time that the Delta gap and the auditory stimuli had been recorded. Maybe he and Mel were not looking at audio hallucinations, but at the evidence of a real live conversation that occurred during the light sleep induced by the implant.

"Can you see what else was going on? Was he talking? Looking at something?"

Mel shook his head. "Without a full EEG, we're shit out of luck." He worked the keyboard, his face wrinkling more and more.

"What's up?"

Mel pushed away from the bench and stood up. "A damn glitch."

"In . . . ?"

"I'm trying to run a trace upstream, to the module inputs, but it keeps taking me to the same IP address as Kevin's." Mel sounded frustrated.

"So? They're all on CloudFort," he pointed out.

"No shit. But each patient is supposed to have his own IP."

"So what's the address?"

Mel drummed his fingers, staring at the screen. "Both tracings point to our runaway bride."

His brain started spinning. "Very interesting," he mumbled.

"I was afraid you'd say that," Mel snorted. "I haven't the foggiest, either."

Suddenly bits of the conversation with the CloudFort rep replayed in his head. The hair on the back of his neck rippled. "Mel . . ." His tongue was too dry to move. "Mel, Gina's module is a device that is 'already recognized by the system', right? Like the CloudFort guy was talking about?"

"So it is," Mel nodded. "We may have just found the portal."

"Stonewalling" was the only way to describe the response Mauricio met when he called CloudFort to get a full copy of Gina's medical record.

"Sir, it's Saturday," the man on the video conference protested. "Decisions about release of records are made by the main office . . ."

"Saturday?" he snapped. "Patients don't get sick on Saturdays? I don't care if it's Carnival. I want those records now."

It took the threat of legal repercussions to make CloudFort turn over Gina Roslyn's information. Even then, there were obvious gaps in the submission.

"I mean all of them," he articulated, staring at the man at the other end of the videoconference line. "Including your internal memos."

"It's not our fault you lost a patient," the man mumbled.

He leaned into the lens. "What did you just say?"

The man blinked. "Nothing. Here's the rest of it."

Another file landed on Mel's desktop.

Most of the downloaded entries dealt with routine sweeps for malware. One stood out because it was in a separate file. He noted the date. The day after Peter reported that Gina had left. He opened the file. Mel looked over his shoulder.

"January 23, 23:05 hrs. Phone con with St. Joseph's Hospital, Phoenix, AZ. Urgent call from Sam Knight, Emergency Room Nurse. Reported patient had neural stimulator overdose. Requested immediate patch-in due to inop server at client's end. Ref tape RT247/x."

There was an audio file attached. He played it. It seemed to have been edited to a few select passages.

"This is Tim Knight . . . Brain pacer failed. A pacemaker-induced psychotic episode." Sound of a large object crashing in the background, followed by screams.

He and Mel stiffened.

"Gina?" Mel asked.

He shook his head. "Not her voice, I don't think."

More exchanges as two men bickered. Then the operator's voice. "In the interest of patient welfare and safety, I'm making the decision to allow the access. Send the link and I'll punch it in from this end."

They exchanged glances.

"I didn't know Gina went to an ER, in Phoenix, no less," Mel said. "There was nothing on her log-in sessions."

Mauricio was tapping his foot so fast, it sounded like a machine gun. "Mel, there is no St. Joseph's in Phoenix."

After a long silence, Mel said, "Well, that's one way to get into the system."

Mauricio got up and started pacing, the tiny lab permitting only a few steps in each direction. Gina had been used to gain access to CloudFort. The poor woman was heaven knows where, and the system had been breached. Thousands of patients could be at risk.

"No worries," Mel was saying. "Now that we know how he got in, all we have to do is find the bastard and get him out."

"Right, Mel. We'll just send him an email," he snapped.

"Hey, don't take it out on me."

He blew out a breath. "Sorry."

"But the email ... not such a bad idea. If I could get a direct download, straight off Gina's module, rather than through those clowns ..."

"Piece of cake," Mauricio snorted. "All we need to do is find Gina."

"When we find her," Mel said, "I will download what's stored in the module ..."

"And get what out of it?" His patience was wearing thin. He wanted results, now.

"There'll be links on there that don't get transmitted through Central," Mel explained. "If I can capture them and run a back-trace through the record, I should be able to figure out exactly what ..."

The intercom buzzed.

Rosie's voice. "Dr. B, are you there?"

"Damn it, not now, Rosie."

"It's Detective Blanchard."

The detective who arrested Sandy. Now what? She was out, and he had told them everything he could without breaching HIPAA. He snapped up the receiver. "Yes?" As he listened, the blood drained from his head, as if during a high-G maneuver. When he was done, he hung up the phone, absentmindedly wiped the sweat off his hand onto his scrub pants, and then turned to Mel. He looked shaken to his core.

"I think I can get that module for you now," he said softly.

43

ICARUS DRONED EVENLY OVER THE ENDLESS landscape of cookie-cutter developments that covered the outskirts of San Fernando Valley. Eventually, developments gave way to the desolate landscape of Mojave Desert. Twenty-six minutes after he took off from Fullerton he touched down at Mojave Airport. In afternoon traffic, the drive would have taken over four hours. Raked with anxiety, he didn't want to wait four hours.

Blanchard greeted him with a cold nod.

"Must be nice," Blanchard said, glancing past Mauricio's shoulder. "Private plane."

"Didn't want to keep you waiting."

"Fly often?"

"When I have time."

"Did you have time to fly up this way a couple of nights ago?"

"I haven't flown in a week." What difference did it make to this guy, anyway?

While they were driving from the airport, Blanchard said, "Paradoxical dysencephaly?"

"What are you talking about?"

"I looked it up. No such thing."

He remembered the symptoms he had made up to keep Blanchard from arresting Sandy weeks ago.

"Not nice, taking advantage, just because you think I'm not as smart as you, Doctor," Blanchard was saying. "I don't forget these things. The guys are still laughing at me for that one. I don't forget," he repeated, touching his bony index to his skull. "Your buddy in Phoenix did warn me . . . about you being slippery. I should've listened."

"Buddy in Phoenix?"

The detective waved it off. "Routine background check."

They pulled up to a two-story office complex that had seen better days. The small faded plaque read "Los Angeles County Coroner's Office."

The aging coroner led them down a narrow hallway, and pushed a door marked "Post Room" open.

The small autopsy room appeared to double as a storage area. The odor of freshly cut flesh, bowel contents, and strong bleach permeated the air. A fluid-stained blue drape covered the outline of a body on the dissection table.

Mauricio watched as Blanchard circled around to the other side, walking gingerly on the tile floor, like a stork in a marsh. The detective fixed his eyes on him, and then gave a quick nod. The coroner pulled the drape back.

The body was of a white woman in her mid-forties. The flesh had been torn in many places by what appeared to be bites. One arm was barely attached. More gnawing marks appeared on her breasts and belly. The Y-shaped autopsy incision that spread from her collarbones down her breastbone to her pubis was sloppily closed with coarse twine. The head and face remained wrapped in surgical towels, revealing nothing above the neck.

"Recognize her?" Blanchard asked.

"Not by the body."

The coroner started to unwrap the bloody towels covering the woman's head. Mauricio was conscious that Blanchard's eyes remained locked on him, as if anticipating his reaction.

The towels lifted. Even matted, bloodied and filled with cactus debris, the red hair was unmistakable. His jaw tightened with such force he thought his teeth would crush.

Little of her face remained. The outlines were there, but most of the skin had been eaten away. Muscles and ligaments around the mouth and the eyes looked like dissections he remembered from medical school. The even white teeth stood out like pearls against the bloody tissues.

Mauricio had seen far worse during a hospital trauma call. But this wasn't an anonymous body. It was Gina. His first patient. His poster girl. Bitter bile in his mouth forced him to look at the face. A lump formed in his throat as he recalled a happy Gina showing off her engagement ring. "What happened?" he asked finally.

The pathologist mumbled something about a couple from LA. "Hiking in the high desert. They found her."

"And?" Mauricio prompted, expecting more detail.

The old man shrugged. "Based on some ground markings, the cops think after the perp dropped her off, she was still alive and able to walk. Or crawl. Then she died, and then coyotes and rats got to her. Or the coyotes first, then she died . . ."

"Cause of death?" he interrupted.

"That is where it gets interesting. On the CT there was an egg-sized area of intracranial bleeding in the right parietal area. And good thing I got the x-ray," he added with a smug twitch, "or we'd still be trying to figure who this gal was."

"Doc here recognized the brain wire," Blanchard said, indicating the coroner. "You're pretty famous, it seems."

"And you, Detective . . . What brings you here?" He sensed a visceral resentment building toward this man.

"After Cat Lady, I'm sort of the brain wire expert around the office,"

Blanchard said.

Did the cops need a wire expert, he wondered?

The pathologist rolled Gina's head to the left, and pointed to a two-inch incision just behind the right ear. The incision was surgically precise, and located exactly where he would have placed the LX module.

"What the hell . . ."

"My feelings precisely," Blanchard said.

"It was closed with two stitches," said the pathologist. "Very professional."

He looked at the coroner. "Mind if I have a look?"

"Look all you want. We already took photos," Blanchard answered.

The coroner gestured toward a bench. "Gloves are over there."

He gloved up and spread the edges of the incision. Several splinters of skull were visible. He examined them closely. The three pieces that formed a small tent in the center of the wound had perfectly regular semi-circular defects facing each other. His brain rearranged the pieces into their original positions: an intact skull with a small hole drilled through it. The diameter, location, and angle of entry were unmistakable. The segments that would have formed the periphery of the hole were smooth, indicating bone healing.

"Looks like somebody was playing doctor," Blanchard commented.

"I drilled that hole," he said.

The detective squinted. "Before she died?"

He shot him a withering look. "What kind of question is that?" he asked, glaring at the detective.

"It's obviously related to her death," Blanchard said eventually. "You said you did it."

"Are you implying I'm a suspect?" Blood rushed to his face. "Because if you . . ."

Blanchard interrupted. "I'm just clarifying, is all. You have friends in high places, Doctor. A gumshoe like me has to be careful."

He took a calming breath. "I operated on her four years ago. I drilled the hole to insert the LX. Somebody pulled it out."

"The x-ray shows your gizmo is still in there."

He had to focus to process the information. "What?"

"Your implant. On her skull x-rays. So that hole is what?" Blanchard gestured at the incision. "Some sicko playing doctor?"

Mauricio looked past the detective. Of course. Pained by Gina's death, he had forgotten an important detail of her medical history. Gently, he rolled Gina's head and palpated her scalp.

"Now what are you looking for?" Blanchard asked.

His heart beating fast, he tried to look nonchalant. "Anything you might have missed, Detective," he said, determined not to discuss his suspicion. I think the hacker just made a big mistake.

He returned Gina's head to its original position, snapped off his gloves and picked up his iPad.

Blanchard's eyes followed his every move. "Now what?"

"Just making notes, Detective," he said as he worked the screen.

Moments later, he closed the cover on the iPad and lowered it, while leaving it on. "Any more questions? If not, I need to use the restroom."

Leaving his iPad behind, he checked his watch and slowly made his way down the hall.

"You all right Doc?" Blanchard asked suspiciously when he returned. "Took you a while . . ."

He gave his iPad a quick glance. All done. "I hope you find whoever did this. In the meantime, I need to get back to work."

44

"Let me see this lucky break we supposedly caught," Mel said when Mauricio landed at Fullerton.

"Gina had two implants."

"I remember. Your first patient and you were all nerves, so you gave me hell because the wire wasn't capturing and we had to slip in another one."

He ignored the dig. "Both of her implant scars were healed and covered by hair. The creep had a fifty-fifty chance, but he took the module we shut down." He handed Mel the iPad. "The question is why take it in the first place?"

Mel gave a little grin. "Because he didn't want me to use the module to download the EEG and figure out how he's getting in. Which is what I'm about to do, as soon as I squeeze out the data." Mel started toward the hangar, his eyes on the screen. "Oh, yeah. You did all right, Mau. Lots to squeeze here."

"Squeeze away," he said, following. "Of the two patients with gaps we know of, one is dead, the other paralyzed. Whether these gaps are related or not, we've got to stop them."

Standing at his work bench in the hangar Mel seemed absorbed by the display on the computer. "I'll bet . . ." His calloused fingers pounded the keyboard, faster and faster. "I might be able to reverse-engineer this thing."

"And what . . ."

"I got it." Mel laughed and uncurled his compact frame. "Why don't I just make a patch? I could . . ."

Mauricio could practically hear Mel's brain grinding toward the solution.

"I could probably block it out . . . That will work."

"Block what? What will work?"

"I'll make a patch that will force the baseline of Delta to stay up, right here. He can try, but the sleep intensity will never dip to the light-sleep levels, which he apparently uses for hypnotic suggestions. The phone call Kevin got—the auditory stimuli. We'll still be able to adjust sleep duration and REM periods, but no one will be able to reduce sleep to make a gap. Capisce?"

He almost did understand.

"If it works, no more gaps," Mel said.

Mauricio drummed his fingers. "You can do it?"

Mel's grin told him his code-crunching guru was onto something. "Have I ever failed you?"

He couldn't recall a single instance. "A patch job," he grumbled. "Just what patients want to hear."

"Stop complaining. We'll call it LX two-point-oh," Mel announced. "Now, with DGBlocker! DGBlocker, get it? Delta gap . . ."

"I get it, Mel." Lemonade out of lemons. "We still won't know how the gaps get there."

"What do you care, if they're blocked? Just plug up the hole, and keep cruising."

"We need to nail whoever is doing this."

"We will. Once we get the patch uploaded, the asshole can hack all he wants. It'll take a while before he figures he's shooting blanks.

By then, we'll have the bastard in our crosshairs."

It was a sweet prospect indeed. "How long?"

Mel rocked his head. "Two, three days, max. I might even surprise you and add something more I've been thinking about."

He had had enough surprises for the week. "Surprise me now. What?"

"Oh . . ." Mel rolled his eyes in a fake dramatic reverie. "Say, some side effect bad enough to make them come running back to their doctors. We'll call it Boomerang."

"Call it Harpsichord, for all I care." He checked his watch. "You have till 9:00 P.M. tomorrow." He headed for the exit.

"That's not even two days," Mel called after him.

"Thirty-six hours, Mel. We can't let our patients be sitting ducks."

Mel stared back, his jaw moving back and forth. He opened his mouth as if to protest, but stopped. "Who needs sleep, anyway. I'll go get some stuff from the lab, and then . . . Don't expect me in tomorrow."

"Fair enough. And Mel? Make it bombproof. One more gap shows up, and I am going to shut the whole thing down and start a recall."

Al slid to the bottom of the van and out of sight as Barcelos emerged from the gate. He had seen the men talking animatedly by the plane, but Barcelos' phone must have been turned off for the flight, because he couldn't hear what they were saying.

But he was deeply troubled by what he overheard once the men entered the hangar, and they were within range of the three remote-broadcasting mikes he had installed days earlier. Mel sounded convinced he could develop a way to block his access to CloudFort. He had seen enough of Mel's work to know that the man was not bluffing. That would be a disaster.

What worried him even more was that Mel seemed to be working from some new data. Al had made sure to wipe his tracks by removing the woman's implant. What was Mel working with?

The loud beat of rotor blades overhead jolted him. Lady Kay, flashed through his mind. The roar got louder. He ventured a glance up through the windshield just as a police helicopter came into view and floated to a landing at the LAPD helipad.

He let out a sigh of relief.

His thoughts went back to Mel. Thirty six hours, Barcelos had insisted. Whatever the programmer was planning had bad news stamped all over it.

After his unauthorized solo venture, that ended in the General's unforeseeable exit, he couldn't afford to disappoint Lady Kay again. Thousands of injured children depended on his success.

"I'll get some stuff from the lab . . . don't expect me in," Mel had said.

A plan started to germinate. He wished there were an alternative, but couldn't think of any. The creation of the blocking patch had to be averted at any cost.

He hoped the deadline to complete the project wouldn't keep Mel from his daily morning spin in Big Red.

45

The Volvo groaned to a halt in the alley between the condos. Mauricio marched into the house, stripping his clothes as he went, trying to rid himself of the stench of death. He pulled the cachaça off the shelf and headed to the garage, taking deep gulps straight from the bottle.

He hoisted the dusty backpack stuffed with climbing paraphernalia so it hung from the rafters like a punching bag, parked the bottle out of the way, and let loose.

Minutes later, the thuds were coming with metronomic regularity. Whomp. Whomp. Whomp. Each time his foot walloped the bag, the walls vibrated. Drops of sweat fanned out from his arms and legs with every strike.

Whomp. Harder. Whomp. A perfectly placed wallop rammed the pack into the adjacent shelf, sending toolboxes clattering to the floor.

He didn't stop. He punched and kicked and smashed, without aiming and without caring. His head spun with anger, disappointment, frustration and fear.

Gina had been murdered, or left out to die in the desert. His patients' security shattered. The LX violated. His private world invaded.

He assaulted the punching bag as if it contained all the evil in the world, as if he could beat it out, and turn back the clock, and undo all that had happened.

"Invaded. Violated. Stolen. Dead." The words exploded with every strike.

It would change nothing, but he had to punish whoever did it.

He imagined coming face to face with Gina's assailant. Suddenly he wondered if he would be capable of killing him.

Once a killer . . .

The thought brought instant nausea.

I'm not a killer.

His foot was flying through the air, aimed at the bag. His brain was flashing on the memory of a long-ago-established taboo. Do not strike another human being. Ever. For any reason.

Once a killer . . .

His stomach convulsed, sending up bile, the bitter fluid filling his nostrils, chocking him . . .

Do not strike . . .

He hadn't meant to kill Paulo. It had been an accident. A blow misdirected by anger.

"Eu matei ele, mae!" young Mauricio was stammering. "I killed him, Ma, I killed him."

"Não tenha medo, Mauricinho . . ." Don't be afraid, his mother was saying as she held him in her arms in the dark hallway of the police station.

Young Mauricio trembled, too frightened to cry.

Paulo had bullied him for years. "Oi, Mau! Você me deixa arrombar Dora? Fix it so I can pop Dora's cherry, or I'll beat you up."

"Vai te fuder. Go fuck yourself," he would reply, and Paulo and his cronies would beat him bloody.

"Come here, boy," his father said after Mauricio got a particularly vicious beating. "If you are going to keep sticking your neck out, let's get you better prepared."

Within six months, Mauricio was the star pupil at the local martial arts school.

By some perverse twist of fate, he was matched against Paulo in the martial arts finals. One-on-one, with rules, he could easily prevail, even though Paulo was inches taller. He also knew that if he did, the after-school beatings would escalate. He didn't care. Just once in his life, he wanted to see the bastard lying on the ground, begging for mercy.

"Vou fuder sua irma," Paulo taunted, seconds after the start of the match.

Mauricio flinched and Paulo struck him in the groin.

The referee whistled.

"If you let my brothers have a turn too . . ."

Another distraction. The blow landed across his nose. He heard a crunch.

"Bastard." Mauricio stepped back and touched his nose with the back of his hand. The hand came back bloody. The air was now coming only through the left nostril. He tightened his newly earned black belt.

Paulo lunged, but this time young Mauricio was ready. He spun around and flew, his leg aiming for Paulo's right shoulder. To his horror, he realized that Paulo was leaning, placing his head in the lethal path.

There was a sickening crunch.

An eternity later, while he was still in the air, came the pain. From his toes, up his leg, toward his groin.

He sunk to the ground in agony, and waited for a retaliatory strike. "The fucker beat me again," he thought, fighting back tears of anger. He had tried to stick up for Dora . . .

The strike never came. In slow motion, Paulo leaned back, toppled over, and crumbled to the ground, unconscious.

That afternoon, Paulo was x-rayed at the hospital in Barcelos and released. A week later, Mauricio was shoeing horses when his father came running. "Hide, Mauricio. The police are coming. Paulo is dead. Run, boy, run."

The warning came too late. He heard the siren in the distance.

Mauricio continued the onslaught on the dangling backpack. At some point during the evening, he thought he heard a knock on the garage door. Tentative, faint. It was probably the neighbor with benefits.

He pounded the bag until his fists and feet were raw, and his legs were Jell-O and his lungs ready to explode. Only when he finally stopped, did he notice the intense throbbing radiating up his leg. He looked down and saw the swelling around his left toes. I must have missed a kick. To hell with it.

He took another swig of cachaça and limped into the house.

There was a message from Leoni on his cell phone. "I've been looking for you. You flew off and vanished. Call me."

He considered it, his brain still fuzzy from the battle with the punching bag. When his eyes managed to focus on the clock, he decided it was too late. She'd probably be asleep . . .

He went upstairs, laid down and closed his eyes.

You didn't call her not because it was too late. You were afraid. Afraid she'd see through you, like she has since the day she appeared at your booth. You didn't trust yourself not to unravel in her arms. You didn't trust her to pick up the pieces.

Trust? Even his mother betrayed him. She promised she would take Dora away, hide her. She didn't do it. If he had known she would falter, he would never have agreed to leave the country.

He rolled to his side. Sleep. He needed sleep, but his heart and his mind were racing. He forced his eyes closed, and started his routine. He was walking through a forest . . .

He wandered up to the river. Ruby red caiman eyes stared at him.

What was supposed to be a calming vision shifted suddenly. His brain conjured an image of the caiman moving, and now for some reason little Dora was right next to him, and she was clinging to him, screaming, and the caiman lunged . . .

He sat up, gasping for air, chasing the dream away.

After another attempt, he realized that tonight his quest for sleep was doomed to failure. Leaning on furniture for support, he limped to the window and glanced out across the alley. The neighbor's downstairs was dark, but the multicolored flicker in the bedroom window told him she was awake.

He wrapped a towel around his hips and one step at a time hobbled down the stairs. He retrieved the cachaça bottle and opened the back door. The cold air sent a pleasant ripple down his overheated body. Wincing from the pain in the foot, he headed across the alley.

Tonight, he was not up for emotional risks. He only wanted the benefits.

46

O N HER WAY BACK AFTER JOGGING around Balboa Island, Leoni decided to make one more stop at the hospital. To see if Mauricio was around, a little voice confessed.

News of Gina's death had rocked her. Her first thought had been, Poor woman, abducted and left to die in the desert. What a world . . . The second thought sent a shiver down her spine. How will Mau take it, if somehow it turned out to be the LX's fault?

She set out on a frantic search for news. The police releases, and a call to Diane at KNOC did little to allay her fears. The official consensus was that Gina must have fallen prey to one of the gangs that were known to prowl the area. There was no mention of Gina's implant, or her connection to NBMC. She wondered how long it would stay that way. She wanted to talk it over with Mau, but he was nowhere to be found. Neither was Mel.

By nighttime, she picked up some posts about Gina on BrainPacers. By morning the site will be buzzing, she decided. If ever the project had a PR emergency, this was it. She called Rosie at home and convinced her to give her Mauricio's address. She drove to Tustin, parked

on the street, walked up to the house and knocked. There was no response, but she heard dull pounding in the garage. She had actually
fallen asleep in her car, waiting for him to finish. She had opened her
eyes just in time to see a man's figure, a towel wrapped around his hips,
crossing the alley between the houses.

"None of my business," she thought as she sped home, gripping the
wheel as if it were a sledge hammer.

The following morning she saw Mauricio standing in line at the
lobby coffee shop, and slid in behind him. "Buy you a drink, stranger?"

He turned. His surprise morphed into a smile as he eyed her outfit.
Clearly body-hugging Capri's, an emerald-green tee, and a runner's
jacket tied around her waist weren't what he expected from his PR person.

"Working Sundays now?" he asked.

"I wanted to drop in and check BrainPacers. I don't like using my
home Wi-Fi," she started to explain. "Not secure."

The smile that lit up his face made the detour worth the effort.

"My turn to buy," he said, evidently remembering the cachaça she
had provided on their recent flight. "What's your poison?"

He handed her the decaf latte she requested, and motioned toward
a table in the far corner of the patio. She noticed his gait as soon as
they started walking.

"You're limping."

He shrugged. "A dumb move last night."

No kidding, she thought. "I could've used your help last night," she
said, then couldn't help adding. "I looked for you, but no luck." Actually
I did see you, sneaking into your neighbor's house, but that's not my
business.

"I didn't get in till late," he was saying.

Like, the wee hours? Why had she even imagined this man would
have an interest in her? Why would she want it? I don't need this, she
kept reminding herself. Her life was settled, her career back on track.

The only thing this man would contribute to it would be heartbreak. She should just fire him from her life.

"Gina's friends on BrainPacers are blogging. I need to know how to respond. Before rumors flare."

"I'd appreciate it if you put out a press release. From Newport, not Pacers. 'We who cared for Gina are devastated. Our thoughts are with her fiancé and her family . . . ' You do that a lot better than I can." His voice cracked. He bit his lips and studied something on the opposite wall. After a while, he said, "The fewer details, the better. The cops gave me a whole lecture about copycats."

She was just getting ready to ask what was there to copy, but he stopped her with a quick shake of his head. She sensed herself pulling back. I'm not in the trusted circle. How was she supposed to do her PR job?

She took a sip of her latte, debating whether she should clutter his head with unrelated news. He should know, she decided. "That lab tech from Boston Medical Center . . ."

His cup froze in mid air. "An implant patient?"

She reached out and touched his arm. "It's okay. Nothing as horrible as what happened to Gina."

She could feel his muscles vibrating under her fingers as he drummed on his cup.

"I read a couple of postings on BrainPacers," she said. "If you can believe the rumors, the woman confessed to selling Vice President Spencer's biopsy results to the Boston Globe. The White House is furious. Heads will roll at BMC, from what I hear."

He was drumming so hard, the liquid was threatening to spill.

"What's wrong?"

"I'll need to look into that," he said flatly, as if making a note to himself.

"Look at it this way. We have over three thousand patients with implants. Odds are, once in a while, one of them is going to do something illegal."

He just sat there, rocking his head. She let go of his arm and leaned back, now wishing she could give him a good slap upside the head, as the saying went.

She tried to cheer him up. "A lady in Utah—also one of our patients—just won a million dollars in the state lottery. So the buzz now is that the LX helps you pick a winning number. If that doesn't drive sales through the roof, nothing will."

She forced a chuckle, but the furrows on his forehead told her he was not amused.

47

T HE ROAR OF MEL'S BIG RED overhead vibrated the roof of the Volvo as Mauricio pulled into the parking lot at Fullerton Airport. His spirits lifted. "He's either doing his morning spin for inspiration, or he already wrote the fix."

The revelation by Leoni that morning about the lab technologist had been gnawing at him. Right after they parted company, he had looked up her record. He was dismayed but not surprised that there was a gap in her sleep cycle tracing, dating back several days. The call to Goodson he placed immediately, tied his stomach into knots. "I'd love to send you the full EEG tracing," Goodson said, but she's nowhere to be found."

He tried to take comfort in Leoni's theory that out of three thousand patients, a few could be expected to go astray. No comfort came. Somebody was messing with his patients, and he needed to figure out who, the sooner the better. Maybe giving Mel a full thirty-six hours was too long.

"Maybe we should just notify the patients immediately," he thought for the hundredth time that morning. And for the hundredth time the thought was squelched by the image of Kevin ripping out his own implant. He didn't want a stampede on his hands.

"I'll be in the hangar, writing code," Mel had told him. "Can't hear the phone with all the noise." He got the message: "Don't call me; I'll call you." But the urge to drive out to the airport and check on Mel's progress proved irresistible.

Now Mel was circling the field, doing touch-and-goes, undoubtedly imagining himself back in the days when he could unerringly plant an F-18 on the deck of a carrier in the Strait of Hormuz.

Big Red streaked past the tower again, the ancient engine leaving behind the familiar smell of burning oil.

The tower controller's voice came over the loudspeaker mounted on the pole overlooking the small viewing patio. "Seven One Echo, cleared for another touch-and go. Nice work, Mel," the controller added.

He heard Mel's acknowledgement. "Seven One Echo cleared for a touch-and-go." Then Mel added. "Last one, Dave."

He paused to watch his buddy plummet toward the runway, squeak the wheels on the numbers, then leap back into the air, and climb at a dizzyingly steep angle, Big Red's engine growling at an ear-splitting level.

"Show off," he mumbled. "Get your butt down here and tell me how you solved the problem."

He punched the access code into the security gate and started to push it open, but his hand froze in mid-motion. Big Red's characteristic low rumble suddenly jumped two octaves. The engine screamed like a race car as the rpm doubled.

Mel's voice, mixed with the whine of the engine, blared from the loud speaker. "Mayday, mayday, mayday . . ."

His heart stopped. Sounds and images played out in slow motion.

Big Red was hanging in the air, rocking from side to side, like a boat on invisible waves.

The scream of the engine turned into a bizarre noise that sounded like metal parts dropped into a giant blender.

The controller's voice, frantic on the loud speaker. "Seven one echo, what's your emerg . . . Oh, shit . . ."

Big Red reared like a horse, going vertical.

Fragments of Mel's voice, barely intelligible.

". . . Failed . . . Can't control . . ."

The screech of metal ripping, coming both over the radio and from the distance.

Big Red's right wing separated. Then the left.

Mel's voice, distorted. "Fuck . . . FUCK . . ." A groan.

The plane began a slow spinning, like a maple leaf ripped off a branch.

Mel's words were barely intelligible. ". . . Broke . . . tell him . . . wrench . . . open door . . ."

Big Red was spinning faster.

Then the words became louder, clearer, as Mel strained to speak against the forces that have been crushing him in what was left of the wildly rotating cockpit.

"Boomer . . . Boomerang . . . sorry . . . love . . . Marty . . . love you . . . Marty."

Then there was only silence, interrupted by the explosions of his heartbeat and the silent scream on his lips.

He heard a soft whistle. He forced his eyes to focus on the spot in the sky where Mel's plane should have been. All he saw was a shapeless mass that was the hull, spinning wildly as it plummeted to earth. Above it, two wings rotating slowly, were floating in opposite directions.

"Falling leaves," he thought, as the incongruous image etched in his brain.

By the time the realization of what happened settled in, he was already in his car, peeling across the parking lot, hoping he could guess the street where Mel's plane—or what remained of it—would be.

He careened west on Commonwealth Avenue, veered right on

Dale, right on Artesia, hugging the airport perimeter, desperately searching for the shortest way to the crash site, as if a timely arrival could undo what happened.

Mel, Mel, Mel—the fucking engine, Mel—I told you so many times . . .

He barely avoided crushing a bicyclist and forced himself to slow down. Getting to Mel was not an emergency. Blaming the engine was useless.

The east side of the airport was a train depot. Warehouses and trailers and railroad cars in sprawling yards behind chain link fences. He had no trouble locating the crash site—it was already well marked by gawkers who appeared out of nowhere, their collections of kids in tow, toting camcorders and cell phones, oohing and aahing and chatting as if they were at a sporting event.

He screeched to a halt at a locked gate. On the other side, a distorted piece of fuselage stuck out from the back of a trailer like a bizarre grave marker. He rattled the gate, glanced around for an alternate entrance, then started climbing the chain link barrier. He made it to the top when he heard sirens approaching behind him. Doing his best to work around the coils of razor wire that topped the fence, he climbed down on the other side, and dashed toward the wreck.

"Stop right there," came the command over the police cruiser's loudspeaker. "Don't touch anything."

Without breaking stride, he circled the trailer, found the stepladder bolted to the back, and moments later he was sprinting across the roof of the trailer toward what was left of Big Red.

From the corner of his eyes, he could see the two-armed policemen running in slow motion, guns drawn.

"Freeze. Police. Step away, or we'll shoot."

He stopped and stared at the familiar leather jacket crammed into a mass of mangled metal. One arm was twisted up in a cheerful wave. Above it, where the smiling face should have been, there was nothing.

In ten minutes the area filled with an armada of emergency vehicles—police cruisers, fire engines, paramedic ambulances, and the ever-present TV vans. There was no fire to put out and nobody to rescue, but it would make an interesting thirty-second flash on the local news.

He stood behind the yellow tape, surrounded by onlookers, wondering if the pain in his chest would be less crushing if he could pretend to be just another gawker with nothing better to do. If he could pretend nothing had happened. If he could make it yesterday. If he only could . . .

He wondered whether Diane would be covering the accident. Then a thought flashed. I need to let her know. Before she finds out from some crass news intern. She had known Mel as long as he had. They had gotten together as couples . . .

Mel's wife. He had to let her know, too. That was his job. He remembered that Mel had a grandson living with him. Had.

Suddenly he knew what else he had to do.

He ran to his car and peeled off, heading toward the hangar.

48

"WE CAN SKIP IT, AND SAY WE DID IT," the pudgy morgue attendant said, huffing down the hallway of the Medical Examiner's Office. "No question of ID here. The NTSB is going to post him anyway. Let them …"

Mauricio shook his head. With the image of Mel's beheaded torso permanently etched in his mind, he had argued with Mel's wife Marty to let him take care of the formality of identifying the body. No widow should go through that ordeal. "This won't hurt a bit," he kept repeating to himself. "Trust me. I'm a doctor." His teeth were clenched so hard his jaw was turning numb.

"Let's do it." He had promised, and there was no way he was going to renege on the commitment, no matter how painful it was going to be.

Why hadn't he pressed Mel harder on the fucking engine issue? Oil leaks on Mel's ancient radial engine were a given. Maybe this time one leak too many.

"How do I know there's oil in there?" Mel liked to joke. "Because it's leaking."

The recurrent conversation flashed through his mind for the hundredth time.

"Mel, one of these days it will bleed out on you."

"So? I've flown gliders before. I can land that thing in less space than it takes you to do a U-turn in that 'Vulva' of yours," Mel would always say.

It was hard to argue with a man who had been pushing aluminum through the skies when Mauricio wasn't old enough to drive. Particularly when the man and the plane consistently managed to whip his ass. Vintage material, both of them.

And now they were no more.

"Sure you want to go through with this, Doc?" the attendant was saying. "It ain't pretty."

He shifted impatiently. The attendant shrugged, turned to a wall of small doors, pulled out one of the sliding trays, and yanked back the zipper.

He took a step closer. The smell of blood and flesh filled his nostrils. Trying to pretend he was back in time, working as a resident in the emergency room, he let his eyes run over the bloodied chest. He noted the shrapnel scar on the left shoulder and the tattoo of a parachute on the right side of the chest. He had seen them many times as he and Mel changed for surgery in the locker room.

Fighting back the bile in his mouth, he looked away. "Where do I sign?"

He was heading out when the morgue attendant handed him a plastic bag. "Want to take these, or should I send it to the widow?" Inside was Mel's leather jacket, blood stained, but inexplicably intact. On top was the metal kneepad that Mel, like all pilots, used to scribble clearances or weather updates in flight. The white sheets were splattered with blood, but the precise handwriting was Mel's. Mel's last words. "I'll take it," he said.

On the drive home, he held himself together by willing his mind to think of nothing. Not LX, not flying, not Mel. Just the white lines dividing the lanes, the traffic signals that changed colors at inconvenient times, the license plates, some standard issue, some personalized. ER DOC. PEDIPOD. STAR2B . . .

He parked the car in its usual spot in the alley, concentrating on aligning it precisely, concentrating on the sound of the garage door opening as he clicked the remote, making a note to have the rollers oiled. Anything to keep his mind off what just happened.

He stepped into the garage. Cautiously, as if walking into an earth-quake-shattered building. He clicked the remote again and let the door down.

Don't think.

He took a few steps forward. Right in front of him, on the garage wall, was a faded picture of Mel and him at a summer fly-in in Mojave. Arms around each other, big grins on unshaven faces. Big Red and Icarus II parked behind them, the older plane's wing hanging over the much smaller Icarus as if shielding it from the scorching sun.

His defenses crumbled. Years of memories exploded, scattered, and came crashing down.

He sank to the cement floor, buried his head in his arms and began to cry.

Leoni's heart stopped when she caught a news fragment about a small plane crash at Fullerton. Her knees buckled. Then the screen showed fragments of a plane that was green. Not Icarus.

It was late evening by the time the identity of the pilot was released. "Mel Morris leaves behind a wife . . ."

She grabbed her phone and dialed, but Mau's cell phone sent her to voicemail. She tried his house number. Nothing. Her anxiety mush-roomed.

She had learned from Rosie that Mau used to see Bruce Levine as a patient. Mel was his best friend. Losing him must have been devas-tating. Could his death drive him do something stupid? Her anxiety turned to panic. Answer the damned phone, Mau.

She hopped into her car, made a quick stop at the deli, and drove to his house. She breathed a sigh of relief when she saw his car, parked between the condos. The house was pitch black, and her knock went unanswered. This time she wasn't going to wait in her car like a jilted woman. He needed comfort; he needed her, even if he didn't realize it. Even if he was dead asleep.

The main door was unlocked. "Mau," she called out. Silence. She crossed the dark living room, trying not to trip, and was about to go up the stairs when she noticed the garage door.

She lifted it opened.

He was sitting on the cement floor, slumped against a backpack.

"Dr. Barcelos?" She stepped through the door.

He looked up and blinked. She hurried to him, squatted down and wrapped her arms around his neck. He seemed to have shrunk down in size since she saw him yesterday. He looks so human, she thought. It was like the Colossus's clay feet had collapsed, and he was now close enough to touch.

"Hi." His voice was hoarse, the eyelids swollen.

"You're freezing," she said releasing him and springing to her feet, relieved that he was alive, scared to leave him alone in his misery. "I'll be right back. You go inside."

It took her minutes to persuade him to sit still on the couch. She covered him with an afghan that was draped on the armchair, and hurried to the kitchen. It was neat as she imagined his operating room was. Simple brown granite tops, oak-colored cabinets, a central island with a six burner stove. Parked in the corner was a pair of cranes carved out of some red wood. And a fading, unframed picture of a dog, propped against the backsplash.

The refrigerator contents were sparse, and she was happy she had stopped at the deli on the way here.

"I brought a Caesar's with chicken," she called out to him, "a tuna sandwich, and . . . I don't know. Soup." It had looked like veggie soup, back at the deli. "Here."

She returned to the living room and parked the cartons on the coffee table in front of him, and went back to the kitchen. After trying a few cabinet doors, she located the liquor stash. Choice of cachaça . . . and more cachaça. She filled a glass, sliced and mashed a few limes, and added sugar. Her hands were still shaking, the nerves frayed by the plane crash report and his disappearance. She poured herself a stiff one.

She settled cross-legged on the floor, facing him, her face close enough to touch his knees. "You scared me!" she said, trying to sound as stern as she could. "I've called everywhere. Where is your cell?"

"In the car, I think."

"And the home phone?"

"I can't hear it in the garage."

"I went to the hospital, I called your ex. I even went to the airport." She squeezed his knee. "You scared the shit out of me, Dr. B!"

"The plane crash at Fullerton. You heard." He looked at her as if seeing her for the first time, and mouthed something that sounded like an apology.

She got up on her knees and brought a spoon of soup to his lips. "Don't let it get cold."

He swallowed and looked pleased. She handed him the sandwich, waited till he finished the bite, then held up the cachaça.

"Just hard to believe," he mumbled after another long pull of liquor. "Mel survived brutal enemy fire, but died practicing simple landings at his home airport."

"He died doing what he loved, Mauricio," Leoni whispered, wishing she had a more meaningful response. But what do you say to a man whose best friend just died? She knew that for Mauricio, a part of the LX project must have died too.

She rested her hand on his knee, and then jerked it back. Right now, he needed a friend, not a clinging woman. "He couldn't bail out or something?" she asked, immediately regretting it. What difference did it make, really? Finding the cause wouldn't bring Mel back, and wouldn't bring Mauricio peace. "I'm sorry," she said, referring to Mel's death as much as to her lack of tact.

"Sorry? For what?" he whispered. "It was all my fault,"

Mauricio noticed Leoni's questioning look. Of all the people, she would understand, he decided. "I gave him a deadline on an LX fix. He was probably sleep deprived when he went up." The pain in his chest made him hunch over. "My fault."

She now settled next to him on the couch and held his hand. "You were both doing what you loved to do. Pushing the envelope. You can't control everything."

She was right, of course. Come out to the edge, it's less crowded out here . . . He and Mel lived on the edge. Mel died. And that is the way it was.

He tried to forced down a few more bites of the sandwich, but his mouth was parched.

"I hope you don't mind," Leoni said suddenly, "but I had Rosie cancel your morning cases. And I created a nice eulogy page on Pacers, for Mel. You can check it in the morning."

"Thanks," he nodded. "I'll use the office time to . . ."

Leoni pressed a finger to his lips. "Tomorrow."

They sat in silence. Her hair swept his face lightly as she leaned back and exhaled.

"You're a driven man, Mauricio de Barcelos," she said.

It wasn't a question. Just a statement devoid of any judgment. Driven? How about committed? Obsessed? "There are things I have to do."

"Have to, or want to?"

"Need to," he whispered softly. Yes, it was a need.

"To survive, because without a mission your life wouldn't be worth living?" she asked.

There she was, probing again.

"Or, is it to stay ahead of your demons?"

"My ghosts." Stop now. It's nobody's concern. They're your ghosts.

Not Leoni's.

"What will it take to appease them?" she was asking.

He and Bruce had worked on this for years. You think you can find the answer in one night, Leoni?

"Whose forgiveness do you need?" she ventured. "Besides your own?"

"My own? That's the least of it." How about Paulo, and Dora, and Gina, and now Mel?

She drew closer. "Why don't you start from the beginning."

The words came pouring out. "How about we start with, I killed a man."

49

Killed a man. Just when she thought she was getting to know all about him, a broadside. The man was like an iceberg. Dark and mysterious and hidden. But she craved to know about everything that lay under that impenetrable surface. The tractor beam that had captured her mind at the tradeshow was now firmly hooked into her heart. Pulling her closer. She was the Titanic, and the iceberg was calling her.

Killed a man. "In surgery?" she offered.

He gave a mirthless laugh. "In anger."

She listened, his truncated sentences sprinkled with Brazilian words, as the story poured out of him. The life on the river, not far from Barcelos. The long walks to school, down a red packed-dirt road. His determination to protect his sister from the bullies. The martial arts competition.

"If only I'd kept my anger at bay, maybe I could've pulled the kick that killed him."

She suppressed an exasperated sigh. Taking responsibility was one thing, but taking on the burden of guilt for something he didn't commit . . ." If Paulo hadn't leaned," she said. "Or if they had a CAT scanner, and diagnosed the bleeding sooner. Or if your village had a skilled surgeon like you." She paused to let this sink in. "It's not all your fault, Mauricio."

"There is more." He stopped, and she gave him time to decide what he wanted to share.

"Paulo's father was the richest man in the area. Cutting rainforest, planting tobacco. Rich. The police were not interested in what really happened. Paulo, the baby of the family, was dead. Paulo's father and his other five sons wanted justice. No matter what it cost. While they were bickering among themselves as whether to send me to Manaus, or deal with me right there, my father managed to spirit me out of town. He promised—and my mother swore to it, they would follow, with Dora. Before I knew it, I was on a boat to relatives in the U.S."

He paused, his voice hoarse. She held the cachaça to his lips. He brushed her away. "I soon realized they weren't coming. I wanted to return, but my father forbade it. 'We didn't spend all our savings so you could come back and rot in our jail. Or be killed. We'll be okay,' he reassured me."

Mauricio stopped again, his body rocking slowly.

"I was fifteen. I should have known better."

"You were a kid ..." she started to say, and then held back. She was there to listen, not to express an opinion.

"There was nothing, for five months. Then I got the phone call." His voice cracked. "They raped her," he whispered. "The five brothers waited for Dora after school, dragged her into the bushes, and raped her."

His body was vibrating like a bowstring that had just released an arrow. She blew out a slow breath and pulled him closer. "She survived?"

"Oh, she lived. Long enough to realize she was pregnant. And then ..."

His voice became as cold and clinical as if he were presenting a case at Ground Rounds. "One night she took our small boat out into the lake. She took her clothes off and folded them neatly on the floor of the boat. Probably didn't want them to go to waste. Then, as far as can be ascertained, she let herself slide overboard, where the caimans kindly ended her life for her."

Afraid to lose control in front of Leoni, Mauricio leaped up from the couch, toppling the drink and spilling it all over both of them. "Ghosts? I practically killed her. Try running from that ghost."

He did his best to lower his voice. "So I made a promise to do something that would be a fitting tribute to her memory. So she would forgive me for not being there for her when she needed me most."

She was looking up at him, as if he were a "dead man walking." She stood. "Only you can forgive yourself, Mauricio."

He smirked. "Truthfully, I thought I was getting there. With the LX succeeding, and lives being saved, I thought I could forgive myself. And now Mel died because of my obsession."

He walked aimlessly toward the kitchen, turned around, returned. Leoni was following his every move.

"Sorry, didn't mean to dump on you," he said, feeling suddenly embarrassed by his emotional outpouring.

"You can't help them, Mauricio. But you're helping others. It's got to count, in the karmic ledger." She walked over to him and took his hand. "Let's get you tucked in. I'll clean this mess up later."

They were halfway up the stairs, before her last sentence registered. Was she planning an all-night vigil? Right at that moment there was nothing he dreaded more than being alone. He hobbled upstairs, his leg pain and his balance strongly affected by the cachaça.

She positioned him on the bed and pulled a blanket over his bare feet. She stood watching him, a silhouette against the dim light of the doorway, the curls glowing like a golden aura. He patted the bed next to him.

"Okay, but a little more space," she said, her voice suddenly thicker.

He slid over, his brain doing a miserable job of coordinating his muscles or was it his thoughts? Her long hair tickled his face as she settled in, and suddenly he became aware of her delicate citrus scent. She leaned on one elbow and ran her hand down his face, his neck, and let it rest on his chest.

His muscles relaxed, the pain of the day slowly giving way to nothingness.

"Sleep," she whispered. "Sleep, my tortured man. Forgive yourself and sleep."

When he woke up in the morning, he was tucked under the covers, wearing nothing but his boxer shorts. All that remained of last night's vigil was a crumpled pillow lying next to him. He picked it up. It had her citrus fruit scent. And it was still warm.

50

Mauricio squinted as the bright-red V-shaped object sailed through the air, describing a perfect arc over the beach. Lexie splashed through the shallow waves, leaped into the air and caught it.

"Here, Lex!" Diane yelled, walking alongside Mauricio. "Bring it to Mommy, Lexie."

Lexie eyed them both, then trotted out of the water and ran up to him. He scratched her behind the ears. "Good girl." Even Lexie can sense my mood, he thought.

The dog shook vigorously, spraying sand and salt water over his pants, made a pirouette and galloped back into the water.

"That wasn't nice," Diane said, taking his arm and continuing down the beach.

He had awakened that morning to an empty bed, a pillow still warm from Leoni's visit, and an aching void in his chest. He thought of Mel, and his mind spiraled into darkness. When Diane called to ask if she could leave Lexie with him, he leaped at the opportunity and offered to meet her halfway, near the Redondo Beach Pier. But the morning walk with Lexie, which Diane and he used to enjoy, did nothing to raise his spirits.

"I have to go to DC for the First Family fireside chat," she reminded him. "The one I got an exclusive to cover, thanks to you."

"Right." He remembered her saying something about airing out the Caldwell family skeletons. "When?"

"It's a bit up in the air. He has a Cambodia trip coming right after it. I'll probably leave tomorrow after the funeral. Scout the place out for a day or two. I'll let you know."

"I'll be sure to watch it," he said, and went silent again.

They continued walking barefoot through the sand.

"You managing?" she asked.

He knew she was referring to Mel's death, and shrugged. Managing was about it. Mel was gone. The man who had been his advisor, companion, and sounding board—his best friend—was ripped away by a freak accident.

"When I get back from DC, maybe you want to come over for dinner?"

The way she made it sound, she might as well have added, and spend the night.

"Di, I'm sort of involved with someone."

"Ah." She was quiet for moment, and then added, "I thought so, the way she looked at you in your office."

A step ahead of me as always, he thought. He had no idea that he would be feeling so drawn to Leoni back then. She had stepped into his life at one of the most embarrassing moments, and remained to help him through one of the most painful ones.

It struck him that besides Bruce and Diane, Leoni was the only person who knew of the tragedy that had left such a scar on his psyche. That was too trusting, with a capital T. He didn't think he would be ready, but there was something about her that touched him at his core.

"Is it serious?" Diane was asking.

He was uncomfortable discussing his feelings about Leoni with his ex-wife. He shrugged his shoulders. From her silence, it was obvious she got the message.

"Anyway, listen . . ." He heard a crack in her voice as she changed the subject.

"While I was prepping the interview with the First Lady, she let it slip that the President wants to reveal a piece of legislation he plans to submit for Congressional approval. Something to do with cutting production quotas for brand-name drugs."

"Di, is this in public domain?"

"I'm giving you a leak on a leak," she smiled. "Maynard Beck may want to know ahead of time, so as not to get broadsided. Are Antidepressants Obsolete? is the lead story on Monday. It has been Patty Caldwell's cause célèbre since Lori got her implant. "Our people are saying it's going to ding the pharmas, particularly Cendoz. You may want to let him know."

It definitely sounded like something that would affect Beck.

"The way Cendoz stock has been doing," she went on, reflecting his feelings, "the poor man doesn't need more bad news."

After Diane left, he continued walking barefoot through the surf, oblivious to the cold foam lapping his ankles.

Lexie rubbed against him, looking for attention. He took the boomerang, and hurled it as far as he could. The red wings spun wildly as the boomerang sailed high over the waves, describing another perfect arc. He caught it before Lexie could.

51

M<small>AYNARD</small> B<small>ECK</small> <small>SQUINTED AGAINST</small> the wind that was blowing across Fair Hills Cemetery, whipping up dead leaves. The wind stung his eyes, making the left one water. Driving to the funeral was time-consuming, but it would mean a lot to his young protégé. He owed him that much.

"Come on, Maynardee," Anabela urged as she worked her way up the wet grassy slope toward the gravesite.

His foot slipped and his left knee complained bitterly.

"You go, I'll join you." His eyes traveled the length of her clinging black dress, tailored overnight for this occasion, down to her toned calves, and to the red-soled Louboutin stilettos digging into the mud. A thousand bucks just for the walk from the limo to the grave site.

He paused to give his knee a break and surveyed the crowd. Almost a hundred people had braved the chilly morning. They clustered in small groups, talking quietly. An assortment of what he guessed were family friends, hospital staff, fellow pilots, and perhaps even a few patients. The man must have touched many lives. He was sad Mel had died the way he did.

Beck knew enough about Mauricio's business to know that losing a chief programmer was like losing your chief chemist. It was a blow that led to instant, often permanent, paralysis. A matador's sword to the soft spot of a charging bull. Perhaps now the young man would be ready to accept his help. But this wasn't the place to renew his offer. He would have him over in the next few days for a face-to-face discussion. Perhaps he would ask his head of R&D, Johanna, to join them and get involved.

He thought of Johanna and all that she had meant to him since he first laid eyes on her across the chem lab bench at Harvard. Whatever his supposed talents, without her, he wouldn't be where he was today—the creator of what was destined to join the pantheon of the five most successful drugs of all times: Lipitor, Zyprexa, Viagra, Fosamax, and now his Anadep.

Fuck the Ivy League bastards who threw him out. He owned the formula, and he had Johanna's talents and her undying allegiance. There was no stopping him. The setbacks of the past few weeks, Caldwell's idiotic proposed regulations among them, were just that. Setbacks, not derailments. Johanna was already pursuing several alternative drugs. Anadep was just the beginning. He was going to become the Bill Gates of the pharmaceutical industry.

He noticed Anabela waving for him to join her. He sighed and started working his way across the muddy slope.

Anabela, Johanna. Maybe he could no longer compete with Mauricio in regards to sheer animal attraction. But he had a far more potent pheromone: he knew how to give women what they craved. For Anabela, it was luxury. The shiny objects of life. With the millions now flowing in daily—hourly, really—it was easy. For Johanna, it was more complicated. All she wanted was to feel indispensable to him. The way things were going since the White House took aim at the pharma industry, she was.

His foot slipped again. Beck shook his head and wondered for a second who would show up at his funeral. He chased the thought away.

There was a lot of life and work still ahead of him.

As he came closer to where Mauricio stood, surrounded by fellow mourners, he noticed a blond woman. Tall and lanky, she wore a conservative black suit and pumps that seemed intended to keep her tall stature from being too conspicuous. The dark outfit emphasized the freckles that dotted her well-tanned skin.

The woman's position, an inch inside Mauricio's space, the backs of their hands almost touching, told him she was more than a casual acquaintance. Thoughtful, intelligent face, caring eyes . . . Good. The boy deserved somebody to support him in this very trying time.

Suddenly a spark of recognition flashed in his brain. Was she the PR woman who had been employed by the CEO of one of the suppliers Cendoz had acquired? His people said something about what a loss it was that she had quit shortly after the acquisition. The recollection was vague. My brain isn't what it used to be, he lamented silently.

Panting from the climb, he took Mauricio's hand in both of his. "Hang in there, my boy." What else was there to say? The fortitude on the young man's face was stunning. The clenched jaw, the deep-set intense eyes.

"Thank you, Professor Beck. It means the world to me."

Even in mourning, Mauricio looked defiant, he thought, feeling a surge of pride as he remembered the day he helped redirect the failing student's career. Have you considered neurosurgery . . . Eons ago. Little did he know how their paths would intersect.

He eased back to give Mauricio more space and wandered off to lean on a nearby palm tree.

Mauricio sensed a ripple in the crowd as the priest began the mass. He listened as several of Mel's flying buddies gave succinct but moving eulogies, and then he gave his own. The common theme was simple. Mel had touched many lives—saving some in battle, improving others in his work. He died doing what he loved.

Suddenly all was quiet.

Then, slowly, the drone of a multitude of airplane engines began to fill the air. It grew and grew, and then the swarm of aircraft appeared, flying toward the cemetery.

A triangular formation of five biplanes was in the lead. Dozens followed at a distance. No two were alike—from vintage aircraft like Big Red, to small twins, the collection was as diverse as he had ever seen in an air show.

The lead formation approached. Then one plane peeled off, climbing steeply into the sky, turning, and flying off into the distance. He recognized the missing-man formation. The triangular combat grouping continued on, the slot to the right and behind the leader now empty—a tribute to a fallen comrade.

He gritted his teeth, determined not to cry for a second time in two days. Goodbye, friend. I'll miss you. He craned his neck as the formation passed overhead, their roar drowning everything.

The sound of Mel's last words came to him, but the memory was too painful, and he stomped on it, hard. Soon it was replaced with the last sounds of Mel's engine, replaying in his head louder than the ones above.

Uninvited, a thought flashed by. Why was Mel flying in the first place, instead of laboring on the software patch?

On the day of the crash, after the initial shock had abated, he dashed to the hangar to look for the accessory drive that Mel used to carry his work. That's where the Delta Gap Blocker would be, if Mel had finished the work. He found the hard drive sitting on the bench next to the computer, disconnected but in plain view.

He took it to the hospital and plugged it into his own desktop. After scanning through the contents, he found a folder labeled "stuff." But all the files labeled with recent time-and-date logs failed to show anything of interest. The pages of code were useless.

He now focused on the planes still passing overhead. It wasn't like Mel to deliver "useless." His heart ached at the thought that Mel died without accomplishing his last task. It would be unfair to the man's life and his memory of him.

He was missing something.

He thought of the last time they flew together. Mel winning the mock battle. The two of them straining as a team to push the plane into the hangar. The engine, leaking oil.

Stop torturing yourself.

He thought of the model plane Mel was building for Mickey. Good thing he remembered to take it when he had ran back to the hangar to retrieve the external hard-drive. Mickey was clutching it at that very moment.

He had surveyed the hangar, hoping to find something else useful. The blackboard with little notes. The drawer misleadingly labeled "Exit Bolt Wrenches." A smiley face pinned to the wall. Mel and his quirky habits. But he saw no further evidence of Mel's work on the Delta Gap Blocker.

He now sensed the answer floating up from a dark recess in his subconscious, that place where ah-ha moments arise. It rose to the surface and burst like an air bubble from some prehistoric marsh.

Of course.

He slowly backed away from the gravesite until he was behind the crowd. All heads were still turned toward the planes. No one seemed to notice his departure, except Leoni, who gave him a strange look.

He hurried to the car.

Out of the corner of his eye, he noticed a man, wearing coveralls and carrying a shovel, limping as he negotiated the steep slope that overlooked Mel's grave. With his fingers on the door handle of his car, he paused and looked back. The silhouette seemed vaguely familiar, but the thought was replaced with a more urgent task: getting back to the hangar.

52

Mauricio's first glimpse of the hangar made his heart ache. NTSB had obviously commandeered the place as a center of operations while investigating the crash. Parts of Big Red were carefully laid out on the floor in a valiant attempt to reconstruct the general shape of the plane out of chunks of metal mangled beyond recognition. What remained of the cockpit still bore the dark stains of the near-instant exsanguination that occurred when Mel was decapitated.

He made his way across the rubble, stepping gingerly as if avoiding grave markers, and pulled open the EXIT BOLT WRENCHES drawer. Inside were several old screwdrivers, a handful of small oily airplane parts, a pair of rusty pliers, and a socket wrench set. He swept the tools aside and lifted the drawer liner. His heart sank. There was nothing even remotely electronic.

Shit.

Just as hope was fading, he found it. A small flash drive, concealed deep inside a 9/16 socket wrench, held in place with plumber's putty. He pulled it out and shoved it into his pocket.

He was headed to the exit when he noticed parts of the propeller laid out on the makeshift workbench that the NTSB had set up in a corner. The wooden parts were wrapped in plastic and sealed with red tape. He came closer. He now recalled the sound of Mel's engine over revving. Over-revving spoke of a propeller failure, not an engine malfunction. A chill swept through him. What if he or Mel accidentally cracked a blade when they were pushing the plane into the hangar? Using the prop for leverage was standard procedure, but . . .

He picked up one of the fragments. The clean shear that he saw, with no scuff marks, meant the blade had broken in the air, not on ground impact. It was hard to see through the plastic, but a detail on the fractured surface seized his attention. Before he realized what he was doing, he was tearing off the plastic wrapping.

The break went transversely across all layers of the maple and fir from which the propeller was made. He looked closer and felt a gut punch. The markings on the broken edge were unmistakable. "Meu Deus . . ."

At that moment, tires screeched outside, doors slammed, and the hangar pass-through door flew open.

"Dr. Barcelos?"

A figure stepped in. He recognized Blanchard, accompanied by a woman and two men, both in business suits.

They introduced themselves. "SAIC Raul Silva, FBI. Agent Christy Vanbruel, FBI. Joel Williamson, NTSB inspector."

FBI? Aviation issues were under the jurisdiction of the National Transportation Safety Board, not the FBI.

"Fancy seeing you in this hangar," Blanchard said.

"Mel and I share . . . shared this hangar for tool storage. I came to pick up some wrenches."

"Oh." Blanchard's beady eyes studied him. "And the first time you were here? Right after the accident? What were you picking up then?"

His mouth went dry. How the hell did they know, he wondered.

"I came back to get my iPad," he said. "It had confidential patient information." It was close enough to the truth to be credible.

The suits exchanged glances. "The object looks bigger than an iPad on the surveillance video," Silva said.

This can't be happening, he thought, cold sweat breaking under his armpits. Old memories bubbled to the surface. The police questioning him after he struck Paulo. The handcuffs. The interrogation. Suddenly the flash drive was burning a hole in his pocket. He had removed something from the scene of an active investigation.

The hangar shrunk to the size of a car trunk. He had to work hard to catch his breath. I have to get out of here.

Somewhere, Silva was talking. "The object you were carrying was wrapped in a tarp."

He forced out the answer. "That was the model airplane my friend was building for his grandson. I thought the kid would want to have it, sooner rather than later. I took it with me."

Don't let them see you sweat. There was no video surveillance at the airport. Certainly not at Mel's hangar. Who saw him?

"Your friend had cameras installed," Blanchard said, as if reading his mind. "Expensive ones. Broadcast to a remote, nicely hidden location, right there in the corner."

"Mel didn't put . . ." He shut up. That's what Lexie was sniffing when she was running around the hangar. Not rats.

"We found it when we were looking for maintenance records," Christy Vanbruel explained.

Mauricio was staring into the distance. They have me at the hangar on tape.

"Dr. Barcelos," Christy Vanbruel said, "if you're uncomfortable answering our questions . . ."

Blanchard threw her a withering look.

She went on anyway. "If you feel that you want to talk to your attorney first . . ."

The suggestion made his heart pump faster. "Ask away," he snapped. "I've nothing to hide."

Blanchard squinted at him, obviously enjoying the power trip.

"Were you ever involved in maintenance on the deceased's aircraft? Say, working on the engine, when the deceased wasn't present."

The implication was infuriating. He sprung to his feet. "You . . ." He managed to stop the word "moron" before it left his lips. "The crash had nothing to do with the engine. His prop broke and tore the engine off the mounts."

In the ensuing silence his heartbeat sounded like a jack hammer. After a pause that felt like an hour, the NTSB guy spoke. "Now Doctor, how would you know that?"

"Because . . ." He had nodded toward the unwrapped prop, then stopped as seemingly unrelated thought fragments snapped into place.

The chess messages that had been popping up on his computer screen. The license plate on the van parked near his parking spot the day he and Mel had their last aerial dogfight. The same van, leaving, when he pulled into the airport the morning that Mel crashed. The hacking attempts. The surveillance video secretly installed in the hangar. Mel, on the verge of coming up with a software fix that would block the cyber-intrusions. And now the markings on the propeller blade.

He looked up. "There was a man there. An avionics guy. Charley Zulu Avionics. Five foot nine, 160 lbs, dark complexion, Latin American or Middle Eastern by looks. Blue van, no windows."

"Wow, what a memory," Blanchard said sarcastically. "Maybe you have a name and a license plate too."

He shook his head. "No, I don't. Wait. Yes. CZM82U."

Blanchard gave a crooked smile. "You just happen to remember that, what, ten days later? Doc, you either have a photographic memory, or you're fu . . ." He glanced at Vanbruel. "You're feeding me a line."

"I just remembered it, okay?" he snapped back. "I thought it was an odd combo for an avionics guy. A little too brainy, you know?"

"No, I don't," Blanchard said, sounding unsure.

"CZ? The international symbol for the Czech Republic? I read it as CZ—M8—2U. You don't need to be a brain surgeon to remember that. 'Check. Mate. To. You.' Find the man who drives that van . . ."

"Thanks for the tip, Doctor," Blanchard sneered. "There were fifty or so vehicles parked here that morning. We'll be sure to follow up with all of them. As soon as we figure out what you were doing in the hangar."

Blood rushed to his head. He took several steps toward Blanchard. But the desire to strike the man instantly brought the weakness and uncoordination that he had experienced in similar situations, ever since the fatal fight with Paulo in Brazil.

He backed off.

Blanchard rose, was towering over him. "Go ahead, Barcelos, make my day."

"What are you trying to say, Detective?" he hissed through clenched teeth.

Christy Vanbruel slid between them. "What the detective was saying is that we'll pursue all leads. You go ahead and go on home," she said, steering him toward the door. "We'll be in touch again."

"I don't care if it was the Holy Pope himself that you operated on," Blanchard yelled at his back. "We will be in touch. Count on it."

He stopped at the exit, his heart racing, his mind numb by the discovery, and turned to the group. "You find whomever drilled those holes in that prop to make it fail. You find him, or I will."

Joel Williamson, NTSB inspector, glared back at him. "We most certainly will."

53

Bc8-f5, Nb8xc6, e5xd4, Ng5xf7+

Hunched over the chessboard in his office, Al was moving pieces at a feverish pace in a futile attempt to relax. Waiting for CNN to catch up with the news—the only news he cared about today—had been exasperating.

With the audio volume on the computer next to him set on low, Al let the hangar recording play for a second time.

"Fancy seeing you ..." He recognized Blanchard's voice. The sound recorded from Barcelos's cell phone was not as clear as the audio from the camera feed in Mel's hangar had been, before the cops ripped it apart.

Barcelos's voice, sounding strained. "Mel and I share ... shared this hangar for tool storage. I came to pick up some wrenches ..."

He paused the playback. Really? You went to pick up wrenches in the middle of your friend's funeral? The look on Barcelos' face as he ran down the hill from the grave seemed like that of a man on a mission. Whatever. To the cops, it would look like a saboteur returning to the scene of the crime.

Al fast-forwarded the recording to the part he had enjoyed most on the first playback.

"CZM 82U."

"Wow, what a memory."

Al had to admit, that was impressive. And there was nothing more satisfying than going up against a worthy opponent.

Smarter than my move, he admitted, chiding himself for using his own van. But with only a few hours to prepare, getting a rental was not in the cards. Anyway, he was relieved that now the cops had identified Barcelos as a suitable suspect to pursue, even if he implied that the van owner was the real culprit. He hoped the cops would take it as desperate accusation to save his ass. The only thing bothering him was, what was Barcelos really doing in the hangar, in the first place?

The morning that Mel's plane went down and Barcelos dashed off to the crash site, Al had slipped into Mel's hangar and copied the peripheral hard drive that Mel had been working on. When he combed through it at home, he found nothing that threatened his CloudFort access. But the uncertainty of what Mel and the doctor could have concocted, outside of the reach of his elaborate surveillance net, was still gnawing at him. Working against those two wasn't like playing chess, where every move was open to inspection. Here, he was operating half-blind, and that left the opponent a lot of room for truculence. Al didn't like truculence.

He glanced at the screen. Where the hell was CNN anyway? They would be broadcasting what could turn out to be his very last case.

Lady Kay's recent comment, "A few more, then we can pull the plug" was weighing heavily on his mind. He didn't want to pull the plug. Since Lady Kay came to him, he had made enough money to build more orphanages than he had ever imagined. With BrainPacers.com, and a little help from Facebook and other social networking sites, he had a treasure throve of good cases. Lucrative cases. To pull the plug, now that he had figured out how to work the system, would be a crime.

An idle thought passed through his mind. What if the tables were reversed, and K&K, instead of the LX, was the target? He stopped playing with the chess pieces, and addressed his computer. "Facebook search, women 40-50, Phoenix, depression."

A $20 dollar piece of malware made Facebook sing: several hundred names popped up on the screen. With a quick cross-reference to Brain-Pacers, he identified the four with the LX implant who were Dumas' patients. He smirked. A tweak of the sleep cycle to put them in a hyper-suggestive state, a properly timed call to convince them that Dumas had touched them inappropriately, and voila. The man would spend the next ten years in court, instead of the lab.

Hell, he could take out the entire Nuvius division. All he needed to find was a K&K employee who had the LX implant, instruct her to send out a couple of memos about some imaginary danger of Nuvius into the corporate network, and then tip the Feds off.

Could this be any simpler? BrainPacers was pure gold. The possibilities were limited only by one's imagination. Suddenly he wondered how much the maker of Anadep would pay to sink K&K's antidepressant, Fonmar.

And then he imagined how Lady Kay would feel.

A ping from his computer interrupted his fantasy. Barcelos' iPhone tracker showed that he left Mel's lab and was entering his own office. Al breathed a sigh of relief. If the good doctor had been trying to upload something, he must have failed, or he would still be up there, working. It appeared that the call to CloudFort Al had placed earlier had paid off.

Minutes later Al heard the staccato sound of Barcelos' fingers tapping a keyboard. Not even a friend's funeral could keep the man from working. The universally understood expletive "Merda!" that reverberated from the speaker told him the good doctor was still having a shitty day.

Al smiled and let his thoughts return to how he might be able to renegotiate his deal with Lady Kay.

54

Mauricio hurried away from the hangar and the authorities as fast as he could without raising additional suspicion, and before Blanchard prevailed over the more sympathetic Christy Vanbruel.

It wasn't until he reached his office at NBMC that he realized that the fingers of his right hand were numb and sweating, and he was clutching the flash drive with his fingers folded into a good-luck figa.

It had taken him an hour to rummage through the flash drive's contents and find what he had been hoping would be there. In true Mel form, it was hidden in plain sight, in a folder labeled "MISC", and identified simply as "DGB+BMR."

It took another hour to figure out how to open the document. The minute he read the subtitle—"Low level limiter for Delta channel settings, with BMR"—he knew Mel had delivered. Whatever BMR stood for, the file was the Delta Gap Blocker that Mel had promised. With luck it would prevent any hacker from reducing sleep intensity to the light-sleep levels that seemed to be at the root of the bizarre behavior exhibited by Kevin, General Schwartz, and the technologist from Boston Medical Center.

He saved a copy of DGB+BMR on his hard drive, pulled out the flash drive with renewed reverence, and bounded up the stairs to Mel's lab. A giant grin was plastered on his face. If somebody sees me, they'll think I flipped, he thought, and then decide he didn't care.

He powered up Mel's monster computer and slipped in the flash drive. He was about to start the upload, but decided to make a backup copy. Mel would have been proud of him, he thought as the disks hummed away.

With the backup complete, he tapped in his CloudFort access code, and now pushed upload. He leaned back and relaxed as the screens ran through the familiar sequence of authentication. With every confirming beep, the weight was lifting from his shoulders. He relished the thought that it would take the hacker days to realize his attempts were futile. And then, if the bastard decided to launch an attack from a different angle, he would be watching.

There was a loud buzz, and the upload sequence ground to a halt. He straightened up.

Moments later, the call window popped up. "CloudFort security," said a harsh female voice. "May I help you?"

"This is Dr. Barcelos," he said, trying to recover from the startle. "I need to update the program."

It took only a few sentences to realize that he was dealing with a hardened bureaucrat.

"New rules, sir," the woman said. "We need authorization from two people on your end. One from a Dr. Mario Ba . . . Bachelo . . ."

"Barcelos. That's me."

"And one from a Mel Morley."

"I have Mel's password. I can type it in for you."

"I'm sorry sir; I need to speak to each of you directly. Mother's maiden name . . ."

"Mel Morley can't speak. He's dead."

"I'm sorry, sir."

"Thank you for your sympathy. Now can you . . ."

"I'm sorry I can't authorize access."

He swore under his breath.

"Of course, if it's an emergency," she added, "I can call the VP on duty, who will come in and authenticate your request, then we will send out a pre-upload notification to the patients on our link, and . . ."

The words security circus flashed through his mind. He considered asking her how long it would all take, then quashed the thought. All he needed was to make a federal case, attract attention and spook the hacker. "Listen, forget it."

"Thank you for your understanding, sir." The woman's tone became more amicable. "A week or so ago we had a security breach involving your hospital. The person lost his job. I want to keep mine."

He was thinking of the irony, when the woman added, "The doctor who called with the same access request, just before you did . . . I had to turn him down too."

His heart missed several beats. "What doctor?"

There was silence while she checked her records. "A Dr. King, from Chess County Medical."

The bastard was a step ahead. But not for long. His jaw muscles tightened. The hacker must have suspected he had a fix, and had taken an extra step to make uploading to CloudFort more difficult.

"You're screwing with the wrong guy," he mumbled.

"I beg your pardon?"

"Nothing." He shut Mel's computer down, yanked out the flash drive and headed back to his office. If he couldn't do a mass upload through CloudFort, he would do it the old-fashioned way. Doctor to patient, one at a time. In the comfort of his own office, where he could keep an eye on the progress.

There was a measure of poetic justice in bypassing the bureaucracy and the red tape. He was starting to enjoy the prospect.

Minutes later, sitting at his own desk downstairs, he entered his password and cued up the list. There were 3578 patients now walking around with the LX implant. Just since that morning, twenty-five had been added by various centers across the country. For once, he wished the rate would slow down. Just till he could solve this problem.

He located the copy of Mel's fix, worked the screens, and pushed upload.

His heart sunk as he completed a mental calculation. At that rate it would take close to sixty hours.

"Total upload time—59.6 hours" a new message confirmed.

"Merda!" he yelled so loud that his voice reverberated through the empty office. First thing in the morning he would try CloudFort again. If their organization ran like most hospitals, Monday crews were miracle workers, compared to the weekend shifts. For now, he was sticking with Plan B. Even one-by-one uploading was better than waiting.

Where to begin was a coin toss. Alphabetical? Chronological? By zip code? By surgeon? The obvious answer popped up: He would start with his own trial patients, who had grown accustomed to his frequent updates and revisions during the early phase of the study.

He eyeballed that list. One hundred and seventy-six. That phase would be completed by early evening. Then he could even pause for a few hours and see if any unforeseen side effects were called in.

He came to Lori Caldwell Thorp's name. Should he include her? He decided to make her number one on the next batch—the post-FDA-approval group of uploads. Start with a winner, his grandmother used to say. He felt a catch in his throat. The real number one, his very first, Gina, was not on the list. It was a silly thought, but perhaps number one was not such a lucky place.

He reshuffled the list, making it chronological in reverse order for the second batch. Starting with the ones that had just been implanted, and working back toward the old-timers. If a few weeks could be considered old-timer. It seemed that protecting first the newest patients, the ones with the least understanding of what to expect, made the most sense.

He was about to start the uploads, but paused and e-mailed Leoni.

"Can you come help me draft a cover letter?"

An hour later, he caught the faint citrus scent even before he heard her, and it dawned on him that he needed her as much for her calming presence as her wordsmithing. Writing a letter had sounded like a good pretext to drag her in to work on a Sunday afternoon. PR never sleeps, as he thought she had said once.

"It's a software update," he said. "Kind of like a patch."

"Ah, patch," she grinned, settling in on the couch. "There's a comforting term. Is that how you want me to word it?"

"Well, enhancements then."

"Enhancements that can't wait till Monday?"

"Just do it. Please."

She gave him a concerned look. "You okay?"

Her touch on his arm sent a jolt through him. Given his confession after Mel's crash, this simple gesture now carried a whole new meaning. Had he shared too much? He hadn't decided how he felt about that. He flashed on the night they spent together. And I slept through it.

"You seem frazzled," she said.

He shrugged. "Mel's funeral got to me, I guess."

Her fingers were warm and soft and lingering on his arm.

"I noticed. You ran from there like you were going to a fire. I was going to run after you, but with all the people watching . . ." She trailed off.

With all the people watching. Was she worried about her reputation or his? Concerns about having exposed himself so openly loomed larger.

She was back on task. "Okay. How about we call whatever you're sending the New Improved LX version, number whatever."

He almost laughed. Mel's greatest detractor was suggesting the same terminology. New, improved. "Perfect," he said.

Minutes later the letter was written and on his desktop.

"Here we go," he mumbled, clicking on the icon and launching the process.

He was supervising the uploads when he heard her phone ring. Moments later she sprung to her feet. "Let's go. CNN is on the way here."

"I'm not talking to anybody about the Schwartz suicide."

She was already at the door, and gave him a nervous glance.

"A commuter plane crashed, and they want to talk to you."

55

"DETAILS ARE STILL COMING IN . . ."

Matthews, the CNN anchor, was live on the monitor in the board room adjacent to the NBMC lobby. "What we know so far is that at 5:00 a.m. Central Time, AirNet flight 344, a D-22 commuter, was en route from Chicago to Sioux Falls . . ."

The TV crew was hastily setting up the camera. Mauricio held his head up as Leoni adjusted the black tie he still had on from that morning's funeral.

"The force of the impact made it impossible to identify the victims, so DNA analysis . . ."

"I don't know anything about this case," he whispered to Leoni.

"Whatever you say will be better than a no comment. You can always cite HIPAA." She ran her fingers through his hair. "You look awesome," she whispered. "Do your best."

"Thirty seconds," the cameraman said.

A Google map with the plane's path appeared on the screen. "Radar contact was lost when the aircraft was just seven miles from its destination," Matthews was saying.

The map was replaced by a clip of the wreckage. Red beams from emergency vehicles crisscrossed the snow-covered hillside. Rescuers' silhouettes darted around the outline of a plane tail, protruding from a ragged crater.

The anchor's voice gave way to a staticky playback of snippets of cockpit conversation that the First Officer, a young woman, had managed to transmit to the ground controllers by squeezing the mike button.

"Captain, we're off the glide slope . . ."

Unintelligible. Then, "Nonsense, young lady." Another garble. "I've flown into here a thousand times . . ."

Traffic controller, cutting in. "AirNet 344, Approach, you talking to me?"

Captain's voice. "Negative, Approach."

A loud squeal as the First Officer keyed her mike simultaneously. "AirNet 344 is requesting climb . . ."

Captain. "Disregard that."

Approach controller, trying to sound calm. "AirNet 344, I show you below glide slope. Suggest you climb immediately."

Controller to Tower on landline: "You better get equipment standing by. This guy is all over the place."

The synthetic voice of the ground-avoidance system blared, "Pull up. Pull up."

Captain. "Shut the thing up. It's wrong."

First Officer, stressed. "But sir . . ."

"You can shut up too, young lady. There's the runway. Right there. Let's just ease her down . . ."

The recording ended.

The anchor started talking. "So far CNN has determined that the First Officer was a low-time new hire. The Captain was a former Air Force veteran, with a history of two medical leaves, and now apparently on antidepressants."

Mauricio felt his body settle into the chair as if in a fog. Not an LX patient. What did they want him for then?

Matthews went on. "The FDA has approved the use of antidepressant drugs for pilots since 2010, but that policy may now be re-examined. As both an expert on depression, and a pilot himself, Dr. Barcelos joins us now from Newport Beach, California. Good afternoon, Doctor."

His mouth still dry, Mauricio nodded back.

"Doctor, I understand you invented a device that cures depression better than drugs?"

"It doesn't cure it . . ." He hesitated. "It relieves many of the symptoms, with fewer side effects than most drugs."

"Drugs like the new one, Anadep?"

"Actually, Anadep is one of the most effective ones available. It has a good safety profile, reasonably rapid onset, and predictable dose-response ratio. As far as drugs go, it's excellent. But they all have side effects . . ."

"So, if the pilot had one of your implants, he would not have miscalculated the distance to the airport?"

"It's not that simple. The LX allows a patient to adjust the input as needed. Perhaps he was over-reacting to the drug . . ."

The anchor didn't let him finish. "A common side effect of SSRIs."

The man was more interested in sounding intelligent than learning the facts. Where was Diane, when you needed an objective interviewer?

"What you're saying, Doctor, is that forty-two innocent people perished in vain."

"I'm not saying that at all."

A parade of pictures of the victims streamed across the screen. The Captain's face caught his eyes. High forehead, deep-set eyes, lips creased into a friendly smile. Andrew Lewis, said the label. The name did not ring a bell, but the features were familiar.

"Can all pilots fly with your implant?" Matthews was asking. "Commercial, military?"

His brain stopped trying to identify the captain, and refocused on the anchor's question. "Uh, right. There's no reason why not. The LX would enable pilots to . . ."

Matthews cut in again. "What a tragedy, that the pilot's doctor wasn't up on the latest therapy. Thank you, Dr. Barcelos." Matthews vanished.

By the time he made it back to the office, his screen was glowing with headlines.

"BRAIN IMPLANTS BETTER THAN DRUGS?—Pilot's physician ignorant of new technology that could have averted the disaster."

"LX DEVICE COULD HAVE SAVED LIVES, INVENTOR SAYS—Newly approved brain pacemaker is adjustable to meet all needs."

"PILOT ON DRUGS CRASHES COMMUTER—Pilot misjudges location of runway. Side effect of antidepressants blamed."

"A NEW, INEXPENSIVE, BRAIN IMPLANT MAY BE THE ANSWER TO DEALING WITH DEPRESSION. Full report at eleven."

He swore under his breath. At a time when he needed a break from publicity, the LX had been thrust back into the limelight. The agonizingly slow software upload would not be able to keep up with the spike in new implants that was sure to follow. Icarus was soaring higher than ever. The heat was unbearable.

56

THE VOLVO'S WIPERS WERE BARELY KEEPING UP with the torrential downpour as Mauricio and Leoni inched up the 405 toward Beverly Hills. A semi swerved in front of him. Mauricio slammed on the breaks, and the car skidded, narrowly avoiding sliding under the eighteen-wheeler's belly.

The touch of Leoni's hand on his shoulder calmed him. "Maybe next time Anabela will give you a little more notice," she said.

Actually, the invitation had been from Beck himself. The text came while he was being interviewed by CNN. "Anabela is having two couples over for a light dinner. Can you make it here by eight?"

After Mel's funeral that morning, followed by the encounter with the authorities at the hangar, and valiant efforts to upload the LX fixes, socializing was the furthest thing from his mind. He called to make an excuse.

"I have something that may interest you," Beck interrupted him, in a tone that Mauricio had learned over the years meant no objections would be accepted. "And bring a date," Beck added.

"I don't have a date."

"What about the stunner you were with at the funeral?"

"She's my PR person, Professor."

"In that case, definitely bring her. I want to see who's behind all those headlines today."

He tried protesting, but Beck cut him short. "Listen, it's a small town. They see you and me huddling after a depressed pilot drills forty people into the hillside, tongues will wag. Trust me, I've been there. But if you and your honey are coming to a preplanned social event . . . that's less suspect. Verstehen Sie?"

He understood, all right. The limelight was ubiquitous.

"The other couple bailed," Beck said when they arrived. "The rain must've been too heavy." He smirked. "Nobody has any cojones anymore."

Dinner was served in the small dining room. Imported melon wrapped in Parma prosciutto, salmon en croute, white asparagus. Washed down with a Louis Latour that was bottled when he was still a resident. Quintessential luxury.

Throughout the meal Beck seemed to take a keen interest in Leoni. "Where did you study public relations? How long have you worked for this bum? Is he nice to you?"

Mauricio felt Anabela's bare foot stroking his calf under the table. The more attention Beck paid to Leoni, the higher Anabela's foot climbed, and the more agitated she seemed to become. It looked like the professor had learned to play her game a long time ago.

After dinner Beck stood up and announced, "We'll be back for dessert," motioning for Mauricio to join him.

"Dinho, meu amor. . ." Anabela cooed. "Can't it wait? We're having your favorite, Baked Alaska."

As they climbed the stairs, he heard Beck mumbling. "Today, it's 'my love' . . . Tomorrow . . ." Beck spread his hands in a "who knows" gesture.

Beck's luxurious study had the scent of rich leather and expensive cigars. It was years since Mauricio had been invited here. The lights were dimmed. The rosewood paneling and thick carpets muffled the sound. It was like stepping into a cave. He eyed the wall of pictures of Beck consorting with dignitaries, celebrities and presidents. On the other wall, heads of exotic African and Brazilian animals eyed him with glassy stares.

Beck poured drinks. "Think you can stand a fine Scotch, just once in your life?" The ice cubes were rattling against the fine cut crystal.

He accepted the glass.

Leaning heavily on the armrest, Beck eased himself into the armchair, and indicated the one across from him to Mauricio.

"Listen . . ." Beck took a long sip, and fixed him with his cold blue eyes. "This is not for public consumption, but K&K is after your ass."

He wasn't really that surprised. He knew Dumas would do anything to derail him, and could probably enlist his parent company for help.

"They are mounting a major PR campaign—your basic mudslinging defamation, but well organized."

His professional reputation was rock solid, particularly since the well-publicized success of Lori's implant. What mud was there to sling?

"I heard the word voodoo medicine is used in one of the ads," Beck said.

"As in brain implants?" He smirked. "That would undermine their Nuvius, which is based on the same concept. Talking about shooting themselves in the foot."

"From what I hear, they're throwing in the towel on their implant. Given your recent success, they're going to rally strictly around their meds. It has a far better profit margin, anyway."

He wanted to thank Beck for the warning, but at the moment the threat from K&K was the least of his concerns. He glanced at the pendulum clock, trying to calculate how many patient files had been updated with the Delta Gap Blocker by now.

"How did you find out?" he asked an irrelevant question.

"One of our reps sleeps with Dumas' admin," Beck said. "Pillow talk beats a memo any day."

He didn't really care. It was 9:00 p.m. By now the DGBlocker would have gone to all of the trial patients, and started with the new ones. Getting there.

"You'd think the FDA would put a stop to that kind of marketing," Beck was saying. "The bastards must have pulled strings to get it approved." Beck took another swig. "It's this kind of corruption that Caldwell should be going after, not pharmas."

It sounded like Beck was going to get back on the soap box. "Are you talking about the proposed quotas he's sending to Congress next week?"

Beck's eyes narrowed. "So it's true?" he said slowly.

"Di mentioned upcoming legislation," he admitted, wondering if he had stepped over a line. A leak of a leak, she called it. She didn't say it was off the record, and intimated that he should give Beck a heads-up.

"What I was referring to," Beck said, "was our President's idiotic idea of limiting patents to seven years, instead of twelve." The ice in his glass was rattling again. "If he thinks that's going to bring prices down . . ." He blew out an angry breath. "So, now we'll have quotas too."

Beck was staring at his picture wall as if the future were written there in bold letters.

"Anyway," he said finally. "You better watch yourself. You've become a major pain in the K&K ass. So they're pouring millions into a PR smear."

"I don't have millions to do anything about it."

"And they know it." Beck fell silent and studied him, his blue eyes hooded by heavy lids. He lowered his voice. "I can see what Cendoz is doing for grants. I want to help you fight back. We think there's room for everybody, implants included."

Mauricio wished he could confess what was on his mind: The only kind of fight that matters right now is one you can't help me with. But he couldn't share his problem, even with his trusted mentor.

"Do what you think is best," Beck said, "but with that commuter crash, I wouldn't put anything past those scum bags."

"Commuter crash?"

Beck seemed to hesitate. "It may be rumors. But if our guy's honey is not yanking his chain—in addition to other things she's probably yanking—then there's reason to believe that Dumas slipped one of your implants into the pilot."

It was a punch to the groin. "How could he? The news said the pilot was on Anadep."

Even as he articulated the words, the pilot's face floated out of his memory banks. Captain Andrew Lewis. Cold sweat beaded on his back.

Right after the LX was approved, a man by the name of Lou Andrews had come in to see him, an envelope full of cash in his hand, begging for the implant.

"Not if you want to fly commercially, Mr. Andrews," he had told the man before sending him on his way. Now there was no question the ill-fated captain was the same man.

"What does K&K have to do with it?" he mumbled.

"Probably nothing. But if he had an implant, and Dumas did put it in, they'll try to drag you into it." Beck chuckled. "Despite what they say in Hollywood, there is such a thing as bad PR."

Beck topped off his own drink and offered him the bottle, but Mauricio waved him off.

He felt nauseated. Now it was obvious why Beck wanted the meeting to be in secret. It was about Mauricio's implant, but also Beck's drug. "I feel like an accomplice," he mumbled. "Did they report this? If not, I have to."

"Hey, don't worry about it for now," Beck said. "Autopsy will show whether the implant story is true."

He started to protest, but Beck held up a hand. "Nothing is perfect. Drugs fail, implants misfire. What, they're going to pull everything off the market? Implants, drugs . . . Let people blow their brains out?" Beck waved him off, indicating it was a discussion for another time. "All I wanted to do was to give you a heads-up, because if K&K dredges this case up, they won't make you look pretty."

"I don't care how I look. This isn't right."

"What, you're going to sue them? Go beat the crap out of the Frenchman? Call the President? Mauricio . . ." Beck worked his frame forward in the armchair, bringing his face closer to him. "Mau, I've always called it like I saw it. Including pulling you away from certain failure as a biochemist. Mark my words. You are a ma-pa shop. They have billions behind them, and billions to lose. I don't want to see you mowed over. If you partner up with Cendoz, our legal team could help you."

He sprung to his feet, his hands shaking. He shouldn't need legal help. He hadn't done anything wrong. "Nobody's going to mow me over."

"Cendoz has resources beyond what . . ."

"It's my product, my battle, Professor." The anger was making it difficult for him to keep cool. Him battling a hacker, fighting for the LX's survival. And here was this crass commercial attack, a threatening cloud ready to burst and muddy the waters. "I'll figure it out," he snapped.

A long moment passed. Suddenly Beck gasped. "Oh, boy. You and I are toast." Wincing, he pushed himself up from the chair, and turned toward the door. "The ladies probably ate all our Baked Alaska."

Beck leaned against the window of his study, watching Anabela saying good bye to the guests down below. An air-kiss for Leoni. A lingering lip lock on Mauricio. He turned and wandered to the desk, the left knee complaining more than usual.

He poured another Scotch. He looked up at the ibex head and chuckled. Trophies on both walls. Four legged on one side, two legged on the other. Friends and enemies. He'd bagged all the important ones. Almost all.

It had been an arduous climb to get where he was standing. Barcelos was not the only one to know hardships. From clawing his way into a community college, working in his father's grocery store to pay for books, making it into Yale on hardship scholarship. Then Harvard Med, on a merit ticket. Then tenure as chairman of the Pharmacology Department. And then they kicked him out. In hindsight, it was the greatest favor they could have done him. Now he was at the top of an even higher hill.

The higher they stand, the harder they fall . . .

The business challenges looming ahead were daunting. The new quota regulations he just heard about would bring his empire to its knees.

He noticed the drink Mauricio had left untouched. It was good scotch. It had to be better than that damned cachaça. What was it that made the young doc so set in his ways?

They were both determined men. When does determination turn into obsession, he mused. When did one's good idea or a good product stop being an accomplishment, and become a rallying point for one's self-esteem?

He downed the drink and poured another, the fine scotch starting to have its effect.

From where he was standing at this point in his career, the height of the pedestal seemed vertiginous. A fall was not an option.

The phone vibrated in his pocket. He winced at the interruption and sent it to voicemail without checking the ID. The evening had been stressful and he wanted peace. He glanced at his watch. Anabela was probably in bed, watching reruns of The Bachelorette, wearing what she usually wore: expensive lotion. Her mind may be on a bachelor, but he didn't care. He downed what was left of the Scotch, and headed for the door. All he wanted now was to enjoy the fruits of his labor.

The phone vibrated again. A text. He swore under his breath and opened it.

"How did it go?"

His face softened. This call was a welcome interruption. He texted back. "As you predicted."

"What about the woman?"

He grinned and texted, "She's hot."

"And you are a bastard." A smiley face followed. "What do you think?"

"Hard to say. She could go either way."

"I heard about the new quota." A frowning face.

"Please verify first." He pushed send, and then added, "I don't think we have a choice."

57

AL PEDALED DOWN THE BOARDWALK as fast as his prosthesis would let him. He needed air. Or a game of speed chess. Or sex. Anything to distract him.

Six hours earlier, when he first saw Barcelos trying to deal with CloudFort, his guard had gone up. Out of paranoia—make that prudence, he corrected himself—he decide to confirm that Barcelos had not found a fix, or if he did, he had not succeeded in uploading it to CloudFort patient files.

He logged in, selected a couple of patients, and altered the settings on their Delta Channels. The program played back the Delta anomalies he had inserted, confirming that his ability to tamper with their control settings had not been affected. He let out a sigh of relief and erased the gaps. Testing, testing.

When he left the hospital a couple of hours later, the cell phone's GPS tracker showed him in Beverly Hills at Beck's residence. The bits of conversation Al captured from the phone were either incomprehensible or irrelevant. And then they turned to nothing but hiss, the phone no doubt left in a jacket in some butler's hands.

The stump at his prosthesis ached as he pedaled, but it was the least of his problems. He had mixed feelings about the commuter crash. On one hand, it was the validation of his work on national television. As he had instructed him in a call during the Delta gap, the pilot misread the approach charts, imagined he was landing somewhere in Hawaii, and plowed the plane into the ground. Mission accomplished. But seeing so many people die pained him. The distinction between the mass destruction he had just committed, and the destruction wrought by foreign bombs on his homeland was suddenly paper thin.

A small regional jet passed overhead on its approach to LAX. He felt a tightness in his chest as he recognized the shape of the plane from the pictures of the crashed commuter, and wished there had been a better way.

"Proof of concept," Lady Kay had said approvingly. "We needed to know that you could force a pilot to ignore his training and years of experience."

It wasn't clear to him why she needed additional proof, and it did not make him feel better. Nonetheless, he had to stay on her good side, at least until his commitment to her was fulfilled, and he could venture out on his own.

He slowed to catch his breath and was ready to turn around, when two men on roller blades slid into position on either side of him. He started pedaling faster. They kept up.

"Hey, Al. Boss wants to chat with you."

Flanked by two men almost twice his size, Al was ushered into a black Mercedes parked in the beachgoers' lot that was just off the boardwalk. When the door closed behind him, he had the distinct sensation of being buried alive. This coffin was quiet and smelled of sandalwood.

"Hi, Al."

As his eyes adjusted to the darkness, he recognized Kay, sitting cross-legged in the opposite corner, flashing her well-toned calves.

"Tell me about the crash," she said, her voice low and soothing. How was your day, honey?

He forced his reply into an even cadence. "It went by the book. With the high-speed impact and the fire, there is no way they will find the implant. If they do, it will be just another case of a LX malfunction. Just what you wanted. 'The higher they fly, the further they will fall' were your words."

She was just staring back, studying him like a cobra. He stopped babbling. Damn her. It was Barcelos' programmer's crash that interested her. She knows. His mouth went even drier. He tried to shift the conversation in a totally different direction.

"I was just thinking . . ." he ventured

She gave him a little laugh. "Tsk, tsk. There you go, thinking again, Al."

He clenched his teeth. This woman had a way of saying, "You're a fuck up," without saying it. He tried to sound calm. "When I took this job, you were talking dozens of cases . . ."

"As many as necessary."

"Well, seems like I'm about to achieve the necessary, but so far the income has been on the sparse side." His courage was flagging. "I was thinking . . . I would like you to consider . . . What would you . . ." What was it about this woman that made him stammer?

She held up a cautioning hand, the elegant long fingers bowed. "Al, before you tell me you want to go solo, I have another assignment."

So he was not a loose end. Yet. But he was past wanting an assignment. He wanted to go it alone. The entire western half of the Badakhshan Province had not a single refuge for injured children. He wanted serious money, not "another case." And more than anything, he wanted to be out from under this woman's thumb.

His voice got stronger. "What if I refuse?"

Her lips pressed together in disappointment. She shook her head slowly. "Al . . ."

"I can work this scam without you, Kay. There're hundreds of cases just waiting . . . And you don't need me anymore, anyway. I've created enough cases for you to go public, blame the implant, and bury it for good."

"That is for me to decide. In the meantime, I'm talking a big case, Al. All the research is done. We know who the players are. The only problem is the timeline. Less than two days. It's not much time, considering the prep work. That's why I need you. You're the only one who can do the magic."

Flattery will get you nowhere. He tapped his fingernails against the prosthesis, making a crisp metal sound. "How much for the magic?"

"What if I told you that instead of orphanages, you could build an entire hospital? In every corner of your favorite province?"

"Not funny."

"Not meant to be funny. And not only hospitals. You'll have enough resources to give your people a real chance to get back on their feet."

He smirked. Getting his people back on their feet was the American government's mission. His was to clean up after the mayhem. To take care of the innocent teens who had been maimed by mines. Those who like him had suffered unjust punishment.

"How does that sound?" Kay was asking.

"A number please."

She smiled. "The number will be large enough to impress anyone. Even that poor woman you've blackmailed two years ago."

"What?" He tried to sound indignant, but Lady Kay didn't buy it.

"Al, I do my homework. Crowley, the man Ms. Wakeling was working for? He was one of our strategic partners." She smirked. "How do you think I found you? Facebook?" She waited for his reaction, but he could think of no comeback.

"And now," she went on, "you're sorry you let her slip through your clutches."

He glanced up. Did she give him credit for being that generous? Letting the woman of his dreams just walk away free? Leoni was on a long leash. You don't know everything, Lady Kay, he thought.

"There is a price for every man, Al. And for every woman. When you tell Ms. Wakeling about the lifestyle you'll be able to offer her . . ."

His heart beat faster. The sudden prospect of Leoni coming to him willingly was tantalizing. "How much?"

"Fifty."

Right. She was yanking his chain. "I can make fifty thou in one gig."

"Fifty million, Al. In Swiss or off-shore banks. Half now, if you agree, half upon completion. By tomorrow night, you could be a multi-millionaire."

His leg began to twitch. He closed his eyes and visualized a chess set, the pieces flying across the imaginary board in a deranged ballet. Relax. Think.

"Al?"

It would take dozens of "interventions" to total fifty million. To say nothing of months of risk. She was offering it all on a silver platter. The choice was clear. "Tell me about the project," he said.

"It's been transferred to your iPad already."

It took him less than a minute to process what he was looking at. "You're one evil woman, Kay," he said finally.

She shrugged. "I like to think of myself as determined."

It wasn't until he got home and fast-forwarded through the other recordings on Barcelos' phone, that he realized that the plan—and his hopes of a big payout—might be in serious trouble. The summons of Leoni to Barcelos' office, the dialog between them, the keyboard tapping . . . His stomach knotted. Barcelos was up to something. All he could do was hope that it would not affect the electronic visit to Cloud-Fort he had to make, at that very moment, nor the next step—to be made the following day.

As he worked the keyboard, he remembered Lady Kay's parting words. "Al, the security video from that motel? I hope you know I'd never use it."

58

I̲T̲ ̲W̲A̲S̲ ̲C̲L̲O̲S̲E̲ ̲T̲O̲ 5:00 A.M. by the time Mauricio made it back to his house from the hospital. He slid the Volvo into the alley, shut the engine off and sat there, his fingers drumming against the wheel.

The previous night, on the drive back from the Beck's, Leoni had been quiet, giving him his space. He was thankful for that. His mind was spinning on how to protect his patients, and he was not about to trust her with that problem.

He had used his iPhone to check on the download progress back at the office: "367 completed, 3,211 remaining," the screen informed him. That meant that one by one, all of his trial patients had been protected, and the program was almost two hundred patients into the post-FDA approval list. With luck, first thing in the morning, he would figure out how to speed up the process at CloudFort without alerting the hacker.

His thoughts drifted to the conversation with Beck and the K&K drama. In his med school days, Beck's advice to go into neurosurgery had been a life-saver. Now, at first glance, his invitation to join Cendoz appeared like a career-saver. Then he thought of Dumas and the Nuvius. The man was a slave to his giant parent, who dictated his every move, planned his every study. Layers of corporate control. If he had been part of K&K, would he have been able to make an on-the-spot decision and save Lori with his implant? Not in a million years. He would be knee-deep in legal alligators forever.

An image of Beck's alligator-hide shoes flashed through his mind, and he wondered if it was caiman hide imported illegally from Brazil.

No way was he going to slide under Cendoz' yoke, he decided. Even if Beck's offer still stood, he would do it alone. Seeking a bailout by aligning with rich interests would be selling out.

Leoni's voice brought him back. "Turn left at the next corner. Otero Drive. Third house on your right."

He pulled up in front of Leoni's condo and walked around the car to get her door. She was outside already standing. She took his hand. "I'm too wound up to turn in. Can we walk for a bit?"

He found an old sweat shirt in the back seat and wrapped it around her shoulders. They made their way down the steep access trail that ran behind her condo and emerged on the shore of the small estuary that connected the river to the Pacific Ocean. Back Bay. It was low tide and the full moon revealed the marshy areas that served as a bird sanctuary. On the other side, he could see the Medical Center on a promontory. To the East, obstruction lights marked the location of John Wayne Airport, closed for the night to commercial jet traffic.

When they stopped walking, he heard crickets. A dark shape of an owl swooped overhead. Leoni snuggled closer, in an apparent effort to stay warm.

"Is this what your home looks like?" she asked.

It took a moment for his mind to grind to a halt, make a U-turn, and realize what home she was talking about. "Take away that tire noise on PCH, get rid of the buildings, add a thick forest over there, and a thousand night bird calls, and the smell of flowers . . . Exactly like home."

"Maybe someday I'll get to see it, your Amazon," Leoni whispered.

"Tell me more."

More than I already gave up? he wanted to ask. You want me to tell you what's it like, after all this time, to still feel like that at any minute somebody could start digging . . . The good doctor is a killer wanted in another country for murder.

She shuddered. "If we were on the Rio Azul now," he started, "this whole area would be untouched by human hands. That marsh over there would be home to a thousand species of birds and fish and . . ."

Hours later, lying in a small grassy depression between two bushes and looking at the night sky, they were finally overcome by the chilly wee-hour's damp air. He stood and pulled her up, one of her breasts brushing accidentally against his forearm, electrifying his entire body. He held her hand, now ice-cold, as they made their way up the steeply inclined bank. On flat ground, she wrapped her arm around his and leaned against him, her thigh matching his with every step.

They stopped at her driveway. She was breathing faster, and he wondered whether she was winded from the climb, or as nervous as he was about the prospect of spending a night together. Leoni had a way of burrowing through his defenses. He wasn't sure he was ready for more than he had already shared with her.

Then he remembered that his phone was still in the car, and that he should retrieve it and check on the upload progress, and that a dark cloud was hanging over the LX. The bulldozer of reality rolled over the intimacy they had just shared. The bubble burst. The day's concerns exploded in his head.

"I need to go."

She nodded, and then her face moved closer. Her lips parted, and brushed lightly against his. Before he could respond, she pulled back.

"Nothing is so bad that it can't be solved," she whispered. "I'm there if you need me."

As he drove back, all he could think of were Beck's parting words. "If you need, Cendoz is there for you."

He pulled into his alley and was about to get out of the car, when he noticed an unfamiliar sedan parked across the street, featureless and grey in the dim predawn light. He opened the door. A figure materialized next to him.

"Dr. Barcelos," the woman said, extending her hand. "I don't know if you remember me. Gayle Morris."

He recognized the redheaded Secret Service agent assigned to Lori. His heart skipped. "Is Lori okay?"

"You tell me." She produced an iPad and angled the screen to avoid the reflection from an overhead light. "Lori's in DC for the family fireside chat. My counterpart sent me this."

Moments later he was looking at a grainy night image of a bedroom, apparently shot with a camera mounted high up. A phone was ringing. He noted movement in the bed. A female figure, wearing a man's shirt that barely covered her buttocks, got up and walked across the room. He recognized her instantly.

"Lori Abrams," Gayle confirmed. "The 24/7 surveillance is the First Lady's idea," she added, as if reading his thoughts. "Wherever she goes. Hidden camera here, and of course when she is in the White House. With the President's blessing. We're under strict orders. Miss something, and we'll be washing dishes in the White House kitchen." Then she added with a bitter smile. "Not that we earned Mrs. Caldwell's confidence, after her last attempt."

Now Lori's back was to the camera. She was holding a cell phone to her ear.

"This was recorded two hours ago," Gayle explained.

At that moment a baby started crying in the background. Lori didn't move, the phone still at her ear. The baby cried louder.

"Must be an important phone call," he commented. "Is her husband still in the Middle East?" That would explain the off-hours call, and the determination to keep listening despite the baby's obvious distress.

Gayle raised a finger. "Watch this."

Lori continued listening to the caller, seemingly oblivious to the crying. Another half minute went by. Lori hung up the phone and headed back to her bed. On the way, her knee struck a chair, toppling it. Lori continued without breaking stride and ducked under the covers.

The baby's crying persisted. A minute passed. Suddenly Lori turned, rose on an elbow, then jumped out of bed and hurried toward the crib. Mauricio noted that now she was limping. She picked up the baby and rocked her, then settled into an armchair, unbuttoned her shirt and helped the baby find the nipple.

Gayle paused the playback and looked at him. "It's the first time since she got off Anadep and had the implant, that I've seen her sleep-walking."

Mauricio started to explain. "It's like patients on Ambien. We've seen people drive to the supermarket and do a week's shopping, without any recollection . . ."

He was reciting the explanation that he gave patients in his office, but his mind was running ahead. Suddenly, he knew. Lori was in light sleep when she heard the phone ring. Then, the caller kept her from hearing anything else. She went back to bed. The semi-asleep period ended, replaced by regular sleep. Maternal instincts then kicked in, and she heard the baby. The limp was from striking the chair that she could now feel. If he referenced the last three cases, it was classic Delta syndrome behavior. His heart started pounding.

"When was her last log-in?" he asked, his voice louder than he intended.

Gayle shrugged. "She likes to do it just before going to bed. Around midnight, I guess."

His brain was racing through the likely sequence of events. The DGBlocker upload had not reached her yet. A gap could have been programmed into Lori's sleep channel. Then came the phone call. But there was only one way to be sure.

He glanced at his watch. Five a.m. here, eight on the East Coast. He started to get back into the car.

"They're getting ready for the broadcast," Gayle said. "Should I let her mother know?"

He rubbed his forehead and realized it was damp. If Lori's LX had been hacked, and the hacker was contacting her . . .

"Gayle, I need you to call them and postpone the event. Tell them to get the White House doc and go check on her. I'll call . . ." Without looking at the records, there was no way to know whether Lori was among those who have already been protected by the DGBlocker. He had chosen to go in reverse chronological order. His gut told him she wasn't. His mind told him he had to be sure before he panicked.

Gayle was shaking her head vigorously. "I can't do that. The broadcast is . . ."

"Screw the broadcast. Go call them, now. And tell them not to let her out of their sight till they hear from me."

He screeched out of the driveway without waiting for Gayle's reply.

59

Racing up the stairwell three steps at a time, Mauricio could think of nothing but what he would find when he opened Lori's record on Mel's scanning computer.

He emerged on the sixth floor, ran down the hall, punched in the combination and dove into the surgeons' lounge. Half-a-dozen surgeons were sitting in battered overstuffed armchairs, watching TV and talking. Half-eaten breakfast trays and donut boxes, and dilapidated newspapers were abandoned on the coffee tables and counters.

One of the surgeons called out to him. "Hey, Mau, isn't that your old lady talking to the Caldwells?"

"Have her ask him about reimbursements," chimed in another.

He glanced at the TV screen. In one of the White House rooms, the President sat relaxed on one end of a large couch, Lori, at the other, looked like a bird ready to fly off. The First Lady in an armchair, close to the President, with the First Dog at her feet, looked in control. Diane was in a separate armchair facing them. A pair of white-gloved attendants poured coffee into cups decorated with the White House logo.

"Folks, like any family, Lori and I have had our differences. It's no secret that Lori's husband, my son-in-law Major Joey Thorp, is serving in the Middle East . . ."

"His third tour of duty," Lori cut in.

Patty Caldwell threw her a stern glance.

Any hope that Gayle would stick her neck out and abort the event had vanished. He found an empty spot in the back of the room.

Someone turned up the volume. His eyes were glued to the screen.

"Make no mistake. In times when the country is in danger, personal sacrifice . . ."

"Mau," said one of the surgeons without taking his eyes off the tube, "didn't you stick one of your wires into the First Daughter a few weeks ago?"

"And pissed off Carl Talon by second-guessing him," said another. A few laughed. Others yelled, "Quiet!"

The camera cut to Lori, tapping her foot, her jaw clenched.

"Hey, Barcelos, the wire isn't working," somebody teased. "She looks like she wants to strangle daddy."

He flashed on Gayle's surveillance video. Oh, shit.

It would take precious minutes to dash into the locker room, change into scrubs, run down the OR hallway and make it to the main terminal and the large screen in Mel's lab for an optimal look at Lori's tracings. If he could confirm the presence of Delta gaps, he would have a solid reason to intervene . . .

No time. He leaped to one of the computer terminals at the back wall. His fingers raced across the keyboard. Lori's record started to unfold across the screen. He glanced at the TV. Lori was shaking visibly. When he looked back at the computer screen, the record was replaced with an ACCESS DENIED message.

Cold sweat coated his back, wicking into his shirt. Feverishly working the keyboard with one hand, he reached for the house phone and dialed Bruce Levine.

Lori's voice was coming from the TV. "When my dad didn't intercede on Joey's behalf and kept him from being mobilized, I was devastated . . ."

His cell chirped with a text message. He glanced down. Sender: unknown. Subject: top priority.

The house phone clicked. "Doctor Levine speaking."

"Bruce, can you pull up Lori Caldwell's record?"

"Oh, hi, Mau . . ."

"Now! Check the record now," he yelled.

Several heads turned toward him.

"Keep it down, we're trying to listen!"

"Okay, I have Lori's record in front of me," Bruce said.

"Check for Delta gaps."

"You mean those breaks in sleep periods we talked . . ."

"Yes, yes. You have to go slowly and expand the timeline. Do you see them? Yes or no?"

"Well . . ." Bruce droned. "I guess there's one . . ."

"When?"

"Sort of hard to see on the small screen. Hmmm . . . Around 3:00 A.M., I'd say."

"Today?"

"Yep. This morning."

That would be right around the time Lori sleepwalked to the computer.

His phone chirped a reminder. Same unknown sender. Still top priority. House phone pinned under his ear, one hand on the keyboard, the other on the cell phone, he managed to open the text.

The receiver slipped from his shoulder and banged on the floor as he began to read the message.

"Dr. Barcelos, I have tried to reconcile with my father . . ."

It was a horse kick to the stomach. He turned to the room and yelled, "How do I get the White House?"

They eyed him as if he were insane.

"Get elected," one of the physicians laughed.

"Someone call 911," he blurted out.

Everything went into slow motion. The people in the lounge, turning toward him, then away. One reaching for a cell phone . . . ever so slowly.

He glanced back to the text message. "By the time you read this it will be too late . . ."

On the screen, the President, the First Lady, and Diane smiled pleasantly, while Lori chewed on her lips.

He banged out 911 on the house phone. A calm voice came from the receiver. "Nine one one, what is your emergency?"

"I need the White House. Now."

"Do you have an emergency?"

He was beyond rational thinking. *Lori, don't do it,* every cell in his brain was screaming.

"Just connect me, damn it."

"Sir, if you use profanities, I will have to hang up."

He took a deep breath. "I'm Dr. Barcelos," he said, forcing himself to articulate, his Brazilian accent making it difficult. "Lori Caldwell Thorp, the President's daughter, is my patient . . ."

On the TV, Lori was now standing, her body tense as a bow. Her forehead glistened with perspiration. Her neck arteries were hammering rapidly.

"Doctor, do you need the paramedics?"

"I need you to place the call," he yelled.

"Jeez, Barcelos, we're trying to listen, man!"

"Pipe down, Mau."

He slammed the receiver and dashed out into the hallway, whipping out his wallet as he went. He found the card the First Lady had given the day Lori was discharged and dialed the number.

A hushed voice answered. "Agent Sides, answering for Mrs. Caldwell."

"This is Dr. Barcelos," he said, his voice adjusting to the whisper. "Lori . . . I think she's going to kill her father . . ."

"Say again?"

"Just stop her. She sent me a message . . . Don't let her near the President!"

The line went dead.

He bolted back into the lounge. On the TV, Lori was moving to a position behind her father, one hand in her pocket. Two figures dressed in blue suits appeared on the periphery of the screen. One was pressing a finger to his ear. The other had one hand inside his jacket. The figures paused in mid motion.

He leaned forward, willing them to move.

Suddenly the image went to static. Moments later, the announcer's face appeared. "We seem to have lost our connection. We'll go to break here, and continue our coverage on the other side."

A commercial for a malpractice law firm started playing. " . . . You may be entitled to monetary compensation. Call 800-BAD-DRUG . . ." Several staff got up for coffee refills. The conversation in the lounge resumed.

He sank deeper into the armchair, helplessly staring at the message on his phone. "Dr. Barcelos, by the time you read this, he will be dead."

60

MAURICIO WANDERED OUT OF THE LOUNGE, head down. How could he have been so wrong? With all that had happened recently, his nerves must have been so raw, he had lost all objectivity, all ability to make a rational decision . . .

After his outburst and call, the broadcast went to a brief commercial and then resumed, with the First Family gathering seemingly undisturbed. "We missed a tender moment during the signal loss," the announcer said. "Lori was hugging her father, whispering 'I love you, Daddy.'"

How could he have misread what was going on?

No, damn it. Any normal person would have reacted the same way. The message he had received on his iPhone, seemingly from Lori, replayed in his mind, branded there by the rush of adrenaline that it had launched.

"Dr. Barcelos, by the time you read this, it will be too late. I've done my best to reconcile. But my father has always been a monster. Today, he will pay. By the time you read this, he will be dead. I'm sorry. You have been very kind to me. Good bye."

He descended the stairs, walking slowly, trying to come to terms with what just happened. He had never felt so powerless as when he saw Lori standing behind the President, her arms wrapping around his neck. Never so conflicted, as when he realized that the President was safe, but his own credibility had been forever destroyed.

He reached his floor when his phone vibrated.

"Dr. Barcelos?"

Already a reporter looking for a pound of flesh? He hung up.

The phone rang again.

"Dr. B, this is Chad Michaels, in the ER."

Now what? Last time he was in that ER he was working on Lori. No, last time he was figuring out what put Sandy into a stupor in the middle of the night. Neither memory was welcome.

"I have Jules Karp here," Chad was saying. "He's complaining of vomiting."

"Who is Jules Karp?" And why the fuck are you calling me about vomiting?

"I think you know him as Spike. LX patient. He said he was re-setting his sleep cycle and suddenly got sick. . ."

"Spike is always resetting his sleep cycle. Make him put it back where it was, and send him home." Right now the last thing he wanted to deal with was Spike's antics.

Chad sounded reluctant. "He says same thing happened yesterday. When he was resetting. He looks pretty dehydrated. Mind if we keep him?"

You can marry him, for all I care. "Do that. Admit him to his primary, give him some . . . Hey, you're the ER doc; you know what to do for vomiting." He hung up.

"Dr. Barcelos, you have . . ." Rosie called out to him as he stormed past her and swung the door open to his inner office.

" . . . Visitors," Rosie finished the sentence.

He stared at the three men in dark blue suits standing in front of him. The room was suddenly hot.

"We're here to investigate your threat to the President of the United States," one of the suits said, taking a step toward him.

He took a step back. His voice cracked. "It turned out to be a false alarm. What would you do if you got a text …" He reached to pull out his phone.

The agent whipped out a gun.

He froze. "Just a phone." He tried to sound calm, but his heart was racing.

"Slowly, sir."

He withdrew the phone, tapped replay and turned the screen so the man could see. "What would you do if you saw this?" he repeated.

The man holstered his gun, looked at the screen, then back at him, then to the screen again, confusion clouding his face.

"If I were whites … You'd be check-mated in three moves," the agent said.

"What …" The screen showed chess pieces facing off from adjacent squares. His throat closed up. He punched the screen. "It was right here … You can check my records …"

"We're checking as we speak. In the meantime, please turn around and put your hands behind your back."

He heard the last sentence as if in a dream. "Are you for real?"

The agent was pulling out his hand cuffs. "Threatening the President is a federal offense, sir. Turn around."

His reptilian brain screaming for him to run, his body turned toward the door on its own volition. "Corre, Mauricio," his father was yelling. Run. One leg stepped forward, then the other.

The agents rushed toward him. "Freeze."

At that moment Rosie poked her head through the door. "Dr. B, the White House … I mean the President's wi …" she babbled. "Mrs. Caldwell is on the line. She wants to speak to you. Alone," Rosie added, eyeing the agents.

The agents exchanged deflated glances. "We'll be right outside this door, Sir."

"Stand by for Mrs. Caldwell," a man's voice said. There was static, and then Patty Caldwell's face appeared on his computer screen.

"Well, Dr. Barcelos?"

The chill in her voice made him cringe. He repeated the text of the message he had received.

"What I hear you saying," Patty Caldwell interrupted, squinting, "is that you believed a text from an unknown sender."

"Mrs. Caldwell, I was afraid there might be an implant malfunction. Or unauthorized access . . ."

Her voice rose. "I thought you said the LX was immune to unauthorized access. 'Virtually impregnable,' I believe were the words on your website."

He felt like a schoolboy being taken to task. "I'm doing everything I can to make sure . . ."

"I don't give a damn what you're doing. I have a hysterical daughter and a furious President on my hands." She took a ragged breath. "Dr. Barcelos, you saved Lori's life, so I'm going to do my best to persuade my husband to let this one slide. But by the time we get back from our trip, I want to hear that you took steps to ensure your implant is invulnerable. Are we clear?"

He nodded.

"In the meantime, we're taking Lori with us."

As she started to move away from the camera, he called out. "Mrs. Caldwell? The agents are here to arrest me."

"Don't worry," Patty Caldwell said. "They're already gone."

61

Still shaking from Lori's on-air fiasco, and shaken from his encounter with the Secret Service agents, Mauricio stormed into Bruce's office. A woman jumped up from the chair next to Bruce's desk. He recognized Sandy McBride.

"Uh, we're in session," Bruce pointed out, visibly irritated.

He met Sandy's startled look. Panting and wide-eyed after the recent near-arrest, he must have looked more in need of Bruce's psychiatric services than her.

"Excuse me Ms. McBride," he mumbled. "I have an emergency."

He held the door open and she hurried out, clutching her purse.

"I hope you have a good reason for this," Bruce huffed.

It took him a several minutes to brief Bruce on what had happened. He left out Mel's murder. There was just so much truth the straight-laced psychiatrist could handle in one session. As it is, the cyber hacking theory was definitely straining Bruce's credence.

"Let me repeat what I hear you saying," Bruce said in his most sincere psychoanalyst tone. "Somehow, for some reason, somebody gains access to the main LX control system at CloudFort. Am I right so far?"

Bruce tented his fingers and propped his head on the tips.

"The how involves using a stolen LX module—a stolen patient."

"Gina?"

"Yes, Gina," Mauricio said, "to gain entry into the system and establish control. It's called the Trojan Horse."

Bruce nodded. "And then the hacker manipulates the channels to alter behavior."

"Not behavior," Mauricio corrected. "Not directly, anyway. He adjusts one channel, the one that controls sleep, to create a short period of time during which sleep is light. The Delta channel gap."

Bruce was frowning.

"He assigns the access time and duration into the outgoing program. The patient logs in as scheduled, and downloads their new settings into the module. Except that now the new settings include an adjustment to the Delta channel inserted by the hacker."

"But why would the patient accept it?"

Mauricio scoffed, "The code is hidden. You'd have to be a programming whiz to see it. And if someone would notice, it looks like it comes from their provider. They have reason to trust what we are sending them. See input; push accept."

"Okay, I get it; I get it," Bruce said growing impatient.

Mauricio continued, "Patient is programmed, goes on their merry way. At a preset time, the Delta channel fires or rather misfires, and they go into a light sleep. A semi-awake state . . ."

"Like what I use for hypnotherapy?"

"Exactly," Mauricio nodded. So far Bruce seemed to be getting it. "At that precise moment—judging by the short duration we see in the gaps, it's just a two to three minute window—the hacker calls them with orders to perform a certain task when they wake up. I suspect he also tells them to forget the conversation. Standard hypnosis."

Bruce studied him, and then let out a short laugh.

"What's funny?"

"Sorry." Bruce cleared his throat. "You have to admit, it does sound like the movie, Dial M for Murder."

"Or The Manchurian Candidate, or a hundred other variations on the same theme. Laugh all you want. It's happening. To our patients. As we speak."

Bruce sat up and assumed a more attentive attitude. "You know, it's the scientific consensus that no one can be forced to do anything under hypnosis that they wouldn't do while awake. And if you believe in free will . . ."

"Free will has nothing to do with it." He jumped up and moved closer, determined to have his partner understand. "The hacker uses the sedation period to alter the victim's perception of reality, not their free will."

"I don't get it."

"Take Kevin. Someone made him believe that he was getting a call from you—his respected advisor. His conscience, for practical purposes. And his conscience was telling him to do the right thing. So he did."

Bruce was shaking his head.

"And the lab tech who leaked the biopsy results . . ."

Bruce interrupted. "That was all about greed. She had, what, two hundred grand deposited in her account?"

"Which she ultimately refused. And her attorney said she remembers a call on her graveyard shift from someone who claimed to be the VP's surgeon, who urgently needed the results. So she gave it to him."

Bruce seemed to be yielding.

"Bruce, if you told me to kill Lexie, I'd refuse. But if you persuaded me that she had rabies, I'd put her down. It's not messing with one's value system. It's about manipulating the perception of what is real."

Bruce stopped shaking his head. "If you subscribe to that, then I could hypnotize a patient into believing that he was a policeman and he had to shoot somebody to defend an innocent bystander and . . ."

"Maybe not with regular hypnosis," Mauricio clarified. "But enhance hypnosis with drugs, and it would work."

Bruce tilted his head, considering. "Granted. There have been reports to that effect."

"And now we know that when it comes to boosting the hypnotic effect, that little Delta channel gap is even stronger than drugs. It opens a direct line to the patient's perception of what is real." He paused to let Bruce absorb it, then added, "With deep brain electrical manipulation that the LX is designed to provide, there is probably no limit."

Bruce persisted. "So, why would anybody want to do that? It's a long way to go for some sick perversion."

"It's probably not a pimply-faced kid sitting on a sofa in the basement. These are high-profile cases, with far ranging impact. I'll bet somebody's paying the hacker big bucks to control behavior to achieve their goals."

Bruce was shaking his head. "Mau, if I didn't know better, I'd say you are suffering from delusions. Maybe we should revisit this theory of yours when your friend's death isn't weighing so heavily."

He bolted out of the chair. After all the explanations, Bruce still didn't get it. "I don't care if you believe me," he practically shouted. "I'm already doing something to stop it. As my research partner, I thought you should know," he added more quietly. "I'm uploading a patch that Mel wrote before he was killed."

Bruce jerked in his chair and set up. "Did you say Mel was killed?"

"In a crash," he hastened to add, hoping he sounded believable. "Before Mel was killed in a crash."

All he needed was to add "paranoia" to Bruce's list of suspicions. He glanced at his phone. "One third of the patients are now safe from the hacking into their Delta channel. And then I'm going to figure out how to go after the bastard and . . ." He cut his sentence short. Bruce might add "homicidal ideation" to "psychotic delusions" and "paranoia."

Bruce leaned forward on his elbows. "You're contacting patients directly and sending them a software patch, outside of the system?"

"One by one."

"Mau, do you realize the panic this could cause?" he asked in disbelief.

"It goes out with a nice letter."

Bruce shook his head. "What, something like 'Sorry Mrs. Jones, your LX might get hacked, so here is a patch for the defect?' All it takes is one Nervous Nelly like Kevin who starts blogging, and . . . It'd be like throwing a fire cracker into a herd of cattle. You'll start a stampede. Did you check with Shelly?"

"Screw Shelly. These are my patients."

"Yours. And mine, and the hospital's. You need to go through channels, Mau."

He threw Bruce a contemptuous glance and headed for the door. "By the time I went through channels . . ." Lori could have killed her dad, for all I know. "Who knows what else could happen."

"Mau, I can't let you do that."

"Not for you to 'let' me"

"I have to notify Shelly."

"That's your choice. I've made mine." He swung the door open. "The upload continues."

Before he reached the first turn in the halfway, he heard Bruce yelling after him.

"Mau! It's suicide! Isaacson will burn you at the stake!"

"Tell him to use my plane to scatter my ashes," he yelled over his shoulder.

62

SITTING ALONE ON HIS PATIO, Beck watched as the waiter presented a bowl of arugula-and-pear salad and sprinkled it with a red wine reduction.

"Would there be anything else, Dr. Beck?"

He waved him off. The waiter nodded deferentially and walked back toward the house.

"A lot of this would have to go," Beck thought as he surveyed his property. The staff. The lush gardens spreading several hundred feet down the hillside to the tennis courts below. The Olympic-size pool, flanked by a waterfall made of giant rocks trucked all the way from Yosemite. The small free-standing cottage, where he found moments of solitude and peace.

He scoffed. Such possessions were just proxies for what he would really lose if Cendoz collapsed. The whole persona that the past few years have created, in the world's eyes, as well as his own, would be in shambles. Above all, he would lose any shred of self-esteem. The sense of who he was. There would be little to live for then.

Beck opened the Wall Street Journal that the butler had prepared for him on a side stand and glanced at the front page.

"President and family traveling to Cambodia. President Caldwell is the first ..."

He ripped off and crumpled the page, dropped it on the floor and flipped to the business section. That was the beauty of real paper. You could take your anger out on it, noisily and inexpensively. You couldn't do that to an iPad.

He wanted to crumple the business section too, although little there was news. "Implants offering stiff competition to pharmas," read the headline. "Parkinson's, seizures, obsessive-compulsive disorders. Is depression the next frontier? 'The entire antidepressant pharma industry should be shaking in their Gucci loafers' said John Alexis, the respected medical-financial expert ..."

No shit. Everyone at K&K, Aventia, and Pfizer had been running scared since that Frenchman started screwing around with those damned paddles. At least K&K managed to sideline the Nuvius with a well-timed acquisition, and bury it with an excess of research-and-development funds. Good investment on their part, considering that a little black box would make their antidepressant obsolete. We should have put a grinding halt to the LX too, he thought.

He recalled his advice to Barcelos. "Forget biochemistry. Go into neurosurgery." Idiot.

He continued reading, like a self-imposed punishment. "Just last week, there was a 9.2 percent increase in patients using the LX neural implants. Forty additional centers are planning to adopt the procedure as the new standard of care. Conservative estimates? If the trend continues, the number of patients treated with LX implants will overtake the number of patients on antidepressants within fourteen months. Both Medicare and private carriers are rushing to make the procedure reimbursable, licking their chops at the potential savings in payouts."

He thought about losing the fleet of gleaming private jets now at his beck and call. The pretty Anabela? She'll run to the divorce lawyer, and without a goodbye kiss.

"Unprecedented paradigm shift . . ." the article continued. "The success of the innovative neural implant field, referred to as 'results-oriented medicine' by physicians, and 'cost-effective care' by insurance companies, will be known as the 'LX massacre' by the pharma industry."

Beck lowered the paper and stared into the distance. For anyone who could read, the handwriting was on the page. Cendoz stock had plummeted 17% in twenty days, and the sell-off was accelerating. The sharks could smell the blood.

Suddenly his left knee was burning with pain, even though he was sitting still. He stretched his leg, wincing. It used to be that he could make love to Anabela in positions that would make an acrobat envious. Now . . . even walking down the stairs was a chore. An old man.

He slammed the fork down. Not yet. He was not ready to throw in the towel. He had a lot more uphill climbing to do to show those Harvard bastards who threw him out what a huge mistake they made. He had to . . .

He recognized the light footsteps approaching from behind.

"Good morning, Johanna."

A hand stroked his cheek, and he smelled sandalwood.

"'Johanna', not 'Jo' today?"

Her hand still on his cheek, she came around where he could see her. She was wearing her simple workout clothes. The cotton pants draped around her slim hips. He wrapped his arm around her, and pulled her closer, feeling the firmness of her yoga-toned buttocks.

"Missed you, Jo."

She kissed him gently on the lips, then pulled a chair closer and sat. "Two days and you miss me already?" She reached her fingers into his salad and snagged a slice of pear. "Where is Princess?"

He shrugged. "Shopping, I guess."

"For more shiny objects? Or for young studs?"

Beck tightened his jaw. "I don't need that this morning, Jo."

She patted his knee. "Cheer up. I talked with Mr. Al the Victorious."

"And?"

"He gets it. He bought my story about the surveillance video at the motel, showing him snuffing out the girl." She smirked. "Didn't even question it. So now he thinks it's do the job, or go to the slammer. He'll do whatever it takes." She ran her hand under his shirt and patted his chest. "And sounds like he's as taken with the 'hot Leoni' as you are."

Beck eyed her appreciatively. Johanna had aged well since he first laid eyes on her, fifteen years ago. He wondered if Anabela would look nearly as good when she turned Johanna's age. Without the perky breasts and the Ipanema Girl hips, the young Brazilian wouldn't even qualify as a shiny object. Johanna had stood by him unflinchingly through his successes and failures and his sexual escapades, and now through this.

"I just got a call," Johanna was saying. "It appears that our doctor does have a fix to block access, and he's been uploading it, one patient at a time."

Beck sat up.

She laid a reassuring hand on his knee. "Relax, love, it's handled."

"How, exactly, 'handled'? We need to be hands-off on this. We can't go near . . ."

"Do you need to remind me?" She threw him a reproachful glance. "He's moving at a snail's pace, going backwards from the newest patients. Cyber Boy is sure that at this rate Barcelos won't get to the intended target until it's too late."

"Barcelos will figure out a way to wreak havoc. You don't know him like I do."

"I know men," Johanna smirked. "I had our PR person call Isaacson and hint that Cendoz grants went only to facilities with squeaky clean reputations. Having a madman on staff, who, according to rumors, has threatened the President, wasn't Cendoz's idea of squeaky clean. Isaacson got the message and will take it from there."

Good woman. The White House had managed to keep the episode

out of the headlines, but rumors were rampant. Johanna always made good use of them.

"In that case we have time to decide."

Johanna shook her head. "That's what I came to tell you. We don't have time. The trip has been moved up. The man is due to fly out in . . ." She turned his wrist and glanced at his Patek-Phillipe watch. "Sixteen hours. We need to green-light this thing now."

A band squeezed around his chest. They were considering betraying a young man who had trusted him like a father. Worse, they were contemplating a crime so heinous, it was unprecedented in the history of turf battles. There had to be a less onerous solution. A smaller bounty to pay for his empire and his self-esteem.

Sweat was beading on his upper lip, and he blotted it with his napkin.

Johanna was studying him as if he were the unwanted residue at the bottom of her test tube.

"What?" he asked, realizing too late that his face was betraying his inner turmoil. He tried to compose himself. "Why are you looking at me like that?

Johanna leaned closer. Her face was inches from his. "Maynard?"

He looked away. "I'm fine."

"Maynard!"

"I just wish there were another way."

"Like your plan A? Trying to bribe Sanjay the FDA guy into a recall, then having to take him out because he was going to rat on you? Or plan B . . ."

"Stop it."

"Or plan B, where the doctor would die in a plane crash? Seemed like a good plan, until you finally got what I was trying to tell you: The minute Barcelos was off the map, ten others would step in and carry on his work. It'd be cutting Medusa's head off—more were bound to grow. Do you have a Plan C? Because I'm at the end of my tricks."

She was right. The threat to Anadep was multifaceted. Barcelos' brain implant was about to take a chunk out of the business. Caldwell's proposed regulations and quotas would decimate what was left. Cendoz wasn't like K&K. The giant conglomerate had a myriad of products to absorb the shifting terrain. His eggs were all in just one basket. And he could hear the steamroller coming. There had to be a way . . .

"Let's find a more cost effective solution," he suggested.

Her look made it clear that she knew he was just stalling. Clasping at straws, to avoid taking the big step.

"How much will it cost us?"

"What do you care?" she asked with a flip of her hand.

"How much?"

"Fifty mil."

He nodded. "You're really good, Johanna." Fifty million was less than a quarter of a percent of annual revenues. A minor line-item that his bean counters would bury in the Promotional Expenses category between Lecture Dinners and Educational Cruises.

"Maynard, I'm talking about wiping both your problems off the board," she was saying. "Neural implant technology will be a four-letter word. For years," she said, pausing to eye him. "Caldwell has been stalking pharmaceuticals since the Harvard pay-off on Anadep. This is your payback. And you're not just saving a product, you'd be saving an industry."

He continued looking away, trying to release the tightness gripping his chest.

After a long moment, Johanna pushed her chair back. "Maynard, I don't know what to say."

"About what?" he asked, knowing what her answer would be.

"About . . . this. About your reluctance. About what it means to us."

"Johanna . . ."

"I didn't stand by you all these years to see you crash and burn at the finish line." She sat up, her back ram-rod straight, the eyes suddenly cold. "What will it be?"

Out of the corner of his eye he saw the Rolls pull into the circular drive. Anabela got out. Two of her assistants started hauling shopping bags out of the trunk.

Johanna followed his gaze and scoffed. "Is that your future? Today, a shiny object. Tomorrow ..." She stood up. "I better get going. Your Princess turns my stomach." She laid a hand on his shoulder. "Last chance, Maynard."

He brought his shoulder up, pressing her hand against his cheek. The hand was as cold as granite. The pressure around his chest was excruciating. The prospect of losing riches and Anabela was daunting. The thought of losing the woman who had been his pillar was intolerable.

"Why do you have to ask?" His voice was subdued. "You always know what I'm going to say."

63

IT WAS EARLY EVENING, AND MAURICIO was sitting at his desk at home, banging at the keyboard. He swore under his breath and pushed away from the desk. The computer was useless. Not surprising, given what had happened earlier at the hospital.

After making his intentions clear to Bruce, he had returned to his office to check on the upload. The counter continued ticking up at the same glacial pace. 1458, 1459, 1460 ... He wasn't even half-done. He stared at the screen, willing the DGBlocker to spread magically down the list like a safety net. 1461 ...

He changed screens and was working on e-mails, when the countdown stopped at 1430. He tried a few keys. The upload was frozen. Moments later, a red box flashed on the screen. "Password expired. ACCESS DENIED." It didn't take a brain surgeon to figure what was going on. The hospital was getting back at him for the White House scene.

He found Isaacson huddling with Bruce in the penthouse office.

"Are you responsible for locking me out?" he demanded to know, his face as close to Isaacson's as the coffee table between them would allow.

Isaacson puffed his chest. "You're damn right I am."

Bruce laid a hand on Isaacson's shoulder. "Shelly, let me." He turned to Mauricio. "Mau, nobody is locking you out. At least not permanently."

"I want the block removed. Now."

Bruce raised his hands. "Mau, I know how stressed you must be. Mel's death . . ."

"That's nothing to do with it. I'm uploading a critical upgrade and you just screwed . . ."

"Stress is stress," Bruce said patiently. "So I was thinking. It might do you good to take a few days off. Get away from the hospital. Maybe take your plane down to Cabo. Or go mountain climbing. Or go . . ."

"Or go to hell," Isaacson suggested from a safe distance.

"I'll take off when I have the time," he shot back. "Right now, you fix my access."

"No can do, Barcelos," Isaacson sneered. "My job is to make sure you don't upset this apple cart."

"I didn't upset the apple cartee." Under stress, his Brazilian accent was coming through again, and he hated it. "I already speakee to the First Lady. She understands . . ."

Isaacson jumped in. "She might understand. I don't. I've worked hard to make this institution what it is today. You're not going to screw this up for all of us, do you hear me?"

The staring lasted an eternity. "Shelly," he said as evenly as he could manage. "I'm going to walk out of here and pretend nothing happened. By the time I get to my office, I expect my computer to be back online."

"Or what?"

"Or my next call will be to my attorney."

"You don't have an attorney."

He turned back to Isaacson, the blood pounding in his brain. "In that case, how about I call the Joint Commission on Hospital Accreditation? Report you for patient endangerment? Blow a whistle, the watchdogs will come running."

Isaacson smirked. "After a stunt like today? You think JACO will give you the time of day?"

He ripped the phone out of his pocket. "Why don't we try," he managed through clenched teeth, scrolling through the numbers.

Suddenly Bruce's hand was on his shoulder.

"Mauricio, do yourself a favor. Do not call."

He shrugged the psychiatrist's hand off. "This is going to stop."

Bruce yanked the phone out of his hand. "Dr. Barcelos, as Chief of Psychiatry at NBMC, I'm recommending that the Administrator place you on a leave of absence, effective immediately."

Out of the corner of his eye, he noted Isaacson's gleeful smile.

"You can't make me," he snapped.

"Want to bet?" Bruce turned to Isaacson. "Shelly, call security. Dr. Barcelos is a danger to himself and to others. I'm placing him on a 72-hour hold."

He couldn't believe his ears. "Are you out of your mind? Besides, you need two doctors . . ."

Isaacson punched two buttons on his phone. "Security and Chuck Talon, on the way," Isaacson announced. "You remember Dr. Talon, don't you? He questioned your sanity the day you treated the President's daughter. We should've listened to him."

They must have been planning to sideline him for a while, Mauricio thought, because when Bruce had mentioned the psychiatric hold, two security guards and two psych-ward workers appeared as if by magic.

Almost beyond control with anger, he raised his arms. "Okay, have it your way, Bruce. I'll take a few days off."

Dream on, you bastards, he thought sitting in his home office. But attempting to log on from his own computer with its own password proved futile.

His monument to Dora's memory was collapsing like a house of cards. The mausoleum of cards.

He had to find his way into Mel's lab and use Mel's password to access the back door of LX system to resume the upload. It would be walking into the lion's den. He would have to sneak in during the night shift, when skeleton crews would be too busy to notice a lone surgeon heading to the ORs. They didn't call it the graveyard shift for nothing.

He glanced at the clock. He had at least six hours to kill.

He went downstairs, poured a tumbler full of cachaça, inhaled the scent, and then dumped the liquid down the sink.

He stripped to his shorts, walked out into the garage, and took a few pokes at the bag hanging from the rafters. It felt good. He punched harder. Ten minutes later he worked up a sweat. His muscles relaxed. His mind began to clear, pushing his troubles back.

He started planning his following move, beyond the time when all patients would have the Delta Gap Blocker installed, to the time he would be able to go after the bastard who was behind this cyber invasion. He recalled hearing the term bee trap, or was it honey pot, or something to do with decoys. He could ask Leoni to help him create imaginary patient records on BrainPacers, figure out how to trace any tampering. Then when the hacker tried . . .

Loud banging on the front door jerked him to attention. He wrapped a towel around his waist and eased the door open. A tall man stood in the shadow of the overhang.

"I told you we'd be in touch," Blanchard sneered.

His tongue went instantly dry. Beyond the door, he heard several sets of tires screeching to a halt and footsteps pounding around the house to the front door.

Blanchard spoke into a radio. "He's here. Come around the back."

"If it's about the call to the First Family . . ." he tried.

Blanchard handed him a sheet of paper. "Doctor, we have a warrant to search your premises."

64

MAURICIO SAW FOUR MEN AND A WOMAN materialize in the pool of light streaming from his kitchen door. "You can't just come barging in," he started to protest to Blanchard. "I have confidential medical records . . ." He could smell the garlic and tobacco on Blanchard's breath as the man inched closer.

"I can't? You just watch." Blanchard lowered his voice to a whisper. "Plane crashes may not be under my jurisdiction. But murder . . ." The detective let the sentence hang.

Murder? An idiotic accusation. No doubt a vendetta for him being outwitted in the Sandy McBride encounter. His pulse quickened. The man was like a piranha latched to a piece of meat.

"Problems?" asked Christy Vanbruel as she rounded the corner.

"None on my end." Blanchard turned to his men. "Start with the garage."

Feeling violated, he watched as the men rushed into his house.

"We meet again, Dr. Barcelos," FBI agent Vanbruel said with a fleeting smile. "When we're done, I'll need you to come with us. You may want to . . . you know . . ." Her eyes darted to his bare chest and sweaty shorts, lingered, and returned to his face. "Slip into something more appropriate?"

"Mind if I shower first?" he asked, looking for anything to buy time and wrap his brain around what happening.

Vanbruel hesitated. "Where?"

"In the bathroom."

"Of course," she nodded. "But I need to see it. The bathroom."

Vanbruel scanned the windowless bathroom with a practiced eye. Her gaze swept up to the skylight. "Okay," she said finally, then spoke into her radio. "Brian, come up here and stand outside while the doctor showers."

"Roger that, ma'am," came the staticky reply. "By the way, we found . . ."

Vanbruel disconnected the radio in mid-sentence. "Shower away. Do not take anything—I mean anything—out of the cabinet without showing it to the agent first. Understood?"

"Yes, ma'am," he parroted, trying to sound casual. His mind raced, reviewing the possible landmines in Blanchard's accusation of murder.

A frightening detail flashed through his mind. The detective's comment, as they were driving to Gina's autopsy. "Your buddy in Phoenix warned me." He had no buddies in Phoenix, except Dumas. What if that hadn't been a "routine background check" as Blanchard claimed? What if the cop had been recruited by Dumas or whoever was pulling the strings, to incriminate him and help ensure that the LX failed? Blanchard could be like the police chief in Brazil. Paid to do a job, but not for the government.

The hair on the back of his head moved. He grabbed the closest clothes he could find—a dirty scrub shirt and an old pair of jeans lying in a pile by the bathroom door.

Vanbruel stopped him. "Do you always shower with your phone?"

He forced a smile. "Only when I'm on call."

Vanbruel squinted, but said nothing.

A giant man with a bald head materialized by Vanbruel's side.

"Give him five minutes, Brian," she said. "When he's done cleaning up, take him to the car."

He glanced at Brian. The man stood a head taller and outweighed him by fifty pounds of solid muscle. A grown-up version of the bullies of his childhood. Trying to get past someone like that was asking for a beating. Or worse.

"Time starts now," Brian grumbled.

"Got it," he winked. "Brian."

Brian looked at him with obvious disdain.

"And, Bri, I can't hear in there when I use my hair dryer. So if you knock and I don't answer, feel free to come in anytime, okay?"

Brian mumbled something under his breath and turned away.

He was closing the door when he saw Blanchard striding up to Vanbruel, brandishing a plastic bag with what looked like a nail.

"What did I tell you?" Blanchard grinned. "Metric bit. I'll bet you it's the one missing from the set in the hangar. Complete with wood shavings." The look of triumph on the man's face was frightening. "No reason to wait."

Vanbruel shook her head. "He's not some scumbag, Norm. Let him get cleaned up."

Mauricio eased the door closed. A metric bit. He didn't own metric bits. His heart stumbled, and then stopped long enough for the blood to drain from his head the way it did during high-g maneuvers. He leaned on the sink for support.

A drill bit with wood shavings. From Mel's wooden propeller. Clear evidence that he had drilled the prop and caused Mel to crash.

If they arrest me, I won't be able to fix the D-gaps. My patients will be victims ... He caught his reflection in the mirror. Lips white, pupils dilated, sweat rolling down the forehead. His whole body was trembling. He took a few deep breaths. Blood began to flow.

Quit bellyaching and think.

He turned the shower to full blast, full hot. A scene from The Fugitive played in his head. "I didn't do it," said the doctor. "I don't care," said the federal marshal.

He was innocent. Blanchard didn't care.

He looked up at the skylight. High, but if he stood on the counter he just might . . .

Moving rapidly, he slipped into the scrub shirt and jeans, and shoved the phone into his pocket. He grabbed the long hooked rod and cranked the plastic dome open. Billowing steam filled the room as cold outside air rushed in.

He climbed on the counter and yelled, "Brian, I have my clothes off and I'm going in the shower now!"

"Three minutes remaining," came the gruff reply.

Even standing on the counter, the skylight seemed impossibly high. Worse yet, it was not directly overhead, but toward the middle of the bathroom. If he jumped and failed to grasp the edges, he would land on the floor.

That was what happened on the first two tries. He did his best to land as softly as possible, but the floor vibrated.

"What's going on in there?" Brian yelled.

"I'm fine. I came out for my moisturizer and slipped," he yelled back, "My butt is a little bruised. Maybe you can check it later, see if I broke anything . . ." he added, playing on the man's homophobia.

On the fourth leap he hooked his fingers around the edges of the skylight. The metal edges dug painfully into his hands. With one flip, he pivoted with his head down, pressed his feet against the plastic dome, clenched his teeth, and pushed. The hinges disintegrated with a loud crack, sending the dome up and out.

If the man outside heard anything, he opted to say nothing.

No turning back now, he thought as he hooked his legs around the edge, pulled up on his arms and emerged on the roof.

The dim shaft of the streetlight outlined three unmarked cars and one police cruiser parked along the sidewalk in front of his house. Two uniformed policemen were leaning into the window of one of the cars, apparently talking to the driver.

Judging from the noises, and the bright light spilling on the driveway below, the garage door was open, the men inside hard at work.

Cautiously, he sprawled on his belly and began scooting toward the ridge of the roof. He had to pull himself up and over it before the men below ended their conversation and looked up. He crawled as fast as he could, cringing every time a tile cracked under his weight.

Thirty years ago he was an expert at slithering through the grass, slingshot in hand, hoping to nail a rabbit. Now the stalking was more challenging, and he was the rabbit.

He gritted his teeth at the thought of what would happen if the agents spotted him. He was already presumed guilty. Guilty and trying to escape? One of those "make my day" moments for Blanchard. What the hell am I thinking?

He realized he was not thinking, and was only reacting to fears planted decades ago. Fears of an unjust imprisonment. Fears about facing charges for a murder he hadn't committed thirty years ago. Or for a murder he hadn't committed days ago.

No way am I going to prison, one voice screamed in his head. Not till the LX is secure.

Not ever, another voice echoed.

He crested the top of the roof. There was no one on the other side. He slid down, letting his body accelerate. There was no telling how long the agent guarding the bathroom door would let his distaste for seeing him naked stand in the way of his professional zeal. At any second, the agent could barge into the bathroom and see that he was gone.

He reached the edge, swung his legs over and dropped into the alley that separated his house from the neighbor's. A short dash brought him to his Volvo, parked in the usual spot between the houses. The car was unguarded. He fumbled under the chassis and retrieved the spare key. Keeping close to the ground, he cracked the door and wiggled his way onto the seat.

He ventured a glance out. He could see figures moving across the windows, in the living room and in the bedroom.

He eased the door closed, slipped the car into neutral and let it coast forward, away from the cops on the street. Once he had rolled out into the back alley, he held his breath and cranked the engine. The old engine hummed to life. He engaged drive and slowly pulled away.

It wasn't until he merged with the freeway traffic two miles from his home, that the realization hit him.

He had nowhere to go.

65

Mauricio stayed in the middle lane of the Southbound 55 Freeway, keeping pace with the late-evening traffic, his eyes spending more time on the rearview mirror than on the cars ahead. It was the general direction of NBMC, but for what? It would be the first place they would look for him. Checking into a hotel, trying to access Mel's computer from his room . . .

No wallet, no ID, no hotel room.

He could park in a dark alley; wait till the FDA office opened on the East Coast. He imagined the likely scenario:

"This is Dr. Barcelos. I want to report a criminal intrusion into the LX program."

"The Dr. Barcelos? The one who threatened the President? Or the one who killed his colleague? Oh yes, the one on psychiatric suspension from the hospital whom the cops are looking for? The one who got the First Mother to shove the LX approval down our throat? Hey, no problem. Just tell us what you want done, Doc. Or better yet, come on in for a chat. You know the FDA building? Right across the street from the police station . . ."

Options for solving the LX crisis before the FBI arrested him were being decimated. And when they did catch him, he would have no more authority than an average low-life fugitive from justice. Suddenly, the unplanned escape seemed like the worst thing he could have done. He should have gone with the FBI, obediently answered questions, explained ... He would probably be home working the computer, before the sun came up.

It had been a stupid move. He was innocent.

His skin crawled as he recalled the triumphant look on Blanchard's face when the bastard brandished the plastic bag with the drill bit as if it were the key to a treasure chest. Or to a prison cell.

His father's voice sounded in his ears. "Adeus, filho!" Farewell, son. "I didn't mean to kill him, Pa."

"Eu sei, menino," his father said. "I know you didn't ..."

He had crawled into the cart. The mountain of manioc tubers covered him, its weight crushing him flat. His father's voice was the last he heard of his family, until the news of Dora's fate. A shameful escape. A life-long exile to avoid a lifetime in jail. And he had been trying to expiate his guilt ever since.

Lights flashing, a police cruiser emerged from the darkness behind him and pulled up to his tail. His stomach went into a knot. I'm dead, he thought as he began to pull over. The cruiser whipped around him and wailed down the freeway.

He slowed the car. What had he been thinking? How long would it take them to find him?

Mel would have taken him in, no questions asked. Diane might take him in, with lots of questions asked, after this morning's stunt during her TV broadcast.

He considered Beck, but he could hear it now. "Young man, do the right thing." Then Beck would tell him to turn himself in, and would offer his legal battalion to help. And they probably would help.

He was flying up a blind canyon, and the walls were closing in.

There was a violent shudder followed by a loud screech as the

Volvo's left fender scrapped against the concrete divider. His eye lids snapped open and swerved back into the lane. This wasn't working. There were more useful ways to die.

He took the next exit. He spotted a closed gas station with a drive-through car wash. He circled around and pulled into the stall from the rear. From here he could see the street, while the car remained in the shadows.

He needed a place to close his eyes, just for a few minutes, and then gather his thoughts.

Where are you, Mel, when I need you most, he thought.

Mel's hangar.

Not. Right now Icarus was probably on top of the cop's list of escape routes.

Leoni.

Before he could catch himself, he had already pulled out his phone and speed-dialed her number.

One ring. Two rings.

Are you nuts, Barcelos? He pushed end.

What was he thinking? It had been barely three weeks since she walked into his booth and his life. He hardly knew the woman. Just because she had been a balsam for his pain after Mel's death was no reason to trust her. Just because she had spent a few hours in his arms listening to stories about his home, or because her hair was luscious and smelled of lemon and her hands were gentle . . .

Bullshit.

He wasn't about to stick his neck out. If Diane could betray him and leave him after twelve years, Leoni could turn him over to the cops in one blink of those gorgeous . . .

His phone vibrated with a text message. Leoni. "Turn off your phone. NOW. And come over."

Twenty minutes later he pulled into her cul-de-sac. When he was abeam the house, the garage door started opening. Leoni appeared, silhouetted by the interior lights. She waved him in. The door came down even before he shut off the engine.

She was barefoot, wearing pale grey sweat pants and a lose green t-shirt that left no doubt that she was not wearing a bra.

"My electricity died," he began to explain. If it ever came to testifying, he wanted her conscience clear of harboring a fugitive.

She silenced him with a finger to his lips. Her look spoke volumes: Don't insult my intelligence, and don't doubt me. She took him by the hand and led him into the house. At the door she stopped and eyed his clothes, covered with dust, cobwebs and gravel. She sniffed his shirt. "I'm not letting you in like this," she announced. "Strip and shower. I'll throw these in the wash."

By the time he came back downstairs, wrapped in a large towel, his hair still wet, the small kitchen table was set for two. A couple of cheeses and slices of prosciutto wrapped around bits of melon, a tin of cashew nuts, a sliced tomato sprinkled with basil and feta. A soft Brazilian motif, Carlos Gilberto on the guitar, was playing in the background. I died and went to heaven, he thought.

"That's all I have," she apologized, indicating the food, and handing him a blue crystal tumbler with ice cubes and a clear liquid.

He recognized the scent of cachaça. Suddenly he felt ashamed that he doubted that she would help him.

She raised his drink toward him. His hand wrapped around hers.

"Leoni," he said quietly. "I did something really stupid today."

"I know," she whispered.

"Not the stunt at the White House."

"I know."

No questions, no recriminations. He studied her face. How could she know?

"They aired it on the news the minute you bailed," she said, as if reading his thoughts. "They're looking all over for you. That's why I told you to shut your phone off."

Of course. They could track me. How stupid.

"If they had tracked you, they'd be here by now. Drink and don't worry." She started handing him the tumbler.

The realization of how far she was sticking her neck to protect him, hit him squarely in the heart. He pulled her against him. Their lips brushed lightly. Then his mouth was hard against hers, his tongue exploring.

The anger, the fear, the fatigue of the past thirty-six hours morphed into an uncontrollable urge.

"Leoni," he whispered.

Afraid to let go, he freed one hand and caressed her face.

He felt her melting into him. He clasped her so hard that the air exploded out of her chest.

"Leoni," he repeated, his voice coarse, his hands reaching under her shirt.

She pushed him away and with one stroke pulled the towel off him. Leaving a trail of her clothes along the way, they made it halfway across the living room. Then they collapsed on the rug, their bodies finally touching, their lips crushing each others.

His world shrunk to a single bubble that held only her. No one else, nothing else, existed. Nothing mattered. No Blanchard, no Dumas, no jail. Only this woman locked in his arms.

She maneuvered her body under his, their skins sliding against each other. She let her legs relax, reached down, and guided him against her.

There was wetness everywhere. Between her labia, down her thighs. Warm, sensuous, welcoming wetness.

His bubble. His safe haven.

She pushed up against him, just as he was entering her. They moaned quietly, their wide open eyes locked on each other.

She began to move slowly. A gentle wave that rocked their bodies as if they were floating on a lake. He pushed against her. She moved faster and faster. He picked up her rhythm, anticipating her upward thrusts.

Within moments, which felt like hours, her whole body stiffened, her eyes rolled up, her neck veins bulged as if about to explode. Then a low moan rose from deep inside her chest, building, louder . . . Her body arched, lifting them both off the floor.

"Mauricio," she groaned, as all her muscles convulsed at once. "Mau . . . ree . . ."

Then everything came to a standstill. Her body was arched, but no muscles moved. Her lungs held the air, neither inhaling nor exhaling. Her heart missed one beat, then another, then another. He watched as her face went from flushed to crimson to purple.

His own mind began to blur. The bubble was shrinking to a single point. All he could feel was her body, in ecstatic rigidity.

Finally, there was one more thrust, and a short, ear-splitting scream that bounced off the walls of the small room. So loud, he could feel his own chest reverberating.

That unearthly sound put him over the top. He pushed into her, grinding his pelvis against hers, crushing her breasts against his chest, his own head rearing back, his moan blending with hers.

They collapsed, gasping, their eyes closed, their bodies reduced to putty.

66

"ROOK F8 TAKES KNIGHT F4. CHECK."

Al watched as the animated graphic black tower lumbered down the far right row of the chessboard displayed on his iPad screen; and, to the sound of crushing metal, it obliterated the knight and his white horse. Red fluid squirted from under the tower as it settled on the spot previously occupied by the white figure. Nice touch, Al thought, giving credit to whomever had designed the program.

Check. In one move, it was going to be checkmate. His breathing quickened.

Early that evening he had cruised past Barcelos' house. He was pleased to see it surrounded by half-a-dozen marked and unmarked police vehicles. The complex maneuver to sideline Barcelos had progressed with the predictability of a well-planned chess game: The suggestion to Lori, during the Delta channel gap call, to hug her father in front of the cameras. The quick visit to the doctor's garage to plant the drill bit used on Mel's prop. The call to 800-78-CRIME, directing Blanchard to the evidence. Nothing had been left to chance. With the doctor under arrest and his credibility destroyed, the outcome of the endgame was inevitable.

One last move remained. He had twenty-four hours left to make it. The morning after, the twenty-five million dollars just deposited in his Swiss Bank account would double.

As he drove home, a ping from his iPad alerted him that Barcelos' GPS tracker was moving. The cops must have taken his phone with them, as they drove the doctor to the police station, he decided. Between the fiasco with the First Daughter and the murder charge, it was safe to say no one would be listening to any allegations the good doctor could conjure. And by the time he managed to catch anyone's attention, it would be too late. That's why I get paid the big bucks, he thought once again. And this time, it was the really big bucks.

Al leaned back, minimized the chess game on his screen, and brought up his favorite picture of Leoni, snapped while she was still under the influence of the Rohypnol on their first and only date. In the dimly lit photo, she was lying on her side, silhouetted by the night-light, her long legs stretching toward the camera . . . He closed his eyes, remembering those sweet moments . . . Business combined with pleasure. Little did he know that a mere attraction would turn into such an obsession. And now with millions of dollars as his irresistible lure, the obsession was about to become a reality.

"Wake up, Al." Kay's voice coming from his Skype message center blasted him back to reality. He clicked on. Kay was staring from the screen. "That trip we've been anticipating? It just got moved up. He's flying out in the morning."

This took him a few seconds to process this change. It was already middle of the night on the East Coast. He had a few hours, at best. An impossibly short timeline. "I need more prep time. There's no way . . ."

"I'm counting on you, Al. Don't disappoint me."

The Skype window went black.

Al let out a long breath and forced his elbow against the kneecap to stop the leg from shaking.

Speed chess. Think speed chess.

He had minutes to figure out how to make the next move. Eons in speed chess time. Nanoseconds, considering the reality of the situation.

Think.

When Lady Kay told him the target's name, he had immediately gone to his computer and programmed daily gaps into the subject's Delta channel. If Lady Kay was correct about the man's habits, he would be doing his log-in shortly after he got up, at 4:00 a.m. East Coast time. He had timed the daily gaps for 3:00 a.m. East Coast time, with plans to continue them until he needed to use one. Little did he know it would be this soon. This was either his sixth sense at work, or prudence born from experience, but now he was glad he had been cautious.

He pulled up the LX tracing. The next Delta gap, which had been programmed in during the subject's logon the previous morning, was in place, scheduled for . . .

He glanced at the electronic clock on the display and tensed up.

Two hours and four minutes left. Barely enough time to figure out how to place the phone call. He could try placing it himself, but if they didn't believe him, his only chance would be blown.

Think.

Suddenly he realized his move. If there ever was a moment to break his promise to Leoni, this was it.

He went to the dresser, rummaged through a drawer, and pulled out one of several identical objects sealed in Ziploc bags. He had hoped he would never have to use them, but the circumstances were exceptional.

Al was heading to his car, when a news alert on his iPad sent his head spinning: "Newport Beach surgeon sought as a person of interest in connection to a colleague's death."

Sought? But Barcelos was under arrest.

A wave of panic started to engulf him, then it rolled over and gently washed out of him on the other side. This unexpected development couldn't alter the outcome of the game. The only person less credible than a murder suspect was a murder suspect on psychiatric leave and on the run. The good doctor had just rammed the last nail into his own coffin.

"I wouldn't trade places, Barcelos," he mused. "Your hospital locked, your best friend dead, your still-in-love-with ex on the other side of the country. Car, plane, phone, credit cards—all traceable at a moment's notice." He smirked. Okay, on a few hours' notice, given the incompetence of the searchers. With nowhere to go and no one to talk to, Barcelos was even more innocuous than if he were in custody. The doctor's position wasn't enviable. And with mere hours remaining till his project reached the point of no return?

Al shrugged and mumbled to himself, "Doctor, your wings have been plucked, and you're going to crash."

67

Leoni opened her eyes. Slowly, her brain refocused. She was lying on the floor of her living room floor, the shag carpet tickling her skin. Mauricio was on his side pressed firmly against her back, his muscular arm draped around her neck, the palm of his hand covering the space between her breasts. The even breathing told her he was sound asleep.

Keeping as still as possible, she tried to blow away the strands of hair matted with sweat against her forehead and eyelids. She remembered what his arms felt like, draped around her. What he tasted like, when she was exploring every inch of his body.

What just happened?

What I've wanted to happen since I laid eyes on this man, she admitted. Only back then it was a purely physical attraction to a man who was just an assignment she had to complete to save her own skin. Now . . .

Mauricio had turned out to be gentle, caring, intelligent, sensuous, and respectful, and passionate about his noble goal. Even with a past that was far more wounding than hers, and with challenges far more daunting than she herself had ever experienced, he had forged ahead, determined to prevail. Now, she felt like she would walk through fire for him.

A few hours earlier, when she heard about his escape on the news, Leoni knew that she had to help him. She was just considering how to find him when he called. Without a second of doubt or fear, she invited him over, wishing she could do more than just offer shelter.

She turned her head toward him, saw how haggard yet handsome his face was, and had an urge to sweep him in her arms and hold him forever. Instead, she touched his hand, with a touch as light as a feather. He was tired and he needed sleep.

His eyelids cracked open. "I thought you were asleep," he whispered.

"I thought you were too," she giggled. It had been years since she had felt like giggling.

Reluctantly, she untangled herself from his arm and stood up. He followed. For a moment they stood studying each other's bodies. Powerful shoulders, muscular forearms, runner's legs. The man reminded her of statues of Greek athletes she so enjoyed drawing as an undergraduate art student.

His eyes now scanned every inch of her body with what seemed like surgical intensity. She tried not to think about her breasts that weren't as perky as they once were, and the belly that was no longer flat.

His finger traced her flank, barely touching, from her hip to her waist, up to her armpit. A touch as light as a butterfly's wings, which sent electric currents in all directions.

"You are so beautiful," he whispered.

She felt her nipples hardening and realized she was turning so that her breast could reach his exploring hand.

Before her marriage fizzled out, she had been the object of desire. Later, there were no desires to act out. The new urges she was feeling were intoxicating.

She took him by the hand and led him up the stairs toward the bedroom. Too late, she remembered that the cleaning lady hadn't been here for two weeks, and the place would be its normal mess—the bed made in a hurry, dirty clothes overflowing the hamper. And then she realized that she didn't care. No need to impress. He already was a part of her life.

She pulled off the wrinkled spread and steered him toward the bed. He stood still, his eyes grinning, teasing her, refusing to take the hint.

"Stop it." She gave him a firm push and he toppled backwards. Without giving him a chance to recover, she collapsed on top of him.

His arms wrapped around her, and she melted into his chest. His fingers began to work down her back, each tiny contact electrifying nerves on the way. Slowly, his hands made their way down to her buttocks, his fingers setting off shock waves that radiated forward, setting her pelvis on fire.

He lingered, touching, stroking, teasing, reaching her most intimate spots.

Finally, she couldn't stand it anymore. "Take me again," she whispered.

He rolled on top of her and pinned her hands above her head. The exhilaration of being helpless and wanted was overwhelming. She tried to push her body up against his, but he resisted.

"I want . . ." she groaned.

His lips were on hers, silencing her.

Damn you. I want you. Now, she wanted to scream, but he wouldn't let her inhale.

And then his hardness was parting her folds. She tightened up as much as she could, knowing that as wet as she was, she couldn't stop his urgent drive, even if she had wanted to.

He eased himself into her and stopped, teasing her. She began to move, feeling herself tightening harder around him than she thought possible. He began to respond, his thrusts measured, controlled, deep, matching hers move for move, and depth for depth.

Soon it became a race, their rhythms taking turn outpacing each other's, his lips finally losing contact with hers as he gasped for breath. And then she was lost again, and he was exploding inside her. They hung on that edge for an eternity, and then moaned in unison. He let his body slump down on top of her and she melted under him.

Leoni woke up because his breathing was raspy. He coughed in his sleep, turned over, coughed again. She slipped out of bed and tip-toed out of the bedroom.

When she came back with a glass of water, he was sitting up, looking around like a lost child.

"What time . . ."

"Twelve forty five. You slept a whole hour," she teased. She handed him the water. "Your breathing sounded dry."

Flicking on the bedside lamp, she slid next to him again. In the warm light, he was even more handsome, his tanned skin like light chocolate.

He put the glass down and pulled her toward him. This time she didn't care that her breasts sagged slightly under their own weight, that the nipples were still erect after their lovemaking, and that his eyes seemed to be taking in every inch of her skin.

He leaned forward and let his lips brush against her right nipple. The feeling shot right through her, as if he had touched her far lower. An instant later, he was moving lower, his lips working their way to just above the narrow strip of hair that bisected her pubis.

"Runway cut," he smiled.

"You're cleared to land," she giggled. "Or do you prefer a Brazilian cut?"

He moved lower. "I love your freckles," he mumbled between kisses. "They remind me of stars. Whole constellations." He raised up and his finger began tracing a pattern. "Centaurus . . ."

The touch was tingling and titillating. She noticed that the arteries in his neck were pulsating faster. He nudged her, and she let her thigh drop to the side, cold air teasing her exposed swollen labia.

"Dipper . . ."

She felt his hardness wedged between their thighs and wished he would find a constellation way south of where his finger now was.

"And this one . . . Cruzeiro do Sul . . . Southern Cross . . ."

Keep going, she urged him silently, feeling her body starting to arch to meet him.

Suddenly his energy vanished, as if someone had flipped a switch.

She opened her eyes and looked down toward him. He was as still and cold as a marble statue, his eyes locked on the spot where he had found the constellation.

It was so quiet, she could hear the clock ticking in the other room.

When he looked up, his eyes were staring right through her, into the distance. The color had drained from his face. The bounding in the arteries slowed to a dangerous crawl.

She touched his shoulder. "You okay?"

"I'm fine," he whispered, his voice cracking.

And at that moment she knew why he was not fine.

68

MAURICIO STARED AT LEONI as if seeing her for the first time. Standing in the garage, wearing nothing but a long T-shirt, her arms wrapped around her chest as far as she could reach, she looked small and frail. And evil, he wanted to add, but couldn't bring himself to think it.

"You are crazy," she was saying. "It's close to midnight. You need more sleep."

What I need is to get away from you. "I'll be all right," he lied. Fighting the anger over her bitter betrayal, he fumbled for his car keys.

Only moments earlier, the freckles on her inner thigh had come into focus, and he had recognized them immediately. The constellation of Cruzeiro do Sul. The unmistakable five stars of the Southern Cross, the Big Dipper of the Southern Hemisphere. With his gut wrenching, he realized that those were the same freckles he had seen in some of the nude pictures that had mysteriously appeared on his computer at the Neuro-Sciences Convention right when Leoni had showed up.

Leoni, working for Dumas?

The woman he trusted to shelter him ... A cold hand crushed his heart as he remembered trusting her with his most intimate secrets. The woman had dumped pornographic images of her own body parts into his computer. And all the malware that came with them that made it easier to penetrate the system. The woman who was becoming his soulmate, turned out to be his worst enemy's ally.

How could you, Leoni? At first he wanted to confront her, to yell, to demand why. But fear of how she would answer stopped him.

As if faced with a cardiac arrest in the operating room, or an engine failure in flight, he felt himself becoming stone-cold rational. If she could sabotage his work, she could just as easily turn him in. He had to get out of here without arousing her suspicion.

"We need to find you an attorney," she was saying.

"I have no right to make you an accessory, Leoni." He had to keep up the act. "It's bad enough that I barged in on you."

"I invited you. Please stay. They must be looking for you everywhere."

"I'll find some place."

"Take my car. They'd looking for your plates."

She sounded so genuine, he almost believed her. "I'll be fine." He opened the door of his Volvo.

She urged him, "Remember, use only land lines."

"I had enough landmines for one night," he tried to joke.

There was a quick flash in her eyes, and he wondered whether he had blown the illusion he was trying to convey—that he still didn't know about her betrayal.

She gave what passed for a smile. "Land lines."

He wondered if she realized that he knew, and they were two people not talking about the gorilla in the room, for fear of waking it up. He was about to get in the car when he noticed a bicycle hanging from the rafters. "Mind if I borrow that?"

"Take it. What for?"

Mauricio had an idea, but he would not share anything with her.

He worked the bike into the trunk.

She wrapped her arms around him. What felt so delicious an hour earlier, was now like a cold anaconda encircling its prey. He did his best to return the hug.

He was dying to ask why, how, and since when. But what difference would it make? He knew the answers would not turn the clock back. His trust had been betrayed. His fantasies about a future with this woman, shattered. He eased her away.

She looked at him, her eyes moist. For a moment, he was taken aback by her intensity. Was he making a mistake? Don't even go there, a voice screamed. When was he going to learn, damn it?

"Mau, I'm sorry this is happening . . . to you. I . . ."

He could tell her lips had started to form the word "love." Right. Of course you do. That's why you partnered with the man who wants to destroy me.

"However things go . . ." Her voice cracked. "I didn't know . . ." She stopped.

He held his breath, hoping against hope that there was an acceptable explanation looming ahead. Prove that you didn't. Please.

"I didn't know making love with you would be so wonderful," she said.

He clenched his jaw and looked away. Definitely, let the gorilla sleep. Talking about what had happened would be more painful than what he was now feeling.

"Don't give up," she said. "Go save your project." She turned, activated the garage door opener, and hurried into the house.

To Leoni, the sound of the Volvo backing out felt like someone was winching out her guts. She dashed into the house, ran upstairs to her bedroom, pressed her forehead against the glass sliding doors overlooking Back Bay, and crammed her hands against her ears.

The sound of the engine faded, as the man she had come to love just drove out of her life.

She opened her eyes. The moon was over the bay, and there was a reflection in the water, but it was hard to see anything through the tears streaming down her cheeks.

One stupid mistake … One moment of weakness, years ago. One chance given to a shy, charming young man with a limp, who promised to fix her loneliness … And the sordid cascade had started its inexorable course. Blackmail, crime. Another blackmail, another crime. Since the damned encounter, her life had switched tracks and she was hurtling along like a runaway train, heavens only knew to what end.

Leoni felt the cold surface of the sliding door vibrating against her forehead as she pounded her fist against the glass.

One. Stupid. Mistake.

If only she had had the guts to tell Mauricio that someone was out to compromise him. He might have been more cautious. Less prone to jump in headfirst and cause the fiasco with the First Family. Less paranoid, and less inclined to ruin his career by running from the authorities.

One mistake? How about a thousand? One for every day of the last three years that she didn't turn the blackmailing bastard into the police. Double the stupidity points for the days she could have confessed to Mauricio.

Could have, but when was the right time to say, "Oh, by the way, that thing with the photos? I did that. Many of them were of me when I had a roll in the sack with a stranger, but think nothing of it." How do you confess that to a man you are crazy about and want him to feel the same way about you?

She stopped pounding the glass and brushed her tears away with the back of her hand. She heard a faint noise coming from the garage. She held her breath.

Footsteps. Her heart leaped. He was back. A chance to make it right. Together they could fix anything. She dashed out onto the landing.

The door below was opening. She grabbed the handrail and took the first step down, ready to leap into his arms, to confess . . .

The door opened.

She froze.

"Al . . ."

69

Aware that at any minute he could be spotted by the police, Mauricio worked his way along deserted streets, toward Huntington Beach, until he located the surface stop for the Metrolink Orange Line.

His original plan to sneak into Mel's lab at the hospital during the graveyard shift was now obviously defunct. The whole place would be swarming with cops looking for him. But the software fix upload had to happen. There was only one place left where he could even consider doing it.

He parked the Volvo across the street from the tram stop island. A few passengers were waiting. He slipped on an old Baja Bush Pilots cap, grabbed his phone, and strolled to where he could see the tracks.

Minutes later, the tram approached. Three long cars hooked together like a minitrain. Los Angeles' rather ineffective response to permanently congested freeways. As the tram slowed to a stop, he started crossing the street, powering up his phone as he went.

An image appeared on the screen. Chess pieces. He ventured a closer look while hurrying toward the tram. A black rook crushing a horse, blood squirting everywhere. This time, he didn't care. Just before the tram lurched forward, he slipped the phone into a basket that one of the women was carrying.

"Boa viagem," he mumbled, wishing his iPhone a nice trip along the forty-plus miles of tram track that stretched across the LA basin. With Metro's recently improved cell phone coverage, the iPhone's GPS would be active and the phone traceable. It would be a wild goose chase for the authorities that would buy him a little time.

He returned to the car, pulled the bike out of the trunk, and adjusted the seat. Leoni's seat. Set to her long legs.

As a last-minute inspiration, he rolled down the driver side window of the Volvo, and threw the keys on the seat. It was not LA's worst neighborhood, but with any luck the car would be stolen, and it would buy him more time while the police tracked it down. He swung his leg over the bike and started pedaling.

Puddles gleamed in the darkness as he passed under the sparse street lights. It was eighteen miles from Huntington Beach to Fullerton Airport. Then what?

If Mel's old computer was still there, if the pirated wi-fi connection was still working, if he could gain access to CloudFort through the backdoor that Mel said he created, if...

If not, dead end. He would be pedaling to nowhere, like a hamster in a cage. As he warmed up, he became aware of Leoni's scent, still lingering on his skin. Leoni, naked. Leoni's freckles. Leoni in the pictures on his computer.

He had Googled the mysterious error message that had launched the parade of lewd pictures at the convention. It turned out that d2-d4 d7-d5 were the first chess moves of the Queen's Gambit. A sequence that proceeded to a bold move that sacrificed the queen to gain a superior position.

Leoni was the hacker's ally. The Chessman's queen. The piece that was sacrificed so that the hacker could gain access to his entire organization.

The hacker's queen. He wondered what else she was to the man.

Wheels screeched as a truck swerved to miss him, the horn blasting. He hunkered down and pedaled faster.

Fifty minutes later, his thighs burning, he reached Fullerton Airport and stopped in the shadow of a small trailer. Of the few cars in the vicinity none looked like police issue. He took a deep breath, pulled down his cap, tapped in the gate combination and rode the bike onto the tie-down ramp.

Icarus was in its usual spot, but now there was a heavy chain draped around the prop, with a red tag flapping in the wind. It was the aviation equivalent of the "boot" that parking police placed on cars, and a most effective way to prevent an engine start. It was reassuring to know that now the authorities had no reason to watch his plane. He wasn't going to be taking it anywhere.

He used the key hidden above the door frame and entered Mel's hangar through the pass-through door. The remnants of Big Red were still there, but there was no trace of the NTSB desks or tools. The chaos struck him in the gut, bringing back memories of his time working with Mel here.

Brushing away the flood of emotions, he moved along the wall in darkness until he found Mel's headlight, tucked behind the beam in its usual spot. He slipped it on. Staying low, he made his way to the work-bench and confirmed that the surveillance paraphernalia that NTSB had found was still lying on the bench, unplugged. He breathed a sigh of relief. No one was watching.

Making the good-luck figa with his fingers, he walked briskly to the desk and fired up the computer. Moments later, his last hope of uploading the DGBlocker was shot down. The wi-fi that Mel had been using was down. No phone, no computer, no wi-fi. And nobody to communicate with. He shuddered as the thought that at last count over 2000 unprotected patients remained. He absolutely had to get to NBMC, find his way into Mel's lab, and upload the software fix.

He desperately needed information about where they might be

searching for him. Damn wi-fi. When you needed one . . .

Suddenly he remembered Mel's fondness for vintage objects. An old ghetto-blaster was sitting on one of the shelves. He blew off the dust, shoved the cord into a socket, and dialed the volume to barely audible.

Already he was breaking news, at least on the local station. "A renowned Newport Beach neurosurgeon, wanted on charges of murdering a colleague, is on the run, as the manhunt spreads to downtown," the announcer intoned. "An Orange Line tram was stopped when the suspect's iPhone showed up . . ."

Like clockwork, he thought, wishing he had a dozen more cell phones to distract search parties.

The sweat from his bike ride was evaporating, and suddenly the hangar felt like a meat locker. He let the newscast continue in the background, and set out in search of something to keep warm.

"In other news . . ."

He smirked. Oh, there's other news besides my heinous crimes?

"President Caldwell and his family are heading to Cambodia . . ."

He found Mel's oil-stained sweat shirt and slipped it on.

"Jorge Ramirez is with us . . ."

He recognized the name. Jorge was the anchor on Diane's station, up early for a radio link. Was Caldwell's trip that newsworthy? Or just part of the election-year quest to stay in the limelight round the clock?

Screw Cambodia. He had to get to the hospital. He started pacing.

"Peter, it's going to be a rare opportunity to bring you live-coverage from aboard Air Force One . . ."

Think. Somehow he had to distract the pursuers enough to make it possible for him to get into the hospital.

On the radio, Peter interrupted, "Jorge, isn't it true that whenever Air Force One flies abroad, she's accompanied by a twin?"

"Isn't it true." The hallmark preface of a Know-it-all determined to impress. He'd come across a few of those in med school. How the hell to get to the lab, damn it? The noose of fear was tightening around his brain.

Jorge's voice. "Exactly, Peter. Since the first Bush era, an identical 747 flies along with the President's plane as a backup. We don't want the most important man in the world sitting on the tarmac, waiting for a connecting flight, do we?" Jorge laughed.

The guy sounded as unpleasant as he looked on TV. No wonder Diane despised him.

"And in the rare event of attack," Jorge droned on, "the second plane serves as decoy. Much like the three Marine 'copters that ferry the President to and from the White House."

The chatter was distracting, but he hoped there would be more news about where the police were searching for him.

"And one more detail, Peter. KNOC has learned that for this mission, a major breakthrough in pilot safety is being introduced . . ."

What, better-padded seats?

"As you know," Jorge continued, "whenever Air Force One flies in international airspace, she is escorted by four F-22 Raptor jets, manufactured by Lockheed-Martin. These jets have a much shorter range than Air Force One, so planes and pilots will be swapped out at intervals—over our base in the Aleutian islands, and then over southern Japan . . ."

Blah, blah, blah. Don't they know all I want is news about me? He was getting punchy.

"What is fascinating is that one of the pilots will be refueling in flight, and will remain with Air Force One during the entire 18 hour flight."

"Jorge, isn't it true that . . ."

He flicked the radio off. In the silence, the image of a decoy Air Force One hit him between the eyes. If his phone could launch a chase clear to downtown, he had an even better decoy in mind.

He made figas with both hands.

70

Al's breath caught in his lungs. The sight of Leoni standing at the top of the stairs, barefoot, in a loose T-shirt that barely concealed her pubis, was tantalizing. She had lost weight since he last saw her, but her breasts were fuller, the legs more toned.

"How the hell did you get in?" she spat.

Al gave a small shrug. "The garage door was open. Looked like you were running an open house."

"Get out, or I'll call the cops."

He stepped inside, eased the door closed, and flipped the dead bolt. If she were going to call the cops, she would have done it long ago. His eyes lingered on her legs.

She took three steps back toward the bedroom. For a moment he thought she was going for the phone, but she reached inside the door, took a bathrobe off the hook and slipped it on. He was about to point out that there was no need to cover details that he had memorized from past encounters, but thought better of it. The fine tremor in her left hand told him he was already stomping on raw nerve endings.

"I need one last favor," he said, trying to sound amicable.

"And I need you to get the fuck out of here."

"Just a phone call."

"Make it yourself."

"I can't. The man we need to call knows you, so he'll take the call if it comes from you." Having to plead was irritating, but time was of the essence. "It's important, Leoni." If she would just listen. "The money it will bring . . ."

"Do I look like I care about your money?"

"Not just my money. We'll be rich."

"We?"

The bitch actually laughed at him.

"Not on your life. I delivered. We are done."

Don't say it Leoni. Not done. We can never be done. "I'm sorry I'm a cripple," he said softly. He repositioned the messenger bag hanging from his right shoulder, and grasped the handrail. The prosthesis bound up when he tried to go up the stairs. He hated how he must have looked.

"With the lifestyle you'll have, you won't mind my limp."

"What the hell are you talking about?" she blasted.

He took a few halting steps up the stairs.

"Leoni . . . If you just help me with the phone call . . ." He kept climbing. If she would just give him a chance to explain. "It's the biggest project I've ever handled. It'll be money like you've never dreamed of."

"Wrong woman, asshole."

"I'm sorry my leg . . ."

"It's not your crippled leg, it's your crippled soul."

"Think yachts, maids, jewels. Monaco, the Riviera . . ."

He reached the landing and stood face to face with her. Her eyes sparkled, her nostrils were flaring. Disheveled blond hair spilled across her flushed cheeks. She was beautiful. He inhaled her scent. "You'll live like a princess." He moved closer and took her by the arms. "And in time you'll fall in love with me," he added softly.

She jerked loose. "Fall in love?"

The hatred in her eyes made him catch his breath.

"Get this," she said slowly, bringing her face inches from his. "If you were the last living man on earth, I would not love you. Do you understand?"

He was counting every heartbeat pounding against his ribcage. Did she not understand what he was offering?

He stepped back, gritting his teeth. "I'll make you love me."

She threw her head back and laughed. "Get lost, you worthless scum."

The roar in his ears was deafening. Worthless scum? He was not good enough. Again.

Fragments of shattered memories exploded in his brain. He had just turned fifteen. It was a warm summer evening. He and Svetlana were hiding in the back of the garage. They had just finished making love for the second time. She was stroking his hair.

Suddenly the garage door started opening. Her father had come home early. They dashed toward the exit, but froze in the headlights like the proverbial deer.

The man jumped out before the car stopped.

"You bastard," he yelled.

Svetlana ran into the house, crying.

Al just stood there. "I love her . . ." he managed.

The father grabbed a pipe wrench and stepped toward him. "Get lost, you worthless scum. Or I'll kill you."

Al circled the car and hurried to the exit. But he couldn't resist a parting shot. "She loves me too. We'll run away," he yelled running down the driveway.

Next he knew, his stepfather was in the car, and the car was backing into him, and he tripped and was falling, and the fender caught his leg and his foot was rotating and ligaments were snapping like bowstrings, tearing, tearing . . .

"Worthless scum?" he mumbled. He sunk his fingers into her arm. "You're in love with him, aren't you? I'll teach you . . ."

He grabbed her neck, forcing her lips to his, but her knee exploded into his groin, doubling him over. The kick that followed sent him tumbling down the stairs.

Leoni watched as the heinous tormentor rolled down the stairs, head over heels. "I hope you break your neck," she thought. She heard a satisfying thud as Al landed hard on his back, the prosthesis wrenching off his leg. The shoulder bag flew open.

She pointed a finger, wishing it were a gun.

"If I ever see you again . . ."

Al got up on all fours and wiped the blood off his mouth with the back of his hand. The prosthesis had fallen off. He sat and struggled to slip it back on.

"Move. Out." Maybe he finally got the message.

Al stood up and retrieved the plastic baggie that had slipped out of his bag, and lifted it toward her.

The blood drained from her face when she recognized the malachite ashtray.

Al let out a chuckle. "Oh, the ashtray I sent you last month? It was not the one with your fingerprints."

"You bastard," she hissed. She started down the stairs. She was going to kill him. With her bare hands.

He stepped back. "Don't make me turn you in, Leoni. Pretty woman like you, in jail . . ."

"Where did you get this?" she managed to articulate.

"From your boss's office. The one I sent you last time was from Chinatown. They had a bunch, actually. This is the one with your fingerprints."

He was probably lying again. "How do I know this is the real one?"

"Dried blood. See, right here along the edge . . ."

She was still two steps above him, but she lunged for the ashtray.

He pulled back and she wound up stumbling, regaining her balance mere inches from him, smelling the onions and turmeric on his breath.

"One phone call, Leoni, and the ashtray is yours."

The nightmare was back, this time bigger.

We will be rich.

There was only one way to deal with it. She squared her shoulders and managed a contemptuous look. "Fuck your ashtray. I've had enough of your threats."

"Leoni . . ."

"You cost me three years of misery and a job I loved. You want my help, tell me about the money."

71

SPARKS FLEW PAST MAURICIO'S FACE and lit up the inside of Mel's hangar, as the carbide grinder battled the case-hardened chain wrapped around Icarus' prop. Mauricio paused to let the blade cool off. Rain drops pelted the corrugated metal roof, the noise almost as loud as the grinder's.

He glanced at his watch. 2:15 A.M. He had to hurry if he was going to make it.

With a final shower of sparks, the disc ground through the link. The heavy chain landed at his feet. He found a roll of black electrician's tape and a stack of white shipping labels and used them to change his tail number from N77MB to N89VF. Then he grabbed a can of spray paint.

"Sorry, Icarus," he said as he covered the pretty red stripes on the front of the wings with a dull green. The acrid fog, trapped in the confined space, instantly sent him into a fit of wheezing and coughing.

Five minutes later he was done. Icarus looked like the much-abused spaceship in *Star Wars*, rather than the beautiful plane he had built with such care. Maybe I'll rename you Millennium Falcon, he thought.

The plan was simple. At this hour the control tower at John Wayne would be closed, and a single-engine plane coming in late would attract no attention. But even if someone spotted him, N89VF would look nothing like the Icarus that the authorities would be looking for.

He wheeled the bike to the cargo hatch. With creative maneuvering and the front wheel off, it fit in perfectly. He leaned against the wing and started pushing the plane out of the hangar.

Fuel? Sufficient. Weather? Shitty. Pilot? Scared. Emergency alternate? None. Come hell or high water, he had to get into Mel's lab, access the back door to the program using Mel's password, and make sure the Delta Gap Blocker went to every single LX patient.

As he taxied toward the runway, the rotating green-and-white beacon on top of the tower played off the raindrops on his windshield, making it look like a giant kaleidoscope. With a final glance at the tower, Mauricio shoved the throttle open. The engine roared to life. He released the brakes and the acceleration punched him back against the seat. Icarus rolled down the runway, the landing light exploding into a pool of white raindrops, the white segments of the centerline disappearing into the darkness as the plane gained speed. Seconds later, the plane bouncing in the wind gusts, the gear retracted with a solid "thunk." He turned off the landing light, plunging his whole world into darkness.

Soon he checked in with Air Traffic Control, using his fake tail number. "Destination, Las Vegas, via Palmdale," he announced.

"November Eight Niner Victor Foxtrot, turn right heading zero eight zero, climb to and maintain niner thousand," a monotone replied.

Mauricio scanned the multicolored instruments glowing in the dark cockpit. So far, so good. Air Traffic Control had accepted his request for a clearance across the San Bernardino Mountains, rather than the easier direct routing. "Vectors around weather," he had explained.

And there was plenty of weather. Icarus bumped and rolled and bucked as it fought its way through broken clouds on the way up to the assigned altitude.

He climbed, the assigned heading taking him directly toward the mountainous terrain he knew so well from his aerobatic play, and that would now offer him a chance to vanish.

ATC was calling again. "Uh . . . November Eight Niner Victor Fox. Verify this is your correct call sign and you are a BE35."

He grinned. It was clear that ATC's computer was spitting out messages that there was no such tail number, or it was not the number of a single-engine BE35 Beechcraft. Controllers were scratching heads trying to resolve the mystery, giving him the time he needed. Six minutes to the hills.

"That's affirmative," he replied.

Clearly, the signal that was being automatically broadcast from his transponder was identifying him as N55MB, an aircraft registered to one Mauricio Barcelos.

He remembered fishing in the river that ran near his parents' house. Flies buzzing, sun shining. The surge of excitement when the cork he used as a bob suddenly dipped below the surface, indicating a fish had taken the bait.

Hopefully, Air Traffic Control was biting. He needed their full attention for his plan to work.

Four minutes.

Icarus reached the assigned altitude and leveled off. He was now on top of the clouds and the ride was smoother. In the distance, the dark outlines of the mountains were barely distinguishable against the black sky. Right and left, gigantic cumulus clouds, lit from below by city lights, loomed like surreal guard towers.

He drummed his fingers on the yoke. Come on, guys. Swallow the bait already. I'm an impostor. The plane belongs to a fugitive from jsutice. Put two and two together, and send out the posse.

As if on cue, a new voice came on the frequency. This one sounded older, more experienced. A shift supervisor. "November Eight Niner

Victor Fox, switch to my frequency one-two-four-point-niner."

The supervisor wanted to have a private chat, off the common frequency. And he was probably dialing his boss, who was contacting the FBI. And all hell was breaking lose down there.

Nine thousand feet directly below was March Air Force Base. He guessed it would take little more than five minutes to scramble a couple of Apache helicopters to force him back down.

Timing was everything. The mountains loomed closer.

"November Eight Niner Victor Fox, So Cal Approach. For traffic, turn right one seven zero, descend and maintain four thousand."

Hook, line and sinker, he thought. They knew who he was. They were trying to turn him around without arousing his suspicion.

"Uh, that was zero seven . . . Say again," he drawled.

Almost there. One more minute and he would be overflying the jagged peaks and gorges where he did his aerobatics. Terrain that he knew like the back of his hand.

"Victor Fox, do you copy?"

"So Cal . . . We're . . . Stand by . . . Clouds . . ." He made an effort to sound even more stressed than he was.

Thirty seconds to the narrow canyon where he and Mel chased each other like kids on a playground.

"Mike Fox, turn immediately to . . ."

"Mayday, mayday, mayday," he screamed as frantically as he could into the mike. Then he switched the radio off, and shoved the yoke forward, pointing the plane into the black abyss below.

If his abandonned cell phone had succeeded in launching a wild goose chase . . . *This* wild goose would launch a posse on steroids.

72

A̲L CLENCHED THE STEERING WHEEL of the van with both hands and peered through the rain-blasted windshield, concentrating on avoiding the flooded spots on the 405. With victory in the palm of his hand, wiping out on the freeway would be a tragic waste.

He had been victorious on every count. Lady Kay was right, he thought. Every woman had a price. Even Leoni.

"How much money? I want specifics," she had demanded.

That was a part of Leoni he hadn't seen. Al guessed that he had pushed her as far as she would go and now she was pushing back. He had seen this in others, why not her? The new attitude excited him even more. "We can live wherever you want."

"Separate quarters." His face must have betrayed his rejection, because she added, "You can visit, when I feel like it."

Fair enough. Maybe the night they had spent together had meant something to her after all.

"My own bank account," she continued her rapid-fire litany of demands. "Ten percent of your deal."

He whistled. Damn, she was different. Ten percent seemed work-able, if he got what he wanted in return. At that moment, thinking of what was concealed under the loosely wrapped robe, he would have given her anything she asked.

"I want to start my own PR agency."

"Deal," he smiled and held out his hand.

She stepped back. "Who do you want me to call?"

Her submission was startling, if not unsettling. He hesitated. A voice in the back of his head was urging caution. This could be a trap. All his instincts were conspiring against trusting her. Al looked her in the eyes. She glanced away. A sure sign of lying. But the eyes were so beautiful and blue, just like Svetlana's.

No, she was not lying, he assured himself. She couldn't be.

Time was running out. He started dialing. "When they answer, tell them you're Leoni. The man will remember you." Who could for-get? "Ask them to put you through to the sleeping quarters, because you have urgent news about a pregnancy test."

"And if they ask . . ."

"Don't take no for an answer. Use your charms. Whatever it takes to get through." He glanced at his watch and started dialing.

"Who do I ask for?" she wanted to know.

He eyed her again. Friend or foe? Either way, they would be in it together. He handed her the phone. The die was cast.

She did as he instructed. If he could have touched her, the night would have been perfect. But there was no need to rush. After waiting three years, he could wait a little longer. The best part was that she was coming to him willingly. He even left the ashtray with her as a sign of good faith. Real or not, she seemed to be satisfied.

Driving the freeway in pouring rain was too treacherous to multi-task on the iPhone, so he turned on the radio. "Manhunt for neuro-surgeon continues . . ."

He switched stations.

"Lo drama al rededor do inventor del implante . . ."

It took three tries to find what most interested him. "The Caldwells are the first, First Family to visit Cambodia, and are going in an effort to promote better understanding . . ."

He swerved to avoid a semi that cut in front, spraying the windshield with water.

"The flight will take them over Canada, then down the Pacific rim, bypassing North Korea . . ."

He noticed that a lone helicopter was following him close overhead. Lady Kay? In his Leoni-centered reverie, he had neglected to call and update her.

We're paying you the big bucks . . . It was a guarantee Lady Kay would ask him where Barcelos was. He could assure her that he was not with Leoni. At least not anymore. Nor was he connected with his cell phone, or with the Volvo that had been involved in a drunk-driver stop somewhere in Riverside.

The chopper was still flying above and in front.

A thought crossed his mind. The plane. He could not count on the likes of Blanchard to secure the plane. He peeled off at the next exit. The chopper continued along the freeway, picking its way through the rain and scud.

Twenty minutes later he pulled into the Fullerton Airport parking lot. Despite the rain he could see that Icarus was gone. He swore under his breath.

Head down, rain running down his collar, he punched in the access code, shoved the security door open and dashed to Mel's hangar. The big door was up. The lights were off. He tripped on a heavy object.

A chain.

He swore under his breath and dashed back to the van. It took mere keystrokes to pull up the records of flights out of Fullerton. N89VF, departed 0245, destination San Diego. Status: unknown.

Al sympathized with Barcelos. The man had probably disguised his plane's identity and was heading to the border for a possible escape to Mexico. All that effort, but it was too late to change the course of the game.

Still, due diligence demanded that he cover all his bases. It would be prudent to give the authorities a hint of where to look for him. The big bucks, he reminded himself. Leoni was counting on him.

He opened the iPhone and looked up the number for Homeland Security.

73

To make the crash credible, Mauricio had to simulate the free fall of a broken plane. Icarus's fuselage groaned under the load of speeds far in excess of the red line.

He strained his eyes searching for visual clues of the approaching ground.

Four thousand, three thousand . . .

It was unnerving enough in daylight at normal speed. At night . . . He didn't dare take his hand off the yoke to wipe the sweat off his brow.

Pull out too high, the plane would remain on ATC's radar, and his subterfuge would fail. Pull out too late . . .

Suddenly, two lights ahead, and growing rapidly. He yanked back on the yoke, the g forces driving him toward the ground, tearing at his limbs, the blood draining from his head. When he leveled off, a car's headlights were barely fifty feet below him.

He turned the transponder off, concealing any identifying signature it might make if a radar did scan the plane at this low altitude. Then pulled the throttle and slowed Icarus to a crawl. Even if he did eventually appear on ground radar, he would be dismissed as a low and slow helicopter reporting on traffic, or a police chopper, searching for the bad guys.

By now, he hoped, all available resources would be heading out to search the remote canyon for what was left of him. He pointed Icarus toward John Wayne Airport and settled in for the fifteen minute flight.

With the ATC radio chatter gone, the cockpit felt deserted. The engine droned evenly in the background as he contemplated the next challenge.

John Wayne Tower was now closed for the night. For once, he was happy about the draconian noise-abatement rules enforced by the hoity-toity Newport Beach residents that halted all late-night jet traffic and closed the tower. All he had to do was land and taxi to an empty tie-down spot as if he owned it. The guard at the South Gate would have no reason to stop a weary pilot riding his bike from his plane to his car in the remote parking lot.

The rest would be easy.

Icarus rolled gently from side to side as it flew among low-lying clouds, barely above the rooftops. In the breaks, he could see the lights of the airport, getting closer and closer.

Suddenly, a powerful jolt rocked the plane. A last vestige of turbulence from the storm, he decided. Then all was smooth again.

Another jolt.

His eye caught a dark shape that crossed in front and above him, like a shark.

A small puffy cloud? Not a plane—it had no lights.

Another jolt, more violent.

There was no mistaking this one. Wake turbulence from a large aircraft. What was a big bird doing this low? Another pilot making the same approach to John Wayne? Nobody should be flying this low.

The shape reappeared behind his right wing, closing in rapidly. He jerked the yoke, and banked sharply.

He spun around in his seat, looking right, left, behind ... Nothing.

The dark shape had vanished.

He turned back on course, his heart racing.

What fucking bozo would be out here, no lights, this low . . .

Suddenly he felt, more than he heard, a low-pitch rumble coming through the skin of the plane. Moments later, an UH-60 Black Hawk helicopter floated into view on his left side, its red and green lights flashing. The giant rotor blades seemed close enough to touch his wing tip. Through the darkness, he could barely make out two helmeted figures in the cockpit. A high intensity beam blinded him as the chopper's searchlight locked on.

What the . . . He couldn't believe it. He was being intercepted. Cold sweat made his hand slip on the yoke.

The chopper rocked back and forth, veered off and away, then swung back. The standard "follow me" order.

He tuned the radio to 121.5. If it was a real intercept, that was the frequency they would be talking to him.

They were. "I repeat . . . Aircraft N89VF . . . Extend landing gear, reduce speed and follow me."

No f-ing way. He banked hard left, cutting in front and narrowly missing the Black Hawk, and forcing him to veer out of the way. Moments later, the chopper was in position again, now at a safer distance. Evidently a midair collision over a densely populated area was not in the pilot's "rules of engagement."

"N89VF, if you do not comply, you will be shot down. Acknowledge."

A cloud loomed, perhaps thirty seconds ahead. He activated the landing gear lever. The wheels dropped, and his body lurched forward as Icarus slowed down. The chopper almost flew past him, but adjusted its speed.

"N89VF, turn left zero two zero."

The cloud was seconds away. As soon as the grey murk enveloped him, he yanked the gear lever back up, rammed full throttle, and pointed the plane straight up. The chopper's flashing lights sailed by below him.

"N89VF, you will be shot down. I repeat . . ."

If you can find me, he thought.

The relief was short-lived. Moments later he was in the clear again. The nearest cloud was at least forty-five seconds ahead.

He heard two cracks. Two fiery objects blasted past him, mere feet away.

Warning shots. He could guess their scenario: They would force him out over the water, and easily blow this homicidal fugitive to smithereens. Tax dollars at work.

He saw the chopper circling behind him, coming in for another pass.

"Stop shooting," he yelled into the mike. "Where do you want me to land?"

"N89VF, turn left . . ."

Suddenly, Mel's voice was barking orders at him. "Look sharp. Don't let him get behind you. Be ready to roll."

Mel, I'm going to make you proud, he thought as he dove into another cloud. "You picked the wrong guy, fellows," he mumbled, corkscrewing the plane to the right so hard he heard rivets popping.

For the next three minutes, which dragged into an eternity, he engaged in a deadly dance, complicated by darkness and clouds and a fear of collision—with the helicopter, or with a missile or the ground. He had no doubt that if he moved away from the buildings and out over open water, where his debris would not injure civilians and cause a scandal, they would nail him. The plan to land at John Wayne and bike to the hospital now seemed like a pipe-dream.

The chopper was keeping its distance.

There was no reason to wait for the inevitable. He turned northwest, toward NBMC, still paralleling the shoreline, still keeping over the city. At one thousand feet, he was in and out of clouds. The marina near the hospital came into view, about a minute away.

Behind him, in the darkness, the chopper began inching closer.

"N89VF you are ordered to proceed to Los Alamitos and land immediately."

He made a figa with his free hand, and prayed that if he stayed over populated areas, he would be entitled to at least one more warning shot. At this range, a shot with intent to kill was not likely to miss him.

He entered a waypoint into the GPS, a few miles off shore, and put the autopilot in standby mode. He didn't want Icarus crashing into a condo complex.

He pressed the mike and tried to sound contrite. "N89VF will comply. Turning to Los Al. Which way is that?" In twenty seconds, he would be over his target.

"Left turn heading zero four zero."

He wadded a few paper charts and piled them on the floor of the cockpit.

"Okay. Turning now." He rocked his wings as if complying. He reached under the dashboard and pried the plastic cover off the fuel tank selector switch. He chuckled. Little did he know when he was building this plane, that being able to find every one of Icarus's parts even blindfolded, would someday prove lifesaving?

"N89VF, I repeat, turn left heading zero four zero."

He turned his head in time to see the chopper sliding behind him. He threw Icarus into a roll and got below the pursuer. The maneuver gained him a few precious seconds, but soon the chopper was on his tail again.

Now, he thought.

He pulled the emergency pins, sending the door flying into space. Then, gritting his teeth he managed to rip the fuel line off the tank selector. Fuel poured out of the line and over the crumpled maps. The engine sputtered, but kept running. He pulled a lighter from the plane's emergency kit and readied it.

He released his seat belt, checked the chute harness he always wore, even when he wasn't practicing his aerobatics and activated the autopilot. Icarus began a turn out to sea. With the door gone, and nothing separating him from the sight of buildings passing far below, he was struck by the frightening exposure. The slipstream blasted his face and chocked him. His muscles froze.

The radio was chattering again. The nearby cloud glowed with the reflection of the chopper's lights.

He looked ahead to a cloud over the marina, and hoped that hiding again would push the chopper pilots to fire another warning shot.

He was seconds from the cloud when the shot rang out, the sound unmuffled and savage. A projectile streaked by. His last warning shot.

At that moment, he flew into a cloud, and everything vanished. He took a deep breath, shielded the lighter from the air blast, lit the flame, and threw the lighter into the fuel-soaked maps. Then, fighting his fear, he leaned out as far as the slipstream allowed, and let himself go.

74

DROPPING LIKE A ROCK, Mauricio saw the chopper cruise overhead. Then the chute popped open, jerking the harness into his crotch, sending a searing pain into his belly. "Should have made a few practice jumps," was all he had time to think before the ground came rushing up. Parking lot, cars, driveways, marina, boats, boat masts ... A painful slam of his right flank onto a sharp object, a twist of the broken toe, and finally he crashed butt-first onto a wooden surface. He opened his eyes and realized he was no longer falling.

At that moment, the clouds just off-shore turned bright orange. A fireball streaked down, disintegrating into multiple segments as it plummeted into the ocean. Seconds later came the boom of an explosion, so intense his chest vibrated.

"We flew too high, Icarus," he whispered, the lump in his throat too large to swallow.

All was still. Boats rocked gently, moored in neat rows, their masts swaying. Not a soul in sight. He heard the distant beat of rotors where the choppers were hovering over a column of smoke that melted into the low clouds.

He shed the harness, stuffed the parachute into a trash bin and limped up the boat ramp. Mel's thin jacket reeked of gasoline and was no match for the cold, pre-dawn wind. He shivered. The pain in his right flank, just under the shoulder blade, was worse. He reached behind and felt sticky liquid. Surface wound from the dock railing, he decided, glad it hadn't punctured the lung.

He made his way across the parking lot toward the street. The massive outline of the hospital loomed in the mist, barely a mile away.

Twenty painful, frightening minutes later, he stood near the trash pickup area behind one of the NBMC buildings. The lack of activity in the adjacent parking lot meant the day shift hadn't started to arrive yet. Several maintenance workers were out on a smoking break by the back entrance, chatting in Spanish. As best as he could ascertain, there was no one resembling a police authority.

Hiding in the shadows, he approached a dumpster and rummaged until he found a plastic bag and two large boxes. He peeled off his jacket. The scrub shirt was soaked in blood. The pain was worse when he inhaled. He gritted his teeth and tried not to think about all the organs located near the wound.

He filled the bag with crumpled paper and slung it over his shoulder to cover up the blood. Then he stacked the boxes in his arms and marched toward the entrance. The smokers eyed him.

"Noches," he greeted them in his best imitation of a Mexican accent, and nodded toward the door. One of the men lowered his cigarette, stepped to the door, swiped his badge and pulled the door open.

"Gracias," he nodded, keeping his face concealed behind the boxes.

Finally inside, he located the laundry room and helped himself to clean scrubs and a long lab coat. In the safety of a bathroom, he rinsed off the blood and changed. Then, lowering his head, he marched into the tunnel that led to the main hospital.

He was halfway there when he heard footsteps behind him. He picked up the pace.

"Hey! Hey, buddy!"

A man was rapidly approaching from behind.

He had no choice but to slow down. "Yeah?" he answered gruffly, head cocked down as if his neck were stiff, revealing as little of his face as possible.

"Wait up!"

A heavy hand landed on his shoulder, sending his heart galloping. He stopped and scanned the tunnel for an escape route.

The man's leg tapped the floor behind him. "Okay, buddy. You're good to go."

He resumed walking and then ventured a glance back. Alberto, the janitor who usually worked in the OR, was picking up a three-foot-long piece of toilet paper that Mauricio's shoe must've been dragging along.

He reached the stairwell in the building that housed the operating rooms and Mel's lab. He was here only yesterday, he reminded himself, feeling like he had been away for months. His steps echoed off the cement walls as he raced up the stairs. He reached the sixth floor, cracked the door open, and checked the hallway. Dim, deserted. Security cameras on either end.

He hurried down the hall, punched in the code to the surgeon's lounge, and let himself inside. Empty.

He heaved a sigh. From here on, clear sailing. Locker room, paper booties, cap and mask. He emerged on the operating room side.

Immediately, he heard the clatter of a gurney being pushed out of one of the ORs, the tubes and lines dangling from the patient indicated that this had been a complicated surgery. He hoped it was the last one for the night. It was close to 3:00 a.m., and in a couple of hours the new cases would be rolling into the OR. Time was short.

When the hallway cleared, he rushed to his operating room. An eerie blue light bathed the cavernous space. The patient table, the aligning and insertion equipment, the computers on the desk, the large TV screen suspended from the ceiling—all were as he had left them.

He scurried around the periphery of the room, out of sight of the camera pointed at the surgical table. OR nurses could be lingering at the nursing station where the monitors were viewed.

He entered Mel's lab. The giant screen came alive at the touch of his finger. It took precious moments to find the original Delta Gap Blocker file that he had left there yesterday, and more moments to exclude the patients who had already received the update. He was so close he could taste the success.

He typed in Mel's password to CloudFort's back door, hoping he could navigate through a procedure that he had never done. Hell, he had never even seen Mel access the back door entry. Talk about the "see one, do one, teach one" mantra of surgical training.

He pushed enter.

Nothing happened. What if the back door didn't even exist?

Right. Upper and lower case. He tried again. He didn't realize he had been holding his breath until the third attempt finally succeeded. A message appeared on the screen. "Mel, you're cleared for approach."

Mel's private humor. He wished this were as easy as landing in the fog. A few more keystrokes, and the "New, improved, LX version 2.0," a.k.a. DGB+BMR, would be ready to go out in one big upload direct to CloudFort, and onto all of those who had not been protected yet.

He waited as the file ran through Mel's diagnostics, the computer whirring evenly.

Suddenly, silence. Then a shrill beep. His heart, already pounding, did a flip.

"Ready for upload."

He felt the stabbing pain in his shoulder as he exhaled. Not a good sign. Later. No time to deal with the wound now.

He pulled up the patient list. Three thousand five hundred seventy eight names began cascading down the screen, the computer chirping reassuringly as each contact information was confirmed, and the new software upload verified. He tapped his uninjured foot, wishing the processor were faster.

The pain in his flank made his stomach churn. Now would be a good time to get some x-rays, start an IV, check for internal organ injuries ... He gritted his teeth, willing the symptoms to subside. Forget the nausea. Stay on task.

A thought mushroomed. Nausea ... The urge to vomit. Spike had to go to the ER because of vomiting. Spike got sick while tampering with his sleep channel. Not his first time tampering, but Spike had never been sick in all the time he had known him. The vomiting had started after the Delta Gap Blocker update was downloaded to Spike's computer. Cause or coincidence? He had been taught never to believe in coincidences.

Go to the ER. Return to the ER.

Boomerang.

That's what Mel said. "We'll call it Boomerang."

Was that the "BMR" that Mel included in his title of the new software? Perhaps the DG Blocker contained another set of instructions, like Mel had implied. Instructions that would make the patient too sick to function if the Delta channel was tampered with. Like by somebody attempting to program a gap.

He cued up a copy of the DG Blocker and scanned the lines of code. Sure enough, buried in the long list were instructions clearly designed to generate impulses in the leads going to the parasympathetic system. Tweak those, and nausea and vomiting were sure to follow.

Love you, Mel.

The list was almost at the end, the names sorted by who had the fix, and who was still at risk, when a small window in the right upper corner of the screen caught his attention. It was Mel's Delta Gap Detector, blinking as it scanned every record, checking for anomalies in the sleep tracings. The previously noted cases were all there. Kevin, Schwartz, Lori. He clenched his teeth. It was their Delta wave gaps that had allowed the hacker to do his damage.

And now there was a new name. His stomach turned as a he realized it looked familiar. He brushed off his concern. Out of three thousand plus patients, there could be two or three with the same last name. He tapped on the keyboard to enlarge the window, and leaned forward to read the specifics. The rustle of clothes behind him blasted him upright.

75

MAURICIO SPUN AROUND. Leoni was standing inches behind him. The obvious question was on his lips, but she anticipated it.

"I heard about the crash on the news. I went to the airport ... And the plane wasn't there ... I knew it was you, and I prayed ..."

She moved toward him, but he held her at arm's length, the memory of the betrayal looming large.

"I knew if you survived, this is where I'd find you ..." Her eyes filled with tears. "It took me a while, but I figured out why you ran out. The photos. You recognized ..."

He winced, reliving the moment.

"Mauricio, please let me explain why I ..."

"Too late." He had no time or love for this woman. He had to get back to the compromised record.

"It's never too late. I can help undo ..." Her eyes darted over his shoulder to the screen. "I know that name ..." she whispered, wiping her eyes and moving toward the computer.

He blocked her. "Of course you do. BrainPacers gave you and your friend all the access you needed."

She looked at him as if he were crazy. "What are you talking about?"

The little act was unbecoming. "Don't play innocent. Is that how you two hacked in? You and your chessman? Using your site to select your victims?" The thought that he had authorized BrainPacers weighed heavily on him. "How much did K&K pay you two? How many more before you blew the whistle and ground the LX into the ground?"

She was shaking her head so violently he thought her brain could tear a vessel. "Mauricio, I knew nothing about it . . . Believe me . . . Let me help you . . ."

He couldn't decide whether her charade was more skilled or more disgusting. He went with both. "Want to help? Stay where you are and let me try to undo the havoc you've wroth."

"Don't shut me out, damn it. Let me show you . . ."

"I've seen enough. The glances, the touches, the endearments." For the second time tonight, he felt a lump in his throat. "To think I trusted you."

"Trust me again." Tears were rolling down her cheeks. She managed to get close enough to grab his arm. "You have to."

The fingers sent a familiar jolt straight to his brain. He wanted to wrap his arms around her, to forgive her even if she didn't deserve it. Instead, he threw her as disdainful a look as he could manage, shrugged off her hand, and turned back to the computer.

"Fox," she said. "Michael Fox."

The hair on the back of his neck stiffened. Lieutenant Michael Fox, USAF, was the name on the record up on the screen that listed patients in whom Delta gaps had been detected.

"I called him," she said.

He spun toward her. "What . . . Why . . ." She was deeper in the deception and the hacking than he imagined.

Leoni came to stand by his side. In a few truncated sentences, she told him about the blackmailer, the threat to her, the recent visit, and the phone call. He felt his anger abating with every sentence, and giving way to an all-consuming fear.

"What did you tell him? The pilot."

She shook her head. "Not me, it was Al. And he walked away. All I heard was something about an Air Force One double. And something about refueling. I think."

The aching pain in the shoulder spread like wild horses galloping across his chest. He pulled up Fox's record to full screen. The defect in the Delta channel tracing gaped like a deadly crevasse in a snowfield. Ninety-eight minutes ago, about the time of Leoni's call.

Bits of recently overheard news meshed with the new information, like engine gears engaging. The President was flying to Cambodia. Air Force One and its twin decoy would be escorted by fighter jets. One of the escort pilots was part of an experimental program . . . Michael Fox. An LX implant recipient.

The impossible was staring him in the face. Oakley had decided to show off his program by sending one of the AAA pilots on a no-sleep trip, unaware that the hacker had tampered with the mission.

"I didn't know why . . ." Leoni was saying.

He waved her off. Perhaps it would all turn out to be another circus act, like the one with Lori hugging her father in the White House.

Or a national disaster that would make the commuter crash look like a footnote. Air Force One was carrying at least twice as many passengers. The President of the United States included. To say nothing of the lifeblood of the program he had worked so hard to implement.

Sweat was running down his back, stinging the wound. He had to get Fox away from Air Force One.

He calmed a little as he realized that one call should do it. He cued up Skype and dialed. With luck, Skype would be harder to trace than a phone call. Either way, by the time they caught up with him, the message would be delivered. The rest was inconsequential. They could arrest him then.

Oakley's immobile face popped up on the screen. "Well, the fugitive physician himself," said the computer-generated voice.

"Brad. Your pilot, Michael Fox, is he flying with Air Force One?"

"I see you and Ms. Wakeling still work together." The digitized cartoon face winked. "At least at night."

"No time for games, Brad. Fox? Yes or no?"

Brad's eyes flashed anger, but his features remained frozen. There was no reply.

"I take that's a yes. Brad, order him back."

"What for?"

"Just do it, Brad. Right now. Make up something. Medical reasons. I'll explain later."

"Explain now."

It wasn't a battle worth fighting. In a few short sentences, he brought Oakley up to speed. "Maybe it's nothing, but we cannot take the chance," he concluded.

"We, Kemosabe?" Brad's computer voice said. "My pilot, my decision. My ass if you're wrong."

"Brad, Fox might be on a mission you'll regret . . ."

"Yeah, yeah . . . That fiasco with the First Family? It's not going to happen here."

It was a gut punch. But he couldn't blame Oakley.

"My triple A boys are trained. Ready to serve. You saw the results. Now the President will see the results. It's my last hurrah. And you're not going to piss on it."

"Brad . . ."

The screen went black.

76

MAURICIO'S HOPE FOR A ONE-CALL solution had crashed.

He raised his hand to run his fingers through his hair and felt blood bubbling from the wound on his back. Shit. The puncture must have penetrated the chest wall after all. If air leaked in, he would be down to one lung. Or worse. A tension pneumothorax could develop, and literally suffocate him. Shit, shit, shit.

Leoni touched him. "You're hurt."

He shrugged her off. "No time."

"How can I help?"

Turn back the clock to the day before we met, he wanted to yell.

Last resort. He would have to try to reach the President aboard Air Force One. Given his recent performance, the chances were nil.

Perhaps the First Lady would listen.

One hand folded in a good luck figa, he used the other to open Skype and dialed the number from memory.

An unfamiliar face appeared. The oval windows and layout of the space told him it was the interior of an aircraft.

"I need to speak . . ."

The agent interrupted. "I'll inform Mrs. Caldwell. Where are you Doctor?"

Grappling with the fear of being located, he rattled off Mel's Skype call-back name. The connection ended.

For practical purposes, Plan B was gone. He was sure that at that very moment, the agent was on the phone to the FBI. They were probably just four floors below staking out his office.

What else, what else? There must be something he could do. If he could upload the DGBlocker-plus-Boomerang to Fox and make him sick, the man would have to drop out before he could carry out whatever instructions . . .

Except that by now Fox had completed his logon and was airborne. Out of reach.

Mauricio's brain was fighting, refusing to accept defeat.

There was something else that Mel had mentioned when they were discussing Oakley's pilots: an extra precaution of some sort.

Think.

He wished his brain were clearer, but the pain and shortness of breath were taking their toll. The solution felt tantalizingly close, but eluded recovery.

Mauricio released a small breath. Carefully, so as not to cause more bubbling. He felt his respiration growing shallower by the minute.

The pilot's respirations were being monitored. All the vital signs were monitored. Lieutenant Fox was being checked frequently.

And then he remembered what Mel had said. "We'll have them log on every three hours."

It could work. It was a long shot, but it was his only shot. He cued up Fox's tracings. Last logon, 05:45 EST. That was 2:45 a.m. local. That meant that at 5:45 local time the pilot would have his second logon for the trip. He cued up the Boomerang portion of the code and dialed in a maximum intensity setting. Hopefully, at his next logon, Mel's creation would lead to incapacitating symptoms, and the pilot would have to withdraw from his escort duties.

The Skype tone startled him.

The First Lady. She did call back. Talking directly to Air Force One was a far better option than guessing logon times.

Patty Caldwell was staring from the screen.

His finger, poised over the keyboard, stopped short of tapping the button to upload the new instructions into Fox's record.

"Dr. Barcelos, this better be important. And accurate."

There was no time to mince words. "Mrs. Caldwell, one of the escort pilots has an implant."

Patty Caldwell interrupted him. "You bothered me in the middle of a meeting to tell me that?"

"But ..."

"The use of your LX by the military is part of Tom's speech later to ..."

"The pilot might have been programmed ..."

"Please don't interrupt. I'm still talking, Doctor."

Somewhere behind him, a door blasted open and someone yelled "Freeze!"

Mauricio tried again. "The pilot ..."

A hand squeezed the words in his throat.

"Fox ..." he croaked. "Return ..."

Plan B was gone. In a last ditch effort, he reached for the keyboard. One keystroke and the upload would go to Fox.

A violent chop slammed his wrist away.

"Security!" a voice barked. "Don't move,"

On the screen, Patty Caldwell sat up in her chair.

"This man will not bother you again, Madam. The FBI and the police are on their way."

"Mrs. Caldwell," he tried.

"Goodbye, Dr. Barcelos," she said. "I'm sorry it had to end like this."

"Patty, wait!" he hissed.

Patty Caldwell's eyes lingered on his. She looked like she was going to ask a question. Then the screen went blank.

The grip on his throat relaxed. He started to turn.

Leoni screamed. "Don't!"

A vicious blow to the temple jerked his head sideways.

77

GRASPING THE EDGE OF THE DESK, Mauricio managed to remain upright despite the force of the blow. He turned toward the voice, and took a step back.

"You're the checkmate guy," he mumbled, recognizing the repairman he spotted at the airport and remembering the license plate.

"Checkmate guy? I guess that's better than chessman," the man smiled, dropping the gun casually by his side. Mauricio noted the silencer screwed to the barrel. "I'd say call me Al, but our acquaintance will be short." The man turned to Leoni, his head cocked, his eyebrows raised in a silent question.

"You're just in time, Al," she stammered. "He was going to . . ."

Al interrupted her in mid-sentence. "Leoni?"

"After you and I talked, I decided to get back in here . . ." Mauricio saw her eyes dart from him, to Al, to the screen, back to Al. "To clean up my computer trail, in case. You know. And then I saw him come in from the back entrance, walk across the lobby . . ." She was talking fast. "And I thought I should follow . . ." There was an unfamiliar harshness in her voice.

Al jerked his head and Leoni stopped in mid-sentence. "There's a wheelchair outside. Go get it, please."

Leoni stepped out.

Mauricio felt his thoughts flapping like a windsock in a hurricane. Whose side was she on? His heart wished one thing. His brain was telling him another. It didn't matter. Right now only Fox mattered. With Oakley and the First Lady attempts dead ends, uploading the DG Blocker to Fox's program was his last chance. Slim and unproven and iffy, and maybe too late, but a chance. The record was still on the screen. All he needed to do was tap a key . . .

"Whatever you're thinking, Doctor, don't do it."

Leoni was back with the wheelchair. A wide body, fit for the morbidly obese. It barely fit into the confined space.

Al raised the gun and signaled. "Let's take a ride, Doctor. Till it's all over, I can't let you out of my sight."

Mauricio eyeballed the distances. The computer was along the way to the wheelchair. If he could distract the man, he might stand a chance.

"It takes more than manipulating the Delta channel, Al," he said, trying to sound calm.

Al scoffed. "Yeah. Takes a well-timed suggestion, too. I got General Schwartz to throw the aero contract to the French, just by having his escort whisper in his ear."

Mauricio glanced at Leoni. Proud of yourself?

Leoni's face was as pale as a cadaver's.

Al seemed to be enjoying the chance to brag. "The lab tech spilled the beans when I convinced her I was the VP's surgeon."

Mauricio gritted his teeth. The CloudFort rep's words echoed in his brain. "Hackers go after high value targets. Depressed patients, not so much." Right. Obviously, these depressed patients were worth their weight in gold.

Al waved his gun. "Anyway . . . In the chair. Now."

He pretended to start moving toward the wheelchair, stalling for time.

Al went on. "And other uses? Unlimited."

"Not with a pilot."

"Oh, you pilots are better than the rest of us? You met Andrew Lewis, commuter captain? Proof of concept. When it comes to D-gaps, no one's immune."

The bastard looked so pleased, Mauricio fought the urge to tear the grin off his face with his bare hands. He took another step toward the computer. Push that button and the problem may be solved.

Al stopped him. "Actually, Doctor, let's have you step back." He glanced at Leoni. "Over there."

Obediently, she started to reposition the wheelchair. In the narrow confines of the lab, it was not an easy task. She was moving past the computer. Her eyes sought his. The two pools of blue-grey screamed volumes. Get over your mistrust and take a chance. Tell me what to do.

Wishful thinking on his part, or was she really trying to help? He glanced toward the computer, back to her, back to the screen. He raised his voice, trying to add more meaning. "We have new safeguards that will prevent patients from complying with your suggestions."

Al laughed. "New safeguards? And I have new wings. In the chair, please. Leoni . . ."

Leoni bumped the wheelchair against him making him stumble.

"Sorry." Leoni bumped him again. "A little room please . . ."

Al took an awkward step sideways.

Mauricio sensed the opportunity. Al's flank was exposed. He had a clear shot. He flexed his legs.

Al turned. Their eyes met.

His stomach convulsed. Murderer . . . You will never again strike a human being. He tried to move, but couldn't. The moment passed.

"That's better, Doctor," Al said, the gun pointing again.

Crestfallen, he looked at Leoni. Do it, he wanted to scream, wishing he had inherited his grandmother's claimed telepathic power. If you are worth my trust, push the button. Now.

Leoni's thoughts were racing. Al was indicating for her to move past him. "Get him into the chair," he was saying.

Leoni hesitated. Why had Mauricio passed the chance to strike? It seemed like a perfect moment. And what was he signaling with his look? He wanted her to do something, but what? Uploading? Safeguards?

She needed time.

Just off her right elbow, Mel's big screen loomed mysteriously, as if taunting her to push the wrong button and blow it all up. From what she had gathered, Lieutenant Fox was the pilot escorting Air Force One. Was something about to blow up anyway?

Fox's record was staring back from the screen. Yes or no?

"Move," Al commanded.

She complied.

Al raised the gun, and Mauricio eased into the chair, wincing as if in pain.

"Tie him down," Al commanded.

She noticed a drawer just under the keyboard and pulled it open. "Hey . . ."

She froze. "I'm just looking for tape. You know . . ." She made a circling motion around her wrists. It wasn't going to work. He wouldn't let her touch anything.

With his free hand Al grabbed a roll sitting in plain sight, and threw it to her. "Use this."

She missed it, bent down, and brought it up.

"Do it," Al waved impatiently.

The moment was now.

She watched as Al reached into a pocket. "Leftover from the case next door," he said, pulling out a syringe filled with milky white fluid.

Mauricio's last vision was Leoni moving toward him. In one hand she held a roll of tape. As she passed the computer, he thought he saw her other hand brush the keyboard.

Moments later, he floated unconscious into the night.

78

DORA WAS CALLING TO HIM. "Mauricio, open your eyes."

Why was his sister speaking English? The act of thinking felt like walking waist-deep through a marsh.

"Mau!"

Why was he sitting on a dirt floor?

A man's voice. "Quiet!"

Pain shot up from his right flank as he took a breath. The air was stale and smelled of garlic and dust. The wound. The fall. Icarus. He tried to open his eyes, but saw only dim slivers of light. His arms were tied behind him, numb and motionless.

Disconnected events slithered through the cobwebs. He was in a wheelchair. Leoni was taping his wrists to the armrests. A man, pointing a gun. A needle was shoved into his arm. A thick milky liquid was injected.

Propofol.

Then the wheelchair was being rolled up to a van. He was trying to call for help. More white liquid. Another memory gap.

A long stagger down a narrow tunnel, rocky walls tearing at his shoulders, the beam of a flashlight casting bizarre shadows.

One eye finally opened, revealing bizarre surroundings. The space was no larger than his garage. Low ceiling and rough walls carved out of the rock and whitewashed. Ali Baba's cave? A den of thieves? He didn't care. All he wanted was to stretch out and go back to sleep. Damned Propofol.

"Mauricio!" someone cried out. Not Dora. Leoni.

"Shut up or I'll gag you." The man again.

He spotted Leoni, sitting on the floor and leaning up against the wall, her wrists in her lap, bound with a plastic flex cuff used by police. She had a large bruise on her left cheek. Her hair was matted.

If his feeble memory served, she had come to the lab claiming she wanted to help him. But then she seemed to be friendly with the attacker. What the fuck?

Their gazes connected. "Are you okay," she mouthed.

Whose side was she on? He nodded. "You?"

She closed her eyes.

He started to assess the situation. He was sitting on the floor, propped against something hard and warm. He craned his neck as far as the pain in the flank allowed. He was leaning against something that looked like a water heater, with a propane tank next to it. He tugged on his restraints. Solid. He felt around behind his back. He was tied to a pipe that was blistering hot on one end, cooler at the other. His chest still hurt, but thankfully the bubbling feeling wasn't there anymore. At least for now the lung puncture had sealed itself.

In front of him, against the opposite wall, was a desk with a computer, a man's back blocking most of a the screen. A wooden workbench with a chessboard and books occupied the center of the room. A small motor—a generator—was humming in a far corner. A ridiculously oversized flat screen TV was mounted above where Leoni was sitting. An exquisite Afghan rug covered much of the packed-dirt floor, in stark contrast to the rustic surroundings.

The man at the desk stood up and worked a remote control. He refocused. It was the man who barged into Mel's lab. Al or something.

The flash of the TV screen and the announcer's voice jolted his senses. "The pursuit of the Newport Beach surgeon suspected of murder may be coming to an end . . ."

He recognized Jorge Ramirez, the anchor at Diane's station. In this bizarre environment, the familiar voice sounded like an echo from the past. A banner at the bottom of the screen read, "Breaking News— Fugitive Physician Presumed Dead in Plane Crash."

Al turned. "Your little trick worked, Doctor. Congratulations."

Ramirez droned on. "During an apparent attempt to fly his private plane into the hospital from where he was on psychiatric leave, Dr. Barcelos crashed into the waters just off Newport Beach. He's presumed dead, and search efforts . . ."

"Good presumption," Al smirked.

"Now back to our exclusive broadcast about the First Family's trip to Cambodia." The image changed to a shot of Air Force One flanked by four military jets, their lights blinking against a deep orange dusk. In the distance, another large plane kept pace with the formation.

"The President and his convoy," Ramirez was saying, "including the twin 747 that always accompanies him abroad as a backup plane, are five hours into their flight. They're now overflying Canada, in what is known as the Northwest Territories. A land of lakes and ice. This is where three of the escorting F-22 Raptors will land, and new ones, with fresh pilots, and full fuel tanks, will take their place. The fourth F-22 will continue with the President, all the way to Phnom Penh, capital of Cambodia. We'll have exclusive live footage from Air Force One after the short break."

Al laughed. "Almost to Cambodia. Our friend Lieutenant Fox has other plans for the President."

The rest of the propofol fog lifted. He jerked on his restraints, oblivious to the pain. "Whatever you're planning, it won't work, Al," he managed to croak through his parched throat. "His training to protect the President is so ingrained that . . ."

"Ha!" Al walked up to him and recited his directions, "Lieutenant Fox, we've learned that a group of terrorists has stowed aboard what they believed was the plane that was to carry the First Family. Their plan was to highjack the plane once it's over sparsely populated area. Once they realize their mistake, they will try to crash the twin into the real Air Force One, flying just behind it, pretending to be the backup plane. Your mission is to eliminate the threat by shooting down the one posing as the President's plane."

Mauricio closed his eyes. "He won't do it, Al."

"But Doctor, didn't you say something like, 'If you were made to believe that your Lexie had rabies, you'd put her down.' With your help, I made Fox a believer."

It was a nightmare. The man heard all his conversations. His cell phone was cloned.

The commercial break was over. Ramirez was back on the screen. "Night refueling is a challenging maneuver that requires skill and constant practice." The image of a tanker plane appeared on the screen. "Fifteen minutes to refueling" the banner read.

"That's his cue," Al pointed. "The moment Lieutenant Fox uncouples the fuel transfer nozzle, he'll remember his orders and …" Al aimed an index at the screen and flexed it.

The thought that this catastrophe was about to happen, right in front of him, in full color on a TV screen, and he was powerless to prevent it, was terrifying. The sliver of hope that the disaster might be averted was growing slimmer by the second.

The man who had masterminded the destruction of his life's work, and was about to murder the President and hundreds of innocent people, wasn't smiling. For him, it was just a job.

He tried to recall details of what happened in the lab. He was talking with the First Lady. Mel's software patch was all cued up. Fox's tracing was on the screen. He was pretty sure he didn't have a chance to upload it before Al barged in. Did Leoni do it, when she stumbled? He stared past Al in the direction where she was sitting and tried to guess the answer.

A familiar voice coming from the TV sunk him to new depths of despair.

79

Every word Leoni was overhearing felt like another nail hammered into her body. Hacking, hypno-suggestions, innocents dying . . . And she was the weak link that had started this whole horrific cascade, way back at the convention.

Suddenly she saw Mauricio's body arching off the ground as if he were being electrocuted, his face twisted in agony. She followed his eyes to the screen.

"...The LX implant that both Lori Caldwell and Lieutenant Fox have ..."

The voice was familiar.

"...Was developed by my husband ... well, now ex-husband ... and it has brought new hope ..."

Diane. And she was aboard the doomed plane.

Leoni shuddered. Mauricio's pain at seeing his companion of twelve years about to die was hard enough to imagine. His torture of seeing his life's dream destroyed was unimaginable to her.

"I'm sorry," Al was saying. "I didn't know your ex was going to be aboard."

The bastard almost sounds like he means it, she thought with new loathing.

Al started rambling something about how he and Mauricio were both obsessed with noble goals, and how they could have been a team. Her anger welled up. How could the slime ball imagine himself in the same league? Helping injured children. He was the kind of person who would fund terrorists just to cause more injuries so he could bolster his self-esteem with more charity work.

"I'll see you in a gas chamber for this," Mauricio hissed.

"You won't see me anywhere, Doctor. I leave no loose ends."

She realized what he meant, and her stomach twisted.

"They'll find you, Al," Mauricio continued.

Al smirked. "Me? They have no idea I exist. You programmed the D-Gap. Your girlfriend called Pilot Fox. It's all your work." He paused to let the words sink in. "They'll stop looking for you, once a few pieces of your charred body float up at the crash site. Criminal doctor meets just fate."

Any hope that they would walk out of this alive went up in smoke. "Al," she called out. "Come here. Please," she added. He believed her the first time she faked accepting his conditions. Would he believe her again?

Al limped to where she was sitting and glared. His mocking eyes were revolting.

"I changed my mind," she forced herself to say.

"Oh, again?" He made no effort to hide the sarcasm.

"I'll come live with you if you let Mauricio go." The thought was nauseating, but if that was the price for Mauricio's life, she would gladly pay it. After all the havoc she had caused, she owed him.

He bent down, seized her arms, and hauled her upright with surprising ease.

"You had your chance, and made your choice," he hissed into her face.

"I made a mistake."

"Yes, you did."

Before she could react, he spun her around and shoved her forward to the center of the room against the work bench.

"I wouldn't want you to miss the big event."

She saw the big screen now facing her.

With two swift kicks he spread her legs wide apart and slammed her face down against the workbench.

"Al, listen . . ." She tried to raise her head. He rammed it back down, harder. She let out a deep groan as the air exploded out of her lungs, and for a moment the room went dark.

When she came to, flex cuffs were binding her ankles to the legs of the bench, and cutting off blood flow.

"You had your chance to come willingly, Princess," Al said. "Now, you'll come on my terms."

"Fuck you!" she managed, the jaw sending a jolt of pain.

He walked around to where she could see him. "Oh, you will. In good time. For now, let's enjoy the show on the big screen. Our little show can wait."

He threaded more plastic straps through the ones holding her wrists, stretching her arms forward till the sockets threatened to pop.

"Can you see okay?"

With her face plastered against the bench, she couldn't look away even if she wanted to. "Bastard," she hissed. Out of the corner of her eye, she could see Mauricio struggling with his own restraints. His bound wrists were secured to a thick copper pipe coming out of the water tank, and all he could manage to do was slide the binding back and forth.

How could this be happening? One minute she was doing PR in Newport Beach, the next she was about to be killed in some God-forsaken cave.

"Al, let him go, and I'll be yours," she tried again.

"Tsk, tsk," Al hissed.

She heard him step away and start inputting something on the computer. If she could overturn the table, and grab something to cut her bonds and make her way to Mauricio . . . before Al stopped her? Pipe dream.

She thought of how deranged and uncoordinated he seemed when she insulted him, back at her condo. Maybe if she provoked him, he would make a mistake and she could somehow get out of her bindings.

"Hey, Al," she said, "You didn't concoct this scheme yourself. Who's paying you this time?"

There was no response. He continued working at his desk.

"How does it feel, being a lowly pawn, working for a master?"

He was now rummaging for something. .

"How do you live with yourself, knowing that people just use you and throw you away?"

What did she say on the stairs at home that provoked him? "Face it, Al. You're a worthless scum."

A drawer slammed hard.

"Worthless scum." The chilly calm in his voice was not what she was hoping to hear.

He walked up to her. Her heart was now hammering against the bench top.

"Remember Gina?" he asked suddenly.

"What about Gina?" Mauricio was so distraught after his trip to the Mojave coroner, that she had made a point of getting a copy of the autopsy report. Gina had been left to die in the desert after her LX was pulled out of her brain.

Nausea overwhelmed her as it all came together. Al was the abductor and the killer by neglect. He must have kept Gina in this very hole for days without anyone finding them.

"Nice place, don't you think?" Al was saying as if reading her thoughts. "Gina didn't mind it."

Days? She recalled a story about a creep who had hid his daughter in the basement of his house in a big city for fourteen years. In this cave in the desert? It would be a long time before anyone found her.

She saw his face. His expression made her nausea turn to retching.

80

AL JUMPED OUT OF THE WAY as Leoni vomited all over the bench. Damn it. He would have to clean it quickly before the stinky mess dripped down on his favorite rug.

Barcelos was grunting in his corner, yanking against the flex cuffs. Good luck. They were LAPD issue. Indestructible.

Caldwell was droning on from the TV. Al checked the crawl at the bottom of the screen. "Coming up: Refueling to begin in eight minutes."

That made it about thirteen minutes to show time. A quarter of an hour till the balance of the fifty mil landed in his account and his life was changed forever.

Leoni retched again, but this time her stomach must have been empty. Her right eye was swelling shut, and blood was dripping down her cheek. He shook his head regretting the violence she had provoked in him.

He walked to the sink, found a roll of paper towels, filled a small basin with warm water and walked back. "First, your face, my Princess." He wiped off the blood gently.

It reminded him of the times he stroked Svetlana's face when they were out stargazing. He wasn't a worthless scum to her, back then. Now . . . With what he had accomplished . . . He felt a sense of pride. I'm a prince among hackers. It would be so good if Leoni could share in the triumph of this moment. But she ruined it by her betrayal. Her loss. She will come around eventually, he decided.

He started cleaning around her chin. She lunged to bite his wrist, but he managed to pull his hand away in time.

"Leoni, don't." He smoothed her hair back. "Don't make it hard for yourself."

Caldwell was still up on the screen, apparently determined to use every minute of air time to his advantage. "During my administration, we have made progress on multiple fronts, but perhaps on none more dramatically than in healthcare . . ."

Diane nodded and smiled, egging the poor schmuck on, in a discourse that had no future.

"For example, take the neural implant," Caldwell rambled on. "We've instructed our military to adopt a device that was originally designed for civilian use, and take advantage of . . ."

Al tuned out in disgust. They were all the same. The Presidents, the Lady Kays of this world. Vultures. Taking credit for somebody's else kill. Look what I did. My idea. Kudos to me, you shameless schmucks.

He faced Barcelos. "Are you listening, Doctor? Your President is trying to claim credit for your invention. It's not right."

He gave another cautious swipe to Leoni's face. This time she didn't try to bite him.

Barcelos was still working on his restraints, not listening.

Al winced. Fifty mil was nice, but this was his finest moment, and where was the recognition? The adulation? The assurances that he was not worthless? Suddenly, he was feeling exuberant.

"I feel your pain, Doctor. We all have people trying to yank our chains. For you, it's Isaacson and Caldwell and that Fed guy. Fiaschetti, right? For me . . . I have this . . . this German Ice Queen. I'll bet you she'll claim all this was her idea. The client will give her a raise and kiss her ass. Me? Not even a thank you note."

He threw the dirty paper towels into the basin and looked up. Suddenly he realized he had Barcelos' attention. The man was staring at him as if Al were about to reveal the secret formula for transmuting lead to gold.

"Ice Queen, Al? Who's the Ice Queen?"

Who indeed? After the last encounter with Lady Kay, he had called Dumas, posing as a venture capitalist, only to find out that the man's project was put on the back burner days earlier. So it wasn't K&K. Back then he felt duped by Lady Kay. Who the hell was she working for, if not the big conglomerate? But at this moment, only the balance in his numbered account mattered.

"I say to hell with Caldwell, to hell with Lady Kay. You and I know right here," he thumped his heart, "who the geniuses are."

"Who is the Ice Queen?" Barcelos persisted.

Why the sudden interest? What did he care, who the Ice Queen was? The poor bastard didn't need to know. It was just a matter of principle. He turned back to the TV, looking for another chance to express his outrage.

"The way I understand the technology," the President droned on, "is that the output from the implant enables our pilots to remain awake for much longer periods of time. With an online session every twenty-four hours to adjust the programming . . ."

Al heard a coarse laugh from Barcelos' corner. "Every three hours."

The interruption was annoying. Al took his eyes off the screen. "What?"

"On the ultra-long military missions, it's every three hours," Barcelos clarified. "So we can monitor the subject."

Al felt a pang of pain shoot up from his ankle. "So it's three. So what?"

"So Fox is logging in every three hours. I uploaded the updated version. The one Mel made for me. Before you came barging into the lab. It's waiting for him, next time he logs on. Your orders will be cancelled."

Barcelos' voice sounded hoarse and choppy, but annoyingly confident. It was the wandering eyes that made the statement suspect.

"You're lying," he said, but the seed of doubt had sprouted. "The hospital locked you out. You couldn't upload shit."

The leg was tapping so hard, he had trouble making his way to the computer on the desk.

"Come on, Al. Mel wasn't naïve. A back door."

The doctor was more savvy than he let on.

"You had no time."

Barcelos glanced away again. He was lying.

He followed the glance. The man was looking in Leoni's direction. A looked seemed to pass between them. "Leoni?" Al bellowed, suspicion mounting.

"So fuck you, bastard."

Suppressing the urge to hit her, Al turned to the computer. A few keystrokes, and he knew he was in trouble. The record showed that Fox's next logon was due at 9:15 a.m. East Coast time. According to the web, Air Force One took off around 6:15 EST. Suddenly Barcelos' bluff about logons every three hours became more believable.

He glanced at the clock. It was 6:05 a.m. in California. He had ten minutes.

To do what? Al controlled his breathing.

His fears that Mel had developed a software patch in his last day in the hangar turned out to be true. Fortunately, whatever it was, it hadn't worked for Fox. Al had seen the Delta gap with his own eyes, and the pilot's response to his instructions left no doubt that he would comply. So why the fuck was the doctor blabbering about cancelling his orders to the pilot?

Barcelos and the bitch were probably lying, he told himself. No app could possibly erase the message he had firmly implanted in the pilot's subconscious.

Or could it? Al felt sweat forming on his upper lip.

"Fox will follow my orders," he said, but he could feel the little snag in his own voice.

"Okay, Al."

He hated the way Barcelos shrugged his shoulders and smiled. His brain began to race. The chess game had just turned into a crapshoot. What if the doctor was not lying? He could not hang his entire future on a roll of the dice.

Al glanced at the timer. Now he had nine minutes to find the truth and take action if need be. He had to abort the programming Barcelos claimed that he had uploaded.

"I want access to that back door of yours."

Another smug grin on the doctor's face. "I don't know what you're talking about, Al."

He stepped over and looked down. "Password. Access. Now."

"Dream on."

He hauled back and rammed the foot into the doctor's ribs. There was a satisfying crunch. The doctor groaned. Leoni screamed an obscenity.

"Password," he repeated.

Barcelos groaned but said nothing.

Okay. If pain wasn't going to work, he could play another game. He hurried to the computer.

"Password, Barcelos."

The man just shook his head and closed his eyes.

Mauricio felt his anxiety mounting as he watched Al poised over the keyboard.

"If you think you can block Fox's upload . . ." He had to pause for breath. "You're wasting your time. Now that he's airborne, the only access is through the military." It wasn't true, but how would Al know?

"Or the back door," Al smirked. "Password please"

"Over my dead body."

"Your choice, Doctor."

"I've already made it, Al."

Al turned away and started typing.

On the overhead screen, Caldwell and Diane's image shrunk into a corner, replaced by a long list of names. He recognized the Brain-Pacers banner heading up the new screen.

"Pick one," Al ordered.

What was the guy asking him to do?

"Pick a patient, Barcelos. He or she will die next time they log on for an update."

He stared, processing how this could be done, but soon the answer became obvious. If the bastard had figured how to program almost invisible gaps into the sleep channel, there was little question he could override the pre-set limits on the other channels and deliver a lethal impulse.

"No favorites?" Al asked. "Fine, I'll pick. Let's work the East Coast. They'll be waking up by now . . ." A record popped up. Al recited, "Thirty-four-year-old mother of three."

The familiar serpentine pattern of LX tracings filled the screen. He could see Al adjusting the controls under each of the channels. A vise squeezed his chest when he read the settings. "Al, that'll kill her."

"That's the idea," Al cackled. "But you can stop it. Just give me the password."

He gritted his teeth and renewed his efforts to break loose from the pipe, careful not to attract Al's attention.

Al was looking at the screen. "Oh-oh. She's just logged on. Think fast."

What was there to think about? Who would live and who would die?

He felt blood running down his wrist, the hot pipe burning his skin as he pulled, but he plastic straps held firm.

"Al, let's talk about some way . . ."

Al pushed the keyboard away. "Oh, well. Too late. She's gone."

The message read: "LX shut down."

The bastard could pick off patients all day long. He did the morbid math. A fatal balance. There were probably a hundred passengers aboard the plane, including the President of the United States, and Diane. There were well over three thousand LX patients on the ground. The realization that Al could get to all of them, and there was nothing Mauricio could do to prevent it, was devastating.

Al was yelling again. Another name was on the screen. "Forty-two year old engineer, sole caretaker for his invalid father. He's next. Password, or the decimation continues."

The choice he had to make was tearing him in pieces. "Al . . ."

"Another one gone."

He could see Al's fingers were trembling as they danced over the keyboard.

"You going to give me the fucking password, Barcelos?"

His eyes went to the TV screen. Diane's image was smiling at the camera. "I'm sorry, Di," he started to say, wishing he could say good-bye in person.

 **81**

Mauricio stared helplessly as Al cued up another patient.

"Next," the bastard announced without even a glance in his direction.

Suddenly a new hope emerged. The odds were almost impossible, but he had no choice.

"You win, Al," he croaked. "I'll give you the password," he said, his voice barely above a whisper. "It's a-four-hash mark . . ." His words faded all on their own as his breath ran out. Damned lung. Please, not now . . .

"Speak up."

He looked up. Now a whisper was all he could manage. "I'm trying. It's lower case a, four, dollar sign, capital B . . ."

He paused, trying to make the password sound realistic. The whole charade had seemed like a good idea, but now he wondered if he had the strength to pull it off.

"Four. Dollar sign . . ." he whispered. "Let me think." He glanced at the clock on the TV. Still six minutes before refueling. If his calculations were correct. "On second thought . . . no."

Al's rushed toward him, his movements disjointed, the prosthesis snagging on the carpet, almost tripping him. "Son of a bitch . . ."

The metal foot smashed into his flank, in the same place as before, but harder. The pain pierced all the way to his brain. He tried to say something else, but couldn't draw enough breath.

Another kick. His right kidney begged for mercy.

"You're nothing . . . but a powerless . . . bully," he managed finally.

The kicks started flying randomly, missing their marks as often as not.

He coughed out frothy stream of blood. A cracked rib must have torn a vessel. He hissed what he hoped sounded like "worthless weakling."

Al was kicking with both feet.

He took the punishment. To lull Al into a mistake, the beating to near oblivion had to be believable. He rolled from side to side in futile efforts to soften the blows. Finally, gasping for air, he laid on his back, too weak to defend himself. He took one more blow to the left flank, the wound on the right side hissed like a punctured tire.

His vision blurred. "You win," he mumbled. "The password . . . In my back pocket."

The kicks stopped.

"Roll over." Al leaned down.

Mauricio rallied what was left of his strength, and yanked on the restraints. The pipe behind him snapped. He heard a hissing sound, but it was not coming from his lung.

Al was standing still, seemingly confused.

Now.

He rolled away from the wall and swept his leg across Al's ankles.

"You . . ." Al yelled, as he toppled over awkwardly.

Hands still bound behind his back but now free from the pipe, fighting for every breath, Mauricio struggled to his feet. The right lung felt like a party balloon.

Al was already on one knee, raising a gun.

Mauricio bent his knees and started to uncoil, aiming the blow at the man's head.

The half-hearted kick that followed was too slow, too poorly placed. The gun dropped out of Al's hand, but not far enough away.

Al lunged for it, landing on his knees.

He tried to follow, but his legs were wobbly. He stumbled, his arms bound behind his back useless to break the fall.

Still on all fours, Al retrieved the gun and inched toward him.

Al's face told him the bastard was as determined as he was.

"The password, fucker. The password, or I'll beat you to death."

And then Al's face morphed into another.

Paulo.

Paulo beating him senseless in the alley.

Paulo's voice echoed, "Let me fuck your sister, or I'll beat you to a pulp."

"Essa vez não," he breathed. This time it would be different.

Rage welled up from the pit of his stomach, and a new surge of strength flooded his body.

Paulo. His brothers had ruined Dora's life. They weren't here to pay for it, but this bastard was going to, for all of them.

He heard a woman screaming,

Was it Dora, the way she must have screamed when Paulo's brothers were raping her?

"Fire," the woman was screaming.

Leoni.

He smelled smoke.

He turned toward the wall. A narrow blue flame was hissing from the ruptured gas pipe. Have to shut it off . . .

The thought was cut short as a brutal blow landed on his neck.

He hunched over. This time it was not an act. All he could manage was tiny breaths, his chest rigid like a barrel.

It was over.

He watched helplessly as Al inched closer.

And then as if by magic, the workbench swung through the air, striking Al's head. The gun flew out and slid away. Al rocked and collapsed, motionless.

Leoni stood awkwardly, her wrists and legs still bound down to the bench, but now closer to the middle of the room. "Gave it my best shot," she mumbled, before collapsing backwards to the floor.

"The fire," she repeated.

The fire, his dulled mind echoed.

With a superhuman effort he crawled to the pipe. Then he turned around, squatted, clenched his teeth, and extended his wrists behind his back over the flame.

The stench of burning plastic and burning flesh filled the room. He felt melted plastic running down his hands.

An eternity later, the flex cuff disintegrated and his wrists sprung free.

His skin still smoldering, he limped to the computer.

One last try.

82

Mauricio bent over the keyboard. Skype was nowhere to be found, but he managed to located the call icon and punched a number from memory.

The connection rang. Once, twice.

On the TV, a flight helmet filled the screen. "We practice refueling even on our shorter missions ..." Even with the audio distortion, he recognized the deep baritone of the young Air Force pilot he met at Los Alamitos. Diane was interviewing Lt. Fox.

Somebody, pick up the phone.

Diane cooed, "Lieutenant, it must be amazing to be the first to try out ..."

The phone was still ringing.

Finally, a click. "It's an emergency," he shouted before the operator could say a word. "I need to speak with Jorge Ramirez."

"What kind of emergen ..."

"This is Dr. Barcelos. Diane's husband. Give me Ramirez."

The line went silent. On hold, he hoped.

Fox was now describing the refueling process. "In a couple of minutes you'll see the hose trail out from the tanker. Then I'll use the sights right here . . ."

"Dr. Barcelos. This is Jorge Rami . . ."

"Patch me through to Diane."

"She's not here."

"I know where she is. Do it, now."

Ramirez vanished. Silence again. He glanced up at the screen. Diane was smiling and speaking, but her finger went to her earpiece. Her expression changed. She opened her mouth.

The camera cut to the studio and a frazzled Ramirez.

Diane's voice came through. "Mau? What is going on?" Her voice was trembling, but it never sounded so good.

"Di, no time. Have them abort the refueling."

Her voice hardened. "Are you nuts? Now what?"

"Di, please . . ." Where was the camera when he needed her to see him?

Leoni's scream drowned him out. "Look out."

He turned. Al was up again, aiming the gun with a shaking hand. Diane's voice. "Mau?"

The shot rang out as Mauricio dove to the ground.

Al hobbled toward him. Another shot. He was already on his feet, sliding to the right, pivoting, gasping for air.

The third shot whizzed past his temple.

"Your woman's next," Al thundered, indicating Leoni.

Oh, no, she's not. Not this time. Every muscle in his body was humming. In the next moment, he was flying through the air.

His eyes registered Al's face, frozen in surprise.

"Die, bastard," Mauricio yelled. The heel caught Al squarely on the temple. He heard the sickening crunch. And, like thirty years earlier, the opponent rocked on his feet, back and forth, then slowly folded and collapsed.

Somewhere far away, he heard Leoni's screams. "Fire."

The blanket covering the futon was ablaze. He glanced around, searching for a fire extinguisher . . . water . . . anything . . . anything to cut her ties.

On the TV Diane was gone, replaced by the tanker, the refueling hose trailing in the slipstream. A few feet away, an F-22 was closing in slowly.

"Diane . . ." The Skype window was blank.

Leoni was screaming again. "Everything is burning."

The fire had engulfed the afghan, the futon, the bookshelf, part of the bench to which Leoni was bound.

He hurried to her, grabbed the first thing he saw on the floor—a paring knife—and went to work on her ties . He aimed the blade from the table leg side, sparing her skin. Moments later, her restraints popped. He grabbed her arm.

"I'm okay," she yelled. "Go."

Diane reappeared on the screen. Through the smoke that floated under the ceiling of the cave, she looked like she was speaking from the heavens.

" . . . we'll return after a short commercial break with our exclusive live footage of Lt. Fox as he begins the challenging refueling process."

"No! Don't let him!" he screamed into the smoke, knowing she could not hear him.

The fire had spread to the computer desk. One of the wooden legs was burning. Before he could react, the desk toppled over, spilling the computer into the flames.

His eyes darted to the screen just as it flared twice and went blank.

The smoke turned orange.

He glanced behind. A wall of flames encircled the propane tank.

"Leoni," he croaked.

He grabbed her hand and dragged her toward the exit.

Behind them, the crackling built to a roar.

"Run," he hissed, his lungs scorched.

The exit was almost within reach when a ball of fire caught up with them.

83

THE MONKEYS WERE MAKING A TREMENDOUS RACKET, banging rocks and sticks against the branches. Birds added to the cacophony, their loud chirping annoyingly monotonous. A stream gurgled nearby.

Something humid and heavy was forcing Mauricio's eyelids closed. He started to speak, but only air blew out.

Panic seized him as he realized he was on his back, his arms tied down. He tried to sit up. A firm grasp held him down. He struggled.

"It's an E-T tube, Dr. Barcelos," a woman's voice yelled from somewhere," to help you breathe."

The weights came off his eyelids, one by one. He forced his eyes open and squinted. A pretty brunette was close enough to kiss.

He tried to focus. People were milling around, making a racket. Monitors were chirping reassuringly. The chest tube protruding from his right flank bubbled cheerfully.

"Do you know where you are, Doctor?" the nurse said, unnecessarily loudly.

His brain ground out a recollection. Al. Explosion. Diane. The President. Refueling ... He made frantic gestures, but the attempts to answer blasted silently out of his breathing tube.

The nurse produced a clipboard and a magic marker. "Write it here."

With his left hand he scribbled, "Air Force One? Okay?"

The brunette looked sad. "Nope. Not okay. You're in the hospital, not in a plane." She pulled out a syringe and squirted something into the IV line.

The monkeys and the birds went to sleep.

When he woke up again, the tube was gone from his throat, and he could move at least half of his extremities. A different brunette appeared.

"Welcome back, Doc. You're at Antelope Medical Center. Surg ICU," she said.

"How is the President?" he hissed.

She frowned. "A shame."

His heart started skipping, triggering the alarm. She turned it off.

"Wasting tax payers' money on those Cambodians, and all he got was a shoe thrown at him."

He let his eyes drift closed and smiled as far as his cracked lips would let him.

"There was a message for you," the nurse said. "A woman by the name of Patty called. Wouldn't leave a number. Said to tell you that Tom and Lori made it safely . . . Hey, are you okay Doc?" She bent down and wiped the tears out of his eyes.

Hours later he persuaded the nurses that he was well enough to be wheeled to Leoni's room.

She was covered in burn dressings. The eyebrows were singed, and the luscious blond mane was reduced to a stubble, but her eyes sparkled just as they did the first day he saw her. The nurse was pushing his wheelchair so slowly that he thought he'd never get close enough to touch her.

As he drew nearer, she tried to lift her head off the pillow. "I'm so sorry," she managed in a raspy whisper.

He silenced her with a finger to her lips, being careful to stay clear of where they were burned.

With her one undamaged hand, she took his and pressed it against her face.

"It's okay," he said. "There will be time to talk."

But what was there to talk about? Whatever had forced her to commit that first offense, Leoni had made her amends. She had managed to understand his faint cue and uploaded the DG Blocker, saving Air Force One. And then she had toppled the hacker, saving his life. She had literally walked through fire for him.

They shared a smile, reading each other's thoughts. "Done."

Suddenly a man's voice intruded from behind him.

"Dr. Barcelos?"

He struggled to turn around. He was too emotionally and physically exhausted to react when Blanchard stepped into his view.

"Detective, I'm not going to answer . . ."

Blanchard held up his hands. "This time it's just a social visit."

What, no handcuffs?

"I just wanted to let you know," Blanchard said. "There's not much left in the cave. Not sure how you two got out, actually. As far as The Chessman . . ." Blanchard paused. "All we found was a charred foot prosthesis. He must have been burned to a crisp."

Mauricio glanced at Leoni. She was smiling, relief painted on her face. He decided to let Blanchard's version of the hacker "being burned to a crisp" stand. There was no point in telling her that if the body had burned up, there would have been bony remains.

"I'll let you know personally if we find anything else, Doc. You just worry about getting well, you hear?"

Blanchard slapped him on the back, and Mauricio gritted his teeth as the pain shot down his entire right side.

"I'm glad I was wrong about you, Doc," Blanchard added. At the door he paused, glanced over at Leoni, and said, "Like to hear the whole story at some point, but everybody's free and clear." He smiled, turned, and left.

The nurse on the evening shift let him use her laptop for a little while. He was about to check his emails, then the perils of using a stranger's computer to access his own account struck him. He went to BrainPacers instead. The blogs were bubbling about police incompetence and mistaken identity, and the ordeal the poor doctor must have gone through. They had no idea.

There was a rambling entry by Spike, with the words "new software" and "puke" used frequently, but no one seemed to have picked up that thread.

Eventually he found it: several references to two people, a man and a woman, who had apparently mismanaged their inputs, and were rushed to their hospital in comas. At least one of them was already back online, singing praises to the safeguards he thought were built into the new, improved software.

Mauricio shook his head. They had no idea.

The nurse collected her laptop, squirted something in his IV, and bid him a good night. He closed his eyes and thought of what a relief it would be to unburden his conscience, air out the dirty laundry, reveal all the details of what really happened to the patients and what almost happened to the world. To throw in the towel and concede the match.

A picture of Dora floated to the surface; the LX was his tribute to her, and he wouldn't give up until his mission was complete.

His mind was fogging over. The meds were taking effect. His last memory was a childhood vision. A herd of baby peccaries, spooked by something, were jumping into a murky river, unheeding the caimans floating all around.

 **EPILOGUE**

Two weeks later Mauricio was invited to a small dinner at the White House. He insisted on taking a date. "To help with my crutches," he told the person who called. It was close enough to the truth.

Leoni looked ravishing in a long green gown, even if it was too loose for her now gaunt body. The gold scarf covering what was left of her hair made Leoni look like a princess. My princess, he thought.

The memory of Al's words sent a chill down his spine. "My princess." He drew her closer as they made their way slowly across the White House portico.

"After that little trip to Asia, we're eating American," Caldwell announced. "Texas beef, Idaho potatoes and California asparagus."

"We were going to have shrimp appetizers," Lori chimed in, "but Dad found out they were from Cambodian waters."

"And Baked Alaska for dessert," Patty Caldwell added.

Baked Alaska brought memories of a recent evening at the Becks. He decided he would ask for a fruit plate. With Brazilian bananas.

The conversation drifted to election politics and Caldwell's health-care cost cuts.

Anything to avoid the eight hundred pound gorilla in the room.

He had debated about how much to reveal to the media about how close the First Family had come to a fiery crash. The Secret Service stepped in and told him to remain mute on the subject. "It's a pending investigation." It was clear that the President was determined to let nothing detract from his campaign message.

He stuck to their party line. A pilot had to drop out. Bad food. Congress launched an investigation into Air Force's culinary practices. Next question?

Between courses, Patty Caldwell asked him to follow her to the kitchen. "To consult on a menu for the Brazilian President's upcoming visit," she claimed.

As soon as they were alone, she grabbed his hand. "All I want to know is that Lori's going to be safe," she whispered.

He gave her a thumbnail sketch of the measures he was taking to secure the LX from any future breach.

John Goodson from Boston Medical Center had called him the first day he had returned to work. "Listen, Mau, I was thinking how to improve the programming . . ." Goodson let it be known that his son had just graduated from MIT, was specializing in IT, and liked California.

"Send him in and let me talk to him," he told his friend.

The young man looked and acted like a young version of Mel, and Mauricio hired him on the spot. Already ideas were forming on a new "fix."

"By the time we are done, it will be as bomb-proof as we can make it," he assured the First Lady.

Before dessert, Caldwell asked him for a minute "to discuss a campaign matter."

When the doors to the private office closed, the President handed him a manila envelope. "You can check it later. Deals with some of your issues." Then Tom Caldwell leaned closer. "I have a message I want you to deliver in person."

The White House limo dropped them off at the hotel. They lingered in the lobby. Her cheeks were glowing, the eyes radiant, the scarf dusted with snow. He smiled.

She squinted. "What?"

"Do I need to be on the run to spend the night with you?"

"You mean, like a whole night?"

How about my whole life, he wanted to say, but there would be time to discuss that.

"My room has a great view of the monument," she said, her voice suddenly husky.

"Mine has a king-size bed."

The day after they returned from DC, Mauricio showed up unannounced at the gates of Beck's mansion. "I have an appointment," he claimed.

The guard recognized him and waved him through. He made his way up the long steps, thankful that he had thought to bring the crutches. There was not a soul in sight. The main door was unlocked. He found Beck sitting on a bench in the garden, studying the coy swimming lazily in the pond.

Beck heard him and looked up. "Ah, Mauricio. Come in, my boy."

He was struck by how much Beck had aged in three weeks since he last saw him. The skin sagged, the shoulders drooped. The blue eyes were lifeless.

Beck slid over and patted the seat. "I thought you forgot all about me."

I tried but couldn't, he wanted to say.

"Anabela," Beck said. "You just missed her."

"I'm sorry."

"Gone," Beck continued. "Back to Brazil, I think." His voice cracked. "Given where my business is headed, I can't really blame her."

That was fast, he thought. The precipitous drop in Cendoz stock over the past two weeks was common knowledge, but surely there was enough left in the family coffers to keep her in shiny objects. Smart move, on her part, considering what he was about to communicate.

"I guess it's back to the lab for Johanna and me," Beck said, staring dreamily into the water. "We'll see what else we can concoct."

"She's not coming back, Maynard."

"Maynard? You finally call me Maynard?" A smile began, and then faded. Beck's eyes flashed alarm.

The man has lost it, he thought. He knows, and he's gone.

"Johanna. Not coming . . ." Beck mumbled. "I figured as much, since she vanished right after they found your parachute in the trashcan. So, she's gone?"

And is now the FBI's best friend, he wanted to say. But those were not the instructions Caldwell had given him.

"I'll make it short." He pulled out an envelope and was about to hand it over, but stopped. "How could you, Maynard?"

Beck looked at him for a long moment. "How did you find out?"

He debated revealing that his naïve trust in his mentor delayed his suspicion way beyond the rational. It wasn't till the hacker had mentioned the Ice Queen, in their final confrontation in the cave, that the horrible truth had struck him.

"How could you?" he repeated.

Beck's shoulders sagged even more. "You flew too high, my boy. I had to clip your wings. It wasn't just about Cendoz and Anadep. It was about me. You understand? Everything I worked for. The risks I took. The liability. The endless regulations." He paused and squinted at the sky. His voice grew stronger. "But thanks to Johanna, I was finally back, on top of my game again. And then you showed up, the upstart. Threatening to derail everything . . ." Beck looked up. "We were all set to buy you out, Mau. But, no, you wouldn't listen."

"Not everything is for sale."

"With a billion bucks on the table?" Beck smirked. "Come on . . ."

A billion dollars . . . Mauricio started counting the coy. Fat and happy. Swimming around, not a worry. Suddenly they looked like piranhas. Back at home in a pond like this, there would be a caiman or two . . . Balance of power.

A billion dollars. Not just his village, the entire town of Barcelos could live happily for a hundred years. And for Cendoz it was a one week's income. Where was the balance? People like him didn't stand a chance in the face of the juggernaut of Big Pharma. What was wrong with this picture?

Beck's voice intruded on his meandering thoughts. "I don't see you calling the cops. Are you considering my offer?"

He gave the old man a pitying look. He knew what was wrong with the picture. The live happily ever after guarantee couldn't be bought.

He handed Beck the envelope that Caldwell had given him.

"Your options for a new deal, Maynard. Pick one." He leaned on his crutches and stood up. "I need the answer by 6:00 a.m. tomorrow. Or the cops will be calling."

He was walking away when Beck called out. "One last piece of advice, Mauricio."

He stopped. Really, advice, after all the pain he had caused him?

"Don't let what happened stop you. It was not your fault. Not the LX's fault."

He listened to Beck in stunned silence.

"We thought the Tylenol scare was bad. A 100-million dollar recall, because of one psychopath who poisoned a few bottles. Now we have hacking." Beck smirked. "It's the fabric of our lives, and the hackers are ripping the fabric up and down the seams." Beck paused to catch his breath, and then went on. "Nothing is safe, and all your medical devices are no exception. What did somebody say? 'Technological progress is like an axe in the hands of a pathological criminal.'"

"Einstein. Einstein said that," Mauricio replied.

"You have a good product, Mau. Even with the hacking, it beats our drugs, hands down . . . Don't give up." Beck exhaled and his chin dropped to his chest. "Just go," he mumbled. "My lawyers will be in touch. To let you know my decision."

Early the following morning Mauricio brought Leoni a cup of coffee, slipped into bed next to her, and flipped on the morning news.

"You miss her that much?" Leoni teased when Diane appeared on the screen. "Now that she's the anchor . . ."

He shooshed her with a kiss.

Beck didn't make lead story. That honor went to the hackers who infiltrated Bank of America and transferred eight-hundred-million dollars to parts unknown.

Next was a piece about a famous brain surgeon who helped the FBI crack a ring of hackers who were attempting to infiltrate a medical data storage provider.

He tuned the rest out until he heard what he was expecting.

"We have sad news," Diane said. "Last night, billionaire founder and CEO of Cendoz…" Her voice faltered. " …Of Cendoz Pharmaceuticals died when the company jet he was piloting crashed into the ocean near Santa Monica Pier. NTSB is investigating . . ."

"Oh, my God," Leoni exclaimed.

Diane was reading on: "We have learned that the evening before Dr. Beck had met with Cendoz attorneys and instructed them to create a six billion dollar—that is billion with a b, —fund to be used to build free-standing clinics throughout the country, to serve patients who are suffering from depression, but are unable to pay for their treatment. The clinics are to include psychiatric, drug, and deep-brain-stimulation modalities. We're told that Dr. Beck was looking forward to inaugurating the first one as early as next month. His charitable contribution will enable . . ."

Leoni was hugging him. "Honey, I'm so sorry. I know how much he meant to you. All those years . . ."

He covered her mouth with another kiss, and then rolled over, pretending to be reaching for his coffee mug.

The President's choices that he had conveyed to Beck were simple: Face prosecution, go to jail and discredit an entire industry, or else.

Beck had chosen "or else."

"Now what?" Leoni asked when they were strolling along Back Bay later that evening. He tucked the crutches under one arm, and leaned on her shoulder.

"Cendoz has a research facility on the upper Amazon. Not far from my home village. Something to do with the pitinga, that little green fish that never sleeps. They're trying to extract a hormone. One of Beck's attorneys called. They want me to take a look at the place. Nothing too involved, just a quick trip or two."

"You can't go back to Brazil," Leoni exclaimed. "With your issues."

"Ah, issues . . ."

He told her about the other contents of the White House envelope. The dual citizenship, Brazilian and American, the paperwork attesting to a legal entry into the country, the court documents from the State Court in Manaus, indicating that manslaughter charges against him had been dropped.

"Nothing like hosting the World Soccer Cup, to make a country magnanimous," he chuckled.

"Nothing like saving the First Family, to cut through the red tape," she echoed.

A flock of seagulls scattered as they made their way closer to the water. He wrapped his arm around her and pulled her closer.

A small plane droned overhead on its way out of John Wayne to heaven knew where.

"Will you teach me to fly?" Leoni asked.

He perked up. "I've been thinking," he said, and told her about the new plane he was going to build. "We'll call it Pegasus," he said.

"And we'll fly to Mount Olympus on it," she said with a smile.

"Or slay another Chimera," he said more thoughtfully.

Author's Note

In case you think the premise of this novel is just far-fetched fiction, here are a few headlines from the very recent past. Who knows what awaits us in the very near future?

10/16/16
"As cyber threats multiply, hackers now target medical devices
Johnson & Johnson notified 114,000 diabetic patients that . . . the J&J Animas OneTouch Ping could be attacked, disabling the device or altering the dosage."
   Trent Gillies, CNBC

04/10/17
"FDA, industry fear wave of medical-device hacks
Regulators and medical-device-makers are bracing for an expected barrage of hacking attacks."
   Casey Harper, THE HILL EXTRA

03/06/17
"DARPA's Brain Chip Implants Could Be the Next Big Mental Health Breakthrough—Or a Total Disaster
Why is the Defense Advanced Research Projects Agency developing a controversial, cutting-edge brain chip technology that could one day treat everything from major depressive disorder to hand cramps?"
   Kristen V. Brown, Senior Writer, Gizmodo
   Kennedy Institute of Ethics

04/02/17
"Super SEALs: Elite Units Pursue Brain-Stimulating Technologies
Naval Special Warfare units began a cognitive enhancement project with volunteers to evaluate achieving higher performance through the use of neuro-stimulation technology."
   Hope Hodge Seck, Military.com

Acknowledgments

My love and gratitude to my parents, Anatol and Vera Lange, for nurturing in me the thirst for knowledge, adventure and exploration that led me to pursue both the science of medicine and the art of writing.

Many thanks to John Nelson for his advice on the structure of the story, and to my agent, Susan Crawford for helping the book get published.

My sincere gratitude to Carol Reed for her tireless proofreading and then promoting the book in a variety of media.

Many thanks to medical school classmate William Goodson, MD, surgeon and writer, for his insightful comments.

Thanks to Chad Lange, MD for his input into the emergency room scenes, and to Christy Lange, Art Critic, for her comments on the design.

And all my love to my wife Amy, for her unwavering support and endless patience during the lengthy birthing of this book.